This novel tells an unforgettable drama that is as alive today as when it occurred. It will capture your spirit and break your heart. It is raw, life-affirming and beautiful and celebrates the possibility of healing the wounds that are tearing the world apart. Read it and know once again the significance of roots, identity and family, and the power of giving back.
—Peter Block
Author of *Community: The Structure of Belonging*

FREE SOIL

*Victor
dream big!
Diane
2011*

FREE SOIL

Diane Jordan-Grizzard

Tate Publishing & *Enterprises*

Free Soil
Copyright © 2010 by Diane Jordan-Grizzard. All rights reserved.

No part of this publication may be reproduced, stored in a retrieval system or transmitted in any way by any means, electronic, mechanical, photocopy, recording or otherwise without the prior permission of the author except as provided by USA copyright law.

Scripture references are from The New Scofield Reference Bible, an authorized King James Version.

This novel is a work of fiction. However, several names, descriptions, entities, and incidents included in the story are based on the lives of real people.

The opinions expressed by the author are not necessarily those of Tate Publishing, LLC.

Published by Tate Publishing & Enterprises, LLC
127 E. Trade Center Terrace | Mustang, Oklahoma 73064 USA
1.888.361.9473 | www.tatepublishing.com

Tate Publishing is committed to excellence in the publishing industry. The company reflects the philosophy established by the founders, based on Psalm 68:11,
"The Lord gave the word and great was the company of those who published it."

Book design copyright © 2010 by Tate Publishing, LLC. All rights reserved.
Cover design by Amber Gulilat
Interior design by Nathan Harmony

Published in the United States of America
ISBN: 978-1-61663-330-1
1. Fiction: Historical
2. Fiction: African American: Historical
10.04.23

Acknowledgements

Eileen Cooper-Reed, Laura Clark, Carole McCullom Jackson, Tricia Smith, Marcia Fleming, Bernice Tolbert, Debby Mason, Kimya Moyo, and Ruby Malone provided hours of editing. Carolyn Jones, RN, MSN and Kweli Moyo, MD, checked my medical facts. Curtis Standifer provided perspective about the Civil Rights and Black Power Movements. Liberian, Phillip Hoff, encouraged me to tell this story.

My brother, Fred, maintained my state-of-the art computer technology.

Sisterbration, Black Women's Literary Group, and OLAD are among my network of sister friends. My bonus daughters, Ki-Afi and Kilolo, are among these amazing women who support each other as we endeavor to become the best versions of ourselves.

My Uncle Elijah Scott is my heart.

My sons, Yosheyah and Gavriel, are my love and inspiration.

My dear husband, Ronald, endured my emotional absence during times when writing consumed me. This book would not exist without his love and support.

Thank you all.

A Dream Deferred
by Langston Hughes (1902–1967)

What happens to a dream deferred?
Does it dry up
like a raisin in the sun?
Or fester like a sore—
And then run?
Does it stink like rotten meat?
Or crust and sugar over—
like a syrupy sweet?
Maybe it just sags
like a heavy load.
Or does it explode?

"Harlem (2) ["What happens to a dream deferred…"]" from *The Collected Poems of Langston Hughes* by Langston Hughes, edited by Arnold Rampersad with David Roessel, Associate Editor, copyright © 1994 by the Estate of Langston Hughes. Used by permission of Alfred A. Knopf, a division of Random House, Inc.

Part One
Exodus

Chapter One

In bondage, even in his mother's womb, he never had more than one choice.

Traders aboard the *Prospect* sold the fourteen-year-old to a sugar planter on the island that would become Haiti. Then, seizures made him fall to the ground; his muscles jerked out of control and he proved him unfit to cut sugar cane in the searing sun. A year later, when the sailing vessel returned to the island, the planter sold the spoiled merchandise back to Captain Vesey.

The boy believed his life to be better, as Captain Vesey clothed him, and the crew named him Denmark. They played with him affectionately as if he were a pet, eyed him up and down, and speculated about his beauty and intelligence. He went silent one day as spits of rain covered the deck and shipmen passed him, one to another, laughing.

From the Indies to West Africa, Denmark stared into the freedom of the Atlantic. With the sun at his back, he consumed the port languages. On days when fog dressed the sky and a vile stench shrouded the ship, Denmark busied himself tidying the captain's cabin, polishing instruments and maps repeatedly and storing them; anything to keep him away from the hold below. His chore in the hold—

shaving the heads of young captives—made him a bystander to flogging, branding, and raping of naked, trembling cargo. It reminded Denmark that he was just an unchained slave. Every time he saw seamen hurl diseased and dead merchandise over the side to feed trailing sharks, he swallowed his screams and retched.

One morning, Denmark found himself hiding his eyes behind the mast as a pregnant woman, thin from dolor and disease, wriggled out of her shackles only to run, call out to her African God, and leap into the ocean's freedom. Against the free call of hawks and seagulls, her piercing wail put a mark on his soul.

In 1783, Captain Vesey, tired of the sea, pointed the *Prospect* toward the rich seaport town of Charleston, South Carolina. He sold the cargo and kept Denmark as his personal servant.

Riding into this strange land on horseback behind Captain Vesey, Denmark took in genteel Charleston planters smoking broad cigars in their livery-drawn carriages. There were mansions fixed with expansive verandahs, a smelly market where sellers beat away black buzzards from their imported Cuban pineapples, a whipping post, and steepled churches. On the side of a magnolia tree, a poster announced a one-hundred-dollar reward for a Negro boy with a "complexion so white that a stranger would not believe he had a drop of African blood."

It wasn't his volition to be a chandler—receiving and cataloging human cargo, alcohol and dry goods, and making minor transactions in the captain's absence—but Denmark served the Vesey family dutifully. Though he didn't consider escape, at night he let his mind wander, thinking of a world without bond people while he whittled small animals out of pine.

Never seeing a black man's dream or prayer come true, he trusted neither. Instead, he studied the Bible: "If thou buy a servant, six years he shall serve, and in the seventh, he shall go out free for nothing." Outwardly, he remained compliant. Inwardly, he resented one man's absolute power over another.

After belonging to Vesey for seventeen years, Denmark tried his luck by picking winning numbers in the East Bay Street lottery and won fifteen hundred dollars. He was thirty-three, physically tall, strong, and energetic when he handed the captain six hundred dollars for his freedom and adopted Vesey's last name. With the remaining money, he opened a carpentry business.

Denmark Vesey entered Charleston's free population a sophisticated, multilingual man, but the Brown Fellowship Society of mostly manumitted mulatto offspring, with their high minds and eyebrows, snubbed him, a former manservant.

The free Denmark sought fulfillment in his deportment, immaculate dress, self-respect, and gaze into the eyes of whites, all outright challenges against Charleston's black codes that went unpunished. Still, nothing satisfied Denmark when he measured his freedom against that of whites. He could not earn as much as whites and had no protections: he could not vote, defend, or bring charges against anyone who wronged him. Only the liberty to do everything that injured no one and the right to equality would satisfy him.

He stayed connected to his slave community and fathered several children. It ripped Denmark's heart and chewed away at his mind each time the planter refused payment for his children's freedom.

Although the seizures that had sold him away from Haiti never returned, the shipboard screams that visited him nightly caused Denmark to thrash his body from side to side and awaken each morning exhausted, drenched in sweat, and numb. Denmark came undone each time an old slave was whipped at the workhouse because his work slowed or when a child was sold in exchange for cash or groceries.

His stride was fast, as if he were running late for some kind of appointment, but he stopped to listen to servants working aboard schooners from the Caribbean and Haitian émigrés who brought details of Toussaint's revolt that squashed slavery in Haiti. The stories stoked Denmark's fire. Finally, he could see an end.

Tales of Toussaint's campaign against slavery spread to Charleston authorities too. Fearing the revolutionary fever would be catching, the militia burned the African Church, invoked terror among its members, and left them demoralized. The mental list of bitter wrongs done to Denmark and his race that began on the *Prophet* was long, and he nursed them until they produced a bloody-minded disposition, a mad spirit of revenge. "We are free, but the white people here won't let us be so. The only way is to rise up and fight the whites. Leave."

By 1821, Denmark had recruited Gullah Jack as a lieutenant in the cause of liberty, saying, "We must organize plantation slaves from powerless servants to rebels with a common purpose. If they won't fight for freedom, they deserve to be slaves."

Denmark boldly revved listeners in his home and in back alleys: "Holding a man in bondage is against the laws of God." He read from antislavery tracts delivered in congress over the Missouri Compromise—"Slavery is a great disgrace to the country"—and from the Declaration of Independence—"That all men are created equal." Using Old Testament scriptures, he taught, "God delivered the Children of Israel out of bondage. God wants you to be free."

Denmark spread his liberation message. "If your liberties were based on hard work, you'd already be free!" He drew strength from thousands who hoped and feared the plan for *the day of the rising*.

A clutch of followers left Denmark's house one Sunday. "You think he's crazy?" one whispered.

The other looked over one shoulder for patrollers, the other for Denmark disciples. "Can't say. Alls I know is he scares me, all that talk o' fightin' and runin.'"

That night, Denmark cautioned his lieutenants. "Listen. Do not reveal our plans to those indulged waiting men who receive presents of old coats from their masters, or they will betray us."

Before Denmark's warning of caution could reach his deputies, plans of the plot leaked to white authorities who in turn prepared the city for battle. Denmark called the plan off.

Nevertheless, after two weeks of solitary confinement, a guard led Denmark on horseback out of the black hole of the workhouse. His tongue drooped from the rope tied around his neck. Guards on either side carried pistols.

As if she were aware of her role, the mare slowed her gait, raised her head, and backed up. Denmark coughed and gagged when the neck leash tightened. He lost his leg grip, toppled backward, and grimaced when two guards yanked him upright by his arms.

The warden rode up and with his riding whip, delivered a lash that sliced into the flesh of Denmark's naked back. He stared straight ahead.

The warden pulled the horse's reins, saying, "Go!" and the horse dropped her head, clip-clopping off at a canter.

A withered Denmark fixed his eyes straight ahead to Blake's Land and the gallows that awaited him. He watched the executioner climb the three-legged structure and throw a hand-braided noose over the top.

He saw the hangman size him up, guess his weight, tie a sandbag of equal heaviness to the noose, and then let it fall to measure the drop. "Too long, death's got to come quick," he heard the hangman murmur. Denmark watched, as the executioner adjusted the rope, and when the length satisfied him, he soaped the slide and climbed down.

On July 2, 1822, rice and cotton planters ended work and turned out in wagons drawn by horses, their bond people in tow, to teach a lesson about resistance and stop loose talk about freedom.

The warden positioned Denmark under the gallows to face the crowd. Hundreds of free men and women wore mourning black. Under the threat of beatings, many slaves wore black cloth pinned inside their clothes; defiant ones wore their black openly. On this day, black solidarity cut across light and dark skin, free men, slaves working for hire, and plantation slaves. Planters were scared.

Dust that caked into sweaty crevices of the magistrate's neck caused him to mop and smear dirt streaks with his robed sleeve. The horse whinnied and threw back her head. Then, with armed sentinels close by and in between chewing tobacco, the magistrate read from the official report:

> "Denmark Vesey, this Court is satisfied with your guilt. You were the author and original instigator of this diabolical plot. Your design was to trample on all laws, to riot in blood, incite a revolt with the intention of burning Charleston, killing whites, and escaping to Haiti. You were a free man, comparatively wealthy, and enjoyed comfort compatible to your situation...Your 'lamp of life' is nearly extinguished, your race is run, and you must shortly pass from here to eternity."

Denmark accepted his fate saying to himself, *I shall go out free,* even though there was neither physical evidence nor a confession.

He swept the crowd with his eyes in search of the house servant who had first leaked the plot information to his master. When their gaze locked, the traitor snatched his eyes away from Denmark, and then, nervously, tried looking back. In an instant, the betrayer's pupils rolled back into his head, and he fell to the ground in a violent seizure. Guilt-stricken, he would go insane and snuff out his own life months later.

Beatings and promises of chaining to the workhouse floor loosened the tongues of some witnesses. After furnishing two hundred names for the plot, some tried to cover up their betrayal by claiming to have heard the rumor and become so caught up in the idea of freedom that they unwittingly passed a bit of information along. Seeing Denmark, those men and women plunged their bodies onto the ground and tried to disappear into the parched Charleston earth.

Denmark saw bondmen and women who had known about the plan and had said, "Kill me then," when their masters tried to coerce information. Others had put on masks of ignorance, telling their owners it was all gossip, and saying, "Who could think up such a terrible thing anyhow?"

Denmark found families in the crowd whose husbands, fathers, and sons had appeared suspicious to authorities and had therefore been interrogated. They remained mute. Still, with only forced testimony, the court found the men guilty. They would soon meet either execution, whipping, or forced exile. Those women and children stared vacantly back at Denmark. Among them, Rain Williams lay prone in the dirt wailing, while her three sons tried unsuccessfully to console her.

Flies swarmed around Denmark. They bit him and

sucked the blood that oozed from his wounds, the sweat that seeped from his body. Denmark closed his eyes against the brilliant early sun.

The hangman climbed the scaffold, looped the noose around Denmark's neck, a sack over his head, and cinched the knot behind his left ear.

Just then, Denmark believed he heard someone call out, "Remember Denmark Vesey!"

He pinned his shoulders back, calmly lifted his head toward the heavens, and shouted, "Remember liberty!"

The warden rode up and poked the horse in the side, saying, "Go!"

The words "Remember Denmark Vesey" never really left anyone's lips, but fear choked the air out of Charleston slaveholders when Denmark yelled his last words.

Chapter Two

The frenzy created by the Vesey plot swept Charleston; hysteria hung like a cloud. At the courthouse, the council planned to put down the resistance spirit. Members roared, "Our worst fears are realized. We sleep peacefully unaware that free blacks are inciting our most trusted and indulged servants to plot right under our nose. How can we know the minds of these people who are our draymen, rope makers, carpenters, cooks, and porters? We need a clearer line between slave and free man. Who knows what might have been?"

Authorities rushed to regain control. They called the blacksmith to add barbs onto the iron gates of their homes and burned Denmark's house and churches where he had preached. The council passed laws, beginning with banning communication between free and bond.

"Denmark cannot become a martyr," they said and made it illegal and punishable for any black to talk about the plot. Hired-out slaves required papers, white guardians were required for blacks over age fifteen, and educating slaves was illegal.

In a closed meeting to discuss the problem of rebellion, a councilman ranted over the council's thunder. "The American Colonization Society bought land for a freedman colony. This is the best answer to our problem. See, read this," he said passing around a newspaper. "Congress gave a hundred thousand dollars to build homes and provide tools and teachers. Black numbers here are too large. The free ones have to go before more plans hatch. Thank goodness there is a chartered ship leaving soon to take as many as we can collect back to Africa."

Then he handed out the *Things Which Every Emigrant Ought to Know about Going to Liberia* pamphlets. "Here, pass these to all free men and women you know."

Rain, overcome with despair, stumbled and crawled her way back from the public execution. The other slaves, twenty-five of them, cared for her three children as they trudged the two miles back to the plantation. Master Allard Williams led the way by horse.

Rain had been purchased in Africa for twenty-five dollars when she was ten years old and Master bought her at the slave mart for one hundred fifty dollars. He named her for the way rain glistened against her tight, blemish-free skin.

Master hired Rain out for babysitting at seven dollars a month. Two years later, he brought her back to learn how to serve his genteel visitors, cook his venison, and pour his three-fingered brandy cocktail. She laundered and pressed Master's waistcoat and Missus's walking dresses. Rain's short legs caused her to fall headfirst into the potato storage every time she reached in. Her favorite chore was punching holes into a piece of tin and rubbing corn across it to make meal for bread.

When Rain was fourteen and her first issue showed, Missus didn't like the way Master sniffed around the young teen, so she sent Rain out to work the rice fields. It took till dinnertime for Master to miss Rain and bring her back to the kitchen. "Git her a starched white apron," he told Missus.

Master had his sawyers make a partition for his privacy in Rain's cabin, and wooden shutters to protect him from weather and malaria mosquitoes. He had them bring in a cotton mattress and blanket.

Master boasted about being righteous, which he showed on Sundays when he gathered his slaves around the rosebushes and sweet, yellow jasmine in the front yard of his estate.

Shielded from the sun and heat on the double piazza, Master rocked in his favorite chair and read from the Bible, "Now listen, God gave man dominion over the lower creatures in the earth. If you are loyal and obedient, my overseers won't whip you." He told Rain, "You needn't run."

Yet one, two, three nights a week, wide-bellied Master stole from Rain in her cabin. It was there that young Rain learned that all property belonged to Master, including her body, to do with as he pleased. And he did.

After the first month of visits, Rain pulled up a fist of dirt, clutched it in her hand, and started longing to see free soil again. She put the unassuming clump in the corner of her tiny room, saying to the family on the other side of the partition, "Don't touch my free soil." From then on, when she heard Master's horse or boots outside her cabin, she set her eyes on the soil, and kept her mind there until his heavy brandy breathing was gone.

Free soil was where Rain came from, where women planted and gathered okra and cassava and tended rice paddies. It was where men hunted antelope, bush cows, and hogs for food, and where she had played making gongs and slingshots to shoo rice-eating birds. When she lived on free soil, Rain coiled and stitched sweet grass and bulrush into baskets and indigo-dyed cloth with her mother.

FREE SOIL

When Rain put her mind on free soil, she heard drums announce the seasons, births, deaths, and celebrations. She smelled the rain forest, and heard cackling in far-off streams. Her free soil helped Rain dream of sprawling land where people moved freely as they worked and played.

Chapter Three

Master's overseer managed the work that produced his unfailing money crop, king rice. From March to November, overseer assigned daily tasks to swamp workers—the number of acres to plant, hoe, and harvest, the length of field to flood and then drain into the river, the number of poles to fence and how high.

A hard-working sawyer named Joshua, whom Master had bought at the slave mart, was skilled at avoiding alligators and snakes while clearing, flooding, and drying the dense swamp. When Joshua wasn't in the swamp, he chewed on a straw, and quietly watched Rain as she worked—moving to and from the laundry room, cookhouse, and the main house. He was smitten.

Joshua started spending time with Rain in between Master's visits to her cabin, and he was the first person Rain told about her free soil. Under a canopy of Spanish moss, which hung from gnarled live oak branches, she talked. He listened to her dreams of returning to free soil.

No matter how many swamps and fences he worked, Joshua watched and waited for Master to leave Rain's cabin. It took hours, though, for Joshua to spend his anger, kicking up dirt down by the wild strawberries, but he always returned to comfort Rain. Whenever Joshua kicked earth beneath his feet, he told Rain, "One day we all be free, and if not in this life, then the next."

After a short courtship, Joshua asked to marry Rain.

Master grunted, "Ya'll can't marry legal, you know."

"Yessah, Master."

"Then I'll let you jump over the broom."

"Yessah, Master."

Joshua bowed his head real low. "Uh, Master. I was wonderin' if you could find it fittin' to lend us your last name." Joshua knew he and Rain could not legally marry, but there was a hint of dignity that even a slave could feel with a surname. "Please, Sah."

Master blew smoke circles from his cigar and stared somewhere way off beyond the swamps and the river.

Joshua stooped his neck and fixed his eyes on a young iris sprouting near his bare feet, and waited. "Please, Sah."

When the newlyweds stepped over the broom, Master surprised them with his name, Williams. He passed out festive sorghum and bread to family and workers alike. Then just before the couple retired for the night, Master told Joshua, "Now, I hired you to another plantation. You'll leave before sunrise. If you behave yourself at the other place, you can visit Rain two Sundays a month."

Rain bore three sons. Yet the pain of labor couldn't compare with the hurt she felt while trembling, looking into each son's eyes as she inspected the color. It would tell Rain if this son was conceived in everything that was wrong in her world or the part that gave her air to breathe.

Joshua folded his hat a hundred ways while he stood outside Rain's cabin waiting for the midwife to holler boy or girl, light hazel or black eyes. He grieved, because he could only lay claim to Rain's third son, Moses.

It was Moses and his half-brothers, Edwin and Benjamin, who tried to console Rain as she wailed in the dirt when the magistrate announced Joshua's execution date for his part in the Denmark conspiracy.

Moses was eight years old when authorities hanged his father and when Rain showed him her free soil. In tattered clothes, he passed out water to the field workers during the day and played with the other slave children at night.

Edwin and Benjamin played near Rain in the house and wore clean hand-me-downs. When they were good, Master let the boys go to school with free children.

※

Moses didn't know which was the more painful: watching Master visit Rain in her cabin, or living out the difference Master made between him and his brothers. Nights when Master entered Rain's cabin, Moses hid in the dank swamp, fighting mosquitoes and thinking of ways to kill him. When he remembered the gallows, he came to his senses, and prayed, "Please, Lord, kill Master."

At night, Benjamin and Edwin sneaked books from the mulatto school to Moses, and by candlelight they taught him to use letters and numbers.

Whether awake or asleep, Moses dreamed about freedom and finding a wife who could help elevate his station. His chances were iffy, because the women on Master's plantation were like sisters, and women on other plantations only dreamed of being free, not getting free.

Moses didn't know what had come over him the morning he interrupted Master's breakfast. With *please* etched into his face, he said, "Master, I was wundr'n' if I could work off my freedom at the carpentry shop, Sah." The question came out thick, scared.

Master's thoughts about his trip to Beaufort came to a halt; he choked on the salt bacon.

"Something wrong with you, boy? You sick? You know how much I make hiring you out? Why, I'd be a fool. You not calling me a fool, are you, boy?" He mumbled obscenities.

Moses didn't wipe at the sweat that was forming across his forehead.

"No, Sah," he answered, and he stood frozen in place until Master rose from the table and went outside to climb into his carriage.

The balmy summer that Master refused Moses's freedom gave way to autumn and turned to late winter. Outside a butcher shop, Moses overheard county patrollers in jovial conversation recount a story about hunting down a runaway with hounds and guns, and then brand and beat him senseless. They laughed about how the slave begged and hollered. Moses was too scared to close his eyes. He bowed his head and recited the Lord's Prayer.

The constant terror of bondage caused Moses to consider joining the African Methodist Episcopal Freedmen Church, which had a reputation for raising money to buy the freedom of its members.

"Where are you, God?" he cried out when he couldn't conjure a scheme to serve God and Master.

While walking the miles to and from the plantation and the carpentry shop, Moses also observed the privilege that the Charleston caste system afforded mulatto freemen and women. Although they weren't first-class citizens, the symbols of wearing expensive clothes, owning real estate and paying taxes exaggerated the advantage of their status. Membership in exclusive mulatto fraternities and schools caused them to hold their head and eyebrows high, self-segregate from slaves, and relish in the deeply drawn lines between white, free, and slave. They didn't draw the line, but it benefited them. Moses watched the privileged. In them, he saw black freedom, dreams. The privileged peered down their noses at Moses. In him, they saw slave, inhumanity, the rank they never wanted to be.

A young, thickset seamstress with high cheekbones and a high-mindedness for success walked into the carpentry shop asking for directions. Moses knew immediately that they would marry. Their masters agreed that Moses would split his Sundays-three with his wife at her plantation and one with Rain, where he continued listening to her stories about free soil.

As news traveled to Master's plantation about tension between the North and South, he tired of Rain and purchased a younger girl. Sometimes, though, Master found himself in Rain's cabin, sitting quietly, seeking comfort in her presence. He never spoke a word about taking grapevine gossip and betraying Joshua's name to authorities as part of the Vesey Conspiracy.

One evening, Master returned from a vacation to Beaufort where he dined and danced. He went straight to Rain's cabin.

While he sat there, staring at the wall, she blurted, "The slaves is sick." Her eyes were wide, her heart pounded. "They got ches' pains, they breathin' is like knives stickin' 'em, and they got feva,'" and then she named the ones she thought would die.

A long time passed before words finally broke through his lips. "Pleurisy is catching like wildfire. In the morning, dose 'em with spirits of turpentine, sweet oil, salt, and cream of tartar. Give 'em an extra spoon of rice and some tea made from the flowers of Missus's yellow jasmine, but don't let her catch you. And keep yourself well."

By the end of the week, ten were dead.

Nervous tension spread throughout Charleston as the grapevine telegraph talked about war. Master sulked over losing his profit to pleurisy. He feared malaria would strike next and he fretted over Confederate bonds he could lose if the Yankees won.

Seeing the opportunity in Master's malaise one afternoon, Rain poured him a second glass of brandy and readied herself.

"Master." She pled with her eyes, even though she stared at the floor. "Please, free my sons so they can learn la'yer, doctor, or min'ster. They smart," she said bowing. "I don't want my boys fightin' no Yankees."

In his drawing room, among shelves of unread books, Master put down his glass. "Bring me some of that turtle soup."

Rain whisked herself down the back stairs and out to the kitchen. Shaking, she told the cook, "Warm this for Master. Hurry."

Rain returned and watched Master slowly sip the soup and down the brandy. Without looking at her, he responded with a voice now old and raspy, "They my slaves. I do what I please. And even if I do, that black one that b'longed to Joshua is too good a worker to let go."

The stabbing pain Master's words inflicted upon Rain's heart felt like pleurisy. "Yessir, Master," she said, staring at the floor.

The idea hadn't been Rain's alone, for she had heard from other plantations that some slaveholders were secretly manumitting their offspring. Her desperation grew as talk of war grew. She fixed Master's favorite foods and polished his collection of Colt and Remington revolvers that he kept for boasting over imported cigars; she washed and ironed his riding coat; and she made herself small and quiet, careful not to rile him.

A month went by before Master called Rain to him. "Now, boys, tell Rain good-bye," he said, and then unfolded the bills to pay transport northward, where Edwin and Benjamin vowed they would pass for white.

Soon after South Carolina Confederates fired the first shot at Fort Sumter, Master fell ill from drinking and old age. He proudly sent his sons by Missus off to join the infantry and then took to his bed. There, no matter how often Missus wiped him down, a putrid odor of decay seeped through his skin and out of every orifice.

When the Yankees came trouncing all over Missus's azalea beds the first time, they ransacked the house looking for money, drank up all Master's liquor, ate up the smokehouse hams, and stole sacks of flour. They took Master's prized artillery.

Master's slaves that hadn't died of pleurisy whispered, "Remember Denmark Vesey of Charleston," as they ran behind Yankees to Union lines. "We shall go out free."

The next time Yankees came to Master's plantation, covering the front yard like bugs, they gathered the slaves and read from a scroll that said, "Thenceforward, and forever shall be free to come and go as they please and get paid for their work."

Master was sick with consumption when news came that one of his sons was lost to war—the other would return home an amputee.

Then on December 31, 1862, Freedom's Eve, Moses, Rain, and Missus watched all night for the Emancipation Proclamation to take hold in the morning.

The next morning, the Day of Jubilee, Rain ran through

the house, across Master's plantation and the next. Her tongue was lapping, trying to taste freedom in the air.

She leaned over a wooden fence, watching soldiers mustering on a rise of land. She heard repeating rifles and a cannon fire in the distance.

Then, "Where you s'posed to be, gal?" shouted another Master. Rain tucked and ran.

By the surrender, Master was dead. He died with a repeater rifle loaded and wrapped in his arms. Missus carried on crying and fainting for days, because she had never paid a bill and couldn't fathom how to manage the swamps and all the debt.

First, Missus laid Master to rest in the family burial ground; then she begged Rain and Moses to help her rebuild. "You, my most petted and faithful of all, you can't leave me. Not now."

Rain and Moses took their sweet time deciphering their free choices, the ones they had and didn't have. A week later, Moses moved his wife and baby son onto the plantation. He would manage the workers who lived and worked on the land, and Rain would help Missus with the house. At night, Moses would work at the carpentry shop making furniture and keeping his own money for the first time. "R'member, Ma, we just waitin' our time."

Instead of paying labor, Missus promised to share crops and profit at the end of the year, if there were any.

Abraham Lincoln had promised "malice toward none" and "charity for all," and the Freedman's Bureau to give freedmen the right to vote and citizenship.

Moses busied himself stabilizing his family while agonizing over the former slaves who wandered back to Master's plantation panting and hungry after their town-to-town fruitless search to reclaim sold and scattered kinfolk. They had nowhere else to go and nothing to live on, not even bread. Moses begged Missus to take a few in, but most had to move on.

Moses prayed, "By yo' grace, God," that the Freedman's Bureau promises would manifest. For the first time in his life, he dared to dream of building his own house. "We gon' get us a mule and a forty-acre patch of our own land, down by the 'bandoned rice fields," he told his mother.

After Lincoln's assassination and the melee between Andrew Johnson and congress over reconstruction and civil rights, the land promised to blacks went back to plantation owners, and Moses's hopes that he would get help to make a new life died.

Chapter Four

Charleston changed before Moses's eyes. He wasn't sure if life was better before or after the war. Inside the carpentry shop, white citizens complained that the North was punishing the South. Outside, Moses watched Jim Crow laws and black codes reestablish the rules of slavery. There was sameness in the boastful stories of vigilante mobs, random murders, and beatings.

Moses soothed himself by helping Denmark's son build a yellow pine church near the site of the original church razed after Vesey's execution.

Then Moses heard talk about blacks making plans for Africa.

One Sunday, Moses and his wife walked through the doorway of Rain's cabin. His wife looked on with approval as Moses cupped his mother's hand and said, "I been saving money since the surrender, and I'm gon' take you back to free soil, to Africa. I don't know which part you from; all the same, we goin,' and I'm gon' take care a' yore every need 'til yore dyin' day."

He stared at the dirt beneath his feet. "Here, we not slave, and we not free. The freedom they speak 'bout only in letters on paper and fights b'tween white men. We can't see it. All that talk they used to do 'bout difference b'tween free black and slave—humph, now all they care 'bout is white and black. White folks mad they lost the war—they mad 'bout free laws the gov'ment passed. I swear, white folks done near 'bouts lost they complete mind."

Inside Moses's eyes, Rain saw her village. She ran over to her clump of free soil, and when she returned, she took Moses's face in her hands. "We goin' to free soil?"

"Yeah, Ma. We gon' have dignity and real freedom, and we gon' live by a clock that we set."

"Thank you, Lord."

Moses applied to the Exodus Association, a group that had replaced the American Colonization Society, which had sent more than fifteen thousand free men and women and freed slaves to Liberia. He obtained endorsements verifying his family's honesty, sobriety, health, and their occupations—carpenter, seamstress, and cook. "Halleluiah!" he shouted the day he bought four thirty-dollar tickets for Rain, his wife and teenage son, Robert, and himself.

Weekly, it seemed that abolitionists opposed to the Back-to-Africa Movement pled on soapboxes, "This plot was started to satisfy scared slaveholders. Be sure," said the abolitionist, "there is no 'back to' if you were born in America. And most of you have lived here long enough to call America *your* home."

Frederick Douglass organized special audiences of blacks with means, saying, "You have the means and respect to fight for brotherhood and equality in America." On a gas lit, cobblestone courtyard, Douglass told a crowd, "Your hard work entitles you to the same freedoms as other Americans, but you have to struggle to make this nation live up to its creed."

Inside the carpentry shop, men who were free before Emancipation argued, "No, sirree, I ain't lost a thing in Africa."

To that, Moses put down the plane he was using to measure a table leg. "Long as I take my family, I ain't lost nothin' here. I say good-bye, America."

Someone challenged, "Ya'll gon' run amuck in Africa with no white folks to keep ya'll in line."

Another shot back, "Humph, you a slave even though you free."

Chapter Five

Moses could barely contain his excitement about fleeing Charleston. Eager to "catch the learning" that would help in his new homeland, he practiced his diction and read the books left by his brothers by candlelight. Daily, he dropped his eyes and tipped his hat at the militia and anyone who might snatch, hang, or even burn him for sport.

Moses was sixty-four, and Rain was eighty-three, when their family boarded the sailing vessel to Liberia along with two hundred fifty men, women, and children.

A minister led the pilgrims in prayer and in reading Deuteronomy: "The Lord swore unto your fathers to give unto them and to their seed, a land that flows with milk and honey."

Moses recited the scripture as the ship sailed by Bedloe's Island. One passenger pointed. "Look, that's the island planned for the statue called Liberty."

For forty-three days, Moses dreamed of a house like Master's and of sending his son to classy schools. Moses dreamed of first-class citizenship and of Rain living the rest of her life without a Master. He promised his wife, "You gonna have tea parties like Missus's." He held his dreams close while he listened to fellow travelers argue over whose dream was more important.

"I'm gonna build schools."

"Schools? This new land needs a political system that takes care of its people."

"You have it all wrong. I'm going to Christianize Africa, save souls."

One merchant flashed his long list of American import and export connections. Nevertheless, they each waxed in the details of their yearning for a new life, details that were rooted in the painful master and servant system they were leaving behind.

When Moses stepped off the ship and onto Liberian soil yearning for liberty and a life free of controls, he was unaware of any rift between the indigenous and the group of settlers he had come to join. He faced out toward the land, the city of Monrovia, as a greeter pushed a Liberian flag into his hand. The alternating red and white stripes on an ocean of blue looked familiar, except for the one white star.

The greeter then handed Moses the Rules of Government, which spelled out how he and his family would join the population of settlers that began with the first pilgrims from America in 1822, observe the established public order between settlers and the indigenous people, and maintain the lines that had been drawn between them. Moses was puzzled by all this, but when he looked at the cover on the book of rules that bore the Liberian seal, he clutched it to his chest. The seal carried an immigrant ship and settler plow, with the inscription, *The Love of Liberty Brought Us Here.*

"We're here, Ma."

Rain gathered her skirts in her hand as she brushed past passengers and officials. When she reached the red dirt, she sat down and cried, "Free soil."

Rain scooped up the rich red dirt, threw it into the air,

and let it rain down on her. Satisfied in her soul, she leaned over and kissed the ground.

The Charleston council member had become a committed colonizing agent after the hanging of Denmark. In 1822, when he and other settlers arrived at six degrees north of the Equator, the land under the huge bulge of West Africa was known as the Grain Coast. Drums sounded the alarm warning of visitors who did not come to trade. They came to stay without invitation. Using crude weaponry, war chiefs organized attacks against them.

In between warding off attacks, the colonizing agents and settlers offered to buy the virgin land. The chiefs refused, attacked the invaders, and contained them in the marshlands, where a horrible stench issued from the mixture of rain and fear, and of the sick dying of dysentery and malaria.

"We're willing to make a good offer for this peaceful land," the agents told a group of regional chiefs.

"No!"

President James Monroe dispatched a schooner containing armed men under the leadership of Lieutenant Stockton. Stockton urged the chiefs to sell. When the chiefs finally acquiesced, Stockton bought the land for three hundred dollars worth of muskets, beads, tobacco, and gunpowder, and Liberia "place of liberty" was born. Colonizing agents supervised how settlers dressed and behaved, and in honor of the president's support, named the capital Monrovia.

In 1847, while Jarteh Togba reigned as chief north of the Mesurado River, the American Colonization Society told the Commonwealth of Liberia that it was time to declare its independence from the United States.

The market in Chief Togba's region was a meeting place for merchants and travelers. There market women gossiped with traders. While pounding cassava, fanning rice, and selling indigo-dyed cloth, the women learned how the place called Monrovia was about to change the way they lived.

Hearing this, Chief Togba crossed Cape Mesurado and walked into Monrovia dressed in his finest indigo grand Boubou robes, kufi, and carried his mahogany-carved chieftain staff.

He demanded an audience, saying, "This is our land, the land of our ancestors," and stared into the face of officials. "You cannot tell us how to live."

The official talked nonstop. At first, he flattered the chief, "You are a stand-up man for your people." Then he explained, "As an officer of the new government, it is my job to bring civilization and Christianity, to educate, and end poverty."

The chief asked, "What is poverty?" When the man finished, Togba described his region. "Ah! Our animals roam, men and women farm, we have plenty food to eat, and enough to give away. The problems you are trying to solve are not ours. I tell you, every man gives and takes his share, and the land sustains us. Because every man can fish and hunt, every man can eat."

The government officer spoke hurriedly, "I'm only doing my job here, but if you agree to collect hut taxes that pay for government services in your region, then you can represent your village, even make decisions that affect your people."

Chief Togba, his eyebrows raised, was dumbfounded. He gathered up the long folds of his robes. He tapped his staff of office on the floor and then raised it to make a point. However, the official, fearing a strike, ducked. Their eyes locked. Neither blinked nor spoke. In the cold silence, the chief patted his feet and pondered the benefits of insurgence. In his head, he counted the men he had lost in earlier attacks and wondered if he could amass a significant show of force against the new government that had guns, munitions, and many men. Togba needed more than anger to fight. He reconsidered.

The official quickly gathered his papers and broke the silence. "Representing your region at the seat of government in Monrovia will help your people. Just try it."

For the good of his people, the chief accepted the arrangement of collecting a hut tax from each villager. In exchange for the taxes, the new Monrovian government promised that Togba could represent his people in Monrovia. For the taxes, they promised to send provisions of supplies, medicine, and machines for growing and cultivating rice to the region.

Soon after Togba collected hut taxes for a year, the officials in Monrovia reneged on every promise. The government promised and promised. Togba waited and waited. Yet the provisions of medicine and machines never came, and neither did the opportunity for Togba to vote or make decisions that affected his region.

Togba visited other chiefs in their region. "These settlers behave like gods with authority over us and then treat us like children. They lie, make promises, and then break them," he told the chiefs. When the chiefs told Togba their stories of suffering and frustration, Togba arose from the gathering, and for the first time in his life, he tasted the bitterness of injustice.

Over the decades, the newcomers and their descendants penetrated the interior populations. They married and shared celebrations and clothes, their ways and their names. Religion was harder to share.

The greatest abuse came when a Monrovia official gathered the nerve to travel to the interior to accuse the aging chief of practicing secret, age-old customs. He ordered the chief to denounce these superstitions and allow biblical teachings in the village.

The rank and birthright of Chief Togba made it impossible for him to bow down. Instead, he said, "We believe in the One God found in all living things. Our land is living, our God is living, and everything we have is our God's donation." Togba refused the Christian Book.

Now old and bitter toward the settlers, Togba passed the chieftaincy to his son, and then summoned his family and villagers.

It was a sunny day, and a slight breeze swayed the palms. Chief Togba inhaled and exhaled, shifted his weight to the edge of his chieftain stool, and made sweeping hand gestures as he talked.

"I'm finished with these settlers. They forced themselves on us. They lie when they say paying taxes gives us representation, but the very nature of their taxes is contrary to the way we live and share this land."

The chief took in a deep breath. "They are stealing our land and replacing our ways with the ways they brought across the big sea. For all these things, I vow that my children and my children's children will never mix with these settlers. My people will never forget our way of life, our relationship to each other, to this land, and our God. We will remain loyal to tribe first, and then true and pure to this soil." He drove his staff into the red clay. "One day, the settler will try to strip our humanity, and before long, he will lose his own. He will trade his soul for selfish greed."

At first, limited transportation made it easy for Chief Togba's clan to follow his deathbed edict to stay pure to the soil and never mix with the settler clans. That changed as his son's children cleared land and intermingled for trade and commerce. Some of his clan wanted to submit to the new ways and religion. Some even dared to step out of the boundaries of their own shadows and into the settlers' dreams.

By the time Moses Williams and his family arrived in Liberia in 1878, and became part of the growing settler class, Anthony Gardiner of Virginia had become the ninth American-born president of Liberia. In those days, government officials walked the dirt roads on Sundays wearing coats, vests and pocket watches, and neckties. Their wives attended church and organized social events. They symbolized modesty and enjoyed the sweet, delicious taste of liberty in the air.

That same year, President Gardiner committed to improving the sour relations between the descendants of both the settlers and the indigenous people, but he was sidetracked by a border dispute with the British Empire.

It took time for Moses to shed the fear that simmered below his skin's surface, time to trust dreaming and making his own decisions. He often caught himself looking over his shoulder for a master to tell him something he couldn't do, until finally, with the money he had left from the voyage, he built a house and opened a carpentry shop. His wife opened a tailor shop, and Rain made a garden in the soil behind the house.

Moses was uncertain how his future would knit itself together. He cared for his family, but he often caught himself thinking about the Charleston slavery system and the lines he had seen between himself as a slave, free men, and whites. The lines he discovered in Liberia were about where one was born: America or Liberia. It seemed strange to Moses that having extraction from America made one highborn and better than being of Liberian roots. He studied his circumstances the same way he and Rain studied their choices after emancipation and reconciled the conflict that bubbled inside him.

Moses sent his son to Liberia College, but he never told young Robert how Rain had been kidnapped as a child, neck-collared, shackled, and carried through the tiny window of no return, or how, like cargo, she had been shipped from Africa to America. Robert never learned of his grandmother's shame from Master's visits or of her sons who disappeared north.

Eventually, Moses rid himself of the ghosts of thralldom and taught Robert to ignore the *rank by heredity* in front of him. "Peace and harmony is better. Don't develop an oppressor's heart," he told Robert.

Despite Moses's teachings, the elevated lifestyle of the settler class was too hard for handsome Robert to resist. The leftover pain, privilege envy, and the overstated free symbols that distinguished freemen from slaves in America had settler descendants creating the same separation from native Liberians. The more liberty the settlers breathed in, the greater the dissonance.

By the time Robert Williams was educated and socialized with the prestigious and the elite, he was proud of his privilege and brandished power he derived from his foreign-born status. He told full-grown indigenous men, "Call me mister!" and he boasted membership in high-society churches and fraternal orders.

Moses, fearing his son lost to the selfish greed surrounding him, was heartbroken. He watched Robert step boldly into his lofty status and become guilty of the same oppression Moses had escaped.

Part Two
Farrow, Ohio

Chapter Six

November 1978—Farrow, Ohio

"Dare to dream the whole dream, Zenobia," her grandmother said repeatedly. "Don't and you won't know which road to take when life throws you a curve. And it will."

"I know what I'm doing, you'll see," Zenobia sassed and hung up the telephone.

If Zenobia Jones had known the road her life was about to take, she would have made up her mind to get out of her own way. Instead, she hoisted familiarity onto one shoulder, expectation on the other, and walked into County General in Farrow, Ohio.

Zenobia ran up to the elevator just before it closed.

"Three, please," she said and pushed inside, even though she hated hospitals more than she hated doctors.

As the elevator crept, the weight of indecision that she carried on her shoulders made her neck stoop, and the elevator's ascent against gravity more forceful.

She was sure eyebrows would rise, because for the third consecutive day, she had assigned her students to study hall. It was the only way she could pretend to be in two places at once.

Outside the door to Ward 3-F, the wing reserved for babies poisoned by lead, Zenobia prepared to see a sick child, the consequence of her juggling teaching and midwifing.

She stuck her thumb deep into the waist of her skirt to loosen the panty hose that threatened to cut off her circulation, and let out a heavy sigh. At the busy nurses' station, she reached under her skirt and rolled the unforgiving nylons over her hips and feet. When an orderly wheeling a bucket of ammonia water pointed to the ladies' room, Zenobia rolled her eyes and stuffed sweaty feet back into her shoes.

Amita lay motionless in her bed as a gauntlet of machines intravenously injected solution into her arm. An upright metal stand held a food pouch with plastic tubes that formed loops, wound their way into her throat, and exposed toothless gums.

As Zenobia approached the hospital bed, she whispered to her friend Clovis. "Hey. Doctor been here yet?"

"Nurse said he's running behind in his rounds."

Zenobia stroked Amita's cheeks. "How's she doing today?"

"I don't know the difference between what I wanna see and what I see. Nurse said she's holding her weight, but looks to me like she's gaining."

A nurse pushed back the curtain that separated Amita from the baby in the next bed. "Doc is ready to see you in the family room—down the hall and on your right," she told Clovis. She then exchanged Amita's liquid food bag.

Clovis had the nervous habit of picking her cuticles, which left each fingertip discolored and disfigured. "Stop it," Zenobia teased, pulling Clovis' hands apart. "No man is gonna want to put a ring on that." She held Clovis by the shoulders as they walked down the hall.

Clovis sat down, pulling Zenobia into the chair next to

her, saying, "Doctor, this is my friend, Zenobia. She can hear whatever you have to say."

"Morning, ladies," the doctor began. "Okay. So it's natural for children to have a little lead in their blood, but the amount in Amita's blood is at a level we consider toxic. She has lead poisoning."

Amita had been in the hospital more than a week. The admitting physician suspected the diagnosis, but Clovis hoped the tests would prove him wrong.

Clovis had read in Farrow newspapers about children dying of lead poisoning after swallowing cleaning solutions, or eating chipped paint from windowsills and walls in the tenements where they lived. It had led to a ban on lead-based paint, but Clovis knew Amita hadn't ingested any of those things. Feeling puzzled, Clovis slumped.

Zenobia held her friend up in the chair. "I'm here."

"We've stabilized Amita," continued the doctor. "No more weight loss, her color is better, and the vomiting is gone. I want to keep her another week, though. If she continues to improve, gains more weight, you can take her home."

"How did she get it?" asked Clovis.

"I believe lead poisoning was passed to Amita in utero. The question is: Where did you contract it?" The doctor tore a sheet from his clipboard. "Call this number at the Health Department and get yourself checked—talk to them about your job. They'll send someone to test your apartment, and if it proves to be unsafe, you'll have to move before you take your baby home."

"What's the prognosis? Is there, you know, permanent damage?" Zenobia asked the doctor, stuttering.

"I won't lie. Amita has quite elevated levels, but it's too soon to tell, so talk to your baby, read to her, love her, and I'll keep a close watch."

Clovis rushed back to her daughter's bed. "I'm gonna keep praying. I know you meant well, Zenobia. But I don't wanna hear 'bout no prognosis. Ima keep praying 'til I know my baby's fine."

Truth was Zenobia had never stopped praying. Looking out the window near Amita's bed, her mind went back to when her prayers and guilt over Amita started. "Take her to the doctor," she had told Clovis when the baby was two months old and cried incessantly.

Clovis had walked the floor for days with her new baby, rocked her, dripped chamomile tea into her tiny mouth. Still, Amita would not be consoled.

The pediatrician said, "Colic," and told Clovis to stop nursing, switch to formula, put Amita tummy down over her knee to burp, and massage her back to relieve the stomach pressure.

When two months passed and nothing had changed, Zenobia called her grandmother and described the problem.

"Now, listen careful," Grandma Jones said over the telephone. "Tell Clovis to go to her baby, real quiet, and take her to the room where she cuddles and talks to her. Lay little Amita on her back."

"Okay," said Zenobia, relaying the instructions to Clovis. She stretched the phone cord so she could see into the bedroom while she talked.

"Now, tell her to talk to her baby, in her most familiar voice, saying the nice things mothers say to their babies. Tell her to stand in front of her baby, call her name, coo, and talk. You got that?"

"Yeah, she's doing it."

"Now tell her to move slowly to the right side, calling her name, cooing, even like, in the same voice her baby knows is hers. Did she do it?"

"Yeah, Grandma Jones. I can see her."

"Now tell her to move slowly to the left side, doing the same as before, and then tell me what happens. I'll hold on."

Clovis hollered, and Zenobia dropped the telephone. Neither knew what to call the problem, but they knew Amita should have moved her head in search of her mother's voice. Clovis repeated the process for the fifteen minutes it took Zenobia to drive them to the emergency room.

The doctors admitted Amita and started the tests.

On the drive home from the hospital, Zenobia beat herself up for the umpteenth time. The previous year was her first year of teaching. It became a disaster when delivering babies collided head-on with teaching. Babies came when they wanted to—stretching past homeroom, first bell, and sometimes way past lunch. She called in sick twelve times during the ten-month school year, using more than her allotted eight days. She was tardy and left early many times, and ended her first year of teaching on probation.

When Clovis told her she was pregnant, Zenobia was already scared of being fired. She tried, as she had promised herself and her principal, to manage her time better, and now she beat herself up for not paying closer attention to Clovis' pregnancy.

For nine months, Zenobia had explained away Clovis' exhaustion, saying it was due to working overtime.

"Slow down, Clovis. Take your vitamins." Zenobia rationalized the anemia, headaches, and constipation as third-term symptoms. "I'll do a complete exam next month," she told Clovis repeatedly, and then rushed off to grade papers. Now, Zenobia clenched her teeth and banged her fist against the steering wheel.

Chapter Seven

Zenobia awoke the next morning with a headache. She took two aspirins and pushed the snooze alarm until she had only forty-five minutes to dress and get to school. She sat on the side of the bed, battling whether to return to the hospital and relieve Clovis so she could eat breakfast, go to work, or visit another expectant mother.

As Zenobia turned toward the hospital, she remembered that she was supposed to proctor a test, and her stomach burned. She made an illegal U-turn, barely avoiding a station wagon full of children, and drove to Farrow High.

With eight minutes to spare, Zenobia parked in her marked stall, trudged up the steps of Farrow High, and made her way through a corridor of students.

"Good morning, Miss Jones," they sang in unison. "You look nice today," said one, causing Zenobia to feel better about choosing school.

Always feeling one biscuit shy of being fat, Zenobia responded, "Morning, sisters, and thank you." She smoothed away an imaginary bulge in the belly of her pleated skirt and checked to make sure no strands had slipped from the chignon at the nape of her neck.

Zenobia headed to her class, realized she had not

checked her mail, and doubled back toward the administration office. She put her leather shoulder bag on the floor and riffled through a stack of mostly junk mail. One envelope bearing her handwritten name, *Zenobia Jones*, on the front, caught her attention. She looked around to see if anyone was watching, stuck her thumb under the flap, and ripped. A letter typed on school stationery read:

November 1978

Miss Zenobia Jones,

Your employment at Farrow High School is terminated effective immediately. A check for your wages and unused vacation will be mailed to your home, and the teachers' union representative will contact you today.

Since she was already on probation, her pattern of excessive absence and tardiness left no need for explanation. She held the letter between her fingers and pressed her arms to her sides to hide wet armpits. She tried to stop the trembling in her legs and did not realize she had bitten the inside of her lip until she tasted blood. Dazed, she looked around to see if anyone was watching her, and discovered the principal's secretary pretending to busy herself with a telephone call. When the bell rang, Zenobia moved toward Room 123 on autopilot.

Fear of failure had started when Zenobia had to stay out of school to heal from plastic surgeries that repaired the birth scar on her temple. She had taught herself to push through long study hours, never missed an assignment, and never failed a grade. How could she fail at her first job?

From the classroom door, Zenobia had almost convinced herself that the termination letter was a mistake and that the woman standing in her classroom was just waiting for her arrival. Suddenly a student, tardy for class, bumped into her, forcing Zenobia to acknowledge her fate.

Her photos, sweater, and Cross Pen set had been tossed into a cardboard box and were sitting on the floor next to her desk. A calla lily lay cockeyed in the box.

Zenobia stood there as her pretense of being a dedicated teacher disintegrated before her eyes.

"What's the matter, Miss Jones?" asked the student standing behind her. "Why are you standing out here? You don't look so good."

The new substitute teacher was standing in the doorway. "Do you belong in this classroom, young man?" she asked.

Perspiration beaded across Zenobia's almond-colored nose. She willed herself down the long hall one foot in front of the other, the same as she had done when she walked away from finger-pointing girls in elementary school, the ones who laughed and jeered at her scarred temple.

Zenobia pushed down the bile that had rushed into her throat and sped up her walk.

As the sun set and chill entered into her apartment, Zenobia rolled her shoulders around, up and down, acknowledging the tremendous weight her principal had removed. She was restless, though, and confused, wondering when her life had twisted and turned out of her control and how, at twenty-six, she had managed to be fired when her college friends had one foot firmly planted on the first rung of the corporate ladder. She wondered what had taken her off course.

During the summer of 1975, Zenobia had granted herself a six-month hiatus between graduating from Farrow

University and finding a job. Bored by her self-imposed vacation, she responded to a flyer stuffed into her mailbox that announced a community meeting. It read, *You have a responsibility to decide the social, political, and economic issues that shape the future of your people.*

The meeting had already started when Zenobia entered the refurbished fire station. She joined others pouring into the packed room, filling chairs and spaces along the wall. A cassette of Nina Simone singing "To Be Young, Gifted, and Black" played in the background.

The organizer was a member of the All-African People's Revolutionary Party. He looked older now, but Zenobia recognized him as the one who had ridden with her uncle to the march on Washington in 1963.

"Thousands, whom we cannot name, have died for the liberation of our people. They died on the shores of our mother land, they died along the transatlantic slave route, they died in slavery, and they died fighting Jim Crow laws that were designed to keep slavery rules in place," the man bellowed from the front of the room. His bald spot put a hole in an otherwise expansive Afro. "Your generation must carry on the struggle so that those who are gone didn't die in vain. The struggle continues."

The crowd erupted into cheers and raised fists.

At first, Zenobia stood to avoid elbow jabs thrown accidentally while people jumped and clapped.

"Our people died fighting for civil rights, and today we are dying from poverty and police brutality!" As he continued, something happened inside her. She found herself clapping too.

Zenobia knew the history, but she had never joined the pieces together. Listening to the organizer, she connected Africans who dove into the Atlantic before arriving in

America to slave revolts. She linked angry mobs that massacred the residents of Rosewood and Tulsa over fear that they would inch out of their place and move ahead of whites to present-day riots that erupted over injustices. *Even when the surface seems calm, discontent simmers beneath, ready to explode. Black or white, it has been one long resistance movement.* She dug into her purse for paper and pen.

"Listen, my brothers and sisters," the dashiki-clad man continued while talking over the crowd. Thick silver bangle bracelets lined both his arms.

"Our comrade, Stokley Carmichael, gave us the term *Black Power* in the '60s, and it's still relevant today. We must define our success. We must bring about the liberation of African people. The slave trade scattered us; your being here makes you an African in America, but we must reconnect with our African spirit, support African people and their struggles in the *diaspora*."

The speaker's words stirred Zenobia's spirit so much that it wasn't possible to listen and write. She shoved the notes into her purse while thinking about the connection that she now made between herself and something called the *diaspora*.

"That's right," shouted someone from across the room.

Zenobia craned her neck, trying to see the face and hear the voices of everyone who spoke.

"Let's hear reports from the diaspora," said the organizer.

Diaspora. Zenobia rolled the word around in her mouth and then said it aloud. Careful not to let the people sitting next to her hear, she repeated the word, breaking it down by syllables, and then spelling d-i-a-s-p-o-r-a. *Sitting right here, I am part of the African diaspora?*

"The Vietnam War is over and we got brothers coming

home battered and broken. There ain't enough jobs for us—what's gonna happen to them?" said a man from the corner.

"Speak on it, brother," shouted someone from the back.

He stood straight and said, "Unemployment is 7.9 percent. That means it's near 50 percent for us 'cause we gave up hope long before they stopped counting," nodding his own agreement.

"Speak on it!" the crowd roared. Someone in the front threw his fist into the air, "I ain't worked in over two years."

"Man, you know unemployment is planned," said a burly bearded professor, taking a step away from the wall so he could be seen.

"You all know *The Man* needs unemployment to justify his bourgeois existence. If we don't watch out, the lumpen proletariat, the have-nots, will take over. *The Man* manufactures have-nots, but he doesn't know the problem he's making for himself, because no one can win a fight with a man who has nothing to lose," he said in a soft tone that contradicted the punch in his words. He tapped his walking cane on the floor and ran fingers through the long hairs of his beard.

The crowd talked over the professor, and someone from the front hollered, "Stop that communist talk!"

The organizer motioned for the room to calm down, saying, "My brothers and sisters, everyone is entitled to their opinion." Then he addressed the man directly, "I believe the socialists meet here tomorrow."

"I have something to say," cried a man from across the room. "Our brother Mandela is still a political prisoner, and if there is any group in the African diaspora that needs our help, it's the African National Congress." Returning an unlit pipe to his teeth, he said, "We have to support them, because we have the same struggle against police brutality."

"True that! True that!" called the audience, waving. The crowd roared, sending electricity throughout the room.

Zenobia couldn't hear for the raucous amen chorus surrounding her. The floor seemed to vibrate and the walls shake. *I'm connected to Nelson Mandela?* "Speak on it!" yelled Zenobia, waving her hand and surprising herself. "Diaspora," she said. This time, a fire ignited inside her, and everything that mattered to her changed.

Zenobia got up, moved through the row. "'Scuse me, 'scuse me," she said and squeezed between two men standing against the wall where she could see everything, take in every word.

A young woman stood to speak. She intended her English to be polished and free of dialect. "I'm from Liberia."

Everyone turned to get a good look at the small woman who spoke with big confidence.

"I'm finishing my last year of education at Farrow University," she continued, taking the time to make eye contact with everyone. "I hadn't planned to speak, but after listening, I had to tell you what's happening in my country."

The woman took in a deep breath and continued. "Despite all our natural resources, infant mortality is high, life expectancy is low, and our women are fifty years behind American women in every aspect of life. If you are going to talk about the African diaspora, and you know how America and Liberia are linked, you have a responsibility to help them."

Except for an older man wearing a kufi who hollered, "Speak on it!" the crowd appeared puzzled.

A woman with blonde cornrows that framed her face spoke next. "We're starting a Center for Women's Studies on campus with a curriculum and research programs where women's issues are studied."

"What will you do for yourself? Stop begging *The Man* for

handouts of low-wage, dead-end jobs. The lumpen—"blurted the big man as he was interrupted by cheers and boos.

"Order, brothers and sisters," said the organizer, walking toward the husky man. The two men whispered, and when they finished, the professor folded his arms and made no more comments.

Returning to the front, the organizer appealed, "Order please, we only have an hour to finish our work."

"Don't forget our schools, brother," yelled a woman in the front. "Schools are a mess. No wonder these kids are dumb. They're not learning a thing."

The facilitator held his hands high like a conductor. "Okay, brothers and sisters, as Comrade Carmichael would say, 'We need organization!' If you want to organize for jobs, gather over there; education reform, there; South Africa, there; and women's issues, over there."

Unaware how much her restlessness had blossomed, Zenobia was ripe for picking. The thought occurred to her that the adrenaline now coursing through her veins had triggered a question about what she should do with her life that hadn't happened at graduation.

She led the way to women's issues, grabbing one woman—"Come on, girl!"—who hadn't quite made up her mind which group to join. There twelve women worked with Zenobia to list ideas that resulted in Zenobia, Cecelia Williams, and two others agreeing to organize for women's health.

Zenobia left the meeting on fire.

Chapter Eight

Ryan Phillips's knock turned into a bang outside Zenobia's apartment door. He shook off the November chill and then looked around to see if he had aroused the neighbors. He waited a few minutes, and banged again.

"It's me, Zen," he said in a loud whisper. "Open the door." He was about to slide his key into the lock when the door swung open.

"Are you all right?" he asked, walking into the stillness and whisking Zenobia into a high-backed wicker chair. He slammed the door behind him and tossed a large manila envelope onto an end table. Ryan's hair was thick, not quite long enough to be called an Afro. He wore tailor-made pants that fit snugly around his butt and draped his long, lanky legs. His trademark Banlon shirt stretched around his muscular chest and arms.

Zenobia was in her favorite oversized tee shirt that read *We Are Africans Period*. Her black, wavy hair, freed from its twisted knot, formed a mane of natural curls that framed her round face. Her large eyes bugged from either too much sleep or too much crying. Ryan wasn't sure. He looked directly into them for signs that he should call her grandmother, or worse, a doctor. He would have to fight with her to do either.

"I've been calling you all day," he told her, eyeing the Princess telephone cord that lay disconnected from its jack. "When I couldn't reach you, I pulled in my replacement coach and rushed over."

"CeCe called to tell me what happened at school yesterday. She said you wouldn't open the door for her. I've been worried, Zen."

Zenobia hated nicknames and told Ryan so the first day he called her *Zen*. She caved, though, when he told her it was because she had passion that he had not seen before and because she showed wisdom beyond her years.

"Talk to me, Zen."

Zenobia rubbed her eyes, and said, "CeCe talks too much," yawned and retreated to the warm spot on her couch.

Ryan knew that with her stubbornness intact, she was still strong—this was no emergency after all; there was no need to fear that she was going to "do something to herself," as CeCe had said when she called. That confirmed, Ryan settled into figuring out what was wrong.

He was as drawn to Zenobia today as he had been the first time he spotted her in the spring of 1977 at a fundraiser for the African National Congress, where she distributed pamphlets—*Your Right to Choose*—to women. He loved her then, and he loved her now. He just didn't understand her.

"I don't get it, Zen. I'm worried, and you couldn't care less. What's going on?"

Zenobia went into the kitchen and rummaged through the almost empty refrigerator. "I'm fine, Ryan. Really. Just got things on my mind," she answered, bending a slice of Swiss cheese to fit on a Ritz cracker.

Ryan's eyes followed Zenobia around the apartment. "Don't worry about Farrow; I can put in a word at Madison High."

She tucked her legs under a crocheted afghan given to her by Grandma Jones and said, "Forget Farrow, Ryan."

"I do have a favor to ask, though," she cooed, telling him about the cardboard box in her classroom.

"You want me to bring you something to eat when I come back?"

"No. In fact, come tomorrow. I need a little space to think things through."

Ryan kissed Zenobia in the sweet spot of her neck, unfazed by the fact that she had not showered since being fired.

Zenobia pulled her hair back, pretending to ready herself for another kiss, when all the while she simply wanted him close enough to get a whiff of his manliness. She loved the smell of sandalwood oil when it mixed with his chemistry and oozed from his pores and sweat.

Ryan kissed her again and backed his way to the door. He winked, forgiving her with, "Long as I know you're all right."

He told her, "That package I put on the table is from CeCe. She said you've been expecting it. Call me?" He held and kissed her again, and closed the door, knowing full well she would not call.

Grandma Jones wanted family business firsthand.

Zenobia replugged the telephone, dialed the first three digits of the number, and hung up when she heard her grandmother's voice, "Dream the whole dream, Zenobia," in her head. She needed a plan.

Zenobia arranged the giant pillows and beanbag cushions that she used for childbirth and breathing classes against the wall. She washed dishes, picked up the clutter, and was satisfied that the apartment was clean.

On the glass cocktail table, she arranged rose-eye agate, andalusite, fuchsite, citrine, and three quartz crystals that she pulled from a purple drawstring sack. She put the envelope Ryan had left on the table next to her along with a photo album, scrapbook, and a stack of letters. Finally, she placed one candle per corner of the table and one in the middle.

Zenobia turned off the lights, opened the end table cabinet, and pulled out a bundle of dried sage. She lit it with a match. It was slow to catch, but once started, the sage smoldered without a flame, soon releasing plumes of smoke and emitting a pungent odor that mimicked marijuana.

Zenobia began the smudging process in the bedroom. She carried the sage bundle from one room to the next, making counterclockwise smoke circles until she reached the front door.

By the time she finished cleansing and making a sacred place to dream her whole dream, the sage had burned down to a leafy butt. She snuffed it out, lit the candles, and positioned herself for prayer. Zenobia petitioned God to forgive her negligence and heal little Amita.

"And God," she said aloud, hoping that He was listening even though she had not darkened the doorstep of a church since she was sixteen. "Please, show me the way."

It was past nine o'clock, and the candle flicker provided just enough light to see.

Zenobia rubbed her hands together and started with the Farrow Daily News article that had been written a year after her birth and announced the largest medical malpractice award in the country, the wrongful act that had left Zenobia scarred and motherless. She stared into one of the candles, remembering the story told to her countless times.

When Grandma Jones, a former midwife, rushed her daughter, Grace, to Farrow General, she begged Grace not to let the doctor induce labor. "Anything worth havin' takes time and work—let nature have its way, baby."

Grace's water had broken without contractions. Fearing an infection would develop, the doctor cautioned against nature. However, a long labor was out of the question for Grace, making it easy to convince her that modern medicine could reduce time and pain. She followed the doctor's advice against her mother's old-fashioned objections.

The doctor (Dr. Hurry became his name in Jones family lore) looked at his watch and told the attendants to prep Grace for delivery.

Grandma Jones pled again. "Please, Grace. Don't be in such a hurry. Ride the pain. Breathe!"

A nurse brushed Grandma Jones aside so she could start the pitosin drip. When contractions grew unbearable, the doctor ordered an epidural anesthesia that rendered Grace's lower extremities numb. When Grace's cervix was fully dilated, the baby's head was positioned low in the birth canal, and yet she did not come.

Convinced that fetal distress would follow, Dr. Hurry commanded the use of forceps. He grabbed the steel spoons and inserted one, then the other, into Grace as if he were preparing to pull packaged giblets from a turkey. He arranged the spoons around the sides of the baby's head. With the head neatly cupped between the instruments, Dr. Hurry pulled and twisted the baby from Grace's womb.

Grace was too numb and scared to help push her baby out, causing the forceps to lacerate the left side of the baby's head and leaving a deep tonglike scar along the temple.

The pincers also lacerated tissues around Grace's womb that went undetected until her temperature reached one hundred five degrees. Despite Grandma Jones's prayers that turned into threats on Dr. Hurry, the injuries led to massive infection that ended Grace's life.

Grandma Jones named the infant Zenobia, after her own feisty mother, bundled her up, and took her home to rear as if the baby had come from her own womb.

The story of her birth always left Zenobia limp and conflicted about feeling guilty for missing a mother she never knew when God had given her so much love and comfort.

Zenobia leafed through clippings of President John F. Kennedy's order for Governor George Wallace to cease and desist obstructing two black students from attending the University of Alabama in 1963. Wallace had pledged in his inauguration speech, "Segregation now, segregation tomorrow, segregation forever." Next were articles about President Kennedy's funeral that same year.

She had endless pictures of her Uncle Scotty during the sixties. Scotty's favorite civil rights memorabilia were the nineteen stitches he had gotten in the back of his head after a beer bottle hit him when he tried to march across the Edmund Pettus Bridge in 1965, for the right to vote in Selma. A picture showed a bandaged Scotty, arm in arm with federal escorts, celebrities, and twenty-five thousand supporters walking the bridge two weeks later.

Zenobia was thirteen when Scotty, the only father figure she knew, came home with his Bloody Sunday scar. She had shown the picture of his wounded head to her classmates, asking what their families were doing to help the struggle.

When Grandma Jones got wind of Zenobia's bragging, she told Scotty, "Get rid of all that mess, 'cause gettin' halfway kilt is nothin' to brag about." Zenobia found the picture and became keeper of the Jones family archives.

Grandma Jones had seen things growing up in Georgia

and knew the consequences of blacks being too outspoken. She put her foot down and told Scotty to give up the movement. Come home and get a real job.

Scotty started snaking toilets for a living after that. He got good at wrapping movement stories around the threaded pipes he wrenched, and eventually he opened a plumbing company that grew out of his walking history.

Zenobia gulped from a glass of water to relieve the catch in her throat that came whenever she saw the pictures of her grandfather, Big John. Although he had died ten years before she was born, his larger-than-life presence lived in family lore. He stood tall even when men a full head shorter than he looked down their noses at him.

Zenobia had stuffed Universal Negro Improvement Association essays into the sleeves of the scrapbook as reminders of Big John's dream to climb aboard Marcus Garvey's Black Star Line to Liberia, where John would find his place in the sun.

As she reread the Articles of the American Society for Colonizing the Free People of Color of the United States, it struck her again that Liberia had been born in America. Yet it was her grandfather's note that emboldened her. She turned over the colonizing document where Grandpa Jones had scrawled, *Some went to be freed, but I will go as a man of my own free will.* She had read these words many times, but tonight as she realized how much her grandfather's yearning to make the world a better place matched hers, she found new purpose.

Her job gone, and Amita sick, Zenobia was hungry to make real the picture she had in her mind. She had applied for everything that would take her to Africa. Unicef sent her a form letter, saying she didn't meet their qualifications. The Peace Corps wanted to assign her to India. She discovered that Xerox and IBM sold office equipment to Liberia and then dispatched employees for technical help. Zenobia had no interest in machines. *However*, she thought, *a corporation might give aid to the needy*. In her search, she found three companies with a philanthropic mission toward health in the third world.

It was midnight, and Zenobia needed a break. With a goblet and a bottle of Mateus, she stared at the wall and then took the 501(c)3, IRS tax-exemption out of the sheet protector.

Zenobia and Cecelia—who demanded she be called CeCe—had become friends at the fire station rally. In six months, they had opened the Midwife Association for the purpose of women helping women who believed that babies should be born safe, in their own time, at home.

With two others, they had trained and registered with the National Directory of Lay Midwives. In her living room, Zenobia found pleasure in coaching women to pant, blow, and deliver babies against the musical backdrop of John Coltrane and Miles Davis.

It wasn't illegal for a mother to have her baby at home because she couldn't make it to the hospital. Having an unlicensed, lay midwife intent on helping a woman deliver was. Helping these women skirt around the rules fed Zenobia's risky nature. Her own gynecologist agreed to back the association in case of complication, but they *never needed* him—a fact that made Zenobia proud.

Zenobia ripped open the envelope from CeCe. "God, please let it be good news." She hollered when she saw the word *Congratulations!*

It came through! Thank, God, it came through! She sat

down, pushed the wine aside, and finished reading the letter from Babies Incorporated.

> Your grassroots approach, endorsement, and support from the Williams family set your proposal apart. We look forward to helping you improve the health status of women and children in Liberia.

Zenobia put the letter on the table, picked it up, read it again, and high-stepped around her apartment. *Perfect timing!*

Covering her legs with the afghan, she took the last swig of wine before opening the letter from Kito Williams, CeCe's sister.

> **Date Mailed: November 1978**
>
> Greetings, Zenobia. I am writing this letter from my balcony while looking at a perfect, blue sky. The temperature is eighty-eight degrees, and from here, nothing obstructs my view of the ocean kissing the sky. There is a schoolyard to my left where I can see young boys playing soccer. Despite our many problems, the innocence in the faces of our children is what I love about Liberia.
>
> I have good news, Zenobia. The president just started an initiative to improve maternal and infant mortality. It is a perfect fit for the Babies Incorporated program. However, if you don't get the funding, my mother and I can make the contacts you need to get involved in the president's project. We want to work with you to prepare Liberian women for the future. In any event, there is work and a place for you here.
>
> I've been looking for just the right house for you to rent—not far from the beach and about fifteen minutes from downtown. Two pictures of rental homes are enclosed.

Let me know your plans soon, but try to come before May, so you can enjoy what's left of dry season. Rainy season is a big adjustment. In the meantime, much love. Tell CeCe hello for me. May the struggle continue.

—Kito

Zenobia was anxious; her body temperature rose and fell with the rush of her emotions: happy... resolved... scared ... stuck. Mostly stuck. Unemployed, with a dream and a paid opportunity, she stood at the precipice of her own destiny. All she had to do was jump.

Chapter Nine

Zenobia arrived ahead of Scotty. She drove through the gated entrance where "Established in 1864," stenciled in metal, was affixed to the brick column on the left side. The sun was barely up. The November air was crisp and cool, and frost covered blades of grass.

Zenobia followed the winding path, past the chapel and maintenance house, until she reached the family plot marked with two large headstones: John Garrett Jones, Beloved Husband, Community Organizer, and Grace Jones, Loving Daughter and Mother.

She put roses in the stainless steel vase set in the ground and pulled her folding chair and blanket from the trunk. She lit a myrrh incense stick and placed it in the dirt.

Scotty intentionally arrived late to their meeting place to give Zenobia her private time. He had started the ritual when Zenobia was ten years old and was the only girl in school who didn't have a mother. He had brought her here and described Grace in every detail: likes, dislikes, boyfriends, and even the rivalry they shared.

Scotty helped Zenobia know her mother and his father, her Grandpa Jones, and from that point on, it was the place where Zenobia came when she needed to feel connected to her past, and present, and to think about her future.

In those early days, Scotty told Zenobia about the dreams buried in Ezekiel Baptist Church Cemetery; its origins established when laws mandated segregated burial grounds. He told her about the church's role in the Underground Railroad, and members who harbored and shuffled runaway slaves northward.

There, too, were the genealogies expressed in large family plots. Tombstones memorialized lives lived and lost, marked by Masonic symbols, Christian crosses, and epitaphs like preacher and church founder, scoutmaster, scholar teacher critic, outstanding character in public life, and founder of the Farrow Universal Negro Improvement Association.

One marker read, "Oldest Colored Barber," and another bore the name of a woman who had run the USO club for black soldiers who were barred from the white USO during World War II.

A large concrete entombment honored one-hundred twenty United States Colored Troops from the Civil War. Small stone markers bore single names: Susie, Auntie, Bob, or Mama and depicted a time when a first name was all they owned.

Dressed in sweats and snuggled deep inside a blanket, Zenobia was in meditative thought when Scotty pulled up in his 1978 Lincoln Continental. He dragged his lawn chair out of the trunk and draped his chocolate brown cashmere topcoat across his shoulders. He set his chair next to Zenobia, grabbed her right hand in his left, and kissed it. Their agreement was that whoever called the meeting talked first. He waited.

"I got fired," Zenobia began.

"I heard. Question is, what cha' gonna do about it? Want me to call my union buddies?"

"I don't want to teach anymore."

To that, Scotty said nothing. He eased his hand from Zenobia's and placed it on the arm of her chair, turned toward her, and listened.

Zenobia asked, "Why did you leave the movement? I know Grandma Jones told you to come home, but you wouldn't have done it if you weren't ready."

Scotty stalled by going to the car to get a thermos of coffee. He poured two cups. "That's a ways back, Zenobia. I—I guess things changed," he said, rubbing his Bloody Sunday scar. "I just had to decide how much skin I was going to keep in the movement. Frankly, I wasn't interested in being shot to death."

"What do you mean?"

"Why you wanna make me relive all that? You know the history."

Zenobia persisted. "Yeah, I knew what you were doing, but I never knew what you were thinking and feeling about it."

Scotty reared back in the chair, ran his thumbs up and down his suspenders, and edged up to the subject. "We've been fighting for the right to determine our own hopes and dreams ever since the first Africans landed in America, fighting for equal rights to life, liberty, and the pursuit of happiness."

She smiled, "You didn't have to go back that far."

"I'll fast-forward. The Civil Rights Act gave the right to vote and go into public places, but white folks were not having it. The Movement set out to change segregation. I was in SNCC and helped organize sit-ins, voter education, and registration."

Zenobia leaned in, studying every grimace on her uncle's face, watching him go to a distant place in his mind.

"I was spit on, had human excrement thrown in my face, chased by snarling dogs." He wrinkled his nose. "I can still smell tear gas and hear the screams from Bloody Sunday."

"Police let that happen? Bystanders too?"

Scotty chuckled. "You're naïve, Zenobia," and continued with reverence. "Half the time the police participated or watched and only stopped before somebody was killed, sometimes not. Churches were burned to the ground because that's where we organized. But we had freedom faith. King said it best. With freedom faith, 'we could hew out of the mountain of despair a stone of hope.' Shoot, we thought we could change things immediately, which gave us the courage to stand up to the threat of jail and hard times."

Scotty hitched up his pants, "Bless my soul, Zenobia, when the brothas, Goodman, Chaney, and Schwerner were killed on their way to register voters in Mississippi, I asked myself if I was willing to risk that much. But I wasn't a Denmark Vesey or Patrick Henry, 'Give me liberty or give me death' kind a brotha."

"You didn't stop then."

"Sure didn't. Those were scary days, Zenobia. Suddenly young brothas joined the Movement and said they wanted no parts of marching and compromising, no peacefully turning the other cheek. They wanted black power. One day we were talking about integration, the next we were doing for ourselves."

"After that, police went crazy with shootouts and so many trumped-up charges that all the legal defense funds in the world couldn't keep thousands of years in life sentences from being doled out to young men."

Zenobia paced with intense quietness. Leaves crunched beneath her feet.

Scotty beckoned her back to the chair, "You got me wound up now; why you want to distract me?"

"What?"

"While all that violence was happening, the only folks talking about 'Give peace a chance' were smoking dope at

Woodstock. Then when Stokley Carmichael said the Civil Rights Act was too little too late, the Movement chant went from 'We shall overcome' to 'Black power!'"

"King was assassinated; Bobby Kennedy was killed before he had a chance to run. All that went on while we partied to message music, you know, Curtis Mayfield, Marvin Gaye, Bob Dylan, Bob Marley, and Gill Scott Herron."

Scotty stamped his feet on the frosty earth. "A lot of blood was shed for change, Zenobia and, like I said, I wasn't interested in being shot dead."

When she could get a word in, Zenobia asked, "You still didn't say what made you get out."

"I got to the point where I couldn't organize another meeting. That's when I did my plumbing apprenticeship and got my license."

Scotty paused and waited for a man to put flowers on a grave two plots over.

"I went to a rally a few years ago where Stokley Carmichael was quoted."

Zenobia asked, "What ever happened to him?"

"He went to Guinea, and when he returned stateside, Stokley was talking about unifying and liberating African people all over the diaspora. We sat up one night while he told us to get 'Ready for revolution.' Said we should keep up with African news, and get a passport 'cause who knows when you might just want to leave here.'"

"That brotha and I covered a lot of ground during the Movement, but I wasn't about Africa. The Movement had to go on without me. I passed the torch."

Exhausted, Scotty stopped. A squirrel hurried across their path, leapt midway up the maple tree, and looked back at the pair just before scurrying to the top.

Zenobia spoke into the quiet. "I'm glad you got out when

you did." She wrapped her arm around Scotty's, and led him down and around winding paths until they'd covered half the sixteen acres in silence. She wasn't sure how long it would take her to hash out all that Scotty had said; she was sure, though, that his torch had passed to her generation in a new form, the diaspora.

Back at the Jones family plot, Zenobia was timid about how the words would taste in her mouth and sound to her uncle's ears. She was sure her dream was harmless—no assassinations, no shootouts. It didn't even include marching. She sipped the last drop of cold coffee, took a deep breath, and knowing once she said it aloud that there was no turning back, she jumped.

"I've been trying to get to Africa for a while now. I just got funds to go to Liberia, where I can work with women," she said without waiting for Scotty to insert a word or mood. "I was wondering, with all you know, what you think I should pay attention to?"

Scotty leaned his back against the tree, folded his arms, and glued his eyes on his niece.

"I can't pretend that I want to teach anymore. There is something so special about helping women birth their babies. They're vulnerable and powerful at the same time. Getting fired was the best thing that could have happened 'cause I never would've quit."

Zenobia kept going. "Plus, not being a licensed nurse midwife makes me worry about being reported. That's not an issue in Liberia."

Worry grabbed at Scotty's heart. He pushed his Stetson back on his head. Thinking about the father-daughter Girl Scout banquets, the Debutante Ball where he presented Zenobia to society when she was sixteen, he could not believe she was growing up.

"All your grandmother and I ever wanted is for you to be able to take care of yourself. Why can't you just go to medical school, become one of those baby doctors—what'cha call them?"

"Obstetrician gynecologist..."

"Yeah, yeah, whatever."

Zenobia handed Scotty the letters from Babies Incorporated and from Kito Williams. "It's not that simple. I have to do this."

Scotty read the letters slowly. "You joining a movement?"

"This is about me." Scotty wasn't her father, but he had been there, following every twist and turn her life took. He was as close to a father as she would ever have.

"Brother Pastor always says that the hardest people in the world to preach a funeral over are the ones who never did anything with their life, never dared to dream, or take a risk. This is a chance for me to put my mark on the world, not a movement."

She laughed. "Besides, after today, I want no part of a movement."

Scotty stuffed his hands deep into his pockets and stared out past the cemetery chapel.

Minutes passed before he said, "Come here," and dragged Zenobia by the arm. He directed her across the gravel road, past the Soldiers of Glory: United States Colored Troops Memorial. He pointed to a small brick marker that read, "Baby—June 5 1949 to June 30 1949."

"Look. What kinda God brings a baby into the world and then takes it away in a month? Huh?"

Zenobia stared at the tiny brick. She wondered whether the mother had been sick, the baby deformed, if alcohol or drugs were involved. Sudden death? Accident? Murder?

"Zenobia, I know what it's like having that burning feeling. I've had it plenty times. But I don't think you should move on this too soon. Liberia is a long way away from your family. Take your time. Think about it."

Interrupting, Zenobia said, "I don't have that kind of time. CeCe's family has adopted me; they're helping with the plans. Plus, we have to start the project by March."

"I think you should wait. But as we stand at the graveside of your mother and my father, the thing I know for sure is that they both ran out of time before they ran out of dreams. I've seen too many dreams dashed. That baby, born and died inside a month, never got a chance to dream. I won't stand in your way."

Scotty rubbed his hands together and put them square on Zenobia's shoulders. "Listen good, Zenobia. I don't know a thing about Liberia, but I know getting out of trouble in another country is different than it is here. You asked my advice—here it is. Have a plan. Stick to it. And stay out of politics!"

"I will," she said gathering the chairs.

"And you better get over to your grandmother's. Word about you being fired is out, and you know how she is about getting family news from the streets.

"By the way," he hollered before he pulled away, "Stokley changed his name to Kwame Toure. You thinking about changing yours?"

Zenobia was happy to return to their usual warm banter.

"Never."

Chapter Ten

Sister Marshall and Sister Hamilton, from the Ezekiel Baptist Church Prayer and Bible Band, had just finished counseling members whom they called the *toos*: women who wore too much makeup, skirts too short and too tight, and who wanted to sit too close to the pulpit so they could send Brother Pastor telepathic signals about their need for pastoral counseling over Sunday dinner. Primed for their next mission, the two women stood on Grandma Jones's porch, adjusted their pocketbooks and Bibles, and readied their tongues. They rang the doorbell.

"Afternoon, Sister Jones," said Sister Marshall, sniffing the air for baking.

Grandma Jones responded, "Sisters."

Sister Hamilton held back, allowing Sister Marshall to lead the way inside.

"You sho keep your house nice," said Sister Marshall. "Guess it's easy since you ain't bought nothin' new," she murmured under her breath.

Sister Hamilton stared ahead toward the kitchen, wishing Sister Marshall would cut some of the sting from her lips.

Sister Jones asked, "Scuse me?"

"Nothing," answered Sister Marshall. "I was just marveling 'bout how comf'table that chair look."

The women sat around Grandma Jones's kitchen table sipping coffee and eating the best pound cake they'd ever had. On the second cup and second slice of cake, Sister Marshall started up.

"Sister Mother Jones, it's my Christian duty to let you know what some of the church members are saying."

Sister Hamilton folded her napkin and placed it next to her empty dessert plate. Her Bible and white starched handkerchief lay next to the saucer. She eyed the cake plate but decided to wait before asking for more. "Amen," she said, pushing her dentures together to keep them from clicking.

Grandma Jones hated gossip, and that was just how this conversation was starting, yet she knew that smack dab in the middle of gossip was usually a hint of truth. She folded her arms and listened for that hint.

Sister Marshall put her napkin inside the grooves of the saucer, and then set the coffee cup on top so that the napkin could catch the drips. Her gulp was bigger than her bottom lip could contain, causing leftover liquid to escape her lips and run down the cup's side each time she drank. Cake crumbs that hung from the corners of her mouth, after she shoved in more than she could chew, fell one at a time as she talked.

"Sister Jones, it's about your Zenobia."

"What about Zenobia?"

"Now we don't mean no harm," Sister Hamilton told Grandma Jones.

Sister Marshall chimed in. "It's just that Zenobia has always been fast. You know, hard to manage, having a mind of her own."

"How's that your business?" asked Grandma Jones.

"Now, Sister Jones, like we said, we coming to you in

the sisterly Christian way," said Sister Marshall, taking the lead. "You remember Sister Johnson, don't you? Well, Sister Johnson's niece, on her husband's side, works in the administration office over at Farrow High where Zenobia works. Well, worked."

Sister Marshall looked over at Sister Hamilton for moral support, but Sister Hamilton was occupied trying to get Sister Jones to notice that her dessert plate was empty.

Grandma Jones put on a poker face, even though she had never held a deck of cards in her hands.

"Sister Johnson's niece told her mother, Deacon Johnson's sister, who told Deacon Johnson, who then told his wife, Sister Johnson," she drew in a deep breath, "that Zenobia was fired because she's been spending so much time illegally birthing those babies that she couldn't get herself to work in the morning."

"She's always been a little hard-headed," followed Sister Hamilton. She pulled a handkerchief from the sleeve of her blouse and patted her forehead. "Don't make sense to me why she doing that midwifing anyway. Ain't no makeshift nurse or doctor worked on me since I come up north. I got my own insurance card."

"You got kids. You know everything they do? You agree with everything?" Grandma Jones returned with rapid fire.

Sisters Marshall and Hamilton looked at each other. They hadn't even started with their talk about the couples at church who were shacking up, living in sin. They thought she should watch Zenobia 'cause she was getting too close to her boyfriend.

Sister Hamilton tried to save the conversation and her opportunity to get another piece of cake with, "Do you think Zenobia ever got over never knowing her mother? I mean maybe we should pray for her." She gave Sister Marshall the cue to help her clean up the messy conversation.

Grandma Jones stood up, put the top on her cake plate, and said, "Ain't nothing about Zenobia's business that belongs to you," and moved toward her front door.

Sister Hamilton eyed the empty dessert plates, wishing the talk had slowed down, but Sister Grandma Jones, arms folded, was already at the door. Sister Hamilton scooped up her pocketbook and Bible, tugged at the bottom of her skirt to release it from her crevices, and waddled toward the door.

Grandma Jones was prone to humming to comfort her spirit and confuse the devil. She hummed, "Take My Hand, Precious Lord."

Sister Marshall threw back the last bit of coffee, dabbed at the spittle on her lip, and moved toward the front door behind Sister Hamilton. Sister Marshall tripped over a shag throw rug and tumbled, face forward, into the oversized living room chair. Sister Hamilton, her pocketbook and Bible tucked into the crook of her arm, rushed over to pull Sister Marshall out of her mess. Grandma Jones worked hard not to laugh at the two full-skirted behinds hovering about her chair.

With a muffled shout of "I can do it myself," Sister Marshall shoved Sister Hamilton with her backside. Looking inebriated, Sister Hamilton rocked in place until she got her balance and stood erect. Then Sister Marshall pulled out of the chair and straightened her clothes.

Sister Hamilton collected herself. "We hope you're not upset. We didn't mean no harm."

Grandma Jones hummed louder, never taking her eyes off the two women.

Sister Marshall had returned her nose to the air and considered saying more: that Zenobia was and had always been a spoiled brat, and that if Sister Jones wasn't careful, stress about the child would be the death of her. However, looking at Sister Jones' stern face and listening to all that humming,

Sister Marshall was smart enough to hold her tongue. So, she just stood at the door with her elevated head and nose and waited for her sidekick to shut up.

Sister Hamilton kept talking, her dentures slipping whenever she pronounced *Z* or *S* and creating a hissing sound. "It's just that I'm afraid Zenobia's going to get herself in some big trouble. Lots of silly women are having their babies at home these days, but last I knew it still wasn't legal, not like the South in the old days." She looked down at the floor as she fidgeted with her pocketbook strap. "You know what I mean? I mean, I'll pray for Zenobia."

With the screen door opened at her squared back, Grandma Jones stood at the doorstep, hummed the last stanza, handed the women their coats, and then closed the door.

"Afternoon, Sister Jones," shouted Sister Hamilton from the curb.

When she was finished cleaning up, Grandma Jones hung her apron behind the kitchen door, poured a cup of coffee, and walked into the room that echoed her life.

She sat in the comfortable easy chair that the church-women had fallen into, the one her husband had brought home to her on a watermelon truck after paying fifty cents a week for six months until it was his. Even though she had reupholstered the chair four times, where he placed it then was where it sat today, nestled amid a shrine of pictures and mementos Grandma Jones had made of her life.

She sat there, comforted by the grooves the cushions made to fit her body, trying to decide if it was finally time to grieve her losses. She started humming the chorus to "His Eye Is on the Sparrow."

It had been almost fifty years since she had left her family, her life as a midwife, and Georgia's red clay. Everybody in Rome, Georgia, was either poor or worrying about being poor. Midwives delivered babies and tended to most of the sicknesses that began with fever and chills. Doctors were called if the fever included fits or swelling or if the coughing gripped the sides and included blood.

Grandma Jones was the best midwife and healer around; she had been known to set a break and had more patients than she had time to see. Her butterscotch complexion and fine hair made it easy for her to enter homes on both sides of the railroad tracks, and she was satisfied with her life until she met and married John Jones in 1931. Less than a year later, she followed him out of Georgia.

John Jones was so black he was blue. Some called him Big Black, but only behind his back. One morning, John Jones and his young bride were in a store buying gingham for a new dress. The storeowner sometimes ignored segregation laws for Big John. Whether it was pity for the African side of John or because the man was hardworking and mannerly, the owner usually bypassed the laws for him.

At the same time, the owner stopped short of making other customers mad about Big John's feeling comfortable enough to spend his money next to theirs, so when the store began to fill up, the owner told Big John to hurry along.

On that morning, a customer who had been eyeing John's wife groped her when she reached for a bolt of fabric. Incensed, Big John balled his fist and knocked the man to his knees with one punch.

"My wife ain't nobody's property!" Big John said, grabbing her and backing out of the store as his fist pumped in the air. As a crowd of rugged, angry men gathered outside the store, Big John hauled his wife like a potato sack over his shoulders and ran through piney woods, cones crushing beneath his feet, until he reached his mother's house, where he deposited his bride on the porch.

"Ma, I want you to take care of my Eunice," he said, leaving his wife. "I gotta git outa here!"

"Run fast, son, 'fore you git yo'self kilt!"

John's mother couldn't read a lick, but nobody could cheat her about money. She ran into the house, pulled out twenty dollars that she had sewn into a mattress, and pressed it into her baby boy's hand. "I 'spect this is as rainy a day as I'll ever see."

Big John pasted a kiss on his mother's cheek and one on his wife's lips. He stopped to look at her—she had the appearance of a deaf mute.

"When I git to where I'm goin,' I'll fetch you," he said to Eunice. Big John then leaped down the porch steps, sending chickens scurrying across the yard.

"Send her directly to me when I tell you, ya hear?" he hollered back to his mother.

Some folks said Big John's arms spread like eagle wings and his body took flight when he jumped onto a moving coal train bound for a new life. It was the last time he would plant his feet on Georgia soil.

When the Baltimore & Ohio conductor announced arrival in Kentucky, Big John prepared to hop off. Just as he started to bail out of the coal car, he saw a weatherworn sign carved in wood and stapled to a tree. The words, "Run, Nigger, Run. And If You Can't Read, Run Anyway," were painted in red for effect.

He decided to keep moving northward and settled back into his graphite bed, while the train rolled passed hills and hollows until it crossed the Ohio River.

Not quite a year later, John sent for his wife, who boarded the colored-only section of the Baltimore & Ohio, headed for Farrow, Ohio. Grandma Jones was stepping in high cotton when she walked into the house John had rented. Scotty was born in 1933. Grace came two years later.

For sixty-three cents an hour, John Jones worked Monday through Saturday, laying and repairing railroad tracks. On Sundays, he volunteered with the Universal Negro Improvement Association, making his community better.

When John dropped dead as a doornail at thirty-nine, right out on the railroad tracks, his widow didn't grieve, because her fatherless children needed her. She hadn't grieved losing Grace, because Zenobia was a precious gift who needed mothering immediately.

Today, the idea that she might die before she was sure Zenobia could find her own place in the world threatened to tie her up in knots and squeeze from her the grief she had pushed aside for so long.

Chapter Eleven

Zenobia returned from her graveside talk and rushed to clean up the gemstones and candles before Ryan arrived.

Ryan set groceries on the kitchen counter, and from there, watched Zenobia in silence. He loved her curves, but she seemed thinner today; he knew she hadn't been eating.

"You hungry, Zen? I brought fixin's for sandwiches."

Zenobia loved Ryan's masculinity wrapped in self-confidence. He was strong, yet vulnerable enough to show a woman he cared.

At first, she just stared at the double-decker turkey and egg sandwich on the TV tray. She picked up half of the sandwich, laid it down again, and grabbed a handful of potato chips.

"It'll wilt soon," he said and poured Zenobia a glass of mint tea. She downed two glasses before he tried to enter the place she had closed off to him.

"So, why do you need so much space?" he asked.

The teacher-midwife tug of war had ended when she was fired, but the mask she had used to hide her guilt over Amita was peeling. Her decision to go to Liberia opened mountains of uncertainty, and Scotty's talk about sacrifice had her thinking. She snuggled deep into Ryan's chest and let go.

Her chest heaved with sobs, and he wiped tears away almost before they had a chance to stream down her face. He had never seen Zenobia cry.

Still sniffling, she was careful to sound strong but not hostile. "I'm going to Liberia, Ryan."

Ryan leaned back on the couch and pretended to listen while trying to quell his own emotions. From their first date, Zenobia had talked nonstop about Liberia, causing him to both expect and dread this day. With all her attempts to get to Africa, he knew that if the Babies Incorporated proposal earned funding, Zenobia would want to go. However, he had hoped that she would reconsider out of concern for the Farrow mothers who wanted her hands in their deliveries.

Taken by the world Zenobia exposed to him, Ryan wasn't conscious that he had been consumed by it. She had shared the composite of rally speeches she had heard as if they were one exciting, long-winded oration. She told him he needed a passport, even though he had never left Ohio. His promise to get one was something he had yet to keep.

"I have to go," she said, giving him her growing list of reasons. "Everything is pointing to Liberia." She finally took a bite of the sandwich, saying, "It's a chance of a lifetime!"

Ryan didn't know the woman who was changing in front of him. Her determination to please everyone else had created turmoil and then backfired. Her otherwise strong veneer had become vulnerable as she crumbled and cried in his arms. Now she was decisive. He waited for the next twist.

Then, without a trace of nervousness and even stunning herself, she said, "Will you go with me?"

Things were moving too fast for Ryan. He had never considered leaving Farrow, let alone the country, and he tried to think of questions that would slow her down so he could think.

He pulled her to the couch. "Can you tell me what you know about your precious Liberia?"

"I'll be honest, what I know I learned from CeCe and the papers my grandfather left behind. Then again, how much do I need to know, anyway? I'm not going forever."

Ryan opened his mouth to speak, but Zenobia's enthusiasm rushed in. Determination and zeal took root inside her. "What I know is that they call it Little America. The government heads look like you and me, and they control their own destiny. The land is so rich in natural resources; people say God kissed it. In a place like that, I can build a clinic and help women raise healthy families. How harmful can it be?"

"How long do you plan to stay, Zen?"

"Two years—tops. That's how much funding we have."

Then Ryan asked the question that would tell him everything he needed to know, "Have you told Grandma Jones?"

"Not yet."

"Then let me take you on a trip," he said closing the balcony curtains. He returned to the couch, taking off his shirt. He took her into his arms and kissed away the starch in her neck, the pout on her lips.

"I want you to go, but I don't want to beg," Zenobia whispered into Ryan's ear. She twirled the hairs on his chest with her fingers and kissed him lightly.

"I was hoping we were through with this conversation for now," he said, getting up. "This kind of decision is hard to undo, Zen," he said, rubbing the back of his hand against her cheek. "I have to think about it."

Zenobia stood at her door, waiting for Ryan to say what she wanted to hear.

"Look, Zen, for a change, there is something bigger than you. You tell me you're leaving in one breath, and I immediately think you're leaving me too. In the next breath, you ask me to come with you. My father has a saying: 'Where you're born is where you should die.' He expects us to stay close and says families fall apart when the help they need is too far away."

Ryan pulled Zenobia close and kissed her on his favorite neck place. "I honestly don't know. Now I need some time; we'll talk."

※

Dressed in tie-dyed paratrooper pants, an orange and yellow Indian cotton shirt, and a wool cardigan to ward off the November afternoon chill, Zenobia opened the door to 1613 Park Avenue. The smell of blackberry cobbler, her favorite dessert, and medicine met her at the door and made her smile. A vat of cobbler always awaited Zenobia when she was troubled or ill, and she was convinced that the dessert healed everything.

Park Avenue was home, the block where the Joneses were the first black family to own. It was a dead-end street where overpopulated blackberry vines trellised fences, fed the birds, and produced enough for each family to freeze, can, and serve up breakfast muffins and desserts, with leftovers to fill wine decanters until the next summer's bloom.

Zenobia jumped double Dutch rope, and played hopscotch and hide-and-go-seek at the dead end of this street where boys taunted her about her scar. Years later, they begged Grandma Jones to let them take her to the movies.

A cocktail and two end tables held Grandma Jones's whatnots—figurines and plates that announced city names and state flags that represented places The Movement had taken Scotty. Over the mantelpiece, pictures of President John F. Kennedy and Martin Luther King Jr. hung on the left and right sides of Jesus. Grandma Jones had put Jesus there when she moved into the house; the others, tributes to their contributions to the Civil Rights Movement, were added upon their deaths. The three men stared down at a bronzed display of Zenobia's first hard-soled shoes placed on the mantel.

On the table next to Grandma Jones's chair was a faded picture of Grace sitting on a pony wearing a funny-looking feathered hat; Zenobia held that image of her mother's innocence in her mind whenever she helped another mother give birth. In that likeness, she saw her own pug nose and toothy smile.

Next to Grace's made-for-pictures pony ride was a photograph of Zenobia with long bangs on her first bike, a tricycle. The only difference between the picture of Zenobia at the Christmas pageant and the one of Grace at the Easter program was the span of time between sepia tones and Kodak color. Next to that, a yellowing eight-by-ten of John Jones showed thick black hair, the feature from his Creek heritage that he had passed on to Zenobia.

The pictures caused Zenobia to recall her Sunday school debate with Sister Marshall on the merits of King David's being the apple of God's eye. Zenobia had tried to keep quiet for all of ten minutes, but it was not in her nature. So she said, with a hand on her hip, "King David slept with Bathsheba, then sent her husband, Uriah, off to war. He was a king; didn't he know her husband would be killed? That's just selfish."

The rest of the class wondered how long it would take Sister Marshall to slap Zenobia straight across her teeth. Instead, the teacher said, "Girl, still yourself in the House of the Lord! It's not your place to question God," and straightened her hat. "I'll have a word with Sister Jones about you. You are way too grown for your own good!"

Zenobia yelled toward the kitchen, "Grandma Jones, I'm here."

"Yoo-hoo!" sang Grandma Jones. "In the kitchen."

Zenobia walked down the flower-papered hallway and stood at the kitchen door, quietly watching her grandmother's expansive body as she turned the pan of cobbler in the oven to let the left side brown. Year after year, Zenobia had stood in that corner, between the stove and sink, learning how to shuck and fry enough corn to fill a Dutch oven or deep-fry the best catfish for miles. As Grandma Jones closed the oven door, Zenobia wondered what she would do if her grandmother flat out said, "No."

Grandma Jones hummed *His Eye Is on the Sparrow*.

Zenobia listened until she heard the words, "And I know He watches me." She dropped her purse where she stood and ran to grab her grandmother.

"Sit down, chil.' Rest your feet," said Grandma Jones, pushing a vinyl placemat in front of Zenobia. "The cobbler will be ready soon."

"You sure we have to wait?" asked Zenobia, looking around for the remains of blackberry custard to lick.

"Get some lemonade from the Frigidaire," her grandmother said.

When Zenobia poured a glassful, Grandma Jones took a long drink and used the hem of her apron to swab the perspiration that had gathered around her nose and graying hairline.

"Whew!"

Zenobia had not been able to bring herself to tell her grandmother about her inner conflict—the need to please and the need to be free. As she sat there, in the safety of love and the comforting smells, her words remained stuck in her throat.

"Reach up there and get that tub of homemade ice cream. I made it with fresh peaches," said Grandma Jones, looking at Zenobia from over the rim of her eyeglasses and wondering why it was taking her so long to get to the point.

Zenobia set the ice cream on the porcelain counter to thaw enough to make a whippy a la mode consistency and then turned around to face her grandmother.

"Grandma Jones," Zenobia began, leaning on the sink, her hands gripping the sides behind her. "I lost my job."

"Humph." Grandma Jones folded her arms under her big bosoms, raised her eyebrows, and fixed her eyes on a linoleum tile. "I lose track of days, but tomorrow is Sunday, which means it took you how long to get here?"

Zenobia put her face close enough to the cobbler to feel the heat. "Do we really have to let the cobbler stand fifteen minutes?"

"Yeah, it's got to settle—same as you."

"I don't know where to begin, so I'll just start," she said, sitting across the table from Grandma Jones and fidgeting with her bracelets. "I like teaching. I even like the kids, and they like me," she said, choosing her words and saying them slowly.

"What is it, precious?"

"I teach because I promised you I would finish teachers' college. I did that, and I was proud because you were proud when you took me to church and testified for what the Lord had done for me."

Zenobia got up, piled blackberry cobbler into a bowl, and heaped two scoops of peach ice cream on top. She returned to the table and continued.

"It's been hard, Grandma Jones."

"You've never been good at hiding your pain, Zenobia, and I've been waiting all this time for you to stop your own war."

"I can't forgive myself for what happened to Amita."

"I know." Grandma Jones pushed away from the table, helped herself to cobbler and coffee, and listened for what Zenobia was going to do about her problem.

"When I deliver a baby, I see a miracle, like the ones you

told me about in Georgia." Zenobia's confidence picked up momentum. "I cry when a mother, tired or not, pushes her baby out. That's what I love. I don't want to let you down, but I can't do that and teach."

"I'm old, precious," said Grandma Jones, her stomach tightening. "I already buried a husband and a daughter. Scotty is fine, but you're my baby, and I don't want you blundering your way through life. Who's gonna take care of you when we're gone?"

She set her shoulders and looked directly into her granddaughter's eyes. "I want you to have your own place in this big world," she said and then spread her arms wide open. "That's all I want—you to have your own place."

Zenobia had never talked to Grandma Jones about her grandfather's archives. Believing there was only one way forward, "There is something else," Zenobia said, sliding the American Colonization Society paper in front of Grandma Jones.

If Grandma Jones could have called up the vigor she had used all those years before to chase Zenobia around the zoo, she would have leapt from the table and rushed out the kitchen door, into her backyard and the Midwestern coolness she loved. If she had ventured outside, she might have sat in the cold concrete chair Scotty had made for her to watch Zenobia play on the swing and jungle gym, and from that concrete post, she could have figured out how such a wizard trick was being played on her.

Instead, Grandma Jones gripped the sides of the table, stared at the paper, and let out a throaty, "Get that away from me!"

The air in the kitchen suddenly felt almost as hot as the oven, and Zenobia—watching perspiration wash down her grandmother's face and her light complexion grow pale—

could not think of anything to say. She was sure she saw Grandma Jones's eyes twitch.

Zenobia had never seen a day when Grandma Jones was not in full control of herself and most of the people around her. Concerned, she ran behind her grandmother to the bathroom where Grandma Jones snatched a packet of Stanback headache powder out of the medicine cabinet.

Back at the kitchen counter, Grandma Jones seemed as if she were possessed by some kind of demon. Her bosomy chest rose and fell to the rhythm of her flaring nostrils; still her eyes did not leave the paper. "I said, get that paper out of my house. Get it out!"

Zenobia did not recognize the guttural voice coming from Grandma Jones. She was wondering whether to call Scotty, when Grandma Jones said, "Now!"

Zenobia jumped up, ran to her car with the paper, and locked it in her glove compartment. Then she eased her way back into the kitchen. The document she thought would link her sojourn to Liberia with her grandfather's dream and secure Grandma Jones's blessing had failed.

Grandma Jones opened the headache powder, which she kept for company because she never had anything that prayer and tea couldn't fix, and chased it down with water. She walked the floor between the kitchen and dining room and rubbed her right hip where the arthritic kink had taken hold. She went to the back door that she kept ajar to cool the kitchen and stood, her back to Zenobia, as if she were in a trance. She hummed *It Is Well with My Soul,* and when she finished, she said, "Sit down, Zenobia."

"I'm not going to ask where you got that society paper, because it's plain to see that even though I thought I had thrown it away, it has conjured its way back into my life. That paper killed my John, just as sure as I'm sitting here."

Zenobia listened while percolating coffee and poured a cup for them both.

"My John was fine working on the railroad, and for the Improvement Association until somebody gave him that society paper. He didn't believe the paper at first."

"Then he talked to old people about their families, and he was beside himself when he learned about the colony for freemen, and that some were freed just so they would leave America. Something way down inside him snapped—said that ain't freedom at all, said paid deportation ain't freedom. Freedom is supposed to be free, takes choice."

"I'm telling you, Zenobia, that paper bound him up and caused him to make a life here and at the same time, make a way to leave. He was never going to save enough to live on and move at the same time, and he couldn't face it. 'Sides, he assumed I was going, which I wasn't. In the end, it killed him."

Zenobia wasn't sure where she got the strength to speak, and though the mood could not worsen, the timing could never be better. "Our Liberian project was funded, and," she paused, "my midwife association chose me to go. I want to go."

Grandma Jones had always known that the time would come for someone to wrestle the Liberian phantom created by her dearest John. She swallowed hard.

"Is it going to pay you enough money, Zenobia? Money runs through your hands like water."

In light of the heavy air that lingered in the kitchen, Zenobia stopped short of her usual *I know what I'm doing* response and settled instead on convincing Grandma Jones of the security of her safety net.

"CeCe's mother, Daisy, and her sister, Kito, are going to look out for me. They're already like family."

Grandma Jones hummed and intermittently sang,

"Precious Lord, take my hand. Lead me on; let me stand. I am tired; I am weak; I am worn."

"Zenobia, I left things out of the midwife stories; like the times I prayed and no matter what was the outcome, I had to make peace with His will." She pointed toward the heavens.

"Same thing you gotta do with little Amita. And this idea 'bout going someplace you never been, have you thought it through? You need a picture in your head of what you are trying to do.

Grandma Jones paused and said, "Pour me another cup of coffee, precious.

Grandma Jones thought for a while before she spoke. "If this is your road, my precious, you'd better learn how to make peace with ugly."

"I will, Grandma Jones," Zenobia whispered. "There is still one more thing."

Grandma let out a deep sigh.

In the most humble voice that she had ever used, Zenobia asked, "Would you look in on Amita for me?"

Chapter Twelve

Zenobia had forced Ryan to decide about his future when he was programmed to win the football season, one game at a time. He missed his best friend, Carl, and decided to seek counsel. Ryan had heard that Carl was back from the army and had last been seen in an old part of town.

Speeding away from his apartment complex, Ryan pulled over when he heard a siren and saw flashing lights in the rearview mirror. He took a deep breath when the cruiser passed to his left.

"Man, that was close!" He slowed down.

Ryan parked and walked over to the Mini Mart, passing a human chain of needy men. One carried a sign saying "Will Work For Food," and another's read, "Homeless Due To War." From the corner of his eye, he caught sight of Carl Haskins.

Carl Haskins was the one in his family lucky enough to get a pre-medicine scholarship, and the only person Ryan knew who was accepted into college and then chose not to go. The draft had already called up more than half the boys in their graduating class when Ryan tried to show Carl how to get a hardship deferment. "Naw, man, piece o' cake," Carl had said. "I'll do my bit, and then get my degree."

At first, their letters were frequent, but somewhere in

between army boot camp and football training camp, rice paddies, and independent studies, the letters between the best friends stopped.

Ryan thought he was looking at Carl, but he wasn't sure. The man whose fingers shook as he dragged on a cigarette didn't resemble the friend he had double-dated cheerleaders and missed curfew with. The man who almost looked like Carl stood next to the Mini Mart, dressed in layers of dirty clothes and wearing two pairs of gloves. Crouched on the cold dirt, he was leaning far too much to one side to be comfortable or normal.

Carl had survived the epidemic of body bags that returned from Vietnam but not the memories. Now trauma shrouded him like napalm. Junk ran through his veins as a means of forgetting about the friend who had died in his arms when they were nineteen and the necklace made of ears he'd worn to prove his manhood.

Missing one hit of the sedative would have reminded Carl of the war and how different his cardboard box home was from the one he had planned. No matter how many televisions or wallets he had to lift, Carl made sure there were enough painkillers running through his veins to keep the memories and feelings at bay. His days were consumed by scratching and nodding, chasing a fix, and looking over his shoulder for the police.

Carl saw his old friend but turned his head.

Ryan stepped gingerly toward Carl. When their eyes met slightly, Ryan remained silent, but his eyes pled, "What happened, man?" The passion for life had drained from Carl's eyes and the court jester smile was gone from his lips. Carl dropped his head and darted across the street, leaving Ryan standing with the begging sign lying at his feet.

※

Satisfaction drained from the elder Phillips's eyes when a twice-torn ligament in Ryan's knee ended his football career, his dream of a Heisman Trophy, and bragging rites at the barbershop. From then on, Ryan had prayed for the day his father's chest would burst with pride again.

His father's pride had gone limp because what the man wanted more than his own life was to see his son exceed his station. That had been his motivation for paying tuition from kindergarten to college. His disappointment was palpable, making Ryan feel like a failure. The air between them had not been good in years.

The injury saved Ryan Jr. from the draft, and when his knee healed, he promised his mother that he would finish college. Ryan was satisfied with his life, teaching physical education and coaching varsity football.

Still looking for someone to talk through his decision, Ryan sat in his car outside the barbershop, trying to shake the image of Carl from his mind.

Ryan opened the door to Phillips's Barber Shop and a thick metal blind with its slats missing and bent clanged against the window and door as he entered. The loose blinds and cowbell tied by rope at the handle announced the entry and exit of every patron and let the elder Phillips off the hook for repairing the blinds.

"Hey, Pops," Ryan said as he entered and went over to his favorite barber chair. He resisted the urge to twirl around in it as he had done as a child, and waited for his father to finish the goatee on his customer.

Ryan Phillips, Sr. sharpened a razor back and forth across the leather strop. "Hello, Son."

"You need me to restock the Cokes?" asked Ryan on his

way to the refrigerator. He passed the thirteen-inch television set just in time to see J.J. on *Good Times* break his knee and shout, "Dyn-o-mite!" Ryan recoiled in disgust and rushed to see why the other barbers were huddled in the back.

"Come over here, son, and learn something. Leave that *Good Times* foolishness alone," called Wesley, who had been in the business with Ryan Sr. since he opened the shop fifty years before.

Wesley turned up the volume on the radio. "Shush! Listen."

> This is breaking news today, November 18, 1978, from the Public Radio Network. Just in from Guyana, South America, officials report an apparent mass suicide among members of the Jim Jones People's Temple where some 913 people are feared dead, including 276 children. Poisoned grape Flavor Aid is suspected. Authorities in Guyana are still investigating this disturbing situation. Please stay tuned for more details.

"Who is Jim Jones?" asked Wesley, turning to finish his customer's haircut. "People are always leaving home, searching for satisfaction where they think the grass is greener. But what I don't understand is what kind of person would follow a man way cross the world and then decide to end his own life."

Ryan Jr. said, "Suicide is definitely a permanent solution to a temporary problem, but I do see why someone would want to travel, experience other people and cultures." Ryan looked over his shoulder. He was sure his father was listening even though he was studying a line that he was cutting into facial hair.

After rounds of "Good night," and "Be careful, don't hurt nobody tonight," Ryan Sr. double-bolted the door and turned over the neon "Closed" sign.

Father and son sat in side-by-side barber chairs drinking Coca Cola and eating bags of Planter's peanuts. Their long legs and big feet dangled over the metal footrest.

Ryan admired his father and was respectful of his quiet nature and the privacy fence he kept around his emotions, even though it restricted their conversations to one-liners like, "How's it going?" "Could be better," "Can I borrow a few bucks?" and "When are you gonna pay me back?"

Ryan had paraded girl after girl in front of his father, never saying how serious he was about them and leaving no sign that one had finally earned his undivided attention. For the first time, Ryan was ready for advice and had no precedent for asking.

"Can we talk about women, Pops?"

The elder Phillips blankly fixed his eyes on the Jazz Greats calendar that hung on the wall across the room.

"I don't think I can be half the man you are," continued Ryan Jr. He waited for a response. When there was none, he said, "You took care of me after Mama left. Then you took her back when she returned penniless two years later."

Ryan Jr. reached, without looking, for the leather strop that hung from the side of the chair and stretched it into his lap. Running his fingers against its smoothness brought him calm. "I was twelve at the time, but I saw you go from anger to disdain, and by the time Mama came back, love again. That's my picture of how a man loves a woman, but I don't know if I have it in me to love that hard, or even if I should."

"You thinking about marrying Zenobia?" asked the senior Phillips, throwing his empty peanut wrapper into the trash. He cleared his throat several times. "Nobody can stop a person who is dead set on being in love. Just don't think you can measure love using a stick other than your own, mine or anybody else's. I had my reasons for what I did."

"A relationship is between two people. You got to love the woman you choose, not the woman you wished she was. You got to know her heart and be prepared to love her every day, good times and bad." The elder looked over his glasses at his son and added, "And from what I've seen, that'll take some doing. A headstrong woman like yours needs a strong man."

Ryan Jr. sat numb, not remembering the last time his father had had this much to say. He was unsure if the last comment was advice or warning.

Ryan Sr. counted his money from the day's haircuts, tips, and booth rentals. He slid the cash into the pocket of his top-coat, opened and closed his switchblade, put it into his right pants pocket, and wiped off his station with a damp towel.

"Your mama made chili for dinner tonight, come have some," he said to Ryan, who sat riveted to the chair.

The vacancy in Carl's eyes had freaked Ryan as much as the homelessness and powerlessness of his existence. Somewhere along the way, some temporary loss of sanity had given a promising physician a cardboard box for an address.

Ryan's father freaked him, too. Owning a business was no small feat, apart from the humdrum of a six-day workweek for fifty years. Even though he appreciated the sacrifice, he was tired of carrying the undiscussable burden of his father's approval.

Ryan hadn't thought about what he wanted out of his own life until Zenobia got clear about hers and proposed the move. Looking at his father for the first time as a man, Ryan no longer wanted to pretend he was chasing a dream his father had for him, and he no longer wanted to feel guilty about it.

In between the images of Carl and his father, Ryan had to find direction.

He called the Department of International Information in Washington, DC. Within a week, he had a list of American schools based in Liberia and requirements for international travel. He raced to the library.

Chapter Thirteen

The only thing that comforted Daisy Togba Williams about leaving Liberia's tropical dry season to come to America in December was that it gave her an excuse to wear the full-length mink coat and knitted wool suits she kept stored at her daughter CeCe's apartment.

Daisy sat in a taxi outside Farrow First National Bank. She checked the contents of the envelope in her lap: her Liberian passport and travel visa, a list of her prior addresses in Ohio, Ohio Master Stylist Certification, Liberian business and International Hair Care Distributor licenses, and the check she would deposit to open a savings account and buy certificates of deposit.

The great granddaughter of Chief Jarteh Togba, Daisy had been born poor and married a handsome, wealthy man of settler origin. A mother at nineteen and widowed with two children by the time she was thirty, she was ambitious and protective, two characteristics that conflicted with her sincere desire to help develop Liberia.

Nevertheless, she didn't have another twenty years to wait for reform. Her business had done well, and if it were to grow, she needed rice and meat in every pot, not a select few. And the women needed enough money left over to have Daisy do their hair and nails.

Daisy had prayed for change when William R. Tolbert became the nineteenth president of Liberia in 1972 after being vice president to William Tubman for almost twenty years. She disliked the True Whig Party, a monopoly government that had lasted one hundred years, and she hoped President Tolbert would keep his promise to change party politics and dismantle one-party rule.

However, Tolbert seemed wishy-washy to Daisy—one minute announcing he would shake things up with frank talk and spread power and wealth, and the next minute, comforting citizens who had been successful within rules that clearly defined who was at the top and bottom. By now, the citizens who'd settled Liberia, bringing their American heritage and customs, were referred to as Americo-Liberians.

Daisy could work with customers who couldn't make up their minds between perms and braids, or who needed flexible appointment times, but she couldn't stand wishy-washy men, saying, "You can't count on them to know which side of the bed they are going to wake up on."

She could benefit from Liberian reform in any fashion, so Daisy supported both underground opposition movements. And because she didn't know where revolution might end up once people got riled with frustration and hope, she had to protect her family. Daisy put the envelope into a leather portfolio and threw her matching purse over her shoulder. Then, carrying her father's pride—which she called determination and others called arrogance—and her mother's rhythmic gait, she asked the taxi driver to wait and walked in the direction of the bank.

Chapter Fourteen

For thirty-four years, Grandma Jones had done without John Jones' emotional strength and guidance. She became mother and father of the family, and nowadays, she told her friends that it was her Christian life that softened her sixty-eight years, "'cause God ain't through with me, yet."

She had taught Scotty and Zenobia that families should get together just because. They gathered just because she cooked, and they made a fuss over how much advice Grandma Jones served along with the food at no extra cost. The falling January temperatures and snow had almost caused her to cancel dinner, except that today was special. Grandma Jones summoned John's strength and called her family together.

Grandma Jones could move safely around her kitchen in a blindfold, but arthritis made her strides shorter, her steps measured, and every now and then, she had to hold onto the back of a chair to catch her breath.

On this day, she rinsed frozen corn before putting two cupfuls into the cornbread batter and poured it meticulously into a baking pan, ready for the oven in time for her granddaughter to smell it baking when she walked through the front door.

Scotty arrived an hour early as requested, parked his Lincoln in front of the house, wiped a smudge away from the passenger side door with an embroidered handkerchief, and walked up the front steps. His newest lady friend, Thelma, would arrive later, giving him time to talk.

"Hey, Mama," he called while knocking. Scotty still had a house key, yet out of respect and fear of startling her, he always announced his arrival.

"Yoo-hoo!"

When not working in his plumbing business, Scotty was suave. His dress hat, leather suspenders, creased and cuffed pants, designer shoes, and shirts were matched and color-coordinated. He looked like his mother and carried his father's hunger to fill every waking moment with excitement.

Scotty kissed his mother on the cheek, sniffed under the lid of each pot, pulled a chair out from the table, measuring the distance needed for his growing paunch, sat down, and poured each of them a glass of lemonade. "So why the big powwow?" he asked and cupped one hand under his chin.

Grandma Jones squeezed herself into the seat directly opposite her son. "Scotty, I've been stewing over this for a while, and I decided that we gotta give Zenobia our blessing to take this trip she's so fired up about."

"She's talking 'bout more than a trip, Mama."

"Listen, Scotty. You know she got that stubborn streak from her grandfather, God bless his soul. She got it in her head that it's her destiny to follow his dream. Brother Pastor don't preach much about destiny, but the Lord sure does work in some mysterious ways. She's going, Scotty, so it's best she go with our blessing."

Scotty had been the man of the family since his father's death, but everyone knew his mother was in charge. "That doesn't take away the worry, Mama. Liberia is on the other side of the world. What does she really know about it?"

"She's got a dream, and that's all she needs. People do a lot more with a lot less."

Scotty went on about how Zenobia had neglected to talk to him before she asked Ryan to go with her. "God knows I want her to follow her dreams too—it's just that this all doesn't seem thought out. What's the rush?"

Grandma Jones peeked under the waxed paper covering the rolls to see if they had finished rising. "Zenobia's feeling guilty about Amita, and she ain't lived long enough to know that there's gonna be harder things to get over. She's got to sprout wings, follow her own dreams, and see what portion God has in store for her. The raising we gave her is set—she might wander off, but she'll come back."

"You gonna let her spend the trust money from the settlement with Dr. Hurry?" Scotty asked.

Grandma Jones picked invisible crumbs from the table while she rolled the question around in her head once more. "There's enough money for two, maybe three more years. She's got to learn to fend for herself. Still, I don't want her over there doing without. I'll let her spend the grant money first. She can call me if she needs more."

"What do you know about Ryan?"

"Alls I know is that he's mannerable, comes from a churchgoing family, and his father has owned that barbershop for longer than Zenobia is old. That, and he came over here the other day to talk to me."

"What about?" asked Scotty, leaning back and tucking his thumbs into his waistband. "Why didn't he come to see me?"

"'Cause he knew you'd give him hell," she said and put the cornbread in the oven; the rolls would go in last.

"It's done, Scotty. We can't hold her back, and I don't want her dying like your daddy, dreams still swirling in her head, her eyes dull, and the fire in her soul stamped out."

Grandma Jones stared out the kitchen door and reminded herself that Zenobia had been born with cauls over the eyes. It was what Georgia midwives called "the gift of second sight," and it meant that God had given Zenobia the potential of insight and wisdom. She was somebody through whom He could work. Grandma Jones knew Zenobia had to discover her gift and learn to use it herself.

"I'll pray, Scotty, that God teaches her what she needs to learn, so she can find her way back home to us."

Zenobia loved the intimacy of their call-and-response ritual. "Grandma Jones?"

"Yoo-hoo!"

Not knowing the reason behind the just-because dinner, she read the mood as a good sign. "Sure smells good—I starved two days for this meal."

"Looks like you could have skipped a few more," joked Scotty, looking at his niece's gut.

Zenobia sucked in her stomach and rolled her eyes toward the ceiling. "You got a lotta nerve," she said, poking her finger into his paunch.

"Set the dining room table, precious—and use the good stuff. Oh, and take out an extra dessert plate."

"One of the church members coming over?"

"Could be."

When Scotty's friend, Thelma, arrived in time to eat, Grandma Jones led everyone into the dining room. Before she took her seat at the head of the table and said the blessing, she pulled three candles out of the buffet. Lighting two, she said, "This one is for my John, and this is for my lovely Grace, may they rest in peace."

Thelma looked at Scotty, who peered over the top of his

eyeglasses at his mother. He looked at Zenobia, who sent a grateful smile toward her grandmother for adding meaning to memories in the making.

"This one is for Zenobia," she started, lighting the white one last. "It's the light that points her way."

When seconds passed and no one had spoken or dared to pick up a spoon, Grandma Jones asked, "What are y'all waiting on? Eat, Thelma, honey. There're no visitors around this table."

Satisfied that their plates were piled high, with gravy spilling over the sides, Scotty patted his right foot under the table—a gesture that confirmed he was enjoying the meal—Grandma Jones started again. "My precious Zenobia, you have our blessing to follow your dream. If it don't happen now, it'll be a dried-up haint that haunts this family like a ghost forever. Shoot, one of your grandchildren could get it in their mind to go."

Scotty passed the macaroni and cheese, reared back on the chair's hind legs, and stroked the inside of his leather suspenders. "Stay focused, Zenobia, don't get sidetracked with somebody else's thing. You hear?"

Grandma Jones cleared her throat, "A-hem," signaling Scotty to stop preaching.

"I'm just worried about you, Zenobia. Remember what I said: do not struggle for struggle's sake. And if you need anything, call me," Scotty said, pointing at himself.

"Whenever you want to come home," Grandma Jones cocked her head toward the front door, "that door you just walked in is always open."

Zenobia fought back tears as she circled the table, hugging and kissing everyone. "Thank you. I won't let you down."

Zenobia was rinsing tired suds from the sink when the doorbell rang. Expecting to see a church sister coming for blackberry cobbler, she walked toward the living room to make the offer in time to see Scotty's stiff handshake. "What's going on, man?"

Grandma Jones showed Ryan to a seat. "Zenobia, we got company," she hollered toward the kitchen, not realizing her granddaughter was already at the living room doorway.

Ryan was a cool drink of dark chocolate milk. His dimples seemed to compete with his close-cut beard for attention when he smiled. He was different from other men Zenobia had dated; he wasn't preoccupied with world politics, and he always called when he promised. Ryan didn't expect the air to move whenever he entered and left a room. It just did.

Watching Ryan in her grandmother's living room, Zenobia thought about the first time they had made love. He had bought a bottle of Perrier Jouët, covered the sheets with rose petals, and threaded his reel-to-reel player with hours of Nancy Wilson, Roy Ayers, and Al Jarreau. That night, they knew they would have to see each other again.

"Don't just stand there, Zenobia, get Ryan some dessert," said Grandma Jones.

"No, thanks, not right now," he said, offering Zenobia a seat on the couch by his side.

Zenobia looked sideways at her grandmother, who, snug in her easy chair, giggled in satisfaction.

"I wanted to talk to you at the same time," Ryan began. "A couple of months ago, Zenobia"—he stopped to smile at her—"asked me to move to Liberia with her. Going to another country is a bigger deal to me than it seems to be for her. Truth is, nothing like this ever crossed my mind. I discussed it with my parents. My mother is fine and my father is set on silence. Then I talked to Grandma Jones."

Zenobia stopped blushing and shot a questioning glare toward Uncle Scotty.

Grandma Jones was focused on Ryan. "Go on, boy," she said, waving her hand at him in the same way that she waved agreement at Brother Pastor when he was preaching a good sermon.

"If I don't go, I would worry about her every minute of every day. But I told Grandma Jones there was no way I could just live with Zen. If I go, we have to go as husband and wife. I don't want to look back at my life with regrets, don't want to ask, *what if?*" he said, looking directly at Zenobia. "I love you, Zen, and I want to give you a reason to love me every day."

He pulled the passport from the inside of his coat pocket and handed it to Zenobia. "Told you I was going to get one."

Zenobia had never considered marriage, but she did trust Ryan to love her every day. "I thought... Since I hadn't heard from you, I thought...," she stammered, looking around the room at the faces looking back at her.

Grandma Jones fanned at Zenobia with her handkerchief, saying, "Just breathe, chile."

"Well?"

"If that's a proposal, the answer is yes. Yes!" she hollered, reaching up to grab Ryan around the neck, smelling his scent. She stood on tiptoes to meet his lips, and then remembering that her grandmother and uncle were there, she kissed his cheek.

Ryan shoved the American School of Liberia informational packet into her hand, saying, "I got a substitute teaching job. It's temporary until they can process my documents in person.

If it goes well, I'll be the boys' physical education teacher. You didn't think I was going to live off you, did you?"

"How'd you do all that so fast?" Zenobia asked.

"Turns out you can get a passport in a couple of days at a distribution center. I drove to Chicago."

Grandma Jones sat back in her chair and fanned.

Scotty pulled Ryan to him, shaking his hand and whispering so as not to invite Grandma Jones's alarm. He paused and then said into Ryan's ear, "I know she's grown, man, and she's got to follow her path, but I been protecting Zenobia her whole life, and I'm going to make sure she knows that if she ever needs me, I'm only a plane ride away."

When Scotty noticed Grandma Jones's piercing look, he gripped Ryan's hand, saying, "Congratulations, man. Welcome to the family."

Chapter Fifteen

Two weeks before the nuptials, looking at their travel visas and packing reference books, Zenobia announced to Ryan, "I'm an only grandchild. It's my responsibility to carry our name, so I won't be changing mine."

She readied herself for the backlash.

Ryan wondered if this was an example of what his father meant by headstrong. "What's wrong with Jones-Phillips? I've seen a few women with hyphenated names."

"Nothing, it's just not mine."

He looked sidelong at her stance, a hand on her hip that jutted out. Ryan studied her face. It was more questioning than firm. He let out a loud laugh.

Zenobia didn't quite join in, but she relaxed the hand to her side and pulled her hip back in.

"I couldn't care less about your name, long as our children have mine. And my son," he paused and continued without hesitation, "my first son will be Ryan Phillips III."

Before Zenobia could respond, Ryan had inched his way to her and moved the box of books from the table to the floor. He kissed her neck and shoulders and breathed *Zen* into her ear. "Zen is the only name I care about."

"You always trying to take my mind off my point," she

said, pulling away. She grabbed a pillow from the couch and threw it.

Ryan ducked and the pillow knocked the telephone off its cradle.

"You pick fights and I end them. That's what we do," he said, cuddling Zenobia.

She reached up, "Come here, you," she said, kissing him long and hard.

※

In contrast to the February cold outside, the church was a showcase of white roses and birds of paradise. Brother Pastor officiated at the wedding at Ezekiel Baptist Church, while fifty family members and friends surrounded the couple. Sisters Marshall and Hamilton sat in the back of the church with their *Bibles* clutched tightly in their laps. They gossiped under their breath, and Sister Marshall whispered, "I bet it won't last."

Sister Hamilton said, "One year tops. Poor Sister Mother Jones, she sure does have her cross to bear."

The women started talking over each other. "What she going to Africa for anyway? What she gon' do over there that she can't do here?"

"Don't know. Guess they can't deliver they own babies."

"Leastwise she got enough sense to take that man with her."

"Umhmm, I heard he's gon' teach gym over there."

"Sho nuff?"

"Think that's how he got those muscles?"

Scotty had already walked Zenobia down the aisle. Tired of the murmurings, he walked up to the women saying, "Shush. I said, Shush!" through clenched teeth and returned to his seat between Thelma and Grandma Jones.

"Well I never…" said Sister Marshall, gall written all over her face.

Sister Hamilton covered her mouth with her white gloved hand and looked at Sister Jones, hoping she hadn't heard the conversation.

Clovis stood maid of honor. Zenobia had given Clovis her furniture, art, and prized jazz and rhythm and blues collection for her new lead-free apartment.

Ryan Phillips Sr. was best man, sporting a scowl and a basic black suit. Everyone else wore African attire as a salute to the journey the couple was about to take.

"I now introduce Ms. Zenobia Jones and Mr. Ryan Phillips Jr.," said Brother Pastor.

"What?" came a gasp from the back.

Scotty turned around giving the sisters a furious look that dared them to speak again.

Grandma Jones held Amita throughout the service, trying to get her to reach forward and grab a Winnie the Pooh rattle. Grandma Jones was happy that life had come to Amita's eyes and color to her skin, and she prayed that Amita's progress would continue.

Part Three
Liberia

Chapter Sixteen

The pilot announced, "Good morning. We're scheduled to arrive at Robertsfield International Airport in just over three hours. I hope you enjoy the movie, *The Deer Hunter*."

Ryan had stopped watching movies about Vietnam the day he saw Carl outside the Mini Mart. "No thanks," he told the flight attendant when she tried giving him earplugs. He turned to Zenobia to talk about Liberia.

Ryan told Zenobia, "I read that Franklin Roosevelt went to Liberia to tell them how thankful he was that the country had been the primary rubber source for the Allied Forces. After that, exports of iron ore, rubber, and diamonds grew."

"Little Liberia? I'll be honest, Ryan, what I know about Liberia is what I got from information my grandfather left behind about the Garveyites and how obsessed they were with the freedom from racism and oppression Liberia represented to them. I know that a lot of artists during the Harlem Renaissance and entertainers like Ossie Davis, who did part of his military tour there, all learned first-hand about the Mother Land in Liberia. Aren't you excited to join that history?"

Ryan chose to withhold his commitment to history, choosing instead to ask the flight attendant for a soda. He swallowed a Chloroquine antimalarial pill. "Auch, a-hem, that's bitter. You take yours yet, Zen?"

"I don't need it."

"You forgot your prescription?" he asked, and handed her a pill from his bottle.

"I didn't forget. Liberians don't take a weekly pill—their environment makes them naturally resilient against malaria," she said, refusing his gesture. "I don't want to act like an American tourist; I wanna *be* like a Liberian, so I can experience the culture as a native."

"I've never heard anything so ridiculous. You can only be a native if you are." He got out of his seat to stretch his legs. Ryan turned toward the bathroom and Zenobia gave him an affectionate pat on the butt. He smiled on the inside.

Ryan's love for Zenobia was so full and the experiences she brought him so new, he often lost sight of the difference between an exciting new idea and something stupid. He put rejecting the malaria prophylactic in the stupid column.

"You scare me," he said when he returned. "It's easy to protect you from the things I can see; it's the other stuff that bothers me."

"I don't need a babysitter, Ryan."

Ryan looked sideways at her in silence.

From her window, Zenobia watched a seagull swooping down to catch fish swimming on the ocean's surface.

"I don't intend to be mean," she said, turning to meet his gaze. "I'm scared, too."

And she was. She needed to redress the mistakes made with Clovis and Amita. She had a lot to prove, and didn't have the courage to tell Ryan all she was thinking. "I'll buy Chloroquine in Monrovia."

"It's not just the Chloroquine, Zen. You take risks. You're idealistic—you dance on the edge. We got a lot to learn about living in Liberia. I'm excited about teaching at the American School. But I'm scared I won't be able to catch you if you fall."

"Thank you for choosing Pan Atlantic Airlines. We hope you enjoy your stay in Monrovia," the pilot announced.

"Guess you're on that edge with me," Zenobia chuckled at first. Then she added, "We'll be fine, Ryan. Don't worry."

الله

A dozen men on the runway below gripped their caps and tugged their collars against the plane's rumbling wind and noise. They lined the tarmac without benefit of protective headgear or earplugs. One waved orange fluorescent sticks, like a giant pinwheel, signaling the pilot to his landing.

"Dang!" Ryan said as the jet screeched and braked to a halt. "We were a foot away from having bags and bones spread across the airfield."

Zenobia nudged Ryan forward so they would not miss their turn to spill into the aisle.

"What's your rush?" he asked.

She leaned into his back—"I got something to do,"—and pushed him into the aisle.

On the pavement, Zenobia felt proud and victorious. She closed her eyes to intensify the smell of Africa, the feel of the high sun. She'd never felt so alive. She opened her mouth to take in her own satisfaction and a blanket of hot wet air snatched her breath, forcing a cough.

Zenobia found the spot that she had noticed from the plane's window and ran to it. As she positioned herself to face the dirt and render a *thank you* meditation, a passenger scrambling to catch the shuttle shoved her into the dirt.

Ryan slung his camera bag to his opposite shoulder,

lifted his wife to her feet, and guided her by the elbow to the passenger transport.

"Come, now," said the driver, flicking a cigarette butt in Ryan's direction. "I don't have all day," and directed the crowd to his shuttle.

Zenobia, scooting next to Ryan, shook off dust and embarrassment. She tried, unsuccessfully, to avoid sitting on the stuffing that poked out of the vinyl seats and wrinkled her nose at the smell of mold.

☙

The dusty, one-terminal building barely contained all the chaos inside. Three jets had landed within the hour connecting passengers from international hubs. There were no electronic boards announcing arrivals and departures, no loudspeakers calling names of lost children or family members, no kiosks offering friendly answers or directions to here or there.

Airport officials greeted foreign dignitaries with a nod and handshake, handled their travel documents, and ushered them through customs and outside to waiting cars. Zenobia heard a cacophony of languages as clusters of "handled" travelers passed her. She stretched to see if she recognized anyone from *World News*.

Ryan told Zenobia, "I'll wait for the bags."

"But we have to go through immigration together."

Ryan watched the ground crew toss luggage from their dollies; the crowd surged forward in search of nametags, labels, and ribbons that distinguished their bags. "Go 'head. I can watch the line from here."

Zenobia ran to the immigration and naturalization cubicle. When she was third in line, she motioned to Ryan. Then while waiting her turn, she recalled CeCe's airport instructions.

"You have to be assertive, not aggressive," CeCe had told

Zenobia about the immigrations process. "Airport jobs are prestigious. Anyone lucky enough to get one is connected to the right person—that makes them special. Give them a dash, and they'll return a favor."

"What's a dash?"

CeCe told her it's what you give in exchange for something you want. To Zenobia's puzzled look, CeCe had explained that when dash gets out of hand, it's a bribe, but it's more like a tip paid forward. You need a favor, pay dash, CeCe explained. You need to show gratitude, pay dash. If you buy a woman's entire market table, she may dash you something to say thanks because now she can go home. When she sees you the next day, she'll dash you a special deal on bananas, peanuts, or whatever. You make her your daily stop, and she'll give you your own price for anything she sells. You can dash with anything, CeCe had told Zenobia. It's the best way to get out of a jam.

CeCe had said, "My mother thinks dash borders on graft. Get used to it; it's a valid medium of exchange, and the way things are done in Africa."

When it was Zenobia's turn in line, she waved to Ryan again.

Ryan ran to immigration, looking backward for their luggage to hit the broken-tiled floor.

The officer, ignoring Zenobia, read from his coffee-stained Observer Newspaper dated March 15, 1979.

Zenobia looked at the line forming behind her and hoped that the officer was only taking a quick break. She waited and Ryan watched across the terminal for their bags. When ten minutes had passed with no acknowledgment, Zenobia opened their documents and slid passports, visas, and certification of vaccination records across the scratched desk.

Someone yelled in Spanish, "Hurry up. I have to be out of this line before noon."

Everyone in hearing range of the irate man turned in the direction of the outburst—some drew their bags and their companions closer.

The immigrations officer collapsed the newspaper and sucked a long wind through his teeth. He crumpled the paper under his elbow, folded Zenobia's documents one inside the other, and pushed them to the side.

"Step aside," he said, while responding to a cute woman who brought him coffee and a smile.

Ryan pulled Zenobia close and watched while the officer waited on three people before picking up the documents Zenobia had shoved at him.

"He's a butt," Ryan said under his breath.

"Shhh," she whispered without moving her lips.

The officer pointed to the spot near the center of his desk where he wanted Zenobia to stand, and he asked, "Can I help you?" as he flipped through the documents.

"How long is your stay?" he asked, still looking over the documents.

"One year."

"One year," confirmed Ryan, still looking over the crowd in the direction of baggage claim.

"And what is the purpose of your visit?"

"Teachers," she said, her eyes moving between Ryan and the official. "We're teachers at the American School in Monrovia." It was the response CeCe had told Zenobia would require the least explanation.

"That's a small bag for such a long visit," the officer said, leaning over and looking at Zenobia's carry-on.

Ryan spotted a man collecting their bags and headed

toward Baggage Claim. Zenobia grabbed Ryan's wrist. "I can't get you through immigration."

Ryan waved toward a stranger who now had all four of their bags. He peered impatiently at the officer.

Zenobia took a pair of men's socks from her carry-on, and handed them to the officer saying, "I hope these will keep you warm in rainy season."

Zenobia ignored Ryan when he asked, "Can you hurry him?"

The officer took the socks, sat back on his stool, and stamped the documents with a thump that startled Zenobia.

"Ninety days," he said, giving them the maximum time he could approve. "Then you mu' go to Labor Ministry for your work permit and to Immigration for a residency permit to stay one year. Don't forget now, work permit and residency permit. They are important, ya hear?"

The officer checked his watch. Eleven forty-five. "Enjoy your stay in Liberia," he said, placing the socks under his arm and putting up a cardboard sign that read "Back at 2:00."

Ryan ran toward baggage claim. Seeing him coming, the olive-skinned man extended his hand toward Ryan. His speech was foreign, his gesture friendly.

Ryan relaxed his stance, saying, "Thanks, man."

He got their bags, took the man's business card, and motioned to a customs official. "Our ride is waiting outside," Ryan said to the officer. "Can you get us through customs before lunch?" He put a package of boxer shorts along with their declaration forms into the official's hand.

Ryan had filled out the forms as instructed, declaring no illegal drugs, weapons, plant products, foreign currency, endangered wild life, or prescription medicines over and above personal usage. He couldn't get over the shock that the two hundred US dollars he had declared on the form was considered legal tender this far away from home.

The officer ran a chewing stick back and forth across his teeth. "Only clothes inside?"

"Only clothes."

The officer stamped the day's date on the forms and waved them toward the terminal exit. "Welcome to Monrovia, Liberia."

Just outside, a group of boys kicked up dust as they romped and shouted, "Mista, Mista," and motioned for Ryan to put coins into their begging bowls. The boys were barefoot, threadbare, and their faces bore snaggletooth smiles. Something about the boys tugged at Ryan; they reminded him of Carl. He wondered why the boys weren't in school.

Then a horn blast, and Zenobia's yank snatched his attention. He turned and led Zenobia into the sweltering humidity.

Chapter Seventeen

"Over here! Over here!" Kito Williams yelled from across the street. "Welcome home." She lifted Zenobia off the ground with her squeeze, even though Kito was fifteen pounds lighter.

Kito asked, "Who is this? You didn't tell me you had a travel companion." Her rapid patois carried a Midwest influence.

"This is my husband, Ryan."

"Your what?" asked Kito, exposing a gap-toothed smile.

Ryan extended his hand. "Pleased to meet you, Kito."

Rejecting his hand, Kito stood on tiptoes to embrace him. "That makes us family."

"How's your mother?" Zenobia asked Kito.

"Long as Daisy is making money, she's fine. And she makes it hand over fist."

When Ryan walked away to load the luggage into the black Chevy Blazer, Kito stared him up and down and winked approval.

Zenobia rolled down the window and stuck her head outside to let sunrays beam onto her face. "It's gonna be hard remembering that I came here for more than sunshine and palm trees," she said, thinking about the hopes and dreams of family and friends she had packed with her things. Feeling a rush inside, she turned her face toward the heavens and could have sworn that Grandpa Jones was smiling back.

She whispered, "Thank you."

Kito pulled onto the dirt road for the thirty-eight-mile drive to Monrovia. "Let's go!"

As if to the beat of High Life music blaring from their eight-track tape decks, taxis and jitney buses darted across the narrow road. Along the shoulder, a mantle of palm and coconut trees, giant ferns, banana, and plantain trees grew. Red, yellow, and white blooms peppered the green foliage.

On the way to Monrovia, Kito drove through the small town of Paynesville where men played checkers outside a small shop, using Coca Cola bottle crates for chairs. A wooden board across their knees served as a tabletop checkerboard; bottle caps were their checker pieces. Children in second or third-hand clothes played—the girls clapped and sang patty-cake while the boys played soccer using an empty soda can. Red dust that clung to their hems exaggerated the tattered and worn look of their clothes.

Ryan asked Kito, "What about those street boys who were begging at the airport?"

"They are 'grown'a boys' or grown up boys, children who are on their own either because they ran away from hard times at home or because their parents send them out each day to hustle for the family."

"Don't worry," Kito continued when she saw Ryan's slacked jaw from her rearview mirror. "They aren't aggressive, but you do want to pay attention in close quarters like the market. They are known to pick your pocket."

Women crossed the street with empty head loads, signifying the end of their market day, while young girls sold greens, rice, okra, and oil in front of small shops along the road.

A broad-shouldered, wide-hipped woman walked side to side with straight-backed balance. She carried a two-foot by three-foot wooden market table on her head and displayed an innate rhythm that came from blood memory. Another woman steadied her head load with one hand and held on to her daughter with the other, while an infant, wrapped tightly to her back, slept.

Kito turned off the ignition. "We have to wait 'til the motorcade passes."

Ryan rose to get a long view of the intersection and the crowd. Children and adults alike stood five deep along the sidewalk. "What's going on?" he said, eyeing the entourage of large black luxury cars.

"It's the President's Holiday Motorcade for J. J. Roberts' birthday. He was the first black governor before independence and the first and seventh elected president after independence."

A record blaring through loudspeakers in the distance sang, "Liberia Is My Home," to a High Life beat.

"That's interesting. Liberians must've really liked him," said Ryan, trying to talk over loud honking horns.

"Yeah, we did," Kito said. "What's even more interesting is that he was born in Virginia." Kito paused a few minutes. "Today the motorcade is for Roberts; tomorrow it'll be President Tolbert leaving or returning to town." She pointed, "Look at the kids jumping up and down. You'll get used to it."

As the motorcade passed and the onlookers went back to their day, Kito revved the engine. "This street is Tubman Boulevard. It'll take you anywhere you want to go. The people refer to the left side of the street as 'ocean side.' The big public hospital is in that direction. It has nine hundred beds, but never mind going there for treatment. Daisy says J.F.K. Hospital stands for 'just for killing,'" she laughed, but Ryan and Zenobia looked startled.

"Here is City Hall, over there is University of Liberia, and just ahead is Capitol Hill. Oh, and that's the Executive Mansion, where the president and first family live."

Kito stopped at the next traffic light. "You've got plenty of time to sightsee," she said, turning around and heading toward Zenobia and Ryan's new home. Two taxis darted by, almost sideswiping the Blazer.

Ryan ducked, saying, "I'm not sure I want to ride in one, but in case I change my mind, what's the trick to catching one of these flying taxis?"

"No trick," laughed Kito. "When you're headed toward town, wave at a taxi going in the direction of the ocean on your left and when he stops, say, 'In town.' Once inside, tell him the street. If you're not sure of the street, just tell him the specific place you're going."

"They look full," said Zenobia.

"That's how the driver makes his money. He picks up until he's full, and you ride while he picks up and drops off until he gets to your stop. If he veers off a block or two, he will eventually get back to the main road." Kito shrugged her shoulders, "It's a good way to learn your way around."

Ryan wasn't satisfied. "There's no shorter way to get from one place to another?"

"Yeah, you can walk. You can charter and pay the driver for the full car. But what's your hurry? You're on Africa time now."

Rubber trees, hibiscus shrubs, and thistle lined the residential section of Airfield Road. Dark blue violets stretched tall and wild; snow-white and pink blooms dotted green vines that hung over the tops of concrete fences. Shanties made of mud and roofs of thatch or corrugated aluminum nestled comfortably between homes of the well-to-do. The giant leaves of coconut and palm trees hovered like fans over the yards of rich and poor alike. In the section of Airfield Road reserved for President Tolbert's private air convoy was a small airport.

Kito started her next lesson. "Now I won't have you embarrassing me with those American 'I don't talk to stranger' ways.

"Liberians greet everybody. When you pass someone on the street, speak. Before you conduct business, speak. And when someone speaks first, speak back. Say, 'Hello,' 'Hello yah,' 'How the body,' anything, just as long as you speak. It's our way of showing that we are all humans."

"And if we don't?" asked Zenobia.

"You'll be thought stupid, for starters. A market woman may say, 'I can' sell you my banana, if you can' speak,'" said Kito, mimicking the country patois and dismissive hand gestures of a market woman. "A taxi driver may say he can' hear you if you talk too proper, if you don't *break the English down*. Bottom line, speak without being condescending."

Ryan asked, "Is 'What's going on?' okay?"

"Are you kidding? We love American slang. The only way to go wrong is by not speaking—shows your ignorance."

"I'm gonna perfect my Liberian patois," said Zenobia. "Soon you won't be able to tell me from a Liberian woman."

Kito pulled up to a one-story bungalow. "Here we are."

Ryan and Zenobia jumped out of the Blazer and ran up to the house.

"Wait for me, Kito," Zenobia called. "I need my hair done, but I gotta look around."

Ryan ran his hand across the three-foot-high cement fence and took time to notice that someone had built a lattice finish into every other cinder. The fence wrapped around the house from back to front, separating it from neighbors.

With Zenobia at his side, he took the four steps and entered the indigo-painted door. Ryan dropped the luggage where he stood.

Wicker and bamboo furnishings, arranged in a conversational pit, welcomed them. African print cushions and throw pillows matched the sunburst design in the curtains.

Ryan looked in the two bedrooms on the left and decided one would double as guest room and office. Ahead was the kitchen equipped with wall cabinets, enough counter space to cook a seven-course meal, and a four-burner range with a gas cylinder attached to its side.

Zenobia took in the smell of freshly painted walls and the warmth of blue ceramic floor tiles in the bathroom. In the windowless room off the kitchen were two fifty-five-gallon water drums.

"Look at this yard," Zenobia called, seeing coconut, papaya, and mango trees from the back door. "We'll have fruit salad everyday."

Ryan pointed to a small coal pot perched on a concrete slab several feet from the house. "I guess that's where we cook when the power goes out."

Back in the living-dining room area, Ryan sat down at the bistro table to test the strength of the wicker chairs, and then he checked the lamps. "Let there be light," he said when brightness appeared.

Zenobia play-hit him, "I told you not to worry."

"That just means I have time to get candles," Ryan told her. "Tell you what. I'll handle getting settled and day-to-day issues while you start your clinic. Deal?"

Zenobia couldn't remember the last time she'd cooked a

meal for Ryan, and she was happy that being married wasn't going to press her into domestic service. "Deal."

Ryan had read in the American School welcome packet that Monrovia experienced frequent running water and power outages. "The brochures say there isn't enough rain water in dry season to generate power for the turbines, which is what makes electricity here. So we have to keep candles and reserved water on hand." To her startled look, Ryan added, "I'll make sure we have light and water."

"More deal."

"Are you coming?" Kito honked and hollered from the Blazer. "I lose money every minute there isn't a butt in my chair."

When she headed toward the door, Ryan grabbed Zenobia's arm and pulled her to him. He stroked her mane and kissed her on the neck. "I'm glad I'm here with you."

"Thanks," said Zenobia, grateful he'd slowed her down to taste the moment. "Our first home as a couple, and I'm happy, too." She reached up, locked her fingers behind his head, sniffed sandalwood, and placed a soft wet kiss on his lips.

Just as Ryan whispered *Zen* into her ear, the horn honked again.

"I don't have all day, Zenobia."

Zenobia ran into the bedroom, opened her carry-on, and pulled out one of the purple pouches she had made before leaving Farrow. She looked over her shoulder to make sure Ryan wasn't looking and pinned a tiny pouch that contained citrine quartz inside her waistband. It would protect and keep her focused.

"You gonna be okay?" she asked Ryan half-heartedly while running toward the door.

"Go 'head. I'll square things away here."

Outside, Zenobia thanked Kito. "It's great. Did I send enough money?"

"Plenty. Daisy and I opened personal and business accounts for you with the deposit you sent. We need to stop at the bank on the way to the salon so you can sign everything."

※

It was three o'clock. Ryan stood on the porch, looking in both directions and trying to decide whether to catch a taxi on Airfield Road or walk to the main street. Across the dirt road, a small man hauled a hundred-pound sack of rice out of a taxi with the words "Blessed by God" stenciled in capital letters on the side in bold black paint. The man threw the heavy sack over his shoulder and entered a thatch-roofed mud house from the side. In front of the house, a young girl sold market items from a wooden table and nearby, a wild aloe vera plant threatened to overtake her stand.

"Hello," said Ryan, stepping around the plant as he approached the girl.

"Wan' buy my groun' pea'? Fi' cen.' Or'ange,' fi' cen,'" she asked shyly while skillfully shaving the peel from the skin of each orange, paring a straw-sized plug out of the top, and then securing the plug back into its place. She swiped at flies that tried to drink juice from her hands and arms.

"I'll buy some ground peas, young lady," said Ryan just as the man returned.

"Say man. Oh, uh, uh, hello yahh. My name is Ryan. My wife and I just moved across the street." Ryan extended his hand.

"I'm Ezra," the man said, studying Ryan's hand gesture and returning a handshake of three clutches that he had learned from his African American passengers.

"This is my small girl, Satta. She's nine years old."

"Nice to meet you, Satta," said Ryan to a toothy smile.

"Say, is that your taxi?"

"Yeah, you need ride?"

"I'm going into town to look around. You going in that direction?"

"You want charta'?"

Ryan laughed, "No, no charter. You can just drop me off, I'll get myself back." Ryan put a list into his pocket and said to Satta, "Bye, young lady."

Chapter Eighteen

Ezra Kaba had been born on the Hotstone Rubber Plantation in Harbel, forty miles east of Monrovia. Everyone referred to the gooey crop grown and harvested on the plantation as white gold. Ezra's family had lived in a two-room shanty, rent-free, for his father's work on the plantation.

Ezra's father, born in Grand Bassa County, had moved to the plantation with his young family to find work. His job was ensuring that hundreds of tappers earned their thirty-five cents a day pay.

Ezra did not know his "year old" when he began tapping rubber trees. He was barely three feet tall and was assigned to work a grove that he could reach. His sister, a half-foot taller, worked a different grove at her height, and so it went on until all eight Kaba children and all plantation residents had assignments that matched their height and experience. Young men agile enough to shimmy up the waist wide trunks worked the tops of mature trees. Ezra's older brother was responsible for organizing the day's latex collection.

On Ezra's first tapping day, just after daybreak, his father helped because the boy wasn't strong enough to use the tapping knife, a sharp rounded blade that protruded from the base of a wooden handle. Ezra's father showed him how to make the downward, diagonal gash just enough to go through the silver bark on the north side of the tree, being careful not to cut into the wood. Little Ezra set his goal.

When he returned to the trees late that first morning, Ezra jumped and clapped at the result of his work. The milky, white substance bled out of the bark and dripped into the collection cups his father had tied below the gashes. Ezra gathered his liquid latex and took it to his brother at the collection point. It didn't pour.

His brother dropped anticoagulant into Ezra's bucket and then poured the softened latex into two two-gallon buckets, saying, "You have to tap early and return to collect before the eleven o'clock sun or the latex will get hard."

The older brother made a shoulder yoke, tying the buckets weighing seventy-five pounds to opposite ends of a bamboo stick. He led a hundred-man caravan, each man carrying his own shoulder-yoke of heavy buckets, on the mile-long walk from the groves to the latex station where the white gold was processed, dried, and readied for export to America.

Residents had lived, worked, and died on the rubber plantation for generations. As years went by Ezra ventured away only for small trips to nearby villages. On a visit to buy flip-flops, he watched a Peace Corps worker buying balloons, boiled eggs, and candy for a group of kids that were celebrating a birthday.

When he arrived back home, Ezra pressed his mother to figure out his "year old," to give him the year, if not the date, that he was born. She remembered being pregnant while serving a party hosted by Hotstone for William Tolbert, newly elected vice president, and his wife. It was an occasion special enough for Hotstone executives to hire plantation workers as servers when, under normal circumstances, those workers were not allowed to enter an executive's home.

She was sure she had delivered Ezra before Superior Tire opened its rubber operations nearby because he was nursing her infected breasts (caused by chemical waste that ran into the river where she bathed and washed clothes) when Hotstone managers ranted about competition.

Ezra added and subtracted the numbers the way he had learned to count the number of latex cups he needed to fill a bucket. He told his mother he had deciphered his month between January and May (after Christmas and before the rains) and his year somewhere between 1952 and 1955, making him sixteen or seventeen years old. He liked the sound of sixteen, so he ran over to the management office, a cabin that doubled as sleeping quarters for international managers, and looked at the wall calendar. It was Friday, January 10. Ezra declared January 10 his birth date and 1954 his birth year.

Ezra stood five-feet-nine inches the year he declared his age; he was a full head above his father. Climbing trees and running over the plantation had made him muscular, and it was apparent, even without his age, that he was a man. He was high atop a tree, smelling the promise of rain, when his father called him down to talk with Boss Man.

"Ezra," Boss Man said, chewing on tobacco that colored his teeth and gums a brownish-yellow.

"Yes, sir," answered Ezra, his back slightly bowed. His eyes, however, watched the tobacco juice spittle that hung from the corner of Boss Man's moustache.

"Your pa is getting old."

Not wanting to disrespect management, Ezra glanced sideways at his father and noticed old scars and leathery skin from years of climbing trees in the sun. His shoulders hunched from hauling too many buckets; still, Ezra did not see old in his father's face.

"You've been a good worker," said Boss Man, looking in

the direction of Mr. Kaba, who rocked back and forth on his heels, nodding and smiling proud like at his son. "It's time to get you ready to step into your father's shoes. You think you would like that? Huh?"

Ezra, standing only a foot away from a spit bucket filled with brown juice, inched his bare feet back to the side until he added space between him and the spittoon.

Mr. Kaba put his eyes on a palmetto bug and listened to the familiar conversation that had occurred between the plantation supervisor, himself, and his own father some twenty years before. It had put a flurry of events into place that retired his father to cleaning tap knives and doing day labor, and it had marked his own rite of passage to the position of plantation overseer.

Boss Man continued. "But right now, I need you to pick up a package for me in Monrovia." He used his tongue to spit a spray of tobacco liquid into the bucket. Bingo! "Can I trust you with a favor, Ezra?"

"Oh, for true," said Ezra. The dimness in his father's eyes blunted his excitement over traveling to the big city. "Yes, sir, you can trust me, Boss Man."

Ezra boarded an almost empty bus, gave a dollar to the driver, and looked around for a seat. Behind the driver sat a smooth-complexioned girl who shot her eyes out the window at a passing car when Ezra looked her way. He took the aisle seat next to her and when she felt his hot gaze, she dropped her head and scooted closer to the window.

From the window, Ezra saw, for the first time, what life was like away from the rubber plantation. He counted seven stops to small towns where the driver picked up women who were either taking market to another town or returning home with an empty head load. Trees, streams, and grasslands crept by as the bus advanced toward the city. One man climbed onto the bus with a goat and a crate of live chickens, three of which he sold to passengers on the bus.

Ezra watched a bush cow grazing and a wild boar cooling off in mud near a stream.

Traffic picked up as the bus approached Monrovia, and Ezra watched taxis tool around each other playing chicken, barely escaping people, and cars. A passenger called out her stop from the back, "Gardnersville," she said, and at that moment, Ezra realized he did not know how to call his stop.

"In town, Ducor Hotel," called another.

"My name is Ezra," he finally said to the girl.

"I'm Sarah," she replied, using her hand to cover a smile that leapt to her lips. She knew the boy needed help but she made him ask.

"I'm goin' to Monrovia."

"Uh-huh."

"This is my first time."

Sarah glanced down at her tightly clasped fingers, sneaked a peek at the boy, and then looked out the window again. "Jus' tell the driver the place or street you are going," she said shyly. "He'll let you down soon as he can. From there, walk or take taxi to the exact place."

"Post office," Ezra called to the driver.

Sarah called, "Wata'side Ma'ket."

Chapter Nineteen

When Kito reached the Always Beautiful hair salon with Zenobia, several men in black leisure suits were walking out of the rear exit. She drove into her reserved space. The men were animated in their gestures, passionate with their words, yet they lowered their voices to a whisper as they passed Kito's car on their way to the parked 1975 Volvo where a driver sat waiting.

Kito overheard one of the men saying, "Our country is filled with natural resources. We should not be poor," and clenched his fist.

Another said, "Blacks around the diaspora long to taste our freedom. We are the first independent African nation, and there is pressure, because the world is waiting to see what we do with our liberty, if we can be self-sufficient."

"It's up to us. No one else can solve our problems," said the first man, his fist still in a knot.

The man with the briefcase spoke to Kito for the group. "Hello, Ma'am." He nodded his head.

"Who was that?" asked Zenobia, sitting up in the Blazer to get a better look as the Volvo sped off.

"Could be anybody," answered Kito, masking her concern about the 'it's up to us,' words she had heard her mother repeat like a mantra.

"He's probably just the husband or boyfriend of one of our customers," Kito continued and broke off a piece of aloe vera from a wild plant that grew next to the back entrance.

✦

Inside, Kito looked for Daisy in the back room that doubled as a lounge between client appointments and a meeting room for her social and civic activities.

The smell of stale cigarettes met Kito before she spotted the pile of butts in the ashtrays. She knew the men had left the mess.

Kito directed Zenobia to take the chair at her workstation. With two hard snaps, she shook the wrinkles from a black nylon apron and draped it around Zenobia's neck, displaying two lines of wording: "Always Beautiful" and "Businesses Working for Liberia" in bold, green, embroidered letters.

"What did they mean, 'It's up to us'?" asked Zenobia.

"It means that we have to do our part to develop Liberia. You have to get your clinic opened. There are too many women planting rice and greens, and cooking to keep their man's favor. It's up to us to guide Liberian women into the twenty-first century."

"I know what it means to us, Kito. What did those men mean? And why were they whispering?"

Kito didn't answer. She peeked out of the front window, closed the blinds, and ushered Zenobia to the washbowl, where she leaned against the wall. She rubbed her leg.

"What's wrong?" asked Zenobia.

"Nothing. My leg is all."

Hearing nothing else, Zenobia pressed, "Well, what's wrong with your leg? Anything I can do?"

Kito finished washing Zenobia's hair in silence. Zenobia, prone to her own brooding, wondered how long it would take before one of them would start talking.

Kito led Zenobia back to her styling station while limping and rubbing her right leg. She parted the hair, opened a wide-mouth jar of hair sheen, liberally applied it to each exposed section, and gave Zenobia's scalp a deep massage. Then she combed the long wavy curls, made a tiny part, and squeezed a drop of aloe vera gel onto the hair before braiding.

Zenobia was sure she would burst in the thirty minutes of nothing but the hum of the hair dryer, the sound of taxis honking, and girls selling oranges and ground peas for five cents outside, when all of a sudden Kito said, "I don't like to talk about it." She paused and took several breaths.

"I had polio when I was little. I spent a lot of time in hospitals in Cincinnati where they were doing research." Kito turned the chair toward the mirror so the two could see each other as they talked. "I'm fine now, but my leg aches and gives out sometimes when I'm tired."

"Polio?" Zenobia shot back, spinning around and eyeing Kito up and down.

Kito squeezed gel from the aloe plant onto the back of her left hand, so she wouldn't have to wrestle with the leaf for each braid, and continued. "I don't so much remember getting polio, just having it. It ran rampant throughout Liberia in the fifties. I had to live on a rehabilitation ward with other polio children. The paralysis in my leg was the side effect of beating the disease. I walked in those darned leg irons for two years, and when they were removed, I had a limp for another year, which if I have to say so myself, I disguised well with very sassy moves," she said, swinging and sashaying her hips.

"My father enrolled me in a research program for surgery to correct my limp and Ma and I flew to Cincinnati. Even though my limp was cured by the time I walked out of that hospital three months later, I had spent so much time in hospitals that I never had any desire to go back," she said, smacking her palms against each other.

Kito sprayed oil sheen over Zenobia's entire head. "CeCe can have her turn getting her American education. I got mine in the hospital."

Zenobia listened intently to Kito and thought about Amita. She wondered if anyone was working on miracle research for lead poisoning. "You don't look like you've ever had anything more than a cold."

"It's just that I can't stand long. That's why I work half-days. Speaking of which, how do you like?"

Zenobia fingered the cascading braids that swung across her shoulders and the cowry shells that Kito had staggered and sewn throughout her hair.

"Pin the braids up, tie them back into a pony tail, or let them frame your face the way they are now?" Kito said, showing her each design.

Zenobia said, "Girl, you laid me out," holding a hand-held mirror up high so she could see the back. "I hate what made you want to stay in Liberia, but I'm glad you're here."

"Yeah, yeah. Don't forget Ma is making dinner for you and Ryan tomorrow night."

Ryan flung his camera over his shoulder as he climbed out of Ezra's taxi on Broad Street. He pushed his hands deep into his pockets and walked, oblivious to passersby who stopped and stretched their necks to take in his unusual height. When he stepped off the curb to walk with the light, a taxi driver honked loud and long and sent him back to the sidewalk.

Ryan read the names printed in big letters on signboards and store windows: "Abdullah's Tailoring," "Ibrahim's Electronic Repairs," and "Closson's Groceries." Outside each shop, a woman sold small markets of bananas, oranges, greens, palm oil, or rice.

On the lower level of an arcade, Ryan bought a *Newsweek Magazine* and a cup of coffee and then sat next to a table full of members of the Unification Church. They huddled, discussing *Unification News* articles, and deciding if Monrovia was a feasible location for a new chapter.

Five boys rushed Ryan with begging bowls. "Mista!" He pulled away from them and crossed the street. Then another boy in flip-flops startled Ryan by shoving something cold into his face. "Wan' buy my wata'? Fi' cen,'" he asked, dangling a half-frozen, water-filled-Ziploc bag that he had dug from the ice chest strapped across his tee-shirted back. "Wan' buy my wata'? Fi' cen,'" he repeated, as water dripped down his dark arms.

Ryan put a dollar into the boy's wet hand. "I'm not thirsty, but this is for your honest work."

"Thank you, thank you," the boy said smiling as Ryan continued walking toward the Carlton, and the YMCA. He crossed over to Gurley Street, where he saw a business center, restaurants, and discothèques.

Then he saw it. Ten or so boys stood, some in flip-flops and others in their bare feet, looking up at a larger-than-life-sized poster of Bruce Lee that was plastered onto the brick side of the Relda Theatre. The words under Bruce Lee's famous stance read, "Knowing Is Not Enough, We Must Apply. Willing Is Not Enough, We Must Do."

The marquee announced *Enter the Dragon*. Stunned by seeing a poster of his favorite actor, Ryan didn't realize someone had walked up behind him.

"Hey, man. What's going on?" asked the stranger, extending a hand. "You like 'kick-'em-up' movies? Bruce is a funny cat."

Ryan knew by the look and language that the man was from the States. When he extended his hand, the stranger slapped his hand into Ryan's, grasped the middle finger of Ryan's right hand between his thumb and third finger, and brought it up quickly with a snap.

"Let me try that again," said Ryan, eyeing the chubby dashiki-clad man who wore a satchel of incense across his shoulder.

"It's called the Snapshake. I'm Kweku. From Michigan. Been here a couple years. You want some incense? Three for five dollars," he said and pushed three packs at Ryan.

"Sure. I'm Ryan from Ohio. What brings you to Liberia?"

"Peace of mind. I came over with a bunch of brothas to start a small business."

"Incense business?"

"Don't knock it, man. It pays the rent." Kweku peeled five dollars from the wad of bills in his pocket, gave it to Ryan for change, and proceeded down Gurley Street.

Over his shoulder, Kweku called back, "Check it out, man. They show the Chinese version of Bruce at two o'clock, English at five. Wait 'til you see the Chinese version of *Way of the Dragon*, with Chuck Norris and no subtitles. You'll fall out laughing."

Chapter Twenty

The first night in her new bed, Zenobia tossed and turned to the sound of crickets and bullfrogs; she was sure they had camped in the grass beneath her window. She pulsed involuntarily to the call and response of drums, shakera, and chordophone in the distance.

The night was hot and dark; it even felt black. She lay in a puddle of perspiration, her sheet and gown stuck to her, and all the while Ryan snored. Finally, she stripped off her gown and threw it, along with her pillow, onto the floor.

Zenobia was moving her foot to the drumbeat. "Ouch!" she said quietly, slapping at a mosquito that bit her thigh. She wasn't sure if the moisture she felt was blood or sweat, but her thigh began to swell and itch. It was hot and hard to the touch.

Sleep abandoned her when someone from down the street turned High Life music on a transistor radio. She grabbed a "lappa" skirt from a bedroom chair and plopped hard onto the wicker couch in the living room. Just then, she noticed a lizard above her. Almost seven inches from its head to its swishing tail, it defied gravity by zipping up the wall and running upside down across the ceiling. Zenobia watched it pounce on a mosquito in mid-flight and devour it.

"Touché," she said, thumbing a magazine.

The next morning, Zenobia appealed to Ryan. "Please, don't forget to buy mosquito coils and a fan when you get back from orientation. Between the heat and mosquitoes, I can't—"

He interrupted, "Why buy a fan when we can't depend on electricity? Besides, I thought you were going to become one with the environment, like a native." He put his palms together in a mocking yoga gesture and said, "Ohm."

"Funny." Zenobia held out her neck for his kiss.

She asked with honey dripping. "You gonna get some African garb, maybe a safari suit, while you're in town? It wouldn't hurt to wear a dashiki to dinner with Kito and Daisy."

"What's wrong with my Banlon and Dockers?"

"Nothing."

Anxious to impress the first lady, Zenobia put on the orange, yellow, and green tie-dyed caftan, one of many outfits that Kito and Daisy had bought and hung in her closet. She tried different pairs of sandals—brown, black, before selecting the orange leather ones. She swept her braids up into a French twist and left one cowry-shelled tendril hanging down her back when she heard Kito pull up.

On the road toward ELWA Clinic, children shooed and ran from scurrying goats and chickens. Several men had started their day, bundling bamboo and sugar cane and stacking it on a truck headed for the interior. Sweaty loggers rushed to mark truckloads of logs with company logos for export. A line of women, their head loads and children in tow, walked the road's deep curves.

Zenobia was lost in thought about how physically hard everyone seemed to work when Kito pointed out the sign

"ELWA Safety First Clinic For Women And Children—Eternal Love Winning Africa."

Kito turned into the gravel parking lot and drove around to the rear of the one-story, white concrete building. She pulled into the last space.

"I thought you said the program started at nine-thirty," said Zenobia, looking at her watch and the first lady's motorcade.

"The invitation said nine, but I was counting on them starting the usual half-hour late," said Kito, breathing out embarrassment. "Guess we're not using Liberian time today."

"What is Liberian time?"

"It means things start when the people who are supposed to be there arrive."

Zenobia wrinkled her eyebrows.

"Come on," Kito said. She led Zenobia up the freshly painted steps, past rows of empty wooden benches that lined the front of the building. A sign, "Welcome to ELWA Clinic," hung over the opened door.

About sixty people mingled inside the lobby that would convert into the clinic's reception and triage room after the opening ceremony.

Some women dressed in crisp traditional African garments, others in outfits seen in any Southern Baptist church on Sunday morning. All wore matching pumps or sandals and clutched their purses close to their stomachs. They used their hands or paper programs to fan air that didn't move despite the prodding of a rickety ceiling fan.

Men in open-collared shirts with half-knotted ties leaned against the walls and doorways with looks of "I hope this is over soon" plastered across their faces. Several scrambled, like goats, to meet the first lady's directives.

Kito spotted two empty chairs near the front and, with

Zenobia trailing close behind, tiptoed toward them, just as a woman stepped onto the podium to begin the program.

The first lady would have looked regal with only the white wide-flowing grand Boubou gown, but the gold lamé embroidery stitched on the seams and ankle-hem shouted monarch. Her matching white head wrap, gele, contrasted with her dark skin and made her look younger than someone who had birthed and raised eight children. The first lady's very presence commanded respect and adoration, and Zenobia took note.

"Good morning, ladies and gentlemen. Thank you for coming," said the first lady in a voice and manner reflective of twenty-six years of political life. "Welcome to the opening of the ELWA Safety First Clinic for Women and Children. This wonderful edifice was constructed with Liberian dollars," she said and then waited for the applause to die down.

"As you know, this is my personal project." She nodded toward the eight women who lined the front of the room, and they smiled back politely.

"These women understand that if Liberia is to remain at the forefront of Africa's development, we must ensure the health and welfare of our women and children. Our children are our future."

The crowd clapped and whooped. Several women nodded to their left and right. Some snubbed their noses at the men who looked down at their watches. One man moved toward the door, dabbing his brow.

The first lady took in the approval and continued. "I want to announce a new government campaign—Reform for Women and Children. Joining our campaign are the World Health Organization, the Red Cross, and several churches."

Two chubby women huddled together, whispering, writing notes, and making plans to talk outside.

"Now, please join me in congratulating these women for a job well done." She paused for handclaps before calling each woman and presenting her with a Liberian Lone Star flag and a name-engraved plaque with words, "All Hail Liberia, Hail," from the national anthem and "Liberia First!"

The first lady stepped down from the podium to a passionate chorus of "All Hail, Liberia, Hail," and to a crowd of handshakes and pictures. Kito rushed over to catch the first lady's attention just as a photographer shoved his strobe light into her face and snapped, securing the last picture for his *In the News* photo spread.

"Long live Liberia, happy land; a home of glorious liberty, by God's command," the crowd sang. As they finished, Kito spoke.

"Hello, Madame. I haven't seen you in quite some time."

The motorcade director sucked his teeth, slapped at the limousine's padded hood, and plopped back into the air-conditioned comfort.

The first lady was ready to leave and was annoyed by the disturbance, but she turned and radiated a half-hearted smile. "Why, good afternoon, Kito. You are quite grown up now. How is,"—she could barely spit the word out—"Daisy?"

"She's fine and sends her warmest regards."

"How nice," the first lady said, her counterfeit smile gone. "Well, it's very nice seeing you, Kito."

"Excuse me, Madame First Lady. I want you to meet my friend, Zenobia. She's a midwife from Ohio and she has a special interest in the reform program you just mentioned."

"Pleasure to meet you, Madame First Lady," said Zenobia, trying to show confidence without being pushy.

"Well, young lady," her eyebrows creased, "I'm surprised. I've never heard of a midwife in America."

Zenobia had never talked to a dignitary. She was nervous. Still she stood firm and seized the opportunity that was in front of her.

"Most of my children were born in American hospitals."

"I'm sure they were all great hospitals, Madame First Lady. Let me explain. My grandmother was a midwife in the Deep South when hospitals were not available to most women." She tilted her head toward the now-empty clinic. "Like here."

Zenobia took a breath. "It's true there isn't much need for midwives in America today, but I've taken up my grandmother's calling. I would love to work in your Reform for Women and Children program."

Kito shot Zenobia a *Wow, you're good* look.

"My nonprofit organization has a grant from Babies Incorporated, a baby products company in the States."

"I'm familiar with the company," interrupted the first lady.

"And we would like to use the money to open a maternity ward here; we would call it 'Sister-to-Sister.' The goals are the same as yours—to reduce infant mortality and improve women's health. We would do it by teaching prenatal care, childbirth and hygiene, and child development, and showing the mother how to use the resources in her reach."

"You know my story," said Kito who had been looking for the place to jump in. "I'm helping Zenobia open the clinic, and getting babies immunized. I'll teach cosmetology to anyone who wants that as a career. I agree with what you said. 'We must prepare Liberian women for the future.'"

The first lady abruptly turned and headed toward her waiting limousine.

"May we take a picture with you, Madame First Lady?" Kito called after her.

The first lady gestured to her driver that she'd only be another minute. "Sure," she said and threw one arm around Zenobia, the other around Kito, while an aide took the picture.

Zenobia added, "My grandmother will be proud to show this picture to her church lady friends."

The driver prepared to step between his boss and the pesky women when she turned and said, "I like your idea, young lady. Have Kito bring you to my office next week. I'll introduce you to my brother-in-law."

The driver closed the door after she tucked herself neatly into the back seat. As he drove off, the first lady pushed the automated window control and said, "Kito, do tell Daisy we must have dinner sometime."

Zenobia and Kito held their laughter until the motorcade drove away and they were safe inside the Blazer, where they could mock the first lady's proper gestures.

"Because of a long-standing feud, Ma would rather have her heart cut out than eat a crumb with that woman. Ma and the first family go through their polite social niceties, but there is no love between them. But enough of that; where did you learn to pitch your program like that, Miss Zenobia?"

"Whatever works."

Chapter Twenty-One

From the time Daisy was twelve, customers had lined up, like human rope, around the two-room mud house where she grew up. The women sat shoulder to shoulder in the hot sun, sometimes ten a day, one after the other on empty Coca Cola crates, waiting for one of Daisy's intricate cornrow designs or hot-comb pressed and curled hairstyles that she copied from Bessie Smith and Billie Holiday album covers.

Neighborhood children started their own businesses—laundry, snack food, and trinket sales—off Daisy's customers while they waited. Her stamina to work long hours had started then, as she used well water for shampooing and charcoal heaters for heating the styling irons. No matter the challenge, she managed to create head-turning crowns of glory.

During one of her long stays with Kito in Ohio, Daisy took a Master-Plus course at the Poro Cosmetology and Charm School. When she returned to Liberia, she became the largest distributor of black hair care products in West Africa.

Now local women, wives of dignitaries, and women as far away as Sierra Leone and Côte D'Ivoire came to Always Beautiful with styles pictured in *Jet* and *Ebony* for Daisy's special brand of curling, weaving, and cutting.

In 1953, Daisy Togba wasn't just pregnant by Herschel Williams, she was in love. Fearing her family and his would ostracize her, she had kept her secret until her navel poked out.

Herschel's mother didn't understand her son's insistence on marrying Daisy. After all, there had been plenty of liaisons with indigenous women that resulted in children. What was so special about Daisy?

"Don't shame your family," his mother had said. "Marry your own class."

Daisy's sister had accused her of selling out their great-grandfather's vow to keep the Togba bloodline pure for the social status that came with marrying a man of settler origin. With that, Jarteh Togba's descendants, Daisy's own family, shunned her for violating his oath.

Despite his penchant for liaisons, Herschel married Daisy. To meld the settler and country cultures that dueled inside her, Daisy prepared country food and served it on fine china. She used her country patois at home and polished her English for the public, until Cecelia and Kito were born.

When the babies came, Daisy hired a country babysitter, cook, and laundress so she could grow her hair business. When doctors diagnosed Kito with polio, Daisy felt the blaming, piercing stares of her mother-in-law right along with the blessing of the best health care her husband's money could buy.

When Herschel died, leaving Daisy with two children, she could have roamed the streets in the same clothes she was born in when his mother made a point of maintaining her disapproval of Daisy, ignoring her and only doing things for the children. Daisy grew tired of straddling two worlds, one minute defending against one side or the other, and the next minute pretending she didn't care.

Daisy called on the doggedness passed down by her great-grandfather and made up her mind to please only herself. She named the priorities in her life: love—her children; passion—her business; and pastime—her politics. She owed Jarteh Togba the latter.

The sun had begun to set, but enough light remained for Zenobia to get the full effect when the taxi drove into the circled entrance of Daisy's home. As she tried to take in everything at once, Zenobia tripped and almost fell over a twenty-four-inch flowerpot. She smoothed over her embarrassment with a smile at Ryan. Then she secured the matching lappa over her caftan all the while goggling at the second-floor balcony and veranda, which started at the front and wrapped around both sides to the back. Flower boxes that draped the veranda seemed gaudy to Zenobia next to the showpiece landscape.

Ryan had just paid the driver when the front door opened, and Daisy appeared wearing a mud cloth caftan, tailor-made to fit her demure shape. Her nails and hair represented the art of a professional stylist; her flawless skin carried only a hint of foundation. Her eyelashes and lipstick gave her the finished look of a queen.

"Welcome," Daisy said, ushering Zenobia and Ryan through the foyer where a Tiffany chandelier hung. "It's wonderful to have you, Zenobia," she said, after a big hug and kiss. "Is this the handsome man I've heard so much about?"

"Yes, ma'am. This is my husband, Ryan."

Daisy hugged Ryan and showed the couple to the dining room. "Dinner is ready."

Zenobia took Ryan's hand and followed Daisy around two Asian-designed and gold-plated vases that stood guard at the dining room entrance.

"Your home is beautiful and warm, like something you'd see in an interior decorating magazine," said Ryan.

Daisy pointed to their seats. "Thank you, we're comfortable. Please, sit down."

The luxury and formality made Ryan want to pull out Zenobia's seat, but she gave him the "I can do it" look that he had grown accustomed to.

"Thanks, Mrs. Williams, for putting our place together," said Ryan. "Kito told us you picked out everything. I can tell that your taste transcends your business."

"Please, Ryan, honey, call me Daisy. It makes me feel old when people your age call me *Mrs*."

"Our house will make it easier to adjust to living here," added Zenobia.

"It was fun—reminded me of putting my own place together when Herschel and I first married."

Kito emerged from the kitchen with her gap-toothed smile. She poured wine into each crystal goblet and then returned wheeling a glass-serving cart.

"Umm," said Zenobia. "This reminds me of the just-because dinners my grandmother makes at home."

"This is real Liberian cooking, and I am happy that it makes you feel at home." Daisy pointed to one of the dishes. "This is my favorite—country rice grown in paddy fields right here in Liberia, not the parboiled kind imported from the States. We call it 'paddy rice.' My father used to say it tastes like butter, which he pronounced 'putta' and my mother always said, 'A woman who can't cook putta is not a real Liberian woman.'

"That's pork cooked in palm oil, and cassava leaf," she

continued, and then pointed to dishes of palm butter with fish, shredded potato greens, and a platter of pumpkin and eggplant stew.

"That's fried plantain," shouted Zenobia, as Kito heaped plantain onto each saucer.

"CeCe showed us how to make this," said Ryan, digging in.

"Here's how to eat a country meal," Daisy said, spreading chopped pepper across the middle of her plate. "Be careful, though, until you know how much heat you can handle." Then she put a spoonful of rice on top of the pepper and built her plate with small portions of pork, fish stew, pigeon peas, and vegetables in a circular fashion.

"Now, you won't always have a finger bowl. I do it for guests new to Liberia," she said, dipping her fingers into a bowl of water next to her plate. She delicately shook off the excess. With her fingers, she swept rice grains into a small pile and then moved a piece of fish and a pinch of vegetables next to the rice. Daisy pushed and patted the food into a bite-size mound, pinched it, and placed it into her mouth without losing a speck.

"Go for it," she said, swallowing. "Use the finger bowls until you get comfortable using your hands. When you're good, you won't need the bowls."

Ryan scooped a large portion of rice and put it on his plate, leaving the pepper and finger bowls alone. He piled on meat stew and palm butter, and bypassed the potato greens that swirled in palm oil.

Zenobia dove into the oily greens, tried to eat them with her fingers, and only stopped when a stream of red-orange oil ran down her arm and threatened to ruin both her white caftan and Daisy's tablecloth.

"So what are you doing with your time while your wife

and my daughter save Liberia?" asked Daisy as Kito called the maid to clear the dishes.

"I start teaching health and physical education at the American School next week," he said, looking at Zenobia. "And I decided to pick up my old hobby—photography."

"He's been stacking undeveloped film cases in the refrigerator since I met him," said Zenobia. "I'll believe it when I see it."

Daisy led everyone into the sunken living room. "Watch your step."

"Tia Maria, anyone?" she asked, and signaled Kito to bring coffee.

Daisy's furnishings rivaled anything Zenobia had seen in the States. The wood tables looked imported from America, the leather sofa and chairs from Italy. The life-sized portrait of a handsome man filled a complete wall. His charming eyes and easy smile seemed to follow Zenobia around the room.

Zenobia played with a cue stick at the billiards table while trying to suppress her gushy lust over Daisy's lavish home.

Ryan slid into a leather chair at the cherry poker table, rubbed his hands across its felt padding, and fingered a stack of poker chips.

"You play?" Daisy asked.

"I can handle any card game," said Ryan, shuffling a deck of cards as if he were a gaming expert. "My game is bid whist. You ever hear of it?"

"No, my husband played poker. He pulled regular all-nighters with his friends."

Floor-to-ceiling mahogany shelves covered one wall and housed a stereo system and music library. Daisy selected an album from the section dedicated to Miles Davis.

"That's my deceased husband, Herschel Williams," said Daisy, pointing to the portrait. "He was a jazz enthusiast, loved African High Life, and he helped finance Liberia's Cultural Troupe. He liked the American bebop sound. However, you can see from the collection of books and memorabilia that his all-time favorite musician was Miles Davis. He used to say that Miles changed music for all times." She put *The Best of Miles Davis* on the turntable and lowered the needle.

"Please," Daisy said, pointing to the leather sectional sofa and ottoman.

When coffee cups were filled, Daisy told the story of Herschel's great-grandfather Moses Williams, who had come to Liberia in 1878 with his wife, son, and his mother, Rain. "Moses opened a cabinet-making store that became Liberia's finest. The Williamses' most fascinating family story was of Rain, whose memory of free African soil got her through slavery, and then with the care given her by Moses, she lived ten years in Liberia. They say she got up one morning, sat outside among the wild jasmine, fern, and hibiscus she tended, and with a cup of strong coffee in her hand, died."

Daisy told Zenobia and Ryan about Liberia's trouble that always fermented below the seemingly calm surface. "I've got to be straight with you, Zenobia. No matter how it looks you will never understand the depth of tension and disunity between the Americo and our twenty indigenous tribes who have different ethnic languages and cultures, ideologies and religions."

Daisy continued, her tone as sharp as her style. "Our 'us and them' society has deeply rooted hostilities that span one-hundred thirty two years. The thorny nuances are complicated and impossible for an outsider to detect. I'll do everything I can to assist you with the clinic. However, I'm telling you, you must promise me that you won't get involved in the political problems. Stick to your work with women because the activism you and CeCe practice in the States will never work here. There will be consequences. I don't mean to be harsh. At the same time, you must take me seriously."

Stunned by Daisy's directness, Zenobia did not speak.

Daisy opened the door for Ryan's concern. "Daisy, would you mind repeating your warning? What kinds of consequences?"

"I don't believe you are fronting me," Zenobia stormed. "You are not going to treat me like some baby."

Daisy folded her arms.

Ryan reared back. "Zen, it's just that—"

Zenobia butted in. "There's no need to repeat, Daisy. Soon enough, my hands will be filled with babies."

"Thanks, Daisy," said Ryan. "The taxi should be outside. It's time for us to go."

Chapter Twenty-Two

Ezra hadn't seen much of Monrovia from his trips to the post office and to Waterside Market for Boss Man's imported tobacco. What he did see of this new, faster and bigger world caused his mind to churn, and before he realized it, the taste of possibility overtook him. Even uncertainty about a new life outweighed the idea that one day he would end up looking into the face of a Boss Man who chewed tobacco while preparing to replace his own withered hands with those of his son.

Ezra quit his job planting Hevea buds, catching sap, and hauling latex. He asked a boy from neighboring Kakata to show him how to drive and teach him the taxi business. The boy obliged and let Ezra use his taxi on his off days.

Ezra proposed marriage to Sarah, moved to Monrovia, where he rented a taxi, and then stenciled "Blessed by God" on the sides. The bow left Ezra's back with every dollar he earned.

On weekends, Ezra made jaunts between Monrovia and Harbel to visit family and to be with Sarah. On one weekend trip, they married, and they agreed she would stay with her parents until Ezra rented a place to live.

Ezra had never felt so free and thought he was rich when he rented a mud and thatched house on Airfield Road.

Despite one of the rainiest seasons ever, he slept every night in the taxi, reserving the inaugural night on their foam mattress for his beloved bride.

☪

Sarah had grown up knowing how to reckon time. The interval between clearing a field and harvesting the planted crop was one year. January and February were "big, cool moons" when north winds dried the air. March and April, rice-planting months, were "sick moons" because the previous year's harvest had usually run low, and malaria loomed high.

May started with sun showers that by midmonth turned into the great rains of June and July, the "wet moons." The August wet moon sometimes found Sarah's family hungry, because the new rice wasn't yet ready for harvest, and the old rice was already eaten. September and October were "rice-cutting moons" with October being used for small garden planting. Rice harvesting ended in November and hunting increased. December, the "small, cool month," saw passing sun showers. After seven years of harvest, Sarah's father let the land lie fallow as he moved his family to clear and plant new rice fields.

Sarah helped keep the family's one-room mud house clean. Using a mortar and pestle, she pounded groundnuts into peanut butter, cooked, and helped her mother sell the amount of rice over what their family could eat without spoiling before the next harvest. It was while Sarah was selling sweet paddy rice at Waterside Market that she learned imported rice from America was putting rural rice farmers out of business.

With that realization, Sarah turned her long-suffering nature into a steady effort to pursue new work. Marrying Ezra and moving to Monrovia was a chance to show her younger brother a different life.

Sarah became pregnant soon after she and Ezra married.

While Ezra drove his taxi and watched night security at an in-town grocery, Sarah set up a small market outside their home.

By the time their daughter Satta was born, Sarah was seventeen and had rented space at Waterside Market. Near the edge of the Montserrado River, Waterside was Monrovia's largest and busiest open-air market. A half-mile hub, it was where tourists, buyers, and sellers shopped, rain or shine.

Sarah had conflicted loyalty toward her family's rice occupation, but she knew she could make good money every day by selling imported rice at Waterside. Using twenty-two dollars given to her by Ezra, she bought a hundred-pound sack. On the ground among six other women, Sarah sold rice, palm oil, peppers, plantains, and bananas.

When the heavy rains came, and while using a cardboard box to shield her and Satta, Sarah made plans to move up in the market, bypass clapboard stands and tables, and take her market inside, where, shielded from the rain and sun, her cash flow would double.

Chapter Twenty-Three

A month after her arrival, Zenobia drank coffee on her front porch while Ezra and Sarah brushed their teeth in the front yard, using well water. Zenobia tried not to stare, but she was amazed by the simple task that she had always taken for granted. Sarah mixed a paste and they used the frayed end of a pencil-sized twig to brush, remove plaque, and massage the gums between their teeth. When they were finished, the twig became a chewing stick that Ezra let hang from his lips.

Zenobia sipped from another cup of coffee, smelled ocean salt in the early morning breeze, and practiced her presentation to the Interior Affairs Minister. She rose to get a better view when she saw Satta in the corner of her eye. By now, Satta was nine and barely four-feet tall, yet she washed clothes for the Frenchman next door as if she had been born doing it. Two things bothered Zenobia about this scene: the child's servitude and child labor. Of the two, child labor troubled her more.

Satta dipped a bucket into a water barrel that stood next to the house. She filled it twice and poured the water into a galvanized tub that she used for wash and then repeated the process, filling the second tub for rinse. She sorted the clothes—white, light, and colored—and laid them at her feet.

The scrub board Satta retrieved from beneath the dirty clothes reminded Zenobia of the rusty one she had seen hanging from a nail over Grandma Jones's retired wringer washing machine.

Satta poured bleach into the water, rested the corrugated board against her knees, grabbed and put a fresh bar of lye soap on top of a white sheet, and then rubbed the sheet and soap against the scrub board, up and down with quick, exaggerated wrist motions.

Satta turned the sheet over in the sudsy water and repeated the process several times before moving over to the rinse tub, where she swished, dunked, and then examined the sheet. Satisfied that it was clean, she clothes pinned the sheet to a line that she had to climb onto a Coca Cola crate to reach. Satta emptied and refilled the tubs for each new load, and when she finished less than an hour later, she leaned the board and tubs against the house to dry, and went home, looking back admiringly at the job she had left flapping under the bright sun.

Zenobia mastered the process in her head and with a couple of hours before her meeting, decided to tackle a pile of dirty clothes. She gathered the tubs and scrub boards that Ryan had bought and placed them in the backyard near an outside water barrel. She left a muddy trail as she made several trips, managing the weight by half-filling the buckets, until the wash and rinse tubs were full. The electricity was out, and Ryan, trying to master the art of ironing with a coal iron, watched Zenobia from the back window.

Zenobia tucked her long skirt between her legs and started with Ryan's pants. She put them into the wash water and air rushed through one long leg, causing lye suds to fly into her face and hair. Catching that pant leg and scrubbing it forced the other to spill out of the tub and onto the dirt.

"It can't be that hard," she whispered to herself and stood to stretch her back and reposition the corrugated board.

Grabbing both pant legs, Zenobia rubbed them between the balls of her fists. She punched and jabbed with determination and when she tried to lift and dunk the long legs, she almost went face first into the tub. After an hour, she was tired, and the single pair of pants was too heavy and bulky to rinse and wring out. Sweat poured down her aching back, and her clothes clung to her skin, which had already started to pucker with a prickly rash and burn from the mixture of heat, sweat, and salt.

As Zenobia zipped by Ryan, heading toward the front door, he mumbled, "On your way to buy a Maytag?"

At that moment, he smelled something burning. *Dang!* He had been smart enough to put only a few coals into the lip of the pressing iron, wait for them to catch, and burn down to ashy red embers so he wouldn't destroy his pants. So busy watching Zenobia's fiasco, he forgot to rest the cast iron on its trivet, leaving a perfectly black iron imprint on the pant leg.

The irony of an electric iron sitting useless on the kitchen counter was not lost on them. "Just how much do you want to be like a Liberian?" he asked, laughing and dumping the coals onto the dirt.

"Funny. I give, though. I'm going to find Satta."

Zenobia showed Satta the mess, and then distressed by the idea of children working for pennies, Zenobia told Satta, "Name your price. We'll pay whatever you charge."

"Fity cent, fity cent," Satta said. "Wash, fity cent, iron fity cent again."

"Fifty cents per load; is that enough?" asked Zenobia.

"Fity cent, fity cent," repeated Satta. "You wan' pay more, you pay my dash."

"Deal," said Zenobia and escorted Satta to her sudsy

disaster. She paid Satta fifty cents in advance for each wash and iron load, plus a fifty-cent dash for each.

Satta tried to hide her laughter, "Thank you Missy Zenobia."

"You can call me Zenobia."

"Thank you, Missy Zenobia."

Swathed in calamine lotion, Zenobia was dressed and ready when Kito arrived that afternoon.

Kito drove away from the curb, saying, "Let's go make us a world."

"What're you so fired up about?"

"My mother has been feuding with politicians for as long as I can remember. She told you about my father's people, and conveniently left out her family's reaction to their marriage. I don't really get it. Her family got mad, said she married for money and privilege and went against an edict that her great-great-grandfather had put down about being forever loyal to their indigenous tribe when the Americo settlers forced new ways of life down the throats of their villagers. That was then, and this is now. I tell you, peace will come with government help of Sister-to-Sister."

Kito was taking the green light on Tubman Boulevard when she had to slam the brakes to avoid hitting a man riding on a three-by-four wooden scooter with roller skate wheels. He canoed across Tubman with his gnarled, atrophied legs tied and seated atop the wooden plank. He used his hands and arms as if they were rowing oars.

"What the…?"

Kito said, "Polio. I bet he could have been treated if the medical services had been available to his family."

The man jettisoned himself over the curb and made his way down the street.

"He looks young, but his eyes look old and hollow," said Zenobia, pulling herself back into the seat.

"And worn and exhausted. I bet he feels fifty," Kito added.

Zenobia trailed the man with her eyes and resolved that she would do everything she could to ensure that all children received the immunizations and treatment they needed.

Kito shook off the outright reminder of what could have been her story. "Before we talk with the Interior Affairs Minister, I need to tell you something."

Kito looked at her watch. *Eight minutes,* and spoke quickly. "President Tolbert's family is filled with indigenous people, like my mother, who married up when they intermarried with the settler-class family. They were expected to drop their country ways and become 'kwi' by taking on the civilized Americo-Liberian ways and Christian faith. "They detached from their country customs by completely accepting Western standards of dress, conduct, and values. The president's family and my father's family have South Carolina roots, and because of that, his family was obligated to invite my mother into their lives. They didn't have to like her, and they didn't.

"Ma had her own ways. She didn't want to adopt 'kwi' ways and she purposely abused their social rules. She worsened an already bad situation when she blamed the government for my father's death. It's funny, though. Now that Ma has seized everything that being 'kwi' affords, she has more high society ways than any of them."

Kito swerved into a space in front of the Ministry of Finance building that housed the Office of Interior Affairs. "A project with an agenda of improving the lives of Liberian women and children should bring everyone together," Kito said, practicing her part with Minister Howe. She adjusted her *gele* and folded the wide sleeves of her Boubou over each shoulder to allow her arms to move and make a space for the heat to leave.

Zenobia smoothed wrinkles away from her purple tie-dyed tunic, threw the briefcase strap over her shoulder, and strutted to show off the embroidery that outlined the kick flap of her matching lappa skirt.

"Out of Order" signs decorated elevators to the left and right of the entranceway. Kito looked up the office number on the directory where there was space for three numbers, but only one number—five—remained.

"Guess we have to take the stairs," said Kito leading the way. The stairwell held the odor of ammonia, urine, and mold that had stewed in humidity for years. There were paper wads strewn across the heavily soiled floor, and water-stained ceiling tiles sagged. "Take a deep breath and run," Kito said, already covering her nose and mouth. "And look out for those brown sagging tiles."

Kito pointed to writings on dingy walls as she ran up the first set of stairs. PAL Revolution was on one side; MOJA Revolution was on the other. "Those are the political groups my mother wants us to stay away from," she said through fingers covering her mouth and nose. An inscription on the second floor read, "We must run while others walk."

Graffiti that proclaimed love between a girl and a boy, names of visitors, and epithets aimed at the Interior Affairs Minister by people who hadn't gotten what they wanted lined the remaining walls leading to the fifth floor. When Kito opened the door marked "Interior Affairs," they lunged through and pushed out the air they had been holding.

Still panting and coughing, Zenobia backed up a couple of paces and took in the office furnishings.

A male receptionist raised his eyes.

Kito pinned her shoulders back. "We're here to see Minister Howe," she said in unmistakably educated speech.

"This way," the receptionist said, ushering the two around his work cubicle and ahead to a set of mahogany tables and chairs. "Le' me tell the minister you are here."

"This is strange," said Zenobia. "With all the rallies I've attended, I've never even come this close to meeting an actual political official. Strange and at the same time, it feels good. I'll be the subject of Grandma Jones's next testimony when I write her about this." She straightened her skirt and eyeballed her presentation once more.

Zenobia followed Kito and the receptionist into the minister's office.

"Good afternoon, Minister Howe," said Kito, shaking his hand and smiling.

"Hello, Kito, and how is…?" he said, distracted by his search for something buried in the piles of paper on his desk.

"She's fine," said Kito, wondering if she would have recognized him through his enormous weight gain without the preliminary formalities of the receptionist.

Stuffed into a leather high-backed chair, the minister's once-firm physique looked like blubber, a gray kufi covered his balding head, and the buttonhole that strained to remain closed cheapened his tailor-made leisure suit.

"This is my friend, Zenobia Jones, the one the first lady told you about. We appreciate you squeezing us in on a Saturday, a testament of your dedication to our country."

"Ah, here it is," said Minister Howe as soon as he spotted Zenobia's written proposal on his desk. He stood and reached for her hand. "Hello, young lady. I trust you are enjoying Liberia," he said, using his fat hands to point them toward two chairs facing his desk. "Please, sit down."

"I just returned from Paris and leave again for Washington, DC, on Monday; however, I couldn't wait to hear what has the first lady so excited."

Zenobia's eyes traveled the office. On one wall hung a bachelor's degree diploma from Howard University and next to it, a master's from the University of Maryland. The wall to the left displayed awards and recognitions, on the right were framed pictures of heads of state and dignitaries. Family photos lined the credenza, and everything about the minister was as proper as his Western education and socialization suggested.

"Daniel, bring two cold Coca Colas," Minister Howe called toward the door. "Let's get started," he said when the soft drinks arrived.

"Liberia is more than one hundred and thirty years old," he began. "And even though we are the oldest independent African nation and have great natural resources, the international community calls us underdeveloped, even third world." He groaned and shuddered.

"I am responsible for the health of all Liberians, ending poverty and disease, building self-reliance. The first lady said you have some ideas that will assist me."

Zenobia hadn't expected the smooth opening. "First of all, Mr. Minister, I have to tell you how welcome I feel in your country. Some of that has to do with the Williams family," she nodded toward Kito. "But it's also the way everyday people treat me on the street. I'm learning your culture; I don't feel like a foreigner at all. Your embrace of America and Americans is clear."

He said, "We are proud of our relationship with America and Americans, and your government's financial support of Liberia," withholding that the president's desire to speed any integration of natives into politics and the economy had motivated the meeting.

Zenobia continued. "Liberia receives US money through the Agency for International Development. American corporations make technology and equipment accessible and there are a few American-based small businesses. My interest is in bringing collaboration between an American company and myself together to directly serve Liberian people. Babies Incorporated is committed to funding my program and shipping surplus inventory. My midwife association brings skills and a burning desire to make a difference in Liberia."

"That's why the first lady was so excited. It's an investment without all the governmental strings," said Minister Howe.

"Exactly," responded Zenobia. "All I need is your formal permission and support to start a clinic called Sister-to-Sister." Zenobia then ran down her five-point maternal health and early child development program:

1. safe, clean births, whether at home or in a clinic
2. breast-feeding over bottle feeding
3. hygiene and cleanliness
4. mother and infant nutrition
5. immunization against measles, whooping cough, tetanus, diphtheria, tuberculosis, and polio.

Zenobia continued, "Women's lives will change, children's lives will change, and women and children will be positioned for self-reliance, which as you mentioned, is important to you. The report you make to the world community about improvements in maternal and child health will be a jewel in the president's crown."

"Wait, now. Daniel, bring another cold Coca Cola and some groundnuts. Go on, Zenobia."

She took papers from her briefcase. "Here are sample brochures—easy-to-follow directions for making rehydration solutions, and breast-feeding techniques. These pictures make communication with non-reading adults easier."

"And where do you plan to put this operation?" the minister asked.

"I, um, Kito and I, saw an abandoned building on Tubman Boulevard, a few blocks from the Executive Mansion, heading downtown. Kito tells me it's been vacant for a while, and my husband said some dry wall and electrical and plumbing upgrades would make it good as new."

"I know the building. It's vacant, but I think it has an owner. I'll have Daniel look into it." The minister looked at his watch and sucked the last drop of Coke from the bottle.

"And how will this idea work exactly?" asked Minister Howe.

"Well, I have startup dollars. Once I have your approval and document what you and I will exchange to set up and operate the clinic, Babies Incorporated will start sending inventory."

"The United States built our Freeport. It's an excellent facility and the best place to store inventory until you are ready to use it."

"Minister Howe, we need permits to renovate the building, and Zenobia and her husband need work and residency permits to stay in Liberia beyond ninety days," said Kito. "My mother, Daisy, and I have given them banking endorsements. However, your good offices extend further."

"Mr. Minister," said Zenobia. "Babies Incorporated dollars will pay for two staffs. I'll need you to pay for renovations and the permits and licenses to make the building operational. Of course, we'll hire all Liberian staff."

"I need Liberians working," the minister said firmly. "You did well. I'll have to discuss the matter with the president and, if he agrees, Daniel will contact you." Minister Howe scribbled notes into the margins of Zenobia's proposal and then shoved it into a desk drawer.

"By the way," he said, "I'm sure you are Christian. I'll have my wife invite you and your husband to our church sometime. We'd love to have you."

"Come, Daniel," the minister called after he had shaken hands and shown Zenobia and Kito to the stairwell door.

"Daniel, get Dr. Jeremiah Browne in here to see me."

Chapter Twenty-Four

The smell of rain usually preceded May showers. It was April, rice-planting season, however, and clouds had already begun to swell and hang over the city. They blocked the sun.

Kito hoisted herself into the Blazer and rested from the stair climb. "Something is happening—I feel it in the air."

"Looks like a storm?" Zenobia said as a breeze kicked open the flap of her skirt.

"We don't get storms; must be rainy season coming early."

Zenobia, impatient, dove in as Kito pulled away from the curb, "Why did Howe stop short of a firm commitment?"

"He has to work a way around the Liberianization Policy, Zenobia. Liberians will never accept a foreigner managing something they can do. Self-determination means hiring Liberians first, if not exclusively."

"But he sounded so interested; he didn't challenge one thing."

"Nothing can happen without his approval—he didn't have to challenge. He could have said no, but he didn't. You wanted his attention, and you got it. American dollars make good business and great speeches. He'll get back to you. Meanwhile, Daniel is going to take care of your immigration documents. You got more than you were looking for in a first visit."

Zenobia was so busy listening and thinking that she didn't have a chance to brace when Kito braked, causing her to bump her head on the dashboard as the jeep lurched forward.

Stalled taxis haphazardly cluttered the street, their doors ajar, fares and drivers missing. At the Mandingo tailor shop, the door swung open and closed, the owners gone missing.

Heat and stagnant humidity did not let up, adding electricity to emotions and stench to the heaping garbage.

"What's going on?" asked Zenobia, looking at the sea of human discontent that spilled into the streets and sidewalks.

Hundreds of boys ran through the streets, turning over market stands, stealing potato greens and rice, and leaving market women to snatch their babies and leap for cover. The boys pumped their fists and raised their voices in unison. "Liberian solutions to Liberian problems!"

Looters ransacked the convenience store; cotton balls, candy, and watches hung from their pockets and then fell to the ground.

A soda bottle rolled across the hood of Kito's Blazer, someone kicked at the rear bumper, and a tall, heavy man, with crazed eyes and cola nut juice dripping from his lips, walked up to Kito's side of the Blazer and tried to push it over.

"We're getting out of here, Zenobia." Before she could turn away from the converging crowd, a Molotov cocktail whizzed over the car, hit the electronics store, and set it ablaze. Kito spotted a small clearance just ahead, mounted the curb, and rode it as if she were a cowgirl.

As Kito rounded a corner, Zenobia pointed out the window. "Look!" A short, weasel-acting man stooped over piles of loot that some twenty boys had collected. It seemed to Zenobia that he was sorting looted items against a list he held in his hand. He admonished the boys for missing things he had instructed them to get. Then, before sending them back into the chaos, he looked over his shoulder to see if anyone was looking. He jiggled his pockets at the boys as if to make a promise of settling when they returned. Zenobia looked over her shoulder in time to see one group of boys run back into the raucous crowd and another run up to the man. One by one, each lay down his begging bowl in exchange for a loot assignment and the gamble at a new way of making a living.

When they heard gunfire in the distance, Zenobia ducked, and Kito gunned the engine, careful not to add hit-and run to the mayhem. She rode two tires in the street, two on the curb, until they were out of the area and headed toward the salon.

"Is that a riot or what!" asked Zenobia, looking over her shoulder. She became relieved as the distance from the chaos widened. "I haven't seen mayhem like this since Martin Luther King was killed."

The two jumped out of the car, even though Kito had barely parked. They ran up the steps and barged into Always Beautiful.

"Get in here," Daisy said and stuck her head outside the door. She looked up and down the street and when she was satisfied that the anarchy would not reach her business, she closed, locked, and secured the door with a chair.

Women clustered shoulder to shoulder in the window, peeking through Daisy's imported miniblinds. Though in various stages of hair preparation, they cared more about the bedlam outside than the fifteen dollars they might be losing on their head.

One customer's Jheri curl activator had dried and become brittle, and Daisy had to reactivate it before rolling her hair onto tiny rods. Another would soon be willing to throw her head into a backyard well if she didn't get relief from the burning chemical relaxer.

"Ladies, please, return to your stations. You will pay double today if you waste my products."

Daisy turned the radio up loud. "We can listen to what's going on and still take care of our business."

"What's happening?" asked one customer, her head halfway under the dryer.

"I knew something had to happen," said Jheri curls now under the dryer. "I'm telling you everyone is angry, unemployment is high, prices are too high, and things were bound to boil over."

"The people are tired-O," said another, slapping her palms, one against the other. "How can one man raise the price of rice? What are the people to do? If you can' buy rice, you can' eat," she said, sucking her teeth so loud and long that the sound could be heard over the dryers' drone.

"Yeah, and all the time the president feathering his own bed and his cronies, leaving nothing for the common man," said Jheri curls, completely out from under the dryer again and pacing the floor. "His relatives are sitting in the best government jobs."

Daisy looked over from her workstation where she was twisting a client's hair into elaborate Bantu knots and paying close attention to the conversation. Not a head was where it was supposed to be. "Can you help me, Kito?"

Zenobia sat on the edge of a chair in between the dryer room and the styling stations. Her head moved in rhythm with the cadence of the talking heads.

"I don't get it. I bought a twenty-five-cent cup of rice today; that's the price I always pay," said one woman. "I'm here from Los Angeles for two years with my copier company. I need to know if I should leave." She pounded her fist against her purse.

Daisy heard rifle shots in the background and looked outside again to make sure the commotion wasn't headed toward the salon.

Several women lifted their dryer hoods and leaned forward to get a good look at the Los Angeles woman. "Jus' listen," said one, and the others settled back into their seats.

"The president grows more rice than anyone. His brother is the largest rice importer, and his family holds the license that guarantees American rice comes here. Increase the price of rice, and he makes money coming and going," said another who had been silent to this point.

"That's right. Tolbert says he is making changes, but I see things getting worse. Our future. Humph! I want my future now!" said the woman in Daisy's chair. "Leave him. I say, leave him!" she said, slapping her hands together. "Whatever happens to him is his doing. Let him go. Humph."

"I bet you wouldn't say that outside of this shop," said Jheri curls.

"I'm not crazy-o, I like living too much."

With that, the women scooted back into their chairs and listened to the radio.

When Daisy finished the client in her chair, she walked Kito and Zenobia into the back room. Zenobia stood while Kito took the chaise lounge.

"Kito, pay close attention to what's going on around you," said Daisy. "This was supposed to be a peaceful protest against the rice price increase. The organizers underestimated how angry people are. Our young, progressive intellectuals are impatient; they want to be heard, and what they want, they want now."

Kito studied her mother. "Are you involved in this?"

"I don't have to be involved to hear about what's going on. It is my business to know," she said measuring her words. "It's up to us to make the changes Liberia needs." She secured the front fold of her lappa skirt and tightened her gele headwrap.

"Since you asked, I did hear there was going to be a peaceful protest today," she said, deciding it was better to offer a smidgen of information, and handing Kito a flyer. "Protesters came around passing out these." The flyer read, "*Change doesn't happen without a demand.*"

"I never saw any of those," said Kito.

"Shhh!" said Daisy, turning her listening ear to the outside. Hearing nothing strange, she asked, "How was your meeting with the minister?"

Daisy's abrupt change of subject irritated Zenobia. She was still reeling from their drive through the riot and Kito's pithy summary of the meeting, so she wasn't sure how to make sense out of any of it.

"I think it went well," she said, looking at Kito for confirmation. "He was interested, didn't say no. I guess that means maybe. He said he would get back to me."

Daisy checked her watch before adding, "You girls should wait until this situation dies down before you go back to Minister Howe. Can you do that?"

Zenobia didn't want to upset Daisy, but she had to ask. "What happens next? There is a lot of anger out there, and based on riots we had in the States after Martin Luther King was assassinated, I can't imagine it will subside anytime soon. My uncle Scotty always said a riot is just the tip of an iceberg."

Kito, busy trying to unscramble the puzzle her mother was becoming, barely heard Zenobia.

"Slow down on your project," said Daisy, ignoring Zenobia's point.

"I've just begun, Daisy."

"Minister Howe has to assess the situation and fix it. He won't have time for the clinic just now."

Kito said, "The minister's staff will take a few weeks to get your visas and see who owns the building anyway, Zenobia."

Zenobia looked at Kito and then shifted her weight from one foot to the other. She was concerned about the riot, but when Daisy told her to slow down on Sister-to-Sister, thoughts of delivering the first baby started to crumble, and a slow ferment stewed in the pit of her stomach. Zenobia looked at the wall calendar: April 14, 1979. Minutes crawled by before she and Daisy finished exchanging looks.

"Yes," she said finally.

"Good. Now, I need to make this money." Daisy checked her two generators; each backed up the other in case the power went out. "Being stuck in my shop is as good a place as any," she said, and smoothed her clothes. "You can't go anywhere either, Zenobia. Can you help relax the customers under their dryers, serve Coca Cola and peanuts? We'll take you home later. Come on, Kito."

When Daisy left the shop that evening, she had made more money than she could fold or stuff into her wallet.

Chapter Twenty-Five

As Ryan approached Satta's table to buy rice, bitter ball, and palm oil, he heard neighbors laughing uncontrollably in the yard next to Ezra's house. They were huddled in the dark, seated on metal chairs and soda crates.

He was staring into the crowd confused about what was going on, when suddenly, he saw in the middle of the pack a television tethered by wire and cord to an electrical pole. He couldn't believe what he was hearing, and the faces on the nine-inch television screen were too small to see. "How did we overcome bad times and nobody told me?" joked Florence, *The Jeffersons'* maid about her African roots.

Then as the crowd broke into a raucous chorus of the musical theme, *"We're moving on up to that dee-luxe apartment in the sky! We finally got a piece of the p-i-ie,"* a taxi drove into the space in front of Ezra's place.

Two men jumped out of the car, leaving the engine running, and doors gaping. They ran to the side door.

Ryan did not move.

"Sarah!" one of the men shouted into the house, loud enough for anyone in earshot to hear. "Your brother shot! Down to Tubman Boulevard, at the riot, he shot, but he not dead."

Sarah had just told Ezra about the market women deciding to buy paddy rice from Liberian farmers instead of paying the imported increase.

Sarah had warned her brother to stay away from meetings where men were organizing frustrated unemployed boys to demand change. Still, she had never expected he could be hurt.

"What hap'en?"

"Rice trouble," the driver started. "The people scared to have empty stomach, so they protest, and the whole thing get out of hand when the police shoot their rifles into the crowd. That's when your brother got shot. In the leg because you know he is too quick," the driver said snap-shaking Ezra's hand.

Neighbors gathered around Ezra's door; one woman screamed and rushed to Sarah's side. Another spun around in place, like a spinning top saying, "I knew 'dis ting would happen!"

"Is there anything I can do?" Ryan asked Ezra, trying to get his attention. "Is there anything I can do?" he repeated.

Satta squatted on the floor; her eyes darted between the men and her parents. She watched silent tears well in Sarah's eyes and stream quietly down her face without a hint of sobbing. No matter the extent of pain or loss, Satta had never seen her mother heave and moan, never heard her cry out, not even when Sarah's mother died from high fever and hallucinations.

"Where is he?" Sarah asked.

"They take some wounded to just-for-killing hospital, but I take your brother to hospital in Paynesville. He say no hospital is going to kill him," moving toward his taxi. "Come, let's go. I can take you there."

Neighbors dispersed to their own houses and waited for their families to arrive with more news.

The rider climbed into the front passenger seat with Ezra, and Sarah slid into the back seat, next to her brother's drying blood, while the driver, hanging halfway out of his window, made a giant doughnut, and squealed past Ryan, leaving a plume of red dust in his wake.

Zenobia ran through the door, eyes bugging, and barely feeling the kiss Ryan planted on her neck. She ranted non-stop about the riot, what the women in the salon had said, and about Minister Howe.

"Daisy said I should slow down, give Minister Howe time to settle the riot and recover all the damage."

"And?" asked Ryan when Zenobia started to fret.

"I can't stop now. What else would I do?"

"Did Minister Howe like the proposal?"

Zenobia started up again like a runaway train. "Yeah, in fact, he invited us to his church," she answered, pouring palm oil and sprinkling chopped red peppers over her plate of rice. "I'll do whatever it takes, Ryan."

Ryan told Zenobia about Sarah's brother. "I'm beginning to worry. I knew we would have to deal with water and power outages, but a full-blown riot over rice is different. Daisy is probably right—it'll take a while for things to get back to normal. Just think about riots in the sixties. There were improvements, jobs and such, but some neighborhoods never rebuilt. I'm not a quitter, and I know the clinic is important, but we can leave whenever you want."

No way was Zenobia going home empty-handed. She rolled her eyes toward the ceiling, crossed her arms, tucking her hands deep into her armpits, and mentally dug in her heels without a word.

Rather than combat her will, Ryan dropped the discussion. He slid his bistro chair next to hers and wrapped his arms around her body. He held her, buried his head in her neck, and kissed her until she slept.

Chapter Twenty-Six

A few days after the riot, Ryan hired Ezra to drive him to town so he could see the damage, and take in a movie if it was open. "Is Sarah's brother alright?"

"He tough, but she worry that he with the wrong group, not the protestors, but the looters."

"You think the riot is over?"

"Can' say. People talking 'bout the gov'ment. They say Tolbert is not keeping his promise to make jobs, or bring the country people and the Americo people together."

"You think it's over, Ezra?"

"Can' say. Bacchus say he want the protest, not the riot. If he and the president can talk as human beings, maybe the riot is over. But I can' say."

"Who is Bacchus?"

"The people love him. He organize the protest."

"It's all confusing to me," Ryan said as he exited the taxi.

"But the rice price come down."

Ryan took pictures as he wound his way around mounds of garbage and debris and headed in the direction of Relda Theater. The charred smell of burned out buildings, market stands, and the stench of sweat and excitement remained. He was lining up the perfect picture of charred stands when he stumbled upon a lethargic dog. Long strands of saliva hung from its mouth as it limped among the rubble. Ryan avoided the dog by walking by a row of old men sitting against the edifice of an abandoned storefront. Their shabby clothes clung close to their bony frames, and their squinty eyes barely focused on Ryan as he pointed his lens toward them. He held the camera in place, but couldn't bring himself to snap. *I could use a laugh* he thought as he gave each man a dollar and walked away.

Ryan was still laughing when the credits from the Chinese version of *Enter the Dragon* rolled. As he left the theater, he smiled at the marquee that announced "*Fists of Fury:* coming soon."

Groups of children, playing their way home from the mission school, knocked into Ryan as he walked down Gurley Street. He was making sharp turns to avoid another dog when a Lebanese storeowner waved him inside. "Come. I have clock radios perfect for Africa: AM, and FM, and six bands with alternating current or direct current power."

The merchant gave Ryan the call numbers for Voice of America and added, "Liberia's Omega Tracking Station is one of the largest transmitters in the world." He wrapped the radio and a pack of batteries in white paper.

Ryan asked, "Where do I get news about the riot? There's nothing in the local paper."

"Next door, next door," the storekeeper answered. "Come see me again."

Inside the newsstand, copies of *World News Service Bulletin* published by European Broadcasting Corporation caught Ryan's attention.

April 14, 1979: The heading read "Rice Riots in Liberia."

The price of imported parboiled rice rose from twenty-two dollars per one hundred-pound bag to thirty dollars. Two thousand protesters took to the streets for twelve hours and the government responded by shooting into the crowd, wounding hundreds and killing forty. Widespread riots, looting, and damage to property and rice warehouses are estimated to exceed twenty million dollars. President Tolbert asks for calm throughout the capital of Monrovia.

April 17, 1979: The heading read "Guinea Sends Soldiers to Aid Neighbor."

A platoon of troops from Guinea was flown into Liberia to quell a weekend of violence and looting. The act angered the Liberian Army, forcing President Tolbert to return the Guinean troops to their home.

Outside, Ryan replayed Daisy's words, "The nuances are impossible for an outsider to see." He looked up and down the street for Guinea troops. He flagged a taxi, and before he could open the door, a fist came out of nowhere, landing solidly on the right side of his head, just above the ear. He clutched the radio and newspapers with his left arm and swung at the air with his right. He missed.

He looked, left and right, for the culprit. From the corner of his eye, Ryan noticed a six-foot-tall woman, naked except for sagging, dirty panties, shuffling in her bare feet up Gurley Street. Her breasts and fat jiggled as she punched the air with her fists and argued vehemently with the concrete, oblivious to the injuries, stares, and finger pointing she left behind.

"Get in," said the driver. "That woman loco," he said, making a circular motion with his finger. "She come every month; catch people who don't watch for her."

"Where to, my man?" the driver asked when Ryan was safely inside.

Ryan was deep in thought, believing the naked woman belonged in an insane asylum. He wondered how many disappointments it takes to put a person on the road to helplessness. What does it take to send someone into the streets to prey on unsuspecting strangers, or turn a promising doctor into a heroin addicted street beggar, turn possibility into desperation and despair, or remove all hope?

"I say, where to?"

"Speed. Catch up to the woman." He leaned out of the window and snapped the picture just as the woman rammed her fist into the head of another man. Papers spilled out of his briefcase and onto the sidewalk.

Chapter Twenty-Seven

May showers ushered in the wet season. Even though she had grown up hearing that, a shower in the midst of sunshine was a sign that the devil was beating his wife, in Zenobia's experience, sun showers had come to mean change. Zenobia missed her grandmother, and she hoped visiting Minister Howe's church on Mother's Day would bring Grandma Jones close.

Even though she hadn't attended service since her best friend was ostracized by Sisters Marshall and Hamilton and shunned from Ezekiel Baptist members for being pregnant at sixteen, Zenobia followed Ryan up the steps of St. John's Baptist Church of Bensonville. The fold in the lappa of her white Boubou opened and closed as she walked, hiding the ten new pounds of rice, which she carried on her thighs. Ezra had told her, "You look like a real Liberian woman," when he dropped them at the church.

In the vestibule, on the left a wooden sign read, "We are climbing Jacob's ladder," "Soldiers of the Cross," and on the right, "To God be all the glory."

Minister Howe saw Zenobia from the deacons' row and beckoned an usher to escort her and Ryan to the front behind the row of missionaries who were dressed in communion white.

Zenobia and Ryan slid into one of the hand-carved, crescent-shaped pews. The pews' shape and arrangement made the preacher visible to everyone. Zenobia's heart sank when she skimmed the church bulletin dated May 13, 1979. It was not Mother's Day in Liberia.

Six deacons stood in the front collecting offerings and tithes, and when the senior choir finished singing from the hymnal, Pastor Kulah strutted to the wooden podium. He straightened his black robes and cleared his throat.

"Church, the subject of my sermon today is *God Specializes*," he said, rearing back on his heels and clutching the rim of the podium. His long robe ballooned around him. "Please turn your *Bibles* to Psalms 46:1–3.

"My heart is heavy today," he continued slowly, tugging at his robes. "I am sure many of your hearts are heavy, too. My spirit is troubled because of the rice riots." He shook his head. "People, this is God's land, and it is abundant. There is enough for all, and He is in the midst of this land."

Congregants looked at each other, mumbled under their breath, and without looking suspicious, they established as much emotional and physical space from their neighbors as possible. Others kept their eyes fixed on the back of a pew and steadied their stance.

"Now, I know this is difficult to hear, but I'm here to deliver God's Word, not mine."

"Amen, Pastor," hollered someone from the rear.

"These dissident groups would have you believe they will let justice prevail. A-huh. Each group says they have the answer."

"Amen, Pastor. Preach the Word," a woman shouted and waved her fan toward him.

"I know it's confusing. Some say the answer to our problem is revolution. Others tell you to reform, and somebody else tells you 'Our future is up to us.'

"But God said beware of false prophets who ferment confusion. Can I get a witness?"

Men stood one after the other in response to the preacher and several women shouted, "Amen, Brother Pastor. Preach! Preach the Word."

Pastor Kulah paced back and forth behind the pulpit. "But God," he said, stomping his feet, "God brought us to this glorious land of milk and honey, and He said 'stand still,' because He is our refuge, and He specializes in the seen and unseen. Can I get an Amen?"

"Amen. Amen. Amen. Stand still!" members shouted back.

Pastor Kulah snatched his head around to look up at the three-dimensional Jesus hanging on the cross in front of a stained-glass window.

By now, half the church was standing and clapping their hands. "Amen. Amen. Preach!" The organist began quietly playing the melody to "God Specializes."

"Saints, you have to trust that God is God. He is the only one who can fix things." Pastor Kulah raised his hands and eyes toward the ceiling in silent prayer.

Some members did a holy dance. Minister Howe clapped and tried to contain his spirit, keeping it from bursting forth.

A young woman, touched by the sermon, sat crying in the choir until the organist nodded that it was time to sing. "God specializes in Things that Seem Impossible," she belted from her soul.

Ryan swayed and clapped his hands with the choir. "Zen, that was the best sermon I've ever heard," he whispered as the choir finished.

"He just told people to turn the other cheek," Zenobia said, her hands clasped in her lap.

Ryan blew a long breath through his nose. "Will you ever enjoy something just for its sake? You read more into everything." He turned his shoulder away from Zenobia and joined in with the choir.

Zenobia paused and then offered an olive branch. "He was trained at Harvard's Theological School. I bet that's why his style sounds familiar."

When the service was over, Ryan told the pastor, "I enjoyed your sermon," and shook his hand.

"Thank you, young man, and God bless," the pastor said, patting Ryan on the back.

While Zenobia was shaking hands and listening to stories about family and friends who lived in the States, Ryan got an earful on the church steps.

"You think Pastor Kulah knows which political side the members are on?" asked one congregant to another.

"Don't know, but he sure blasted the protest movement, talking about wait on the Lord. Humph."

One said, "I heard that the Liberian Army sided with the protesters and that Tolbert lost military support when he called in the Guinea troops."

"My brother is in the army, and he said the president doesn't trust them anymore," said another.

"I'm telling you, this thing is not good. I heard Tolbert is going to release the protesters, give them amnesty, and their rights to organize and express themselves."

"That's dumb. They will just organize against him."

"All that money, he'll buy them off."

"If he starts that, he won't know where to stop. His own party is angry because he said he was going to integrate the common person into the political system."

"I'm telling you, he can buy me off."

"My friend, I'm going to do what Pastor Kulah said and

wait on the Lord. Plus, I heard that the progressive protestors are making a deal to create a mutual plan with Tolbert."

"I say leave Tolbert, let him go. He deserves what he gets," the congregant said, slapping her hands dismissively.

Just then, Minister Howe's staffer opened the limousine door and summoned Zenobia and Ryan.

Chapter Twenty-Eight

Zenobia stood in the rain looking at her signboard, "Sister-To-Sister: Where Mother and Child Give Birth to Their Futures—Your Government at Work," which reminded her of a giant business card on stilts.

Zenobia strutted around in a tie-dyed caftan, reminiscing how far her project had come in five months. "Take a picture," she told Ryan. "Grandma Jones will turn the church out when she testifies with this one."

Daisy had been right about Minister Howe being busy after the riot. He conducted an investigation and in June gave the president the Report of the Presidential Commission on National Reconstruction, which stated 'let us all join to build the new Liberia.' With the Commission implemented, Minister Howe returned his focus to Sister-to-Sister. He ordered supplies and sent a special work crew to construct new walls and enlarge the windows in what would become examining rooms.

The August wet moon was monsoon-like and caused constant work delays. Still, Zenobia was happy with the progress and flitted around, running her hands up and down unpainted walls. She was most happy when Daniel arrived at her door with work and residency permits for her and Ryan.

"January," she called to Ryan through a doorframe.

"January what?"

"Opening day for Sister-to-Sister is January 5, 1980. I will have delivered some babies by the time I've been here a year."

※

As the two headed toward the main road, Zenobia looked back at her dream that was manifesting before her eyes.

"Have you ever wondered why there are so many expatriates living here?" she asked Ryan.

"Yeah, fact is, if you have even a little money, it's easy to live here. Most of the teachers at the American School were part of the Garvey, Civil Rights, or Black Power movement; some are the traveling spouses of embassy or U.S. Aid for International Development employees. No matter their employer, they came to live out the freedom of their dreams. Everybody loves the tropical weather and white sandy beaches. One teacher told me she just quit her job one day, bought a ticket the next, and moved here with her son. She says she gets self-satisfaction every day."

"Do you think Daisy could live with the same extravagance in the States?" Zenobia asked Ryan.

"Who knows how much money Daisy has, but it's clear that in Liberia, you are either related to the Americo class and have access to opportunities to fulfill your dreams, or you are in the indigenous class and don't. There is nothing in the middle. I heard that it is possible for some indigenous people to get fostered into an Americo family and then gain access to opportunity, but those that aren't that lucky, like Ezra, don't have a shot at accessing anything but hard work."

Ryan paused a minute. "I wonder if Ezra ever dreams about Satta getting enough education to have a better life than his. I can't imagine life without a dream, without hope."

Ryan thought about his own dream. He brought Zenobia's hand to his lips, kissed it, and said, "Zen, I've been taking a lot of pictures lately. I have seen all types of people, who they are, and the huge gap between wealth and poverty, sanity and insanity."

"Pictures? For what?"

Ryan said, "Don't know yet," even though he was sure his hobby had turned into a plan.

"Airfield Road," Zenobia said to a driver that splashed a puddle when he swerved toward them. She shook the rain off her umbrella, slid into the back seat with Ryan, and didn't notice the rain-drenched man standing across the street from Sister-to-Sister. He had watched her and Ryan at the building and saw them get into the taxi.

"Hello-yah," Zenobia said to everyone in the taxi and continued talking to Ryan in her practiced patois.

"We'll have a party to cel-ebrate the birth of Sister-to-Sister," she said to Ryan. "Better yet, we will start a se-ason of the sun party tra-di-tion every November to cel-ebrate the end of rainy season. I'm telling you, we will invite all the people we know, and serve only Li-berian chop, no Ameri-ca'n food what-so-ever," and slapped the palms of her hands.

Zenobia framed the shape and size of a new hairstyle with her hands. "I'll have Kito cornrow my hair into e-lab-o-rate braids and ask Daisy where to buy the best mud cloth caftan. People will come from all over to talk world politics and play bid whist."

Zenobia talked about the party until the window passenger, who had been studying her, dared to say, "I say, Ma'am, you look like one real Liberian woman."

Zenobia's smile beamed satisfaction.

"What tribe are you?" the man continued.

The driver honked at a nearby taxi, then veered to the left, barely missing a water-soaked pothole and shooting water into the face of a pedestrian. He was distracted by the rain and traffic, but the driver watched Zenobia through his rearview mirror, and he, too, waited for her response.

It had begun for Zenobia at the rally where she heard and then let it reverberate through her soul that she was an African by time and geography who now lived in America. It had turned her life around. From that day until she stepped onto Liberian soil, what Zenobia wanted most was to become an African version of herself; to look, think, feel, and meld into an African woman, 'one real Liberian woman.'

Her thoughts returned to the taxi where she wondered what had happened. Was it something in her gesture, a slip in her patois that allowed the passenger to peek inside, to provoke the question? Since Zenobia couldn't figure out how to disappear into the taxi floor, she pondered her answer. All she could think of was diaspora.

Knowing Zenobia's heart, Ryan looked for a way to rescue her. "We'll get down at the next stop, driver," he said. The driver looked at him quizzically.

The passenger waited.

Zenobia wanted to proclaim, *I am an African*, but how could she say this to a man of African soil, of generational tribe, and family clan. "I, I, um, am an African American," she uttered just as the man sucked his teeth and mumbled, "American, just like I thought." He opened an umbrella and exited the taxi.

Chapter Twenty-Nine

The rain tapered off in October and small gardens popped up all over Monrovia. Minister Howe sent Daniel to Zenobia's door with directions to hire nighttime security; rogues had broken into Sister-to-Sister and had stolen windows, doors, and bathroom fixtures. Electrical outlets had been ripped out of their sockets and strewn across the floor. "Minister Howe ordered replacements, but Freeport delivery will be slow," Daniel told Zenobia. "You should hire nighttime security."

Zenobia hired Ezra to monitor the renovation site, and then asked him to drive her to Always Beautiful.

"Let's go to Waterside," Zenobia said when Kito finished the last braid. "I can't be happy about my clinic, and so I may as well spend money."

Zenobia gasped at the nakedness of the building when the taxi drove by Sister-to-Sister. "Let me down," she said to the driver. "Right there."

The driver made a U-turn in the middle of Tubman Boulevard. "I'll pay you to wait," she told him.

Zenobia walked Kito through the missing entrance door. They stepped over wire and downed drywall. From the middle of what was supposed to be the reception room, she looked up and saw clouds through missing ceiling tiles. Light raindrops fell on her. "It's worse than when we started renovations. How could this have happened?" she asked Kito.

"When I was little," Kito said, "the whole neighborhood would watch for rogues stealing clothes from a clothes line or food from the kitchen while their neighbors slept at night. When they caught one in the act, people chased him through the streets, throwing rocks and shouting, 'Rogue, Rogue,' to shame and embarrass him. Along the way, crowds joined in the chase for blocks. Sometimes it worked and the rogue stopped." She looked around at the ruins and said, "Rogues are usually just beggars, hungry people, trying to feed themselves and their family. This is vandalism. I don't know what to make of it."

Back in the taxi, the driver told Zenobia, "Somebody spying outside this place here. The man asked me your name, but I an't know it."

Zenobia began to slump and Kito caught her. "Minister Howe should have a solution. He's losing money, too," Kito said. "In the meantime, we have a party to plan."

☙

The only place in Monrovia where Zenobia still felt like a tourist was Waterside Market. A cacophony of sights, sounds, and smells, the first few minutes at Waterside always overwhelmed and repulsed her senses. Customers and market women haggling over prices, merchants shouting, music shops playing High Life and reggae rose to such a pitch Zenobia couldn't distinguish one sound from another. The caustic smell of raw and smoked fish, monkey and goat meat, tobacco, spices and sweat all made Zenobia's stomach queasy. Pickpockets and moneychangers who sold foreign currency there at black-market prices made her jumpy.

Specialty shops catered to the strange tastes of expatriates by selling imported canned meat and fish, imported sodas, chewing gum, leaf tobacco, Cheez Wiz, European and American movies. Sellers of eight-track tape players and cassette tapes, rainbow-colored Hoola Hoops, and Converse tennis shoes met high demand. Even though Liberia's weather would never be suitable, vendors stocked turtleneck sweaters in every color and size.

A clapboard stand specialized in items that allowed young Liberians to live out dreams based on American situation comedies. Youth bought bell-bottom pants and jumpsuits, psychedelic clothes, and platform shoes.

Kito signaled the driver to let them down in the textile section. As they walked an alley path and through a maze of stalls, Zenobia vacillated between holding her breath 10–15 seconds and breathing deeply so she wouldn't hyperventilate before her stomach calmed. Kito said, "Here."

Inside, Zenobia was comfortable again, and the two friends moved eagerly through the aisles, examining row after row of exotic designs, colors, and textures from Egypt to Sierra Leone, South Africa to Algeria. Zenobia chose a hand-woven Kente cloth from Ghana with golden threads woven into a rich purple background.

"My man will look regal in this," said Zenobia, winding with Kito around the next corner and down a narrow beaten path. At the dead end of the nook sat a tailor shop.

"Alfredo, this is my best friend, Zenobia. Zenobia, this is Daisy's personal tailor."

Alfredo shook Zenobia's hand wildly. "I can' see Missy Daisy for long time," he said. "She travel stateside?"

"No, she's here—just busy."

"That mean she make plenty money," Alfredo said.

Zenobia sketched a caftan for her and a dashiki for Ryan on a piece of paper. "Can you sew this?"

"I can sew anything you can draw," Alfredo said. He took Zenobia's measurements and asked, "What about the man?"

Zenobia stepped to the door and waited until she saw a man of Ryan's weight walking by the shop. "He's that weight," she said, "but two feet taller," and gestured with her hands.

Alfredo got a glimpse of the man in time to see his back. "Ah, your husband is big," he said, puffing up his own chest and shoulders.

Alfredo marked on Zenobia's design and said, "One week. Don't worry—I make it good."

Daisy had three regulars to finish before she could end her Saturday business—a haircut, a wet set, and an up-do. The women amused themselves with small talk about weekend plans, while Daisy stretched her back, put a cassette tape of Miles Davis into the eight-track player, and took in the first riff of 'So What.'

Just then, a van driver wheeled onto the curb in front of the salon. Three men spilled out, rushed the steps, and ran into Always Beautiful. Two reached behind each dryer, saying, "Sorry ya," to the customer, while unplugging and rolling the dryers out the door and into the van.

Wet set raised her hands, as if surrendering to her own personal robbery, haircut let out piercing sounds, and up-do balled her fist. None of the women made a move to leave their seats.

Daisy lunged at one of the men. "Wait a minute!" she shouted, and looked into his face. She tried to recognize him, his ethnic speech, or his manner. *Have I seen him at a meeting somewhere?*

The last vandal, at Kito's styling station, unplugged the curling iron holder and carried away the complete set of Marcel, spiral, flat, and barreled irons. With his free hand, he reached behind his back and grabbed a rack of hair-cutting shears.

Daisy rushed him and pounded his head, neck, and shoulders with two of her heaviest brushes. Her hands were too greasy to take hold of his back, so she threw the brushes at him as he mounted the moving vehicle.

"Daisy, who did you anger?" asked haircut, when the men and their threat were gone.

"I'm telling you, I've never seen anything like that," said up-do, checking on the condition of her hair, and deciding if she would let Daisy finish.

Daisy stuck her head out the door and looked up and down the street. When she was sure the van had disappeared, she double-bolted the door, drew the blinds, and straightened her clothes. She leaned against the wall and said, "No mind, ladies. I have more dryers in the back. This small problem will cost us only one hour, and I assure you, you will leave my shop beautiful as always."

Chapter Thirty

Old Ma folded her grand Boubou robes around her, tucked her sack of medicines under her arm, and went into the Monrovia office of the World Health Organization just in time for her noon meeting.

The group dedicated to making pregnancy safer and improving sexual and reproductive health in Liberia had come to Yekepa to ask her politely if she would work with them because she had the ability to bridge indigenous customs and western medicine. That's what they told her, but Old Ma knew that they wanted her because in her fifty years, she had delivered more successful village births, circumcised or not, than anyone.

It hadn't been her choice to become a medicine woman. When she was five and, on her own made a healing headache tea for her mother, her gift of healing was noticed. Older medicine women taught her how to recognize healing plants, trees, and herbs, how to make poultices, and teas. When they finished passing on age-old ways of healing, she became an Old Ma. Her own mother made sure she learned the wisdom and responsibility that came with being an Old Ma. Even though she knew concoctions for evil roots and potions, her mother convinced her that God would strike her dead because her gift was for God's healing through her hands.

When the Liberian American Swedish Mining Company built the mining community in Yekepa, Old Ma was selected to be "western-trained" by the physicians there and became the only 'country woman' with complete access to the Yekepa Hospital.

The gift of healing brought her to Monrovia today. She was amazed that the world's best doctors were trying to learn the properties of plants she used to make balms that healed the scar tissue of circumcised women. The doctors referred to it as secret because they hadn't figured it out.

The nurses called Old Ma an agent of change when they recited their motto "When women thrive, the society benefits," and asked about her secret talks with village women.

"First I know, 'cutting' is an ancient tradition. I have to respect that. I know that if it is ever possible for a girl to refuse, which is extremely rare, her tribal clan immediately shuns her. Any mother who refuses to have her daughter 'cut' is disobedient to her husband, the child's father. So I whisper with respect," she told the nurse team. "I teach the truth about the woman's anatomy. I tell her that her 'secret of joy' will not grow out of control if left alone, and that leaving it alone will not make her daughter dirty or wild. Then I point out all the examples of pain, infection, and death from the procedure, which she already knows."

As Old Ma walked the stairs to the second floor, the smirk she carried on her face was for the amusement she got when watching degreed professionals try to conceive a formula that mirrors her sensitivity and patience with women. *It can't be bottled.*

Chapter Thirty-One

With clouds completely receded and rain evaporated from the air, Kito arrived with serving trays of rice, palm butter, groundnut stew, cassava greens, black-eyed peas, egusi, and fried fish for the first annual November season of the sun party. She put the food on a table, including Zenobia's fried plantain, and arranged it like a buffet.

Word of the party spread, and expatriates from the Caribbean, Europe, the Americas, and Continental Africa swarmed the Airfield Road house, giving it the look of a United Nations summit. The price of admission was sharing a greeting exchange in one's primary language: Hola, Jambo, Bonjour, Shalom, Bom dia, Marhaba, God dag, and Dumela.

A Nigerian guest called Ryan and Zenobia's home Harambe House, meaning "let's pull together," as a tribute to the eclectic group that gathered and found a place for camaraderie and a venue to argue world politics.

A loud whistle came from across the room when a tall, butterscotch, big boned woman with Caucasian features entered the living room. "Who is that honey?" a man asked to no one in particular.

Beads and golden studs, woven into the woman's braided locks, looked like an Ethiopian basket atop her head. A ringlet dangled over her right eye, and the ornate embroidery sewn around the neck of her caftan almost matched the design of her hair.

"Come on in, Tasha," called Kito as she introduced her friend to Zenobia and Ryan.

"Habare gani," Tasha said, giving her greeting in Ki-Swahili and trying to be more exotic than her American background. She pretended to reapply lip-gloss while using her cosmetic pack mirror to eye the men standing behind her. "Nice party," she told Zenobia.

Ryan, in the embroidered dashiki, exhibited an Ashanti kinglike posture. He took his place at the bid whist table and started trash talking. "I hope y'all realize that nobody can beat me 'cause my great granddaddy invented this game." He shuffled the cards and dealt them around the table. "No kitty," he said, pushing the matching kufi back from his forehead.

"My main man is a serious player," said Keith, an office machines executive. He played a card and held his hand close to his chest. "You cats like living here?"

"I love it," said Kweku, the man who had met Ryan at the Relda and who finally told Ryan that he lived with a religious community that had been in Liberia more than twenty years.

"For twenty-five cents, a kid brings me fresh young coconuts every morning," continued Kweku. "Here, papaya grows in my backyard. In Detroit, fresh fruit comes from the grocery. Still, the biggie for me is that I haven't heard the *N-word* since I got here. Man, you throw in the beach and weather, life doesn't get any better than this."

"Man, the strangest thing happened to me at the market," said Keith. "I was buying bananas from the woman I get them from everyday. She has the sweetest honey bananas. You know, the short, fat ones they call lady fingers?"

"Yeah, yeah, get to the point," snapped Kweku.

"She wanted to give me her baby; asked me if I would take her daughter back to the States with me. You ever hear anything like that?"

"What'd you say?" asked Ryan.

"What do you mean, what did I say? I paid her for my bananas, gave her a good dash, and told her she had to be crazy 'cause nobody just picks up a baby in the market and takes it home."

Ryan shuffled the cards and dealt them again. "Are all of you planning to stay?"

Regardless of Ryan's lowered voice, Zenobia heard his question. She poured a round of palm wine to stay in earshot of the conversation.

"I get hazard duty pay from my company," said Keith. "It's almost double my salary, plus a hazard duty stipend for living in a third world country. I am not going anywhere before my two years are up. I might even sign up for two more."

"Are you kidding?" asked Derrick, an English teacher with the Peace Corps who worked in Bassa County helping to translate the Bassa language into writing. He slammed cards on the table. "Boston!" Then he scooped and shuffled them for the next deal. "I like being single and I got me a Liberian woman who takes good care of me," he said, winking.

Zenobia directed her guests to the buffet, the liquor table, the barrel of palm wine. "I'd be careful," she warned, "unless you and palm wine have already met."

When Marvin Gaye belted from the stereo, 'What's Going On?" the entire crowd sang, 'Brother, brother, brother."

Ryan asked the men, "What did you think about the rice

riot?" Before anyone could answer, he said, "Tripped me out, just like Kent State."

Abdul, an exchange student from Côte d'Ivoire asked, "What's Kent State?"

"Student activists demonstrated against the Vietnam War," said Keith. "The National Guard opened fire on them right on campus. Killed four and wounded nine. It showed me that humans are capable of doing most anything. But I agree with my man, Kweku. These folks can do whatever they want, because this *is* as good as it gets for me."

Ryan asked, "What do you all think about the conflict between the Americos and the Indigenous? Sometimes I wonder if I'm considered an Americo."

Keith was the first to answer. "Man, that conflict is just how the country got started. After all these generations, I think everybody should call themselves Liberian."

"Ryan, man, you are no more an Americo than I am," said Abdul. "We're both here enjoying the benefits of African Independence. You are African-American; I am Ivorian and neither one of us came to stay. The settlers paved the way for us to be here."

Derrick continued. "I often compare the story of pilgrims landing on Plymouth Rock while Indians occupied the land with the story of the American Colonization Society settling in Liberia. What baffles me is how any group thinks they can claim an already-inhabited land as their own. No wonder there is conflict."

"Show me a place where there isn't conflict, and I'll show you a place where everybody is asleep," said the younger Abdul.

Zenobia couldn't hold back. "Out of the mouths of babes. Where is the talk about what you're doing to help the people who live in this paradise that you love?"

Just then, a crowd from the street swarmed the front

steps and porch, and guests who were out back ran toward the front. Someone shouted from outside, "Hey, Ryan, you got celebrities. It's Ansa and the Jazz Notes Band!"

Zenobia's mouth gaped, "Who?"

"Come on in, man," said Ryan, and escorted the dark-skinned, thinly built Ansa to where the band would set up. Then he nudged Zenobia to a corner. "I wasn't sure Ansa would show up, so I didn't mention it. He has a new baby, and his money is short. I told him he could book parties with our guests, if he plays for free."

"Can he play?"

"He cooked at the school assembly."

A guest ran from the backyard, carrying a bottle of Jack Daniels. "This is really something. Man, I'm 'bout to spend the night!"

Chapter Thirty-Two

The January north winds had dried the air, but came short of changing the unhappiness that was closing in on Zenobia.

Christmas had left Zenobia moody; it was the first time that she had not had Christmas dinner with her family. Without snow, the tropical climate seemed a strange contradiction to Midwestern winter holidays. Then the influence of Islamic and indigenous religions downplayed the Christian season and gave Zenobia pause to miss home. There were no television commercials pulling her into tinseled malls to buy the latest gift, no smell of pine, no carols or *White Christmas,* no Salvation Army kettle drive jingle, and no toy stores that enticed children inside with lists of items that neither their parents nor Santa could afford.

Daisy and Kito closed the salon for a week and flew to the Bahamas; Sarah and Ezra worked a half day, she at the market, and he in his taxi, and then they made meat and gravy, rice, and biscuits. Zenobia and Ryan gave Satta books, writing paper, and pencils.

Zenobia and Ryan were enjoying a glass of imported wine when "Old Man Beggar" danced on stilts down Airfield Road. "Old Man Beggar" wore a mask and baggy clothes, and moved from house to house, drawing crowds of onlookers to fill the hat in his hand with "treats." The couple ran outside and laughing, they threw pennies into his hat. Later that Christmas night, Zenobia realized that she could not measure her distance from home in miles. She retreated into herself.

When Daisy returned from vacation, she tried to improve Zenobia's mood. "Honey find something else to fill your time."

The more Ryan tried to console Zenobia, the more she snapped. The more Zenobia pushed Minister Howe about completing Sister-to-Sister, the less he was available.

"There are abandoned projects all over Liberia," Minister Howe told her. "Even a rich man could run out of money or die before his building is complete—rain, rogues, supplies lost at the Freeport—anything can cause delays. You must be patient—this is Africa."

Ezra told Zenobia, "Somebody doin' that de-lib'rate to you, Missy Zenobia. And someone is spying at the building-o."

"Who would do such a thing, Ezra?" she asked, "And why?"

"Don't know, but it's true. You can' open the clinic this month or the next," he said when he reported that there was nothing left to steal.

Sarah told Zenobia that she had seen a man walking around Sister-to-Sister early one morning when she was on her way to Waterside. "He look ugly, Missy Zenobia," Sarah said. "Mean."

Zenobia didn't know what she'd do if she caught the person red-handed. She wasn't about to chase him through the streets, hollering "Rogue." She told Sarah and Ezra, "If I find out who's doing this, I'll tell Minister Howe. He will know what to do."

When the inventory of diapers, blood pressure cuffs, stethoscopes, baby clothes, blankets, and sleeper sets arrived from Babies Incorporated, Zenobia paid a cash dash to Freeport officials and Daisy gave discounted hairdos to their wives to ensure the supplies went untouched.

Then Ryan came home with mail that broke Zenobia's melancholy mood. He handed her an envelope.

Date Mailed: January 5, 1980

Happy New Year Precious,

I missed you at Thanksgiving and Christmas dinner, but I liked the Christmas cards you sent. The fake Christmas trees and African women dancing around them with hardly any clothes were funny. I haven't seen a warm Christmas since Georgia.

Thank you for sending the pictures of your work over there, which I pass around the church every Sunday, just in case somebody missed them the previous week. Sister Marshall is so jealous she just about can't stand her own self. You remember her no-count daughter, Charlene? Well, she run off with the preacher's son to Atlanta. Sister Minnie and Sister Hamilton is just about eating every bad word they ever spoke about you. I speck it taste pretty bad going down, too.

I never let on that I knew they spoke badly of you. Serves 'em right, though, that every chance I get, I rub those pictures of you right into their faces. I like all of them, especially the one with you and the first lady of that whole country, and the one of you in front of that clinic that's gonna help those poor women and their babies. And I like the one outside the Minister's church. Is he the Pastor or just the Minister?

Clovis and Amita ate Christmas dinner with me. Clovis likes her manpower job, and since she lost some weight, she looks good in your clothes. Amita is in a special preschool for lead babies and my heart almost jumped out of my chest when she heard my voice and smiled. Doctors say she's gonna be fine, not retarded, just a wee bit slower than other babies. We'll see what God says.

Scotty is fine and he says he's gonna marry Thelma. We'll see about that, too.

I'm glad you're going to church, Precious. Keep God in your life and don't get too full of yourself, 'cause the world has a way of rolling right on over the one who thinks they are sitting on top.

Tell Ryan his mama come by to see me the other week. She's missing him pretty bad. His father too, except he won't say.

Kiss him for his mama and me.

Stay out of trouble and keep those pictures coming. I love you.

—Grandma Jones

Chapter Thirty-Three

After hiding her dread that the clinic would not open in January, Zenobia was agitated. Nights of sleeplessness had distressed her. As soon as the sun rose, she ran to the main road and hailed a taxi. When the taxi drove past the ELWA Women's Clinic sign and into the yard, thirty women—pregnant, nursing babies in their arms and small children in tow—were already sitting on the concrete porch bench.

Zenobia burst through the purple door, where ten more women stood in line to receive a colored dot and a number.

"Your color is blue and your number is five," the receptionist said slowly and clearly. "When it is your turn, I'll say blue five. You understand?" the receptionist asked. The woman, who looked to Zenobia to be five months pregnant, nodded.

Zenobia waited a long ten minutes and then stepped in line between two women. When she reached the receptionist, she introduced herself. "My name is Zenobia."

"I believe you stepped ahead of these women," said the receptionist, sucking her teeth.

"Actually, I am not here for a clinic appointment, I would like to speak with one of the nurses."

The woman examined Zenobia from head to toe and back again. "Do you have an appointment with one of the nurses?"

"No, I do not. But, uh, I—I would like to apply for a job. I would like to work here."

The receptionist got up. "One moment," she said to the woman behind Zenobia. She said nothing to Zenobia.

When the receptionist returned, she ushered Zenobia into a room. "Wait here."

A desk and four chairs stood alone in the sweltering, windowless room. The rickety ceiling fan did nothing more than move hot air around and agitate the ends of loose papers.

Curiosity overwhelmed Zenobia, even though she tried not to appear nosy. She peeked at the contents on the desk: packs of pencils and notepads, a stack of pediatric tropical disease brochures, and childbirth reference books.

Taped flyers that announced upcoming events lined the wall where Zenobia stood. Pamphlets tacked to bulletin boards listed signs and symptoms of malaria, its prevention and treatment, and recommendations from the World Health Organization and the Red Cross for childhood immunizations. A list named ways to detect symptoms of disease caused by airborne, waterborne, or bloodborne pathogens.

Information in a pamphlet, *Female Mutilation is a Human Rights Cause,* held Zenobia's attention. She had heard about it, but had always thought it was some barbaric practice found in the African hinterland, and could barely believe the World Health Organization was openly addressing it. "Genital cutting is seen as a way of ensuring that a woman is clean, chaste, and ready for marriage. Uncut women are associated with promiscuity and lack social respect," the article read.

A woman in a short white laboratory coat walked in. "Ahem. Hello, I'm Annie," the woman said, carrying a stack of literature about the return of polio. She extended her hand. "I am the head nurse at ELWA."

Zenobia took Annie's hand. "I'm Zenobia," she said,

composing herself while starting to return the Female Mutilation article back to the wall.

"You can keep it—we have plenty. How can I help you, Zenobia?"

"Well, I attended your grand opening, and I had to rush afterward, so I never had a chance to personally congratulate you on this wonderful accomplishment."

"Thank you. It is a blessing from God. We are doing His work," Annie replied. "I'm sure you noticed we have lots of patients. Is there something I can do for you?"

"I was wondering (*how you did all this?)* if you have any openings. I have three years of practical midwife experience in the States."

"What brings you to Liberia?" asked Annie.

"My husband works for the American School, and we are guests of Daisy Williams—you know, the woman who owns Always Beautiful Hair Salon. Her daughter and I are best friends."

"Sure, every fashionable woman knows Daisy."

"Well, I've missed working with women and thought I would stop in to see if you needed a hand. I could volunteer, and then I'd be available whenever you needed permanent help."

Annie tucked a clipboard under her left arm and rubbed the bottom of her chin. Several minutes passed. "We are very busy here as you can see," she said finally. "There are four of us—one Jamaican, a South African trained in England, and two Liberians. I am Liberian. We get along very well and our relationship with the government is exceptional, as I am sure you noticed with the first lady.

"We are teaching basic systems of colors, reading, and numbers so the women can follow their treatment and medications. We have more inventories and a better record of live births than the local hospitals. We immunize, distribute vitamins, and teach sanitation, breast-feeding, and weaning techniques. It would be very difficult to think about doing anything that would disturb all of that. But I'll tell you what. From time to time, we get into a jam where we are needed outside the clinic. We'll put you in our directory, which will enable you to deliver a baby in an emergency. But you can only deliver those whose names are on our Safety First list."

Annie pulled a current list of one hundred eighty names and handed it to Zenobia. "These are women who are currently in our care. We update the list monthly. It will be your responsibility to maintain a current list."

Zenobia scanned the list and noticed that Sarah's name was not there.

"I can't say how often you might be called upon, but in the meantime, here are a couple of programs you can get involved with," said Annie, handing Zenobia a *Breast Is Best* brochure. "These programs are sponsored by the World Health Organization and the Red Cross."

At the front desk, Annie said, "Our nurses are involved with the problem of female mutilation. It's not as bad here as in other African countries, but it is here, and it's hard to penetrate new ways of thinking because it is seen as a cultural rite and obligation. I'm sure you know circumcision is not good for women and you should be familiar with it to be a midwife in Africa. There is a weekly meeting at the Red Cross office downtown, if you are interested."

"Thank you. Thank you so much," Zenobia replied, her head reeling. "How can I—"

Annie looked at her watch and cut Zenobia off. "I must go now, Zenobia. Thank you for stopping by. And oh, don't forget to drop off your credentials for our files."

Annie walked toward the examination room where five

women with screaming babies were awaiting her return. *Arrogance. Thinks she can just show up and jump in.*

Zenobia brushed by patients, the receptionist, and ran out of the clinic door. She waved to a taxi that had let out two women and tried to ignore the anguish growing in her stomach.

Chapter Thirty-Four

Around midnight, a cloud, unfamiliar to Liberia's tropical paradise, formed over the Atlantic and caught people off guard. Winds of dissent stirred and the sea trembled, coughing up more than a hundred years of retribution. The unusually high wind carried the smell of ocean salt into Zenobia's window, and palm fronds rustled loudly.

Zenobia awoke from her sleep to an empty bed, and looked out the window at the strange dry-season sky. It was dawn—the heavens tried to lighten, but a black cloud had eclipsed the sun and all signs of encroaching danger. She lay there, ignoring the prophetic weather and thinking about the importance of the *Breast Is Best* campaign in protecting babies from dysentery. Poor mothers, intent on stretching milk formula because of its expense, were diluting it with contaminated water and unconsciously causing the severe illness. *Breast really is best*, she thought.

She pulled the sheet covers around her legs, and she was looking for the cotton spread when singing and gibberish shook the windowsills. Zenobia pushed the curtain aside, expecting to see another cultural celebration, but her mind froze.

A barefoot man walked down the street with a full-sized airplane propeller on his head. He carried it with ease, forcing Zenobia to squint her eyes to see if it was real. Two men trailed the first, carrying the plane's wings. It was real.

Ryan ran up the walkway, his bag of leaking rice measuring the trail of his fear. He vaulted up the steps, bolted into the house, and threw himself against the bedroom door.

"Zen, Baby, there's been a coup!"

"A what?"

Zenobia couldn't decipher the meaning. Outside the bedroom window, children bustled down the street, playing with airplane seats, having turned the nearby airfield into a playground. She wanted to laugh at the absurdity.

Streams of people zigzagged across lawns, brandishing their spoils: furniture, food, jewels, and clothing. A little girl stuffed in an office chair with reams of paper and a Remington manual typewriter, wheeled by Zenobia's window. The girl's smile and flailing arms and legs were reminiscent of an amusement park ride; her friends ran laughing to catch up.

A deep line creased Zenobia's brow. "What's going on?" she asked when she could find words.

"I got up early to go to the market at the end of Airfield Road. When I got there, the women could barely sell their products for talking over each other. My pineapple lady said soldiers stormed the Executive Mansion, just after midnight, and shot President Tolbert in the head." He took a breath. "Zen, she said they cut out his guts!"

"Okay, okay," Zenobia said, mentally trying to put it all together. "Tolbert was assassinated. That's what you're telling me, right?" She followed Ryan around the house as he secured windows and bolted doors.

"People get assassinated in America," Ryan said, grunting to tighten the lock on the living room window. "Here, when a president is gunned down in his house and in front of his wife, it's a coup!

"The market women said the soldiers took the first lady hostage. Nobody knows where she is; now they're looking for all the cabinet members."

Zenobia slumped into a wicker chair in the living room.

"Don't wimp out on me now," said Ryan.

Zenobia ran in circles around the furniture while Ryan tried to catch and calm her. She stopped to peek out the living room window. The chant was at once deafening and sobering. "Tolbert is dead! Tolbert is dead!"

She watched drummers make a circle in front of Ezra's house, yet there was no sign of Ezra, Sarah, or Satta. The drums sounded celebration. Rhythmic stilt walkers and acrobatic dancers moved to the beat, exchanging stunts from one side of the street to the other.

Where the Frenchman lived next to Ezra, a man dug a pit and lit a fire while two others slammed a goat, still dripping blood, onto the ground. Within minutes, the smell of goat choked the air.

"What do we do in a coup?" Zenobia called to Ryan, who was in the bedroom throwing clothes into suitcases.

Their loud, breathless staccato outbursts overlapped.

"You're asking me? You're the one ready for revolution. What did Stokley, Kwame, whatever his name is, say? We're in a revolution right now!"

"That's not fair," Zenobia said. "I know, the Civil Defense Emergency Response!" she added, remembering the cold war air raid drills at her elementary school. "Aren't we supposed to find a safe, windowless corner?"

The outside chants came loud again. "Tolbert is dead! Tolbert is dead!"

"We need to go to the room off the kitchen with the water barrels; no windows there. He slapped his leg. "No electricity!" Ryan urgently rifled through the kitchen drawer.

"We don't have enough batteries for the flashlight and the radio," he said, slamming the drawer.

They retreated to the room and cowered in the corner with the radio. "This is Master Sergeant Samuel Kayan Doe, Chai'man of the People's Redem'tion Council and Head of State of Liberia. What we have done on this day, April 12, 1980, has never been done in the history of Liberia, but because of uncontrol'ble corru'tion and viola-tions against our people, it was much necessary. The first thing we will do is increase the salary of all enlisted men and law enforcement officers. They will make two-hundred-fifty dollars per month now."

Ryan pulled Zenobia close.

"To restore order and calm," Doe continued, "I am starting martial law. No one on the streets from six o'clock in the eve'nin' until six o'clock in the mo'ning. The people who assisted me in this take-over are the new gov-e'ment heads," he said, naming the new cabinet.

Ryan and Zenobia leaned in to hear the cabinet names over the laughter and drums outside. The radio weakened with each name.

"Now, listen carefully," said Doe. "I have some other names to read. If I call your name, you mu' come to the Exec-utive Ma'nsion. You mu' come im-e-de-ately so we can talk to you. If we have to come for you, it will not be easy."

Doe read a long list of names; his tone and intent were clear. Minister Howe was among the names.

Ryan jumped up. "We'd better destroy everything that connects you to Minister Howe, the first lady, everybody you've been working with."

Again the chants, "Tolbert is dead! Tolbert is dead!"

"Get the pictures, Zen." Zenobia's heart beat double-time. She knew Ryan was right; still she wasn't ready to destroy the dreams those pictures embodied.

"What about the building permits? They have Howe's name on them."

Ryan thought for a minute. "You'd have to get building permits from his office, anyway. Plus, you'll have to prove you had permission to use that building."

In that instant, the thought of losing the clinic occurred to Zenobia. "Prove to whom? It's a mess, but it's mine. Prove to whom, Ryan? Huh?"

"Quit trying to pick a fight, Zen. I didn't start this, but I could kick myself for not seeing it coming."

Zenobia didn't know who to blame, yet the more the realization set in, the more she believed a coup could put her dream out of reach. Fear consumed her.

"All I know is that you have to destroy everything that shows more than a business relationship with anyone in Tolbert's government. Now!"

Zenobia jerked backward at Ryan's emphasis.

Ryan made two piles, one for the fire, and the other for the suitcases.

"What are you doing?" Zenobia asked. "It's not time."

"You're being ridiculous, Zen! The only time we have here is the time it takes to catch a plane."

"A plane?"

Ryan parceled the contents of a drawer into each pile. "Face it, we are foreigners and being here is a mistake. But right now, we have to destroy evidence that could tie you to the government. I'll start the fire."

The chanting grew louder. "Tolbert is dead! Tolbert is dead!"

As Zenobia scrambled through papers and pictures, tears welled in her eyes. "It's your fault, Ryan. You should have talked me out of this." She bit her lip to stop another word from spilling out.

Ryan looked up from the piles. "What? What did you say?"

She shook her head back and forth trying to bring her senses back. "Nothing. Forget it!"

Ryan knew it would have been pointless to talk Zenobia out of anything, let alone try and change the trajectory of her dream. It didn't matter though; Tolbert was dead and neither of them knew the difference it would make in their lives.

Ryan turned his attention back to his work. He slipped out the back door, looked around and saw no neighbors. *Where is everyone?* Without a sound, he perched the coal pot on top of a concrete slab, stacked pieces of coal inside, and bunched steel wool on top.

Zenobia was glad that Ryan had taken charge. She handed him the pictures, one at a time. He lit the picture of the first lady with a match and used it to torch the wool pad. Zenobia was sure she would faint. The pad and the first lady went up in flames, engulfing the coals and sending red heat and smoke leaping from the black pot. Ryan looked around to see if anyone had noticed.

Zenobia clutched each item before she handed it to Ryan, her diary of meetings with Minister Howe, and when she was more comfortable with the idea, she put the scrapbook in, the one she hoped to use to show people the value of dreaming big.

Zenobia was angry at Ryan's insistence upon leaving and resisted his initial move toward her. However, for the first time in the past year, she had to admit to herself that she was fresh out of ideas. She clutched the citrine on her waistband, prayed that her own fire would not die, and reached for Ryan.

They hugged and watched the blaze dance on their memories.

Chapter Thirty-Five

Zenobia and Ryan were snuggled in each other's arms near the reserve barrels of water. Ezra's loud knock startled them.

When Ryan unlatched the door, Ezra said, "Morning o-o. I have rice for you," and he laid the hundred-pound sack at Ryan's feet.

"Thanks, man," said Ryan, hiding his slight struggle with the bag. The leftover smell of goat caught in his throat and he coughed. "Are you all right?"

Zenobia peered around Ryan's arm, "What's happening now?"

Across the street, next to Ezra's house, Zenobia saw a soldier sitting with his booted feet propped comfortably on the Frenchman's veranda. Two women passed, chattering about their haul—clothes bundled under their arms, Italian knits, Indian cotton, and leather shoes that Zenobia was sure she had seen worn by her neighbors.

"Is it true?" Ryan asked. "I mean what they say happened to the president, is it true?"

"Are Sarah and Satta all right?" asked Zenobia.

"Fine, Missy Zenobia. We all fine. Sarah is sellin' at Wata-side this morning. The Frenchman and his family, gone; the British family; the Jamaican family, gone. All gone to d'Embassy.

"When the people run to the Embassy of their country, the soldiers move into their empty house," Ezra continued. "The upcountry people, they come to Monrovia to be closer to the new gov'ment and put up a small house right next to the big house that the soldiers already take over."

Zenobia butt in, "Good thing we are in our house. Or we would have squatters, too."

Ignoring his wife, Ryan said firmly, "We're going, too, Ezra, to the States."

"Not today-o. Samuel Doe stop communica-tion and transporta-tion. Everything shut down. It will be some time before you can make phone call or take plane. They say Americos try to escape by car. All the borders are blocked."

Zenobia was relieved. She directed her questions toward Ezra. "I gotta get some air. It's okay to go out, isn't it? Can I take a taxi to Sister-To-Sister?"

Across the street, a Catholic priest was shooing children, like chickens, off the streets and into the church for Sunday Mass. Zenobia twisted her nose at the pungent odor that came from a pot of road kill stew that was boiling a few doors away.

"Stay here, Zen. I'll see if it is safe." Then Ryan asked Ezra. "Is it okay, man?"

Ezra backed toward the steps and away from the palaver. "It's not safe today-o. I brought rice, and Satta is coming with bitter ball, smoked fish, palm oil, and some coals. I ride my taxi to town and then tell you if safe." He looked at Zenobia, "I check on the building."

Eight o'clock on Monday morning, Ezra arrived with news. "You can go to town now," he yelled from the front steps.

"Soldiers say everyone can go and come, because they want things to be normal again, but you mus' be home at six o'clock. They not playing-o! And the ma'ket is too dan-ger-ous for you. People meetin,' discussin' the problem. We will bring ma'ket to you."

"Ezra, I can't ask you to do that."

A soldier trying to catch the attention of a young woman carrying a head load of greens distracted Ryan. The soldier teetered in a drunken stupor, lost his balance, and crashed, face down, at the foot of the steps. Just feet away, women talked loudly about the new government as they sat at looms weaving intricate patterns of colorful threads into yards of cloth to sell at Waterside.

"What?" Ryan asked, finally listening.

Ezra repeated, "I said I bring your ma'ket, and I do it b'cause I want to."

Ezra called, "Come Satta, bring the vege-tables." He looked at Zenobia with pride over his use of the word that she had taught Sarah and Satta for meal planning.

"I'm 'coming to go' see the body now."

"What body?" asked Ryan.

"The president," said Ezra, walking down the steps. "In front of the Ex-cu-tive Ma'nsion for everybody to see he dead."

Zenobia and Ryan gasped, "What?"

Ezra jumped into his taxi. "For true, you can go in town, nobody looking for you. Be home by six."

Ryan tiptoed onto the porch, looked up and down the street, and beckoned Zenobia to join him. Chairs, couches, and tables decorated front lawns and marked the territory of squatting soldiers.

"Where are the neighbors?" Zenobia asked.

"I'm worried, Zen."

Wet uniforms lay drying across a row of hibiscus bushes

in front of the Frenchman's house. The muted army colors gave sharp contrast to the brilliant purple and white blooms. A coal pot held a cauldron of stewing meat on the Frenchman's porch. Ryan led his wife into the house.

"I'm not scared," she said, reaching for Ryan's hand.

"I know you aren't. I'm scared for both of us. The neighbors we've known for more than a year knew to go to their Embassies. How did they get a heads up and we didn't?"

"Because Kito and Daisy are our sources of information and because Liberian papers hide the truth."

"But the coup wasn't going to be announced in the newspapers, Zen and Daisy couldn't have known it would happen. Every government has an agenda, and we don't know the agenda of this one. Other than people of the soil, we don't even know who the new officials are."

"When Kennedy was assassinated, Johnson became president. Same party. Same government. She added, "This is a definite change of the guard, but..."

Ryan interrupted, "Doesn't matter who is in charge; we are not Liberian. We don't know what's going on because as foreign visitors, we don't have a side to pick in this fight. If we had a side, a vested interest, we wouldn't be so blind."

To that, Scotty's cautionary words played in Zenobia's head. *"Make sure you know how much you're willing to sacrifice—know how to get out of a situation. Stay out of politics and focus on your own stuff."*

Zenobia crossed her arms and was in deep thought for several minutes. "You are right about not having a side," she said. Then she uncrossed her arms and leaned back in resolve. "If I could pick a side, it would be for the regular people. The clinic is to help them, so I'm not ready to give up. I'm not ready to leave. Who knows, this government could be easier. They probably have something to prove."

All the windows were open; the April air did not stir, nor did Zenobia's will. Ryan could barely remember the day Zenobia surprised him by falling limp into his arms, and then as if something overtook her, a stronger determination than he had ever known from her burst forth. Now just days ago she had blamed him for her problems. He knew that protecting her without her cooperation would prove impossible.

Ryan held Zenobia in his arms, "You can't always have it your way. I've never been in a foreign country. I've never been in a coup—I don't know the rules of this game. I'm not even sure if the whole thing is over. Please promise me, promise you will pay attention and not take chances."

"Don't lecture me, Ryan."

"I need a promise."

"Okay," she said, pulling away. "Just don't talk about leaving. Not yet."

That afternoon, Zenobia kissed Ryan as he put her into a taxi headed toward town.

"Before six," he said to her and then hailed a car going in the direction of the American School.

She replied, "Before six," and said to the driver, "Executive Mansion."

It was two days after the coup, and the sky seemed eerie: the sun shone bright and yet dark clouds gathered in the distance. The dense foliage along Tubman Boulevard had not changed. Hibiscus was in bright bloom, wild orange tulips were iridescent, and shrubs that bore scarlet flower balls sprinkled the roadside. The people, though, seemed quite different to Zenobia—their steps higher, quicker, their smiles brighter, and children's play seemed freer.

Tolbert's body on public display had drawn crowds numbering in the hundreds. She got out of the taxi and mixed with the steady cord of people queuing up, not to mourn, but to verify that the Americo era was over. She joined them, walking toward the presidential home, even though the humidity and frenzied excitement stifled her.

Zenobia listened to a group of women.

"I touched him—saw his bloated head with my own eyes. Had a bloody hole in it the size of an orange," one gestured.

A woman with a toddler in each hand said, "Too bad for him, but it is our time—time we had our own president, a man of the soil."

"I hope my sister gets here from the interior tomorrow," said another. "Before long, blowflies will lay their maggot larvae and infest his body. I've seen it happen, then the animals and birds will come, and there will be nothing left to bury but his dry bones."

A man walked up. "Did you see the magic symbol that's carved into the president's cane?" he panted. "It's the compass that lies over the square that they say gave Tolbert his secret powers, the Freemasons Society symbol."

A woman blurted, "Secret power? What kind of secret power gets you killed while you sleep in your own house by your own soldiers and with your own wife right there?"

Zenobia had never seen an unembalmed body, and she wasn't sure she wanted to see this one. Despite that, the throng of people who piled out of buses and rented taxis with electricity in their voices, who rested on the ground and in the grass after walking for miles to stand in line as witness to the death, drew her. Among the rank, she stood, and had almost made up her mind that if she never reached the body, it would be worth it to stand there long enough to hear all the reasons why people had showed up. Then it hit her.

Reality set in when a stench so vile and so putrid that it

strangled her air made her cough, and her head hurt. Her stomach churned and heaved and her mouth went dry and cottony. *No matter what he did, he didn't deserve ending up rotting on the front lawn of the house.*

Zenobia decided she would not be a spectator to President Tolbert's post death humiliation, and she stepped out of the line. As she moved out of the multitude, and there was a rush to fill her void, Zenobia overheard a woman. "I tell you, I had to see for myself the man who stands for all those who robbed the common person of his dreams and choices. It is up to us." She hawked and spat hostility onto the red dirt.

Zenobia tried to shake off the odor that clung to her nostrils, clothes, and skin. She hoped that by walking the blocks from the Executive Mansion to Sister-to-Sister, the smell and her mind would clear.

From only a few feet away, she could see that the only thing left of her signboard was its goalpost-like frame. Inside, she stepped around broken window shards. Doors were toppled and she saw where a small fire had been set. Her dream lay in a mangled mess at her feet. The tears refused to fall.

Zenobia turned around to get a look at the jeep that drove up to the door. Five unarmed soldiers climbed out.

"What do you know about this building?" demanded the biggest one.

"I, I um—I'm Zenobia. Zenobia Jones," she started. "I was just…" She fidgeted with her bangles. "I was just looking around for the owner to see if it was available for rent," she stuttered. "I'm from America and…"

One of the soldiers scooped Zenobia up by her elbows, shouting, "It's her," and shoved her into the jeep.

The men talked fast, mixing Liberian patois with an ethnic dialect Zenobia didn't understand. She looked at her watch. It was only two o'clock, within curfew limits. *Do I have Miranda rights? Do I get a phone call? An attorney? Breathe!*

At City Hall, her captors lifted her squirming body and escorted her up two flights of stairs. Even though the people milling around the hallways hardly noticed her, their presence gave Zenobia a pinch of comfort. She was rushed through a door with a nameplate that had only three letters, "MA__R" of the word MAYOR remaining. She was tossed into an empty chair.

Her eyes watered from the stink of body odor and cigarette smoke. The hurry of men moving furniture and themselves around created such a blur that it was hard for Zenobia to make out everyone in the room, and then she noticed a man combing long fingernails through sparse chin hairs. He stared at her.

She took short breaths to avoid taking in the stench, touched the citrine, and wished she had one of Grandma Jones's prayer clothes.

The weasel-looking man with a receding hairline sat atop a wooden desk, hanging short legs over its side. The elevated platform, on which the desk sat, made it easy for him to look down, condescendingly, at anyone else in the room. As Zenobia watched him watch her, she shifted her weight nervously, all the while wondering why he looked familiar.

He began, "Afternoon. My name is Kimeh," attempting to portray an education that he did not possess. "I know your name is Jones, and you and I have interest in the building you are renovating."

He's the man that's always standing across the street from Sister-to-Sister.

"Let's get down to biz'ness," Kimeh continued. "You see,

that building has been in my family a long time. My uncle owns it, yet Old Man Howe seemed to believe the government owned it."

"Who is your uncle?" asked Zenobia, confident she could clear things up by throwing out the name of an important person she had met with Minister Howe or the first lady.

"Dr. Jeremiah Browne," he answered.

"Dr. Browne?" repeated Zenobia, realizing on second thought she must not acknowledge anyone in Tolbert's government.

Kimeh repeatedly rubbed his hands together and put them into his pockets as a compulsive ritual. "Minister Howe bribed Jeremiah into working for you."

Zenobia had seen those mannerisms before. *He is the man who sent the small boys to loot at the riot!*

"First, it's an insult," he flipped his wrist as if shooing a fly. "Then it is impossible for my uncle, a Liberian who owns a building, to work for you, a foreigner," he said, studying Zenobia. "You must work for him, or in this case, for me."

Kimeh climbed down from his makeshift platform, waved a hand to dismiss his men, and inched his chair next to Zenobia.

When Kimeh placed his hand on her arm, Zenobia considered begging her captors to stay.

"I want to a make deal," he laughed, rubbing his hands and putting them into his pockets. "Is that what you Americans say, 'let's make a deal?'"

He looked Zenobia in the eye. "I want the same deal you made with Howe. You fix the building; I deliver your permits and supplies."

Kimeh looked older than his forty years and reeked like someone who'd eaten, slept, and smoked cigarettes in the same rumpled clothes for days.

The bile Zenobia had pushed down where the president

lay in state tried to return. She decided the wormy man looked weird, not dangerous, and if he had planned to hurt her, it would have happened already. She sized up the distance between her and the door and resolved she would not show fear.

"I have no such agreement with Minister Howe. I paid him rent. That's it. Besides, I abandoned the project, because there is too much damage. I have no more money," she said, all the while wondering if there was a deal they could strike.

"Give me the money you agreed to pay Howe, and I will see to it that you have everything you need. You can come to Kimeh for everything," he said, winking.

"I have to talk this over with my husband."

Zenobia stood and seeing no opposition, she put one foot in front of the other and edged her way toward the door.

"This is not your husband's business. My proposal is between you and me."

"My husband and I are partners. I can't make money decisions without him," she lied. "Should we discuss this further?" she asked, already at the door. "Mr. Browne?"

"Yes. I'm Kimeh Browne, nephew of Dr. Jeremiah Browne. You come here in two weeks or we will find someone else to do biz'ness." He waved Zenobia's dismissal.

Chapter Thirty-Six

The Monday morning after the coup, Always Beautiful was packed with clients who had missed Saturday and those who were rescheduling their regular appointments to meet curfew time lines. Daisy posted new hours: 8:00 AM to 5:00 PM, and she reserved the morning for women who traveled the farthest distance.

Although she had not found the vandals who stole her equipment, she had discovered since the riots that new dissident groups had formed to have their say. A new brand of old and young rebels had emerged, moving slyly, seizing opportunities by operating on the periphery and between groups, getting and leaking information to whoever offered the greatest personal gain. Loyalty was at a premium, and Daisy whittled down the individuals with whom she worked to a loyal, faithful few.

Daisy was twisting a French roll when a man came into the salon. She stopped. The two went into the back room, and when they returned, the man slipped an envelope into his suit pocket and drove off in a black Volvo.

Kito recognized the man as one who had been to the salon before. She studied her mother.

The superintendent was leaving the American School when Ryan arrived. "This is messed up, man," said the Washington, DC, superintendent. "This is a panacea, a black paradise, and these fools had to mess it up," he said, as he got into his Peugeot and handed Ryan one of the posters he had just stapled to the school's front door.

Ryan crumpled the poster that read, "Closed. Reopen in Fifteen Days. Staff Meeting at 8:00 AM, Friday, May 2," and then threw the camera bag over his shoulder. He checked his watch and whistled for his driver to turn around. "In town," he said and climbed in. "My God is love too," he said, noticing the message painted on the taxi door.

When the driver pulled off, Ryan asked the question he had been pondering. "Why do you put those words on your car?"

"It is my prayer," the driver replied. "All the taxis, the thing they want to happen, their prayer or their praise—that's what they write on the taxi."

The driver adjusted his rearview mirror to look at Ryan. "My God is love, and He show it when He give us a Head of State who is a man of the soil." He lifted his head high and added, "Samuel Doe is a Krahn man, same as me. If my tribe is President, then I am President."

Ryan wiped the camera's viewfinder with a handkerchief and then tested the focus by looking at a coconut tree, a child playing tetherball, and two Mandingo men mired in conversation. Without taking a picture, he adjusted the lens for light.

"Where in town?" the driver asked Ryan.

"Ducor Hotel."

"I'm taking Chessman and Russel Avenue to town. The dead body biz'ness make too much traffic on Tubman. Okay?"

"It's absolutely okay."

༄༅

"Put me down here," Ryan said when the driver reached Broad and Randall streets where tall rain trees lined both sides of the street, and where people hurried in and out of buildings. Reggae, rhythm and blues, and High Life music played inside small shops, on street corners, and in cars. Ryan paused when he heard two children shout, "Tolbert is dead!"

Inside a Lebanese small shop, Ryan bought a *World News Service Bulletin.*

> **April 14, 1980: The heading read "President of First African Nation Executed."**
>
> On April 12, 1980, twenty-eight-year-old Master Sergeant Samuel K. Doe led seventeen noncommissioned officers to storm the Executive Mansion. They seized power, murdered, and disemboweled President William R. Tolbert, nineteenth president of Liberia, and chairman of the Organization of African Unity while his wife watched. Doe stated he overthrew the Tolbert regime due to "rampant corruption and continuous failure" to solve Liberia's problems. The act ended one hundred-thirty-three years of one-party rule and settler privilege.

Ryan tucked the newspaper under his arm, joined a tour group at the foot of Ducor hill, and climbed the incline until they reached the summit and the highest point of the city.

At the top, Ryan saw a bricked overlook that surrounded the Ducor Inter-Continental Hotel. He found a spot on the wall, away from the activity of market people selling to tourists, and for the first time since arriving in Monrovia, he tried to listen to his own thoughts, to consider how thirteen months ago, he had traveled across the world from safety to a riot and military coup.

Ryan felt celebration in the air. It didn't feel right to him, though. Somehow, in all the triumph, something was missing. He wondered if all the fanfare had made them unaware that something else, something more massive, was boiling just under the euphoric surface.

Ryan shook his thoughts, stood, and looked around. He thought the height and thinning air had suddenly snatched his breath. The city that nestled under a beautiful, majestic sky stunned him, made him feel as if he stood on top of the world.

He removed his sunglasses and put the viewfinder at his right eye so he could look at the city through the lens. He held his breath and secured the frames of children playing, showing toothy smiles; *snap*; a crippled, toothless beggar sitting on the ground; *snap*; the Catholic and Baptist Missionary Church steeples; *snap*; a boy carrying a cooler of five-cent water bags on his head; *snap*; two taxis racing each other to a stoplight, forcing others to let them pass; *snap*. He saw a taxi with "God Bless My Taxi" on its side door, and another, 'Respect Human Values'; *snap, snap*.

Small shops announced quality photo prints; *snap*; a Mandingo fine jewelry shop; *snap*; tailor shops; and a country chop (food) shop that claimed authentic Vai cooking; *snap*. Things were back to normal. Too normal.

A woman who had pretended not to watch him giggled when Ryan asked to take her picture. There was something in her big eyes and thick-lipped smile that reminded him of Sarah. He held the camera away from his face so he could take in the strong heart and spirit that shone through her eyes, the resilience and courage, the hope and fear, the peace and at the same time, strength.

Ryan took his time studying the perfect picture. When

she thought he had changed his mind, she steadied her head load and dropped her smile.

"Please let me take your picture. Has anyone ever told you how beautiful you are?"

A smile came from her heart again, and Ryan snapped several frames before buying her load of oranges and passing them out to tourists.

Behind the hotel, Ryan looked over the cliff that dropped sharply into the Atlantic where a higher-than-usual tide crashed angry waves against jagged rocks and left frothy foam swirling around the cliff's base. *Snap. Snap…*

Ryan was satisfied that he had seen Liberia for the first time.

"Taxi!"

Chapter Thirty-Seven

Ten days after the ocean opened its bowels and spewed angry dissent that ended President Tolbert's life, an aftershock came. A forceful wind blew across the sea to the shore. The sea retched forward and hurled generations of pent-up frustration and revenge, like living projectiles that pierced their way into every corridor, street, home, and mind.

Thirteen men endured humiliation and beatings, and after summary trials, they were found guilty. Guilty of one hundred thirty-three years of settler class greed, of stealing humanity, and ending hope; guilty of looking outside for solutions to Liberia's problems; guilty of passing down the same indignities onto indigenous men and women that they had learned in slavery; guilty of deferring dreams.

Thirteen fathers, husbands, sons, and uncles seen by some as distinguished, having the highest degrees; seen by others as traitors, guilty of committing the highest crimes.

The sky changed to stormy black as the men were stripped, marched publicly, and tied to electrical poles. Their wrists were wrenched behind their backs and around the poles with wire; their ankles bound by rope. Soldiers took their good time—five minutes—to open fire and spent four hundred rounds into thirteen enemies of the people.

It was the icing atop a nasty cake. Gunshots rang out from the ocean to the interior announcing a change of the guard—from settler to man of the soil.

The men's reddish liquid oozed down the splintery posts until it became congealed rivulets of dirty, brown sludge, uniting them in death. The soggy sewage streamed into sand crab crevices and emptied into the sea while a crowd of spectators cheered. Tasting the blood, the ocean roared, twisted, turned, and tossed giant waves of revenge that thundered against Liberia's coastline.

Before the thirteen were dumped into mass graves, their mothers, sisters, wives, and daughters came crying, begging forgiveness. But they were turned away for giving birth and nurturing thieves. The women were ripped with fear; pain and loss were apparent in their eyes. Without the chance to say a loving word of goodbye, one woman ran to the ocean's edge and bowled over. She gripped her stomach and moaned. The other women clung to each other and howled; "I'm sorry. *I am so sorry.*"

When no one listened—the women screamed a century's worth of *I am sorrys*.

And they were sorry.

Despite the ocean's warning, emotional debris littered the land, derisive hope suffocated the air. No person, place, or thing, no action would ever be the way it had been before this day. Still the people slept.

Ezra told Ryan about the execution. "I see it with my own eyes." Even so, what Ezra described was beyond anything Ryan could believe until he read *World News Service Bulletin* the next day.

April 23, 1980: The heading read "Tolbert Cabinet Publicly Executed."
On April 22, 1980, ten days after a bloody coup that ended True Whig Party rule and so-called Americo domination in Liberia, thirteen members of President William R. Tolbert's cabinet and family were publicly executed. The international press was on hand to observe former dignitaries paraded naked through the streets, tied to poles on the beach, and shot dead. Witnesses to the spectacle cheered, and the men's wives wept over a mass grave.

It was a week after the execution. Ezra awoke to the noise and stood at the side door of his house. He noticed lit candles and kerosene lamps as his neighbors stirred and peeked slyly through half-opened doors to see what the commotion was.

Ezra walked outside and almost tripped over a giant box turtle that stood in the road when he stepped beyond the aloe vera plant and onto the road.

The prophetess almost bumped into Ezra as she ran down the dirt road in her bare feet and bathrobe. Her arms were flailing, her voice piercing. Ezra barely understood her rant.

"*Wake up!* I had a dream last night. A vision," the prophetess hollered. "We killed them. They paid—now we pay. The pay forward and backward does not end. It never ends. Trouble is coming. We will see fire, destruction, and people running—children fighting and dying. Liberia will cry blood. I tell you, Liberia will cry tears of blood. Pray for Liberia. Liberia needs prayer!" she yelled as she ran toward the next block.

Chapter Thirty-Eight

Tasha Jenkins stepped out of the taxi and smelled the air. She hoisted a backpack onto her shoulder and peacocked up to Zenobia's door.

Zenobia had to stand back to talk to Tasha rather than bend her neck to look up.

"You remember me from your party, don't you?" asked Tasha.

"Sure do. What brings you back?" inviting Tasha into the living room. "Want a Coke?"

"Thanks. Um—um—um," Tasha said gulping. "I can't believe how thirsty I am. Can I have another one?"

Tasha crossed her legs and kicked her ankle, causing the flip-flops to make a plopping sound. She admired the living room furnishings, and when Zenobia returned with the Coke, Tasha began, "I live in Yekepa. You ever hear of it?"

"Don't think so."

"It's a mining town in the interior, more like a big city up by the Nimba Mountains. They say the iron ore up there is the best in the world. It's a planned community that America, Sweden, and Liberia put together."

Zenobia pondered. "A big city in the interior sounds like an oxymoron."

Tasha touched up her lip-gloss. "It's got all the conveniences you'd find in any cosmopolitan city, and it's the only place in Liberia I'd live."

Tasha swept the lock away from her eye with an exaggerated stroke. "I teach at the Yekepa High School for the Peace Corps. We get kids ready for scholarships to go to school abroad so they can come back and run the mining machines. Anyway, Kito does my hair and since the curfew, I can't get to town, with my hair appointment and errands, and back to Yekepa in time. Kito thought you might let me bunk overnight from time to time."

Zenobia thought about the days when Scotty had been in the Movement. Activists traveling from one city to another stayed at Grandma Jones's house for the warm bed and home-cooked meals. There would have been no Movement if lodging and per diems had had to be paid. Zenobia had met exciting and famous people sitting around Grandma Jones's dining room table.

"We have a spare room, but I'll have to talk it over with my husband when he comes home. I'm sure he won't mind."

"Kito said something about you opening a clinic." Tasha then told Zenobia about the Women's Association in Yekepa. "It's called 'From Mats to Mattress,' and it teaches rural women to read and take care of their families.

"We can trade. You let me stay here when I come to town; I hook you up with the woman who runs the program in Yekepa. You can stay with me when you're there."

Zenobia hadn't thought about her grandfather in a long time, but she was sure he had had something to do with Tasha's showing up.

"I've got errands. I'll be back before six." Tasha turned at the door, "Oh, by the way, I'm from Illinois. Chicago. See ya," and she was gone.

"Ohio," called Zenobia to Tasha's back.

Three weeks after the coup, expatriates, no matter how much time they had been in Liberia, tried reading the signs—the grip of a handshake, the number of invitations to dinner to chat about politics—to see if the new government had done anything to substantially change their life. Rumors circulated that the former first lady had wandered the streets calling out the names of her dead husband and children until an Americo family took her in.

Americos as a group feared reprisal. Rumors abound that soldiers, high on kola nut, ransacked random homes, tortured and killed their residents. International communication and flights had resumed; however, most Americos slipped out of the country over land via the Côte d'Ivoire, Sierra Leone, or Guinea borders. The French, British, and Nigerian expatriates who lived on Airfield Road and who had retreated to their respective embassies in the still of the night returned home to find soldiers squatting on their property, wearing their clothes and jewels. Seeing this, they told their drivers, "Airport Please," where they waited days for a flight home.

Sarah was now six months pregnant and Ezra worked extra hours driving his taxi so she would have enough money to rent a stall on the inside of Waterside Market when the new baby came.

Ryan came home with the first government-released mail since the coup.

Date Mailed: April 23, 1980

Zenobia, I've been watching the television day and night. I've been reading every newspaper Scotty brings to me. Everything says that those nice people you knew are dead. What kinda mess are you in over there?

We're going to send the Red Cross to find you if you don't call and tell us you are all right. Scotty told me your time is four hours ahead of ours. I do not care what time it is. Call.

You can always come home.

I love you.

—Grandma Jones

At six-thirty, the morning after Zenobia received her grandmother's letter, she entered Liberian Telecommunications and nudged an officer. He was sleeping with his rifle snuggled deep in his chest.

She whispered, "'Scuse me," trying not to frighten him, and then moved into one of five narrow telephone booths. She dialed the numbers for an international operator-assisted collect call, which connected her to a London operator, who in turn placed the call to Farrow, Ohio.

"Is this you, precious?"

"Sorry to wake you so early on a Saturday morning, Grandma Jones, but I didn't want to wait any longer."

"Are you all right? I've been reading about all those people dying. I saw that new president on the news. He said all the other presidents been treating his people badly for a hundred years. I keep looking in the paper and the news for some mention of you and Ryan. There's nothing."

Zenobia measured her words. "Reporters from around the world are here telling the story. But we couldn't call out or receive calls, plus we couldn't send or receive letters until now. It's how they control communication inside the country and keep tabs on who is coming and going. Nobody's been able to leave the country until now either."

Scotty had told his mother not to push Zenobia about when she was coming home; it would only give her a reason to dig in her heels. Grandma Jones knew Scotty was right, so she bit her tongue to keep from asking if Zenobia was leaving too. She now cleared her throat, and said, "A hundred years is a mighty long time to be mad, precious. You sure they can get over it any time soon?"

Zenobia breathed in and exhaled. "A-hem. I met a man in the new administration. He's going to help me pick up the pieces of the clinic."

"What pieces?"

"You know things that still have to be done to get the clinic finished."

"It's been a long time. Did you think it was gonna take this long, precious?"

"They call it African time, Grandma Jones. Everything moves slower here. But it's important to me that you don't worry. Really. I am fine. Ryan is fine. Daisy is looking out for us real good, and our neighbor goes to the market for us every day. The curfew is six in the evening 'til six in the morning. Things are absolutely safe. No more fighting, I promise. Things are back to normal—we just have a new government. That's all. I'll explain the hundred-year conflict in a letter, but I don't want to run up your phone bill. International calls are too expensive."

"I'm glad you called. I just had to hear your voice, and I'll be overjoyed anytime you decide to come home. Tell Ryan to write his mother."

"I will. I love you, Grandma Jones, and I promise to write more often. Bye."

"I love you, too, precious. Don't make me call the Red Cross."

That was it. When Zenobia hung up, she had nothing left, no comforting words to encourage herself with, nor energy to soothe her own heartache. The apprehension left in Grandma Jones's voice had added to Zenobia's misery. She walked several blocks, thinking, before she hailed a taxi.

There had been no emergency ELWA births; the Breast Is Best meetings hadn't resumed after the coup.

As her desperation grew, Zenobia reached for the slightest hope for her clinic. She began convincing herself that she needed Kimeh Browne; by the time Zenobia reached home, she was considering Kimeh's offer.

Kito arrived at Zenobia's house, saying, "For God's sake, Zenobia, give yourself a break. Come on, let's take a walk."

"Fourteenth Street Beach," Kito told the taxi.

Kito grabbed Zenobia's hand. "This way," she said, leading her the short distance to the beach. They walked barefoot around crabs darting in and out of holes and women lying topless under the sun.

The skies were deceptively clear for May. Zenobia and Kito tiptoed, curling their toes in the warm sand, until they found and climbed a rock made accessible by the low tide. The two sat atop the boulder, as if it were a perch, and watched the sun shimmer on the waters. Small waves splashed beneath them.

Zenobia broke the silence by sharing her thoughts about Kimeh.

"Stay away from him, Zenobia," Kito said. "He's a soldier. He may be slow to kill but quick to jail you and Ryan! I'm telling you, Zenobia, nothing good can come from him. Nothing."

Zenobia wouldn't let it go and hoped for Kito's approval. "I don't have proof, but I know he is the one who vandalized

Sister-to-Sister." She withheld the fact that she had watched him send boys into the riot. "But think about it, Kito. What if, in some strange and convoluted way, he can help me because of his own self-interest?" She paused. "If I can find a way to 'scratch his hand and let him scratch mine,' he could be my answer to the clinic getting back on track." She set her jaw firmly, "I just have to find a way to keep him honest."

Kito threw a seashell into the ocean. "That is the most convoluted thing I've heard. If he destroyed your dream, you should be mad. I'm telling you, he is trouble."

As fishermen miles down the coast dragged nets full of the day's catch into the harbor for market, the salt breeze cleared Kito's thinking.

"There's your advice right there." She pointed to a seagull that jabbed his beak into the sand and came up with a mouthful of sand flies. When other gulls shrieked and encroached upon his meal, he ambled to a new location. "Move on."

"I have some crazy news," Kito offered after a long silence fell between them.

"What?"

"Daisy is some kind of secret agent."

"Get outta here. She is overbold, but she's no agent. Daisy doesn't have room to be an agent for anyone but herself. Think about it, she does everything out loud. There's nothing secret about her."

"Those hotheaded men who want to change Liberia overnight keep coming around. I thought the coup would relax things; thought people got what they wanted, except now I think resistance is growing. It's in the air; I think it all went underground. To Always Beautiful.

"I overheard a conversation in the back room. They said for self-sufficiency Liberia should rely on its own food production. That's what Daisy means by African solutions to African problems."

"And?"

Kito sucked on an orange until juice trickled down her arm. "Daisy wrote a big check for rice farmers in Voinjama."

"Talk about putting your money where your mouth is. What's the harm in that?"

"I just don't like those men. They seem mad all the time, sneaking in and out."

"Daisy has a good heart for what she believes in. I'd like to see the person who crosses her, though. Come on—let's walk over to the Eighteenth Street beach so we can see the Zairian brothers that hang out behind the embassy."

"Shameful," said Kito, play-hitting Zenobia. They locked arms and walked past smooching couples, picnickers, and topless women.

Chapter Thirty-Nine

"Zen," Ryan called. He looked in the bedroom, "Zen."

"In the back," she called, where she was folding a basket of clothes with Satta, teaching her to spell and write her name.

As Ryan approached, he overheard Zenobia telling Satta that she could go to the Episcopal school because she and Ryan would pay the annual one hundred twenty-dollar tuition, the thirty-five dollar registration fee, and buy the green jumper and white blouse uniform. Everything would be paid in time for Satta to start before the December to February school break. Satta was giddy.

Ryan couldn't hold it any longer. He spoke to Satta and then declared to Zenobia, "The country is broke."

"Broke?"

"Yeah," he said and read the newspaper article aloud.

> **May 9, 1980**
> **Republic Of Liberia**
> **Ministry Of Finances**
> **Notice Of Inspection Of National Identification Cards**
>
> This is to inform all proprietors and heads of financial institutions, land and air transport compa-

nies, trading firms, big and small businesses, public corporations, government ministries and agencies, schools, embassies, marketing associations, communities, amusement centers, hotel managements, companies, and members of the floating population within the city of Monrovia and parts adjacent that the Special National ID Card Task Force team will commence inspection of identification cards on Monday, May 26, 1980. Any citizen or resident alien who is five years of age and above and not exempt under the Government Decree, must present his or her ID Card to the Task Force.

You can purchase a five-dollar card from the Deputy Commissioner for National Identification Cards.

—Signed: Deputy Commissioner
of National ID Card Program

In a matter-of-fact tone, Ryan said, "The school superintendent distributed identification cards to the staff today, while whispers flooded the auditorium, whispers that the government's money is hidden away in personal foreign bank accounts. The identification card program, five dollars each, is supposed to raise quick cash."

"Why do you listen to such gossip?" Zenobia snapped, stacking coals into the bottom of a coal iron while Satta, her excitement waning, looked on. "Kito told me they've always had ID cards, just never enforced the rules is all. What's eating at you?"

"It's not the cards, Zen. I smell general desperation."

"Thanks, Satta," Zenobia said. She hugged and paid Satta. "I can make it from here. Now let me see your gorgeous school smile." Satta smiled like the sun and then bolted for home.

"I don't like this," Ryan said when Satta was gone. Worry and frustration were in his eyes and forehead. He paced. He hadn't been about wishful thinking; he hadn't followed

Zenobia to Liberia on a whim. Ryan expected to see an economic boom, Western modernization, and foreign investors.

"Listen, Zen, I traveled halfway 'round the world to be with you while you achieve your dream. There's no blame—I chose to do it. It's just that I can't believe you're too stubborn to see what's right in front of you. We've been blindsided at every turn. Nothing is the way we planned. We walk around, thinking things are normal, then bam, a riot, bam, a coup, bam, a public execution. What's next? Huh, Zen? What's lurking around the next corner? I need to know that we're on the same page, that we can talk and decide together what to do. You don't see anything wrong with a government that is broke? You aren't the least concerned?"

Ryan went into the windowless room where he kept a second water barrel to cool beverages; he popped the bottle cap and stood outside thinking and taking a long swig of Club Beer. *I am determined to understand Liberia for myself.*

Zenobia remained quiet. She knew that he knew she wasn't going to budge. No need to say it.

Finally, a cooler Ryan said, "Let's stick with the basics. Our permits need updated stamps. I'll get mine done through the school; you want me to get yours?"

Zenobia held on to the measly possibility that Kimeh could help her. He was simply an obstacle that stood between her dream and reality. After fourteen disheartening months, holding hope against hope, her senses completely dulled, Zenobia saw only what she needed. She dared not let go.

"I'm working on a contact in the new administration. If that doesn't work, I'll go to Immigration myself. I'll take care of it. Don't worry."

Zenobia ushered Ryan into the house. "I'm with you Ryan," she said, rooting for the scent of sandalwood and swathing him with kisses. "I just can't give up yet."

Chapter Forty

Zenobia couldn't sit another minute on the sidelines of her chance to leave her mark on the world. She threw her purse over her shoulder and marched brazenly and unannounced into Kimeh Browne's office and demanded his attention. His minions went scurrying to their corners.

Kimeh kept his eyes on Zenobia while closing the door. He rubbed his hands and dug them into his pockets. "What brings you here? Ready to make a deal?"

"I'm ready to meet Dr. Jeremiah Browne. If Minister Howe was going to hire him, the three of us should agree on the arrangements. Then we make a deal."

Kimeh slinked toward Zenobia.

When Zenobia said, "I dare you!" with her eyes, he moved himself gradually back to his perch.

A sudden commotion on the other side of the door made Kimeh jump. He opened the warped door to a dozen men hugging, snap hand shaking, and slapping the backs of his men.

Zenobia had hoped to use a meeting with Dr. Browne to test Kimeh's ability to walk her documents through Immigration as Daniel had. Seeing his complete distraction, she prepared to leave.

The men in the hallway parted, like the Red Sea, to let Zenobia walk through them. She recognized Ansa.

"Hello," she said.

As Zenobia descended the stairs, one band member whistled and made the universal hourglass gesture for a well-shaped woman. Ansa told him, "Cool it. That's my main man's wife. Respect her."

"Excuse these men, ma'am, and give my regards to Ryan."

"Come back next week!" yelled Kimeh at Zenobia's back.

"My main man, Ansa," said Kimeh, waving to his men to get Coca Cola for everyone.

They all broke into boisterous laughter, chest bumping, and hand slapping.

"My main man, Kimeh. How's it going?" asked Ansa, hitching up his pants.

"Good, everything's good," replied Kimeh, hitching his pants, too. Kimeh mimicked the American style and slang that Ansa had picked up from the range of musicians who had come and gone from his band.

"Man, for the two weeks since the identification mandate, curfew or not, your identification cards allow us to move all over Liberia," said Ansa.

A dribble of saliva slid down Kimeh's lip when Ansa pulled out a wad of American dollars and peeled off two, four, five twenties. "Here you go, my man."

Kimeh stuffed the money into the shirt pocket of his wrinkled leisure suit.

When Ansa turned to leave, he raised his hand to trigger the snap handshake response. Kimeh hesitated.

"You gonna leave me hanging?" asked Ansa, his hand dangling.

"I need a favor," Kimeh stammered. "My daughter is getting married in November, and she's dying for you to play." He threw a play punch at Ansa.

Ansa said, "Sure, Kimeh, you're my main man," as he walked through the door.

Kimeh hitched up his pants. "I scratch your back, and you scratch mine."

"You got it, my man. One hand washes the other," called Ansa, running down the steps with his band close behind.

Zenobia hadn't heeded her body's urgent demand for attention. She had ignored the looming mood, the chills and aching joints for two days and by the time Ryan arrived home from school, her attempts at stopping the pounding in her head had pulled her into a desperate sleep.

The eerie quietness and drawn curtains told Ryan something was wrong. The heat emanating from her bed and the smell of sour perspiration scared him. He rushed to Zenobia; finding her trembling and cold, he called Sarah for help and sent Satta to find Kito.

Sarah filled a pan with cold water and placed compresses on Zenobia's head. "She okay, Mr. Ryan."

When Kito arrived, she shook a thermometer and pushed it between Zenobia's cracked lips. "It's Sarah and me," Kito whispered.

Zenobia tried to help Kito by opening her dry mouth but found she didn't have the strength to lift her thick tongue. "Feels like light bulbs screwed into my eyes; everything hurts," Zenobia mumbled before succumbing to sleep again.

"One hundred and four degrees," Kito said to Ryan. She opened each of Zenobia's eyelids to reveal yellow where the whites were supposed to be. "It's malaria, and she's jaundiced."

"Malaria? Jaundice? How'd she get that?" asked Ryan.

"The female mosquito puts the malaria parasite into your bloodstream when it bites. It sits there, waiting patiently for your resistance to run down, and then when you're weak, it takes over," Kito explained. "And jaundice travels with malaria."

Ryan's nostrils flared. "That's not what I mean. She's supposed to be taking Chloroquine," he said remembering the argument on the plane. "She's so hard-headed. Is it true Kito that Liberians don't get malaria because they live here and are immune?"

Kito laughed until she realized Ryan was serious. "Zenobia knows that malaria kills every day. I take the same pill you're talking about." She checked Zenobia's eyes again. "Don't worry, she'll be fine."

Ryan pulled a chair next to the bed and clutched both Zenobia's hands. "What am I going to do about her stubbornness?"

Kito showed Ryan how to drip cool water onto Zenobia's scalp and put wet compresses across her eyes, forehead, and along her shoulders and arms.

He followed Kito's instructions, soaked the towel again, and placed a kiss where it had been. Ryan caressed and wiped Zenobia's neck and shoulders with another compress before repeating the ritual. "Now what?"

"The Chloroquine and aspirin will make her sleep 'til morning. I'll stay the night to watch her fever. When it breaks, she will have extremely achy joints and muscles," Kito answered. "She must drink plenty of water. I promise you, she will be back to herself in a week. Right now, I'm hungry."

"The chop is ready," said Tasha, curtseying and pointing to the rice, groundnut stew, and potato greens Sarah had prepared.

"How is she?" Tasha asked.

"It's her hard head I'm worried about," said Ryan, motioning for everyone to sit down.

"Malaria is a rite of passage," said Tasha, "A down payment on tropical paradise, if you ask me. I was hard-headed, same as her, thought nothing could break this down," outlining the contour of her voluptuous body. "It only took one bout with the big *M* and some nasty herbal medicine for me to take that bitter Chloroquine pill. Now I take it religiously."

Kito washed her hands with lye soap and then sat at the table shaking her head. "Zenobia is sick with malaria. But she's mostly sick at heart, full of disappointment over having nothing but a coup to show for her time."

Ryan was taller than the women around him were, yet worries curved his shoulders and made him seem short. "Zen refuses to believe the project is over. I can't even count how much money she's thrown away, hers and Babies Incorporated's. And it's not just the building; she's got supplies sitting at the Freeport with nowhere to go."

"Zenobia is going to spend all the time and money it takes to make Sister-to-Sister happen," said Kito.

"Maybe it's none of my business," Tasha inserted. "It seems to me this is as good a time as any for her to go with me to Yekepa. I told Zenobia about the Mats to Mattress Program and the woman who runs it, Old Ma. Frankly, I think it's what she's been looking for all along."

Kito looked at Ryan and shrugged. "Maybe."

"I'm sure she can work with Old Ma immediately."

"My mother used to say that there's more than one way to skin a cat. One way doesn't work, try another," she said, brushing a lock away from her eye as she cleared the dishes.

"I like it," Kito told Ryan, who was heading toward the bedroom to change Zenobia's compresses.

"I'll stay until Zenobia gets well and then take her to Yekepa," said Tasha.

Ryan opened the bedroom window just a bit to let in fresh

Free Soil

air and the smell of rain. He checked Zenobia's temperature—one hundred—and replaced the moist compresses.

"Get well, baby," he said, holding her hands. "I have a dream, too."

Zenobia tried to lift her head from the pillow. It would not budge. The voices she heard sounded like an orchestra without direction, loud and clanging. In between fitful sleep, she saw Sister-to-Sister rise in splendor, like the Empire State Building, and then fall into rubble like a Mayan ruin—a baby lay in the wreckage calling out to her, "*Mommy*."

Grandma Jones crawled onto sweat-soaked sheets and rubbed Zenobia's temple, using the same love balm she had applied when Zenobia was sick with fear and worry about whether doctors could hide her ugly scar.

She whispered into Zenobia's ear, "My precious, you're so good at digging in your heels, you don't know when it's time to let go. Figure out what you need and ask for it. I love you, Zenobia." And then she climbed out the window.

Chapter Forty-One

A week later, Zenobia conceded loss and agreed to meet Old Ma. She stuffed a few changes of clothes and birthing supplies into a duffel bag, Tasha slung her bulging backpack across her shoulder, and the two climbed onto a yellow jitney bus headed for Yekepa.

Tasha sucked her teeth at the gawking passengers. "Don't worry about their stares," she said, pulling a lock away from her eye. "They're jealous that we have stuff and they don't."

Zenobia stiffened her back. "We probably look excessive to them," she shot back, while wondering if she had ever met a woman more self-absorbed.

Zenobia took in the new experience. As the jitney headed northeast from Waterside Depot and Monrovia, the paved road ended, the city shrank, and she could no longer smell the sea. Passengers bounced to the sway of the bus, and several banged their heads against the windows when the driver swerved to miss a water-soaked gully.

Zenobia was lost in her thoughts as she almost worshiped the specter of wild tropical flowers, the giant ebony and mahogany trees in the distance.

Tasha tried to release the sting of Zenobia's excessive

comment by changing the subject, "Do you know what happened to Kito's father?"

Only half listening, Zenobia asked, "What do you mean?"

Tasha leaned in, whispering, "You didn't hear it from me, but a woman at the Yekepa Iron Ore Company, the one who told me about Always Beautiful Salon, said Daisy's husband, Herschel Williams, was a big-time manager for the company. Everybody liked him, said he was fair to his workers. Liberian managers didn't make as much as their foreign bosses, but they made ten times more than the workers did—you know, the ones who were actually mining and transporting the ore. Mr. Williams felt bad about their meager salaries, and he believed the best booster for his workers was his unfailing fairness. He was the only Boss Man who honored their breaks and gave them time off when they needed it without taking their pay, things like that."

Tasha brushed her dress and looked down her nose, saying, "Mining is probably the dirtiest work there is." She pulled out her nail file and started working on her left hand. Aware that she had captured Zenobia's attention, she continued.

"Anyway, Herschel Williams worked in Yekepa during the week and traveled back to Monrovia on the weekends. It happened on a weeknight, Kito's tenth birthday, to be exact. He paid a driver double to take him to Monrovia in time for the birthday party Daisy had planned for Kito. It was one of Liberia's worst rainy seasons on record. Torrential rains had flooded the roads, and as you can see, there's no pavement outside Monrovia 'til you reach Yekepa. The driver swerved hard to avoid a waterfall that ran through a ditch and ran smack into a tree. The impact killed them instantly."

Zenobia's twisted face spoke for her.

"Now, like I said, you let somebody else be the first to tell you, but Daisy Williams blamed the government for the bad roads. She said the Iron Ore Company was supposed to pave the roads between Yekepa and Monrovia as part of the deal they cut with Sweden and America to mine and export the ore. She said government and corporate officials pocketed the profits and left the people to suffer."

Still dumbfounded, Zenobia asked, "Didn't her husband have insurance?"

"You're funny, Zenobia. Humph, Daisy was her own insurance plan."

"You can imagine Daisy's pronouncement didn't go over well," Tasha continued. "That was about fifteen years and two administrations ago, but the gap between Daisy Williams and government officials grew as wide as the Atlantic. She put up a fuss for months, threatened to send letters to the media in America and Sweden because they shared ownership in the Iron Ore Company. She threatened to expose how they took Liberia's natural resources and sent the profits home. She drafted a letter and sent it to their headquarters to show how nasty her statements could be. Each company feared the press, so the executives met with the president, agreed to a settlement, and cut Daisy a fat check."

Tasha stared out the window for a few minutes. "People say Daisy is one Liberian woman who thinks she can have the same things as men." Tasha paused and added, "Imagine that."

Just as the June rain slowed to a drizzle, a man from the back called out, "*Hayya Allah Salat, Hayya Allah Salat,*" and the bus driver veered over to park in a dense grove. The jerky move snapped Zenobia out of her stupor.

Passengers grabbed hand-woven raffia mats that had been stowed under their seats. Holding on to prayer beads, they climbed down the bus steps, lined up, women together, men together, alongside a thicket of evergreens, and kneeled.

"Allaahu Akbar, God is Great, Laa ilaaha illa-Lah, there is none worthy of worship except God."

"What's this?" asked Zenobia.

"He's calling Muslims to pray."

Zenobia hoped that God would hear her among the others; she bowed her head, opened her hands to receive a blessing, and prayed.

As the bus began its ascent toward the Nimba Mountain Region, Zenobia tried to digest the story of Herschel Williams. She had never seen mountains and grasslands more luscious and had to acknowledge that something powerful had had a hand in creating the phenomena around her. On her left, an antelope drank from a natural watering hole, and up ahead she saw that netting around a rice swamp kept birds away. Yet in the midst of all this greatness, she wondered what Kito knew about her father's life in Yekepa.

"Wait until you see the city," said Tasha, finishing her nails.

"Driva' let me down. I got pee pee," yelled a passenger.

"You might as well go, too," said Tasha. "No rest stops around here. Come on, I'll show you—just be glad the rain has stopped."

Tasha led Zenobia away from the other women to a section of overgrown hibiscus shrubs. She reached into her backpack and pulled out a wad of toilet paper. "Here," she said, pushing a few sheets at Zenobia. "I keep some with me all the time."

Tasha spread her legs wide enough to accommodate her hips, pulled her skirt up just over her hips, squatted halfway, and bent her knees outward to keep her balance. She glanced down to make sure her ankles were clear but kept her head up so she wouldn't topple over.

"Now you try," she said when she was done. "You might

want to take off your underwear first. There's just no easy way to juggle all that and your aim."

Zenobia wasn't inhibited—she had delivered too many babies for that—but urinating in public was just plain gross. She followed Tasha's directions and was about to squat when a lizard ran past her foot. Her knees bent, her skirt bunched around them, and she lost her balance when she tried to move away from the lizard. She fell over into a thicket of wild fern.

"I can hold it until we get there," Zenobia said, reaching for Tasha's hand and brushing away mud and embarrassment. The two women walked back to the bus looking as if they'd just taken a casual stroll.

※

An entire world sprang up from the foot of Mount Nimba—the air was thinner and cleaner, no smell of salt. Seductive mountains encircled Zenobia wherever she stood. Their scenes warranted frames. The sky was bluer and the thick foliage took on such a profound green, it looked blue. From the hillside, she took in a deep breath and looked toward the heavens.

"Thank you."

"Let's walk," said Tasha, leading Zenobia toward Sandy Clark Square, Yekepa's hub for gathering and entertainment. "These buildings are new and no modern convenience was spared."

The smell of freshly mowed and sprinkled grass tickled Zenobia's nose as the two walked by imposing rows of residences.

"Over there is the international school where I teach seventh grade," Tasha said. They walked by the modern library and passed Yekepa bank where customers rushed to beat closing time.

"The hospital is up ahead," said Tasha, pointing beyond the square. "If I ever get sick, I mean sick enough to need something more than Old Ma's medicine, I want to be right here where they have state-of-the-art medicines and equipment; the doctors are some of the best trained in the world. Over there is an indoor/outdoor recreation center where the primary sports are tennis, soccer, and golf."

"What's that?" Zenobia asked.

"Machines digging out the iron ore, giant shovels scraping and pouring pellets into truck bins for hauling. You'll get used to it soon; blends right in with the bullfrogs and chirping crickets."

"Most everyone here is from somewhere else, but the majority group is European nationals," Tasha continued. "You either work for the mining company, or you work for the people who do."

Tasha walked several yards before stepping over a brick wall. "This way."

They walked what seemed like a mile down a winding road. The houses became smaller and shabbier, with less space between them, and red dirt replaced lawns. "Liberian managers, service staff, and some miners live in these houses during the week or longer, if needed. Everybody else lives in the village."

Tasha pointed toward the village entrance, a mud wall surrounded by hibiscus shrubs and feverfew orchids. The way in led to a narrower path that then merged into dense grassland. "Old Ma lives over there," Tasha said, pointing to an area in between affluent Yekepa and the village.

"She'll meet you here in the morning."

Chapter Forty-Two

As soon as Ryan had seen Zenobia and Tasha off to Yekepa, he hired Ezra for the day. "Come on man, I have lots to learn about Liberia and you are the best person to teach me."

"Where to?"

"You show me what I need to know. Okay?"

Ezra filled his taxi with gasoline and he sat tall in his seat as he drove down Benson Street beyond Capitol Hill. He stopped in front of an expansive three-story concrete building with ground-to-roof pillars at the entrance. "That's the Gran' Lodge," he told Ryan.

"You mean the Masonic Grand Lodge? I can see the symbol at the top of the building."

"It's a bad place. Secret place," he said pointing. "Evil. All the gov'ment people line up behind each other to decide how to make the country people live. Only secrets inside. No countryman can go inside without special request. Now the soldiers ban everything there."

"Come on Ezra. I'm not a Mason, but I know plenty of them in the States. They call it a secret society, but they are not bad people."

"Bad, Mr. Ryan. Bad sign. Secrets. Bad people."

"Okay, man, I'm with you." Ryan said and snapped his camera.

When Ryan finished taking pictures, Ezra drove down the coast, southeast from Monrovia to Buchanan, Grand Bassa County.

Ryan broke the long silence. "Zen and I have been surprised by the turn of events since we arrived. We didn't anticipate any of it: the riot, the coup, the execution. Can you tell me what's really going on? Without information, I can't make good decisions about our future."

Ezra thought hard as he drove alongside the railroad that linked the iron ore mines in Yekepa to the shipping port in Buchanan. Finally, he opened up. "Everyday I see taxi carrying loads of guns upcountry. We were happy for the man of the soil, but the only person Doe is puttin' in jobs is his own Krahn man. And I hear things. They say…" Ezra lowered his voice to barely a whisper. "The soldiers with so, so power, they kill the people they don't like and dump them in a big grave behind the Mansion. With so, so power and no money, they steal anythin' they want."

"That's scary. How does so much go on and no one knows?"

Ezra looked at Ryan sideways. "People know. You can' know cause no Liberian will tell you except me. The newspaper can' tell, but in the market, on the street, everywhere the people talk."

"Did anyone know about the attack on Tolbert?"

"The rice riots stir the people; make them want what they never had, no more waitin.' But soldiers tell me they make the plan to kill Tolbert just before they do it, and they kill the men who work for Tolbert because they do everythin' for themselves, not for the people. The one man they didn't kill lived with Americo family, but his ma and pa from the country."

"We're here. You can take many pictures in Gran' Bassa. I'll take you to your friend, Derrick."

Ryan and Ezra ate coconut and boiled eggs with Derrick and the Bassa children as they dramatized a Bassa proverb. Ryan laughed as the children acted out. "He who steps in (a river) first shows the depth of the current." The children then begged Derrick to let them act out their favorite story—the choice to do good or to do bad to every stranger they meet. Courtesy to a stranger, the children stressed, is always the best course because he could be the bearer of good fortune or carry an omen. Derrick would spend the next months translating their language through stories about moral character and accountability on earth into storybooks to teach children to read.

"I have treat for you," Ezra told Ryan before they returned to Monrovia. "Sarah's sister make stew with fish straight from the ocean, and *fufu* from the cassava. You will be real Liberian man next time you see Missy Zenobia," he said laughing. "Come, I will take you."

Chapter Forty-Three

The June skies opened up and rained harder than anything Zenobia had experienced in Monrovia. It was a downpour that hammered so hard, neither she nor Tasha could sleep.

By daybreak, the rain had tapered into a drizzle, and dark clouds forced the sun behind them.

Zenobia didn't know what to take, so she lined her fishnet bag with a yard of fabric and packed alcohol wipes, cotton, and dental floss. She started to throw in a stethoscope but changed her mind.

"How will I know her?" Zenobia asked Tasha as she left.

"She'll know you."

"Morning ya," a woman called to Zenobia as she neared the narrow path.

Zenobia held out her hand and sang, "Morning O."

"This way," said the woman.

Deciding to shut up until she could breathe and have something substantive to say, Zenobia pulled her rejected hand back and followed, barely keeping pace.

Old Ma's spirit seemed soft, but her walk was hard. She didn't move with the gait of a market woman or one who'd given birth to many babies. A mesh bag, similar to

Zenobia's, dangled over her shoulder and bounced to the rhythm of her gait.

A bandana covered Old Ma's hair; small brown tufts peeped under the back knot. She was plump, on her way to fat, and her full skirt swished when she walked. She had breasts that looked like they could feed a litter; her skin was a smooth copper.

The two passed rows of houses—shingled tin roofs, mud, and thatched—each with one to two rooms for sleeping.

"In here," said Old Ma.

Rainwater dripped from the shingle of a one-room house. A girl swept debris—stray leaves and sticks—away from a patch of dirt that constituted the front yard. Two boys played soccer with a can.

From the doorway, Zenobia saw a woman sitting on a spotless dirt floor; the only thing between her and the dirt was a plastic mat. Sponge mattresses given to her by the Mats to Mattress Program lay against mud walls. She held a baby in one arm, and with the other hand, she turned an empty rice bowl upside down on a wooden table to keep flies away.

Zenobia made a mental note about the baby. *Three months old.* She didn't know what to make of his bulging eyes.

"This is Esi," Old Ma said to Zenobia.

"Morning ya," said Zenobia.

"He's got open mold," said Old Ma, nodding at the mother and pointing to the top of the baby's head.

The baby's soft spot was sunken, moving in and out with the rhythm of his pant. An herbal paste, plastered over his head, was now dry.

Zenobia stepped back and closed her eyes. "What's his name?"

"Boima."

"Boima," Zenobia repeated, planting the pronunciation in her head. "He's beautiful. May I hold him?"

The woman smiled shyly and handed her son to Zenobia.

Brushing her fingers across the top of his head, Zenobia could feel that the skull bones had not closed. That was normal for a young baby; it was the depth of the opening that bothered her.

She opened Boima's eyelids. His eyes were dry. His skin was dry and limp between her fingers. "He's dehydrated. That's why the opening is so deep," she told Old Ma.

Old Ma pulled herbal paste from her bag and smeared a fresh covering on Boima's head.

"Is there a spoon and clean water around?" Zenobia asked.

Old Ma called to the boys outside. "Come, now, I need well water, the one down to the rehabilitation project." She handed them a large covered calabash. "Fill this to the top, cover it, and bring it back here. You hear me?" she said. "Make sure nothing gets inside. Hurry, now."

When the boys returned, Zenobia cleaned the spoon from the rice bowl with an alcohol wipe and then wiped it with a clean cloth diaper that she pulled from her bag. She dipped the spoon into the well water and allowed droplets to fall into Boima's mouth. For the next hour, at five-minute intervals, she dropped life into baby Boima. He smacked his lips and sucked desperately.

Zenobia showed Esi how to repeat the process, and Old Ma made Esi promise to use only clean water.

"You did well," Old Ma said when they were outside. "I've been telling Esi to give Boima clean water for days now. She wouldn't listen. Said her mother told her to use the paste that's on his head. Yesterday I pled with her, telling her that her son could die if she didn't use the paste plus water. Sometimes people prefer a stranger to someone they know. Like I said, you did well."

"Thank you," Zenobia said almost prayerfully.

☪

Tasha came home from school and found Zenobia sprawled across the living room floor, construction paper, markers, and scissors everywhere. "What's this?"

"Old Ma took me to see a dehydrated baby," Zenobia told Tasha, barely containing her excitement. "I'm making pictures of the rehydration solution to give to the mother in the morning so she can make it herself."

Zenobia read the recipe to Tasha. "An eight-ounce Coca-Cola bottle of boiled water; add to the water one bottle cap each of salt, sugar or fresh orange juice, and baking soda. Everything's in the market.

"This picture brochure shows how to make clean water without boiling. You put a tightly capped bottle of water in the sun for five hours." Zenobia had drawn pictures of bottles under the sunrise, in full sun, and at sunset to depict the amount of time they should remain.

Tasha walked carefully around the scattered posters. "I've watched heavily accented doctors rattle off medical instructions to women who I knew didn't understand a word. They needed these flyers."

"Yes, Tasha, but even more than that, they need empathy."

Tasha returned to the living room with two cold Coca Colas. She noticed Zenobia's changed mood. "What's going on?"

"I was wondering, why did you ask me to come here?"

Tasha took her time answering. "Everything you did backfired. It shouldn't have been that hard, and I thought Old Ma could show you a better way."

"It's hard to know if Old Ma needs me or if I'm just a

sidekick. Today she had me deliver the same message to a woman who hadn't listened to her."

"Do you think she was testing you, trying to see if you knew your stuff?"

"I don't know."

"The Yekepa Women's Association is responsible for the Mats to Mattress Program. They make sure Old Ma has everything she needs. There is no program without her. Old Ma knows what she is doing, and nothing gets away from her. She cannot take risks. Trust her, follow her and you will be fine."

Zenobia was half remembering the emptiness she was feeling just before malaria overtook her. She was already imagining the babies she could deliver with Old Ma. Finally, she allowed her heart to open up with hope again, hope that she would finally get to do what she had come all these miles to do.

"Zenobia, did you hear me? I said guess what happened to me today. A student who had been failing received a scholarship," she said. "He had felt defeated until I taught him to read. Today, he was proud of his scholarship, and I felt good, too."

She turned her thoughts back to Tasha. "Is that what you like about teaching? I love my work. Do you love teaching?"

"There's no other way out for these kids. The only way for them to have a better future is education. With education, they get a glimpse of something bigger and better than their circumstance, and then grow beyond it. Simple as that."

Even though Boima was alert when Zenobia arrived in the village the next morning, she showed Esi how to make the rehydration solution. "Use this for two more days," Zenobia told her, made two marks on a piece of paper, and then drew the number 2.

"Isn't he still nursing?" Zenobia asked Old Ma when Esi rejected Boima's pull at her breast.

"She wants to wean him so she can switch to formula."

With that, Zenobia doubled back and left a "Breast Is Best" brochure with Esi.

Old Ma walked with a comfort that came from knowing her own heart, and an enduring confidence in who she was. She waved at women who stopped fanning rice or looming cloth to speak as she and Zenobia walked by. One woman rushed her. "Here, Old Ma. Take this rice. My baby is fine now. Thank you."

"Thank you, too."

"Come on," Old Ma said, leading Zenobia into a house where she had delivered a baby the day before. "Hello, yah," Old Ma said to the new mother. "Is she breast-feeding good?"

"No, she can't catch the nipple," answered the mother. "Should I buy formula?"

Zenobia leaned in to watch the woman push her baby girl's head toward the dripping nipple. The baby did not latch on.

"Hello yah. My name is Zenobia. You mind if I try?" Zenobia used her fingers to show the mother how to touch her breast to the center of the baby's mouth. The baby opened her mouth, but when the mother put the nipple inside, she did not latch.

"Something is stuck in her mouth," said Zenobia. "Can I hold her?"

Zenobia picked up the baby and held her heart-to-heart for several minutes. She talked and cooed, and then she laid the baby in the bend of her left arm so she could examine her mouth.

When Zenobia slid her finger under the tongue, she noticed that the membrane extended to the tip. "She can't latch because her frenulum has her tongue attached to the floor of her mouth; she can't lift it," Zenobia told Old Ma.

Old Ma took the baby. "Stay here, Zenobia."

"I want to examine the baby in the sunlight," Old Ma told the mother. "I'll be right back."

Old Ma looked inside the baby's mouth. It was only the second case of this in her experience, but the procedure was simple, no more difficult than the circumcisions she performed on infant boys.

Old Ma folded her ample body and sat on the ground. She leaned her body against a coconut palm and wrapped her skirts around her legs and feet. Then she laid the baby across her knees, opened a cellophane packet of yellow powder, and retrieved a small pair of blunt surgical scissors from her bag.

When Old Ma snipped the thin membrane that fastened the baby's tongue to her mouth, the infant let out a yell that sent her mother running from her mud house. Old Ma then put two pinches of the yellow powder under the tongue, held the infant tight to her bosom, and within minutes, the baby was asleep.

"Your baby's fine, now," said Old Ma to the mother standing there wringing her hands. "The powder will make her sleep and stop the bleeding. When she wakes, she'll catch your nipple and drink your milk."

"Thank you, Old Ma!" the mother said, crying.

"Come get me if you see blood," said Old Ma. "I don't think you will, but just in case. You hear me?"

"I will Old Ma. I will."

"I wanted to see you clip the membrane," said Zenobia. "I know that's what you did, but I've never seen it done."

"These women rarely see the inside of a hospital. My surgical scissors are the only tools safe and clean enough to do a good cut, but the sight of them going into her baby's mouth would have made that mother crazy," Old Ma said. "I know what's best for my mothers, Zenobia. I'm glad you were here to distract her."

Old Ma continued. "This is our last stop. You can come in, but don't say anything unless I signal you," speaking over her shoulder and leading Zenobia inside.

"I delivered her baby two years ago," Old Ma whispered under her breath. "Now she wants to have this one at the hospital."

"Why?"

"She's been afraid of pain since she was a child. Then she started listening to the talk that goes on inside those rich homes she cleans; she thinks she's entitled to what they have. If she could, she'd tie her legs into a slip knot to keep that baby from coming before she got enough money to deliver at the hospital."

Zenobia shivered.

"Some of my mothers want things handed to them, don't want to work through hard times to get to the good."

"Does she have money for the hospital?"

"No, and if she did, it wouldn't matter. The hospital only admits villagers when I say there's a complication I can't handle." Old Ma paused for effect. "There isn't one. I'll deliver her when it's time."

"Old Ma, I'm curious."

"Yes?"

"On every road, there are houses where you don't take me; you don't even talk about the women inside."

"There are things you don't know." Anticipating Zenobia's next question, she continued. "Things you're not ready to learn."

"Get dressed," Zenobia told Tasha when she came home. "You remember Ansa, who played at our Seasons party last year? He's performing at Gertrude's tonight."

"Now, that's what I've been missing," said Tasha. "The chance to let my hair down."

Partygoers crowded onto the street and streamed into the only restaurant and bar establishment in Yekepa. It doubled as a supper club and was where young, old, white, black, workers, and bosses freely mixed for the promise of a good time.

Zenobia and Tasha could hear High Life beats before they passed the blinking neon sign, "Friday, June 27, 1980 Ansa and the Jazz Notes—One Night Only—in front of Gertrude's Bar and Grille."

Chapter Forty-Four

After weeks in Yekepa, Zenobia and Tasha headed back to Monrovia in the early morning downpour.

Zenobia rifled through the picture brochures and couldn't wait to show Ryan. "First Nine Months," "What to Expect During Delivery," Rehydration and Nutrition," and "Breast Is Best"—she was impressed with herself.

Tasha poked Zenobia in the side when the bus pulled over. "Look."

Trucks with rain-soaked soldiers in full military gear were brandishing weapons and standing guard on either side of a roadblock.

Cars and taxis, absent drivers and riders littered the road.

"Checkpoint," said one soldier.

Zenobia and Tasha looked at each other. "Checkpoint?"

A soldier climbed onto the bus, eyeing each passenger. He walked over to Zenobia and said, "I need to see your identification card. You too, miss," he said to Tasha.

"Of course," said Zenobia and sat up so as not to look frightened. She rummaged through her purse and brought up an empty wallet.

"We are American citizens, living in Yekepa," said Zenobia. "We are on our way to Monrovia just now to collect our identification cards from Mr. Kimeh Browne. He gave us verbal permission to travel, without incident, until we returned to Monrovia."

The soldier nodded his approval to another. "Make sure you have your permissions when you travel this road again. No more exceptions," he said to them, and moved to the next passenger. "Identification card, please."

Zenobia looked over her shoulder to see several passengers dash the soldier money in place of the card.

"That was close," said Tasha when the bus drove off. "Where are your travel documents, and who is Kimeh Browne?"

"He's someone in the new administration who's gonna get my documents."

Tasha turned around to see the long line of cars going through the checkpoint. "Why can't you get your own?"

"Minister Howe got them last year. I just hate the hassle." She shrugged her shoulders and did not mention her plans for Kimeh.

"I don't understand that about you, Zenobia. You take the long way around when a straight line would do. I know what you mean, though. It took months for me to get used to changing office hours, priorities one day that drop to the bottom the next. That's why I let the Peace Corps take care of everything."

The driver abruptly stopped in front of men huddled on the road. Soon as the men took seats on the bus, leaving their mud-splattered taxis behind, the driver announced, "There's a gas shortage. The next bus to Yekepa may be delayed. Sorry, ya."

☙

The date on his Observer Newspaper read Thursday, July 31, 1980, and from the second floor window of his poached office, Kimeh Browne watched people rushing about their day as usual. He circled the desk, first one way and then the other, carving a pattern into the dusty floor with his tracks. While hitching up his pants and combing his whiskers with his nails, he noticed the growing space around his waist.

Kimeh was looking for the same break he had looked for as a "grown'a boy," grown-up boy on the streets fending for himself. Accused of having sex with a schoolmate at the age of thirteen, Kimeh ran away from home rather than face the dishonored father, or go to jail because he could not pay her father for despoiling his daughter's virginity. Kimeh had lived hand to mouth, selling cold water and market bags at Waterside until—due to his desperation or their need—the army took him.

Having been a street boy, he knew their nature. Still, organizing them into a rogue crew had proved hard. He couldn't keep them from pilfering goods for their own profit before reporting to him. One boy tried to steal from Kimeh right under his nose.

The new head of state had ignored Kimeh for a cabinet position and had passed over him for other government posts. Now four months after the coup, his name had not surfaced when the director of Liberian Electric Company was hired.

Kimeh made a list and pounded on the desk saying, "I deserve my rightful place in this society!"

Zenobia Jones was ignorant of the mess around her. He put a check by her name because he had already stopped her project. The fixtures and drywall fit his renovated home.

Jeremiah Browne, Kimeh's uncle, had a conflict with Minister Howe over the building. Howe had assigned the building to Jeremiah under stipulation that the government would pay his tuition to Emperor Medical School in London. Jeremiah would return with his medical degree and open a clinic. When Jeremiah dropped out of school and returned home an alcoholic, Howe reneged. Still Kimeh believed that if his family couldn't have the building, no one could.

Kimeh bore down hard when he wrote Minister Howe and then licked the pencil tip. The revolution had taken care of him.

He wrote the head of state—he was a man of the soil whose only loyalty was to his own Krahn tribe. Kimeh needed his own power and that took money to keep food and supplies at the Gbarnga Checkpoint.

Ansa—Kimeh had money as long as Ansa had work across Liberia.

Chapter Forty-Five

Zenobia burst into the door, "Ryan! Ryan!"

"Hi, Baby," he said, coming from the back where he was eating the soft meat from young coconuts. He pulled her close, brushed perspiration from her neck, and planted a kiss in its place.

Zenobia pulled his lips to hers and kissed him hard. "I missed you."

"Me, too," he said, smiling. "How come you're late? You hungry? Thirsty?"

"The bus picked up extra passengers, a gas shortage, I think."

Ryan handed Zenobia a newspaper. "There is an international oil crisis. The Shah of Iran is out. The Ayatollah is in, and every nation is controlling the price of oil to reduce demand."

"While the rest of the world impacts Liberia," she said, ignoring the paper and snuggling under Ryan's arm, "I am finally making a difference with village women. I should have been there all along. Old Ma is very wise, a younger version of Grandma Jones. She's a midwife and a healer." Zenobia then told Ryan everything about Yekepa, everything except the fact that she didn't get her identification cards.

Tasha jumped out of a taxi at six o'clock. Before Zenobia could offer Tasha black-eyed peas and rice, Ezra yelled into the door, "Missy Zenobia, Missy Zenobia. You mu' come deliver my Sarah!"

"Come in, Ezra. I already told Sarah that I couldn't deliver her. She isn't on the ELWA list."

"I know, but she ready to drop the baby now," he pled. "No other midwife nearby. I can' make it to the hospital—no gas for my taxi—I can' birth her! Please, Missy Zenobia, my Sarah has hard time with babies."

When Zenobia didn't answer, Ezra said, "I'll hold your foot," and reached for Zenobia's ankle.

"Stop that, Ezra," Zenobia said, backing away from him.

She grabbed her birthing bag and teas from Yekepa. "I'll need help," she told Tasha.

"Don't look at me! I'm a teacher."

"Tell Sarah I'm coming, Ezra. Get lye soap, and boil two buckets of water."

"Thank you, Missy Zenobia."

"I need you, Tasha," Zenobia said without a question in her voice.

Tasha rolled the sleeves of her caftan over her shoulders, and tightly folded her arms until Zenobia emerged from the bedroom. "You sure we won't get into trouble?" she asked. "I thought it was dangerous delivering a woman you don't know."

"It's Sarah, Tasha. Besides, we don't have a choice. If the baby is ready, it's coming." Zenobia dragged Tasha through Ezra's side door.

Inside, mud walls kept the room cool; a small, wooden table for eating sat in one corner with three neatly stacked stools. Foam sleeping mats leaned neatly against another wall- the one Ezra had bought and kept unused until Sarah moved to Monrovia lay freshly sheeted. Everything was 'broom-swept-clean,' free of debris.

Zenobia stilled herself, closed her eyes, and took a deep breath. "Hi, Sarah," she said, "This is my friend, Tasha. How are you doing?"

Sarah was on her hands and knees, doggy-style. Perspiration beads lined her cornrows, sending a stream of sweat onto the plastic mat underneath. A plug of mucus lay in a pool of water beneath her.

"The baby coming," Sarah said and then clamped down on a chewing stick.

"Sure is," Zenobia said, moving Sarah to a dry sheet and barking orders.

"Tasha, pour hot water in that aluminum bowl so we can wash our hands. Ezra, bring the lye soap."

Sarah groaned because the last time she had screamed and cried out, the time when she was ten and when her protest should have mattered the most, it had gone unheard. When Sarah groaned again, Zenobia asked Sarah to turn over. She rubbed her hands together to warm them, touched softly, and then circled Sarah's stretched stomach to feel the baby's position. The baby stiffened in response to Zenobia's hands, bringing another contraction. It was not breach.

When the contraction was over, Zenobia massaged Sarah's lower back and then made a pallet of newspaper and sheets, careful to smooth out the lumps. She placed the plastic mat on top and added another sheet. Tasha helped Zenobia tuck the sides and corners.

Zenobia traced the baby's position again. Sarah smiled.

"Your baby is almost here, Sarah."

Another contraction came in response to Zenobia's touch. "You've already birthed one baby, Sarah, so you know the pain that's in store. When it catches you real hard, just bite down on the chewing stick. Hollering and fighting the pain makes it worse. You can trust me. I won't let you suffer. Just think about the beautiful baby you're gonna have."

Sarah bit hard with the next contraction.

"That's good, Sarah," Zenobia said. "Ezra, bring more chewing sticks."

Zenobia moved her right hand down Sarah's stomach and to her vagina to measure how she had effaced and dilated. Zenobia stopped when Sarah started to push.

"Don't push yet. Can you breathe for me?" She demonstrated how she wanted Sarah to breathe through the pain. "Wait until I say push."

Zenobia attempted to measure the cervical dilation. Then she stopped. Her heart jumped and raced, perspiration circled her underarms and neck, and her breathing halted. Her stomach churned, sending bile to her throat and down again. She forced her throat not to gag and steadied herself.

"Come Tasha, hold the kerosene lamp closer," Zenobia managed to say, enunciating each syllable. "I changed my mind. Put the lamp on the table. I need your hands."

As the temperature seemed to rise in the room, Zenobia called upon the strength of Georgia midwives. She wished she could speak to Tasha in a language Sarah wouldn't understand, except that she didn't know the language of shock. Zenobia slowed her breathing and her speech, measured each word, and tried to make this birth like all the others. She silenced the scream that wanted to leap from her core and steeled her feet so they wouldn't run across the street to the safety of her husband.

"Tasha," Zenobia breathed, "Come closer."

In the light thrown off by the kerosene lamp, Tasha saw why Zenobia was stalling.

The contractions came faster and harder, less than a minute apart.

Zenobia took her time tracing Sarah's birth canal in hopes that she was wrong. She discovered a scarred, bumpy surface where Sarah's pleasure covering, soft tissue, and small lips were supposed to fold and protect. Her "secret of joy" was missing.

Zenobia could tell that Sarah's surgery had included clipping and sewing. Satta's birth had stretched Sarah, and the scar tissue that remained made passage for the new baby difficult.

"Okay, Sarah, we have to take this slow and easy—*Please God*—relax your face and your lips like this." Zenobia put her lips into the shape of a relaxed o. "You remember how I showed you to breathe?"

"Uh-hum," Sarah said feebly.

"Good, keep doing that, and keep your lips relaxed."

"Tasha, get the olive oil. Put a couple drops on your fingertips and massage right above the perineum like this. Don't stop."

"Okay, Sarah," said Zenobia. "When the next pain comes, push as hard as you can, then stop. Go ahead and scream, if you need to." *God knows you deserve to!*

Tasha massaged while Zenobia slowly inched Sarah's wounded tissue over the baby's head as it crowned. Sarah pushed, just as Zenobia instructed, until the baby's head popped out.

Zenobia looked into Sarah's scared eyes. They were strong. "You're almost finished. When the pain comes again, it's going to feel like a circle of fire. It's not fire, only your baby's shoulders. Rest now, until the pain and fire come, then I want you to give me a big push."

"I'm doing good?" Sarah asked.

"You're doing better than good. You're doing great."

Tasha contorted her body so she could massage Sarah and stay out of Zenobia's way.

"Keep massaging," directed Zenobia.

Zenobia eased Sarah's tissue around the baby's neck and prepared to rotate the shoulders simultaneously with the next contraction.

Sarah chomped down on the chewing stick with the next fiery pain. She thrust the baby forward.

"Thank you, God!" mouthed Zenobia.

Zenobia wrapped the baby in one of the sheets and handed him to a dazed Tasha. "Rub that chalky covering into his skin. Gently now, and keep him warm."

Zenobia took a second look at Tasha, "Stay with me, we're almost done. The afterbirth is next."

Outside the air was humid. Ezra paced, making another path in the dirt and playing with the holes in his pant pockets. He rolled his head around his shoulders, shushed Satta, and swore he would find enough money every month for birth control pills because the medicine woman's tea had not kept Sarah from getting pregnant again.

"I want a son," Sarah had insisted after Satta was born and she had pretended to drink the medicine tea.

When Zenobia pinched his butt, the baby grimaced, kicked, and wailed. His heart rate and breathing were strong.

"Sarah, you got a beautiful, healthy baby boy." Zenobia saw bravery in Sarah's smile. "Can you nurse him?"

"Ah-hmm," Sarah said, smiling.

Tasha was beyond thinking on her own.

"Lay the baby across Sarah's chest so he can latch," Zenobia told Tasha. Then Zenobia tied dental floss around the umbilical cord, three times, and pulled until it separated from the placenta.

The baby latched onto Sarah. After a few minutes, he

let go to rest his jaws. With the next strong and long draw, a contraction expelled the placenta. Zenobia wrapped it inside one of the soiled sheets.

"Anything coming, Sarah?" asked Zenobia.

"A little bit."

"Drop some into his eyes and then feed him the rest."

Sarah looked puzzled.

"The liquid that comes before your milk is medicine that keeps your baby strong and prevents infection that might happen during birth."

Sarah trusted Zenobia and followed the instructions.

"Thank you," said Sarah.

"I thank you, Sarah, for trusting me to deliver your baby."

Zenobia yelled outside. "Ezra, I almost forgot. You have a fine son, and his birth date is August 1, 1980."

"Thank you, Missy Zenobia. Thank you."

Zenobia handed Ezra the placenta-filled sheets. Ezra took the bundle from Zenobia, walked behind the house, and buried it deep under an evergreen.

"We're going home now, Sarah. Ezra is making tea for you. I'll come back in the morning." Zenobia moved toward the door with Tasha, and then turned around. "Is there anything else you need?"

Sarah answered, "Thank you."

In the middle of the road, Tasha fought back waves of sickness that wanted to retch forward with the anguish she had managed to hold back so far.

Zenobia rubbed Tasha's back, coaxing her to leave everything in the dirt.

In that moment, Zenobia heard her grandmother's words, as strong as if Grandma Jones were standing on the road with her. "The time is gonna come when you have to make peace with ugly. You have to pray that His Will be done."

Zenobia stood there feeling the warmth of the night air, the brightness of the stars. She turned on her heels. "Go on to the house, Tasha. I'm going back to Sarah."

Zenobia cut three leaves from the aloe plant. "Do you mind if I sit with Sarah for a while?" she asked Ezra.

"Go 'head, Missy Zenobia."

"I have medicine that will make you feel better," she told Sarah.

Zenobia held the aloe leaves upright to keep their water intact the way Old Ma had shown her. She washed the first leaf and sliced it, thin, without damage. Zenobia put six aloe slices in a clean warm cloth and showed Sarah how to lay the compress against her.

Sarah lay there, holding her baby son, dozing and thinking about the time she had learned that her screams would never count. It was when she and six other village girls were ushered—with dancing, drumming, and food—into a sacred hut with their mothers and the village medicine woman. One-by-one each girl was clipped, her womanhood stitched. In an attempt to show strength, the other girls yelped and whimpered. Their mothers gave them tea for drinking, an herbal compress to prevent infection, and then nursed and dressed the bleeding wounds.

Sarah was different. She screamed loudly because no matter what explanation her mother gave her, she could not make out how the surgery could help her. She thrashed and twisted her hips against the medicine woman's heavy weight and pressure from the cold sharp instrument. Sarah cried out while the pain intensified, and then, when the woman was finished, Sarah lay still and quiet.

"I did it—my mother, her mother, and all the mothers in our village have done it," Sarah's mother explained. "It's our way. You'll feel better when the pain is gone, and then you'll be ready for a husband," she repeated as Sarah wobbled and hobbled along, careful not to reinjure herself.

For months, Sarah wrapped herself up and became a prisoner in her own somber, silent cocoon. She barely spoke above a whisper, and when she figured out how to go on living with only half of herself intact, her speech returned with the resolve that she had lost her right to oppose anything she did not want. She went on living, resolute that she would never again cry out because when it should have mattered most, it had not. She was left with silent tears.

When Zenobia clasped Sarah's hand and held it, a brilliant beam broke through Sarah's countenance. This time Zenobia knew that Sarah was saying thank you for generations of wounded women.

Tasha left for Yekepa the next day. "No need to send a message," she said. "Whenever you're ready, show up."

Chapter Forty-Six

Daisy opened the back door to the salon and welcomed the October air. She sent Kito to the Freeport to receive a shipment of shampoo and moisturizer and then turned over the "Closed" sign. She didn't like the way things were going. She hated to admit to herself that Liberia's problems would not end soon. She set out Coca-Colas and waited.

Three men arrived arguing, "It's not just the filthy streets. Government payroll is months behind, still there is no economic development, no medicine at the hospitals."

"Is this what men of the soil took over to do?" asked Daisy. "While Doe enjoys the taste of his pretentious power, the people have a new breed of hardship. Water rarely runs, electricity seldom flows, and unemployment is higher than I've seen in years."

The others all chimed in.

"The United States is committing hundreds of millions to Liberia to protect its Cold War interests. None of that money will get into the hands of the people."

"All we have is corruption; as much in the army as among the civilians. If there is no discipline in the military, where do you find it? Security is a joke."

"Lack of discipline breeds factions and creates plastic gods."

"We need free-flowing communication between the rulers and the ruled."

"We need jobs, roads, education, and medicine for the everyday person."

"How quickly people forget. When you forget your past, you can't see a future. We already know it will take generations to repair the damage of more than one hundred years of Americo-Liberian rule. But Doe is not the one to turn things around."

"Doe is surrounding himself with his own Krahn people. We need a government elected by all the people for all the people."

"Gentlemen, gentlemen," interrupted Daisy. "We're not here to recite all that's wrong. What are we going to do about it? It is up to us, you know. Our investment in paddy rice resulted in a strong crop. It'll take years, though, to switch habits away from imported rice."

One of the men interrupted Daisy with, "Political groups are merging. We've been approached to merge with another party. What do you—?"

"Never," said the man whose face had become familiar to Kito.

"Ma. Ma," called Kito entering the salon. "What's going on?"

Chapter Forty-Seven

This time the November season of the sun party was more than a celebration of dry season. Ryan had presented his dream project to Zenobia—advance copies of his coffee table photography book, *A Land in Peril: Seeing Heart through Eyes*.

Ryan had signed a deal with International Geographic to illustrate Liberia's government transition from settler to men of the soil, to put the country into a new focus for the world. In this special edition photo journal, Ryan captured Liberia's natural bounty; the abundance lived by Americo families, contrasted with Liberia's blight and suffering, the fear and hope of her people. Through the light of their eyes, Ryan captured people who loved their land, despite the fact they owned so little of it.

The book illustrated hardship—barefooted children wrestling rubber trees with pride and determination, market women carrying headloads to the market and returning with empty tables at the end of the day, loggers and miners, boys selling water and girls doing laundry for school tuition and for buying rice for their families.

Through their eyes, Ryan captured perseverance despite frustration, the courage to keep going when fear said stop.

Men and women showing tenderness to each other and

their children filled the pages. One caption highlighted a mother's stern discipline toward education. "Get your learning. Don't be lazy."

Religious places of worship—Catholic, Islam, African Methodist Episcopal, Baptist, Lutheran, and Church of God—were colorful and vivid on the pages.

Masks, drummers, dancers, baskets, cloth spinners, weavers, and dyers, coal pot cooking portrayed the range of ethnic cultures. One could almost hear the palaver on the pages of market women haggling with buyers over 'the real' price. The centerfold was of Zenobia and Sarah grinding peanuts and palm nuts in a mortar and pestle for palm butter and peanut soup.

Ryan devoted a section of the book to beggars. Some physically deformed by birth or by polio, kids who were hungry and haggard, hustling for food and money. Sick old men leaning against buildings with a begging bowl at their feet. A few were waiting to take their last breath.

The hardest pictures for Ryan to take were of men and women, boys and girls, traumatized by helplessness, they were roaming the streets and talking to the air. His genius captured faces where the light had dimmed from their eyes; their spirit had descended into some deep dark place where it became trapped and where dying began.

In a new leisure suit made by Alfredo, Ryan stood taller than his six feet; he was proud of the mark he was making on the world with his art.

The usual crowd gathered. They played cards and dominoes and ate from Kito's buffet.

Tasha arrived, wearing a Kito creation atop her head.

The room broke out in laughter when Keith yelled from the bid whist table, "Ryan, you gonna quit that teaching job so you can take more pictures?"

"It's about the message, not the book," added Kweku. "Remember Bruce's Kung Fu philosophy: 'Flow like water; be water, my friend.'"

"One step at a time, man," said Ryan.

Kito pulled Zenobia into the kitchen with urgency in her voice. "Daisy said the military has banned all intellectual activities that criticize the administration. She says the book makes you stand out."

Zenobia pushed air between her lips. "Honestly, Kito. It's a book, a book of pictures. Ryan hasn't criticized anyone."

"It is said that a picture is worth a thousand words."

"Don't bring him down, Kito." Zenobia was unable to take her eyes off Ryan. "He's done nothing wrong."

Just then, Ansa yelled from his truck, "Say man, we still invited?"

"'Round the back," Ryan called. The band walked through the guests, snap hand shaking, backslapping, chest bumping, and hugging.

Zenobia ran outside to Ansa. "Are you friends with Kimeh?" Zenobia whispered.

"If you know Kimeh, you know he has no friends."

Zenobia frowned. She wanted to ask, needed to ask Ansa what he meant. She didn't trust him.

Tasha was anxious to take Zenobia back to Yekepa. Excited about their growing friendship, she pulled Zenobia away from the crowd. "Did you get your papers taken care of?"

"I am going with you tomorrow. You saw how those soldiers acted when I threw Kimeh's name around." She held her hand up for Tasha to return a high five.

Ansa overheard the conversation while he was tuning up his trumpet. "You need identification cards?"

Tasha looked up and down at Zenobia, but neither spoke.

"I'll see what I can do." Then Ansa played "Windjammer."

"Thank you," he said to the crowd when he finished. "This cut will be on my new album."

✥

Zenobia and Tasha were packed and ready to leave when a taxi pulled up blaring, "Who Owns the Land? My Papa's Land, Who Owns the Land?" The driver bobbed his head and snapped his fingers as he walked up to the door.

"Yes?" Zenobia asked before he knocked.

"Morning. My name is New York," he said. "Ansa buy my gas and hire me to take two women from this house to Yekepa. I'm ready to go, if you are." He handed Zenobia two identification cards. "Ansa say these are a gift for your hospitality."

Chapter Forty-Eight

Kimeh used every influence to give his daughter a better wedding than anything she had seen. The African Unity Conference Center prepared a full-course buffet of Liberian and American foods for three hundred invited guests. Foofoo, egusi, cassava leaf, palm butter, greens, pumpkin and groundnut stews, goat soup, and fish (dried, salted, and stewed). Barbecued ribs, pork chops (fried and smothered), candied yams, macaroni and cheese, and collard greens connected the guests to American soul food.

White linen covered each table. However, the tablecloth under the ice and fruit sculpture turned a rainbow color when the air conditioning malfunctioned and turned the arrangement into soup.

On the happiest day of his daughter's life, Kimeh looked like a boy in a tuxedo. He hoped his pretentious gestures would add substance.

His wife, in traditional African dress, strutted and rubbed elbows with her guests even though most of them had come to watch her little husband pretend to be big.

Kimeh had chosen a wife who could make up for the social class he lacked. He'd never read a book in his life, while Mrs. Kimeh Browne had a teaching degree and carried herself like a Rhodes Scholar.

Uncle Jeremiah was already so drunk that Kimeh threatened, "I'll take you out back and put an end to your misery if you embarrass my daughter!"

"Okay, brothers," Ansa said to his band when the cake had been served. "A producer for Fela Ransome-Kuti is in the house. Let's show him what we do."

As soon as the band struck the first chord, Uncle Jeremiah tiptoed to the wedding cake. With a plastic knife, he cut a slice right through Saturday, December 6, 1980, and then slipped on spilled punch. When he tried to catch himself by grabbing hold of the tablecloth, he slid under the table, and brought the remainder of the seven-tier cake down with him.

Kimeh ran from the dance floor, picked his uncle up by the scruff of the neck, and led him behind the Conference Center. Kimeh kicked Jeremiah, saying, "You know you wasting your time living—now you wasting mine!"

Jeremiah was too drunk to do anything but throw defensive punches aimlessly into the air.

"Be a man," Kimeh continued, now pummeling him. "I let you live in my house, but what do you give me in return? You abuse my name, my family. You are embarrassing me so. Do you want anything in life?"

On one elbow and with a hangdog demeanor, Uncle Jeremiah said, "I can spoil you in one second. I can tell things."

Kimeh was a hothead, but he wasn't mad enough to give his uncle an excuse to tell all he knew. "Leave here, go! We'll settle this thing tomorrow," said Kimeh, pulling his uncle from the ground and brushing dirt from his coat.

As soon as they heard "I Shot the Sherriff," the crowd that had gathered around the fight ran to the dance floor. The band played Afro-beat, High Life, African-Caribbean rhythms, jazz, and a tribute to Bob Marley: "I Know" and "Redemption Song." They showed off by paying homage to Fela with "High Life Times" and "Black Man's Cry." Men, women, and children sang, danced, perspired until dawn, and then left clicking their tongues about Ansa and the Jazz Notes.

Kimeh slipped out the back door with his wife while Ansa talked to the producer about recording an album.

Ansa caught Kimeh out of the corner of his eye and hollered after him.

Kimeh dragged his wife toward the waiting car.

"Ah!" he slammed his fist into his hand. "Man! I don't believe it," Ansa called and ran out.

His nostrils flared as he cursed. "Kimeh's been sucking me dry for months. Now he disrespects me. Don't worry, guys. I'll pay you," he told the band. "And you can believe, I'll get mine."

∽

The next day, Ansa sent the band away after only an hour of practice. He lit a cigarette in his backyard and listened to his brother. Ansa wondered if he'd ever get used to the rage that had begun coursing through his veins.

Trembling, Ansa's brother told him, "Political factions are surrounding Gbarnga." The brother stood his son in front of Ansa while he recounted the story. "My boy was walking home from the Baptist School near Gbarnga when a man claiming to be a soldier tried to put an AK-47 into my boy's hand. My boy said '*no*' and ran, but the man caught up and overpowered him, grabbed my boy's right hand, the hand that he uses for writing, and bent the thumb and two fingers back until each one bulged. His hand made a popping sound, and went limp. My boy cried out, but the soldier put the gun to his head and told him, 'Next time I come here, you better be a man. You pick up the arm like I tell you.'"

"Look at my small boy," Ansa's brother continued, "His knees are always knocking. He jumps at anything, he can't sleep. He used to be smart, now he can't remember his lessons. He just stares at the sky."

Ansa jumped up; his rage was boiling. "Our family knows everybody in Gbarnga. You don't know who did this?"

"The checkpoint brings new people everyday. Most are not soldiers, just men with guns."

"Leave your son with me and my wife," Ansa told his brother. "We will care for him."

Chapter Forty-Nine

The day Zenobia returned to Yekepa, the sun was still up, and Esi was waiting. "Old Ma want you to come," she said and led Zenobia down a path thick with tall grass and into a house.

Old Ma was already leaning over a woman. An infant, swathed in old clean cloth, lay still next to his mother.

"What's going on?" asked Zenobia, rubbing the bar of lye soap across her hands.

"Another baby is coming," said Old Ma. "See to the boy."

Zenobia put two fingers under the baby's arm and counted five seconds—the pulse was slow, breathing irregular. When the baby didn't react to the flick she gave his butt, she recalled the cardiopulmonary resuscitation class from several years before.

She placed a piece of clean fabric on the floor, put the baby on top, and knelt over him, tilting his tiny head back to open the airway. When she was sure she felt faint breathing against her cheek, she softly covered the baby's nose and mouth with her lips, and blew easy, every three seconds. The boy's chest rose with each breath. In between her breaths, Zenobia rubbed the boy's back vigorously with her fingers and thumped his feet. Finally, after several rounds of breathing and rubbing, the baby grimaced and wailed.

"There you go—that's what I needed," she whispered.

Old Ma pulled the second baby, a screaming girl, from the woman. She pointed to the yellow around the baby's eyes. "It should be white," she told the mother. She showed the mother how to put a lappa over the baby and lay the baby, stomach down, across her lap. "Sit under the sun every day from noon to two o'clock. That's the healing sun. Do it five days and the girl's eyes will turn white. Make sure you drink plenty clean water, and nurse your babies good. You hear?"

"You did good," Old Ma said to Zenobia as they left. "Real good."

Outside, Zenobia asked, "I just read that the sun's rays act as an incubator. Is that why you told her that?"

"That's right. The twins are pre-mature, but healthy. The sun will help knit everything together. Like I said, you're doing good."

***

"Have you thought about why you're in Liberia?" Zenobia asked when Tasha joined her on the front porch.

"Peace Corps."

"No, I mean why here—Liberia. You could have been assigned anywhere in the world. Why Liberia?"

"My parents and I don't get along. When I barely graduated college, I didn't have any plans or goals. I joined the Peace Corps so I could see the world on somebody else's dime, especially since I didn't have anything else to do. My father said the Peace Corps would help me grow up." After a long silence, she continued. "I've never thought about a question like that. But when I see you after a day with Old Ma, and I watch Ryan's reaction to his book, it all makes me wonder what I should be doing, and whether I can have more of the same feeling I get when my kids learn to read

FREE SOIL

and then go abroad for more education. What about you? Why are you here?"

"Chasing a dream, I guess. I've been here almost two years and for the first time, my dream is bearing fruit. I can't understand why I didn't come to Yekepa in the beginning."

"That's easy. You didn't know about it," answered Tasha and left Zenobia outside with her thoughts.

Zenobia gazed out at the clear darkness. The Big and Little Dippers shone brightly against the evening sky.

A slight breeze that cooled the night caused Zenobia to shiver a bit, and palm branches to flutter. There was just enough half-moon light for Zenobia to see an orange-and-brown-colored owl. Its eyelids blinked before it took flight and left a baritone hoot trailing in its wake. Zenobia swore the owl had winked at her.

Zenobia and Tasha chartered a taxi to Monrovia. They were in a deep discussion when, "Jesus Christ!" the driver shouted.

At the Gbarnga Checkpoint, military jeeps, trucks, and some twenty soldiers stood guard, using their AR-15s, semiautomatic rifles, MAC 10s, and shoulder launch missiles to wave travelers to stop or move on. Two soldiers had hand grenades and stilettos clipped alternately around their waist belts.

Empty buses, taxis, and personal cars lined the road- their passengers stood outside their vehicles pleading for understanding.

Zenobia asked the driver, "Is there something wrong?"

"Identification checkpoint."

The driver inched his way through the line until a soldier with an AK-47 draped over his shoulder pointed at the spot on the ground where he wanted him to stop.

"Identification, please," said the soldier.

The driver opened his wallet to show his identification card and a picture of his daughter.

"Thank you," said the soldier.

Tasha rolled her window down a bit, opened her wallet and showed her residency, work permit, and identification card.

"Thank you," he said.

A second officer, pointing a rifle, walked to the other side of the car and looked at Zenobia. "Identification."

Zenobia opened her wallet to show the soldier the card given to her by Ansa.

"Get out of the car," said the soldier, with hand grenades clipped around his belt. His words were fast and choppy. "Now!"

The driver jumped out from his side; Tasha and Zenobia poured out the back, leaving their things inside.

A volley of gunfire could be heard in the distance, causing everyone to comb the sky with their eyes and hunch their shoulders. Some ducked and hit the ground.

The first soldier looked suspiciously at the women and told the driver to step aside while he examined Tasha's documents a second time. "She's okay," he said, using the barrel of his rifle to nudge her to the side.

"This one is no good," said the other soldier, planting himself between Zenobia and Tasha. The women had to bob and weave their heads around his body to gesture and talk.

"I'm sure it's okay," Zenobia said. "Kimeh Browne issued this card personally."

"Do you think I am joking?" the soldier repeated. Tasha and Zenobia jumped. "This card is no good here! Kimeh is no good here."

Two more troops in castoff uniforms gathered and asked, "What should we do?"

"I am an American with the Peace Corps, and I teach in Yekepa," began Tasha. "My friend is American, too, and she has been visiting me. I'm escorting her to Monrovia, and I'm sure, officer, that she will get the documents she needs as soon as she gets to Monrovia. It's just a mistake." She signaled to Zenobia to shut up about Kimeh.

The soldier stretched his arm and pointed his finger in the direction of Yekepa. "She can go back, but she will not pass through here!"

"Uh, maybe I can give you something for your trouble, officer," said Zenobia, digging around in her purse. "Here, sir." She handed the soldier a five-dollar bill. "My husband is waiting for me in Monrovia. He'll be worried if I'm late."

"You think you can insult me? No dash," the soldier yelled, and pushed his face into hers.

"She abus' you," shouted a soldier. "She think she can buy her way. You wan' make an example from her?" he said, brandishing his gun.

Zenobia and Tasha were the only passengers causing a scene. Most travelers either turned around together or split up when one did not have the card. None tried to convince the soldiers to let them pass.

"Cocky Americans," said one soldier so Zenobia and Tasha could hear.

As the line grew, more soldiers arrived to keep traffic moving.

"Your husband is your biz'ness," the soldier spewed, answering Zenobia, and then he threw his rifle over his shoulder. "Without ID, you will not pass here."

"You can do whatever you want," the soldier told Tasha and the driver. To Zenobia, he said, "You wasting my time," and pointed the gun nose toward Yekepa. "Go now!"

Hearing another volley of gunfire, Zenobia and Tasha hunched their shoulders together.

The driver dumped Tasha's and Zenobia's belongings onto the ground and sped away.

A four-wheel jeep, filled with men and guns, drove up. "What you want us to do, boss?" asked one who jumped out.

"Do not let one person from this rejection line pass through," the head soldier scowled. "And this one here," he pointed to Zenobia, "Remember her face, she can never get through. Tell your Kimeh that," he told her.

One man stepped up to Tasha and breathed nasty air into her nostrils. "You wan' make date, ride in my jeep?" he asked in a lowered voice. "You make date, and I'll see you and your friend can pass through," he said, watching over his shoulder for the boss.

"I'm getting sick," Tasha gasped, feigning a headache. "The sun is too hot. I'm sure I will faint."

When Zenobia said, "We're going to Yekepa," the soldier relaxed his lust.

Zenobia and Tasha grabbed their bags and headed on foot toward Yekepa. When she was sure enough distance was between them and the checkpoint, Tasha shouted, "I've never been so humiliated!"

"Humiliated? They scared the mess out of me. Now I'm mad."

Tasha took quick steps. "I'm humiliated 'cause I got ID and you don't! The whole thing didn't have to happen," she said, and flip-flopped red dust onto her caftan as she walked ahead.

"Why did Ansa gave me those cards anyway?"

"It's his fault? If you had found that man, whoever he is, you would have had the same phony cards. Besides, if you had *real* identification, none of this would happen. And why do you make everything about you, Zenobia?"

At first Zenobia didn't answer. She was tired and unsure if she could make the walk back to Yekepa. "Stop fussing, Tasha. Did you hear what he said? How will I get home?"

"Hello, yah!" called a bus driver who'd been turned around. "You wan' ride to Yekepa?"

᎒

"It's getting worse," Old Ma said, when Tasha and Zenobia returned.

The sun was high the next day when Old Ma brought Esi to Tasha's apartment. "I know how to handle this."

Chapter Fifty

Keith wiped beads of sweat from his forehead as he knocked on Ryan's door. "Say man. The brothas are going to see how much palm wine we can drink in one sitting. You can crawl the one block back home if you can't walk. Come on."

"We playing cards?"

"Just palm wine."

Ryan locked the door. "Sounds serious."

Derrick was already woozy when Ryan and Keith arrived. Keith talked as he poured.

"My friend at the American Embassy told me that they are going to issue an announcement for Americans to leave. My company says it's up to me. I'm conflicted, though; don't want to jump ship if I don't have to."

Pouring more wine, "What are you talking about?" Ryan asked.

"This thing is bigger than any settler-indigenous conflict. Tubman was president for 27 years before Tolbert. He opened doors to foreign investors who made small improvements in schools, health, and roads, the little infrastructure we all enjoy. He was the first president to allow the indigenous to vote. With all that, Liberia became a fast-growing economy. It looked like an economic boom. Tubman gave huge incentives to foreign investors, which created the corruption that made it possible for them to exploit rubber, iron ore, and timber, and then send pure profit home to their respective countries. The country grew economically without any real development. Liberia was strategic during World War II because rubber was critical to the supply line of the Allied Troops."

Derrick interrupted. "Slow down man. Here, take a drink and catch your breath," handing him the jug of wine. "That's not news. I learned all that in my Peace Corps orientation."

It suddenly hit Ryan. *Why didn't I develop relationships with American Embassy staffers?*

"Yea, but when Tubman died and Tolbert became president; he wanted independent status in the world. He established relations with Russia and Eastern bloc countries," Keith continued. "He was chairman of the Organization of African Unity, but he severed ties with Israel. Don't you think that made him vulnerable for assassination?"

"There you go with those conspiracy theories," said Ryan. "What I want to know is what's going on right now."

"People are dying," Keith said while pouring another round. "You heard Doe on the radio the day of the coup when he read the list of people he wanted to come to the Mansion? Well, based on some unorthodox system of reprisal with no day in court, the army snatches people, tosses them into army jeeps, and strips them to their briefs. People just go missing. Imprisonment, beatings, and murder follow. Human rights violations."

Ryan didn't say a word. *Is that what happened to Minister Howe?*

"I'm clear that Liberia is no longer a beacon of hope for African independence," Derrick said. "Think about it. Americo-Liberians never rose to more than five percent of the population. Yet they managed to block everyone else's access to economic and political power. The people were in a 'nothing to lose' situation. They were bound to rise up. The coup just blew the top off what has been simmering more than a hundred years. Stability is over."

"Sounds pretty grave to me. I'm ready to leave, but Zen…"

Keith looked at Ryan startled. "Now that is why I'm not married. I am not beholding to anyone and this conversation has cleared my head. I won't be here any longer than it takes for the Embassy announcement."

"The Peace Corps motto is 'the toughest job you'll ever love' and I love working with those smart Bassa kids. They are the future of this country. Stability is over, but if I need to leave, the State Department will evacuate me. I'm going to wait it out."

Ryan reared back on the legs of his chair and chugged another glass.

Chapter Fifty-One

Ryan was sorry he drank that last glass of palm wine as he fumbled with his sandal buckle the next morning. He threw down two Tylenol with a Coke, and called Ezra. "I need to pick up the week's mail from the Post Office," and cursed.

"You mad?"

"I go to the Post Office every week to see if we have mail from the States. There is never any mail from Liberia because all business is face to face. So I'm only looking for stateside mail when I go."

Ezra looked puzzled.

"At home, if the mailman comes to your door, you have mail. If he doesn't, you don't. You see, Ezra, it's very simple."

Ezra asked, "Someone come to your door with mail in America?" and went on laughing for five minutes. "Things so, so easy in America." Then he didn't laugh.

Alone with his letters, Ryan was quiet for the ride home.

Date Mailed: November 28, 1980

Dear Son,

I bought copies of your photograph book. I keep one at the barbershop and all the guys come in talking about how they always knew you were going to make it big some day. They lie by telling me you get your smarts from me. But it feels good, anyway.

I keep a copy in every room in the house too. The pictures make me feel close to you. You were always good with that camera.

I know Zenobia has tamed you, but don't forget about home. Your mother is fine and misses you an awful lot. She says, hello.

I'm proud of you, son. Really, I am.

—Love, Dad

Date Mailed: November 29, 1980

Hallelujah Good News Precious

You will never guess who is sitting up at my kitchen table eating some of my best blackberry cobbler. Amita. Clovis is here, too. She says hi and she says Amita is some kind a miracle. But it was God and me working together. Amita is smiling real pretty, too.

They had Thanksgiving with us, and I've been watching little Amita so Clovis doesn't have to spend all that Manpower money on childcare. I talk to Amita, read to her, and pray. It took her awhile, but she's walking and talking. You know God specializes in things unseen. She's gonna be just fine.

I'm glad things have settled down there because you can be in danger at home, Precious.

Your Uncle Scotty is doing fine. He says he is waiting for you to come home so he can marry Thelma.

We had elections this month, and Jimmy Carter lost. Man named Ronald Reagan won and he's gonna be sworn President in January. He used to be a movie star in Hollywood. He says rich people's money will trickle all the way down to me. We'll see.

> This is coming up on the second Christmas you been gone. We thought you'd be home by now, precious.
> —I love you, Grandma Jones

Ryan was so consumed by repeatedly reading the letters from home that he was startled when a woman jumped out of a taxi and appeared in front of him.

"Hello, ya," he said.

"Hello, ya," Esi replied. "You look the way your wife said," and handed him the note from Old Ma.

Saturday, December 13, 1980

> Your wife is in trouble. Armed factions, vying for power, are all around Bong County. Yesterday, she was denied transit due to identification from an opposing group. Tasha is staying in Yekepa with her.
>
> There is a woman in Monrovia, Daisy Williams, who owns a hair salon, Always Beautiful. Go to her, she can help you.
>
> Your wife is a target if she travels, because it is already known where she got her documents.
> —Old Ma

While Ryan's emotions swirled, Kimeh waited in his office for his minions. He dragged heat from the last cigarette in his pack, coughed out smoke, and waved it away from his face.

Kimeh was broke after the wedding, and he was so scared Uncle Jeremiah would tell about his exploits upcountry that he used the little money he had to find a place for his uncle to live.

Kimeh believed that when the time was right he would hold Ansa's foot, beg forgiveness. Kimeh was sure he could pay half the money and arrange for the rest. Ansa always told him, "One hand washes the other," and that's what Kimeh intended to do.

❦

"Things are not looking good, Chief," a staffer told Kimeh.

"We went to get money from Gbarnga Checkpoint. Our men are not there."

"Who is there?"

"Soldiers, Chief. That's all we know. They have pistols, bayonets, and AK-47s!"

Kimeh slapped at the man. "Then give our men bigger guns—Get whatever they need."

The men looked at each other. "Chief, we don't have,"—they looked at Kimeh's bulging eyes—"we don't have money."

"Then get some! Get it and get that checkpoint back! Now, leave me so I can put my mind on this thing," Kimeh shouted.

The men bungled out the door and down the steps. They walked three doors to a small shop where Kimeh could not see them from his perched window seat. They collected seventy-five cents between them and bought a Club Beer.

Kimeh had to get out of the office before anyone came looking for him. "I need to meet those soldiers," he said aloud. "I'll convince them to join me."

❦

Ryan shoved the note into his pocket and frantically looked for Ezra. "He working," Satta reported. Ryan ran down Airfield Road until he saw a taxi, "In town."

"Where in town?"

"Always Beautiful."

When Ryan passed the Sister-to-Sister ruins, hurt for Zenobia's disappointment and naiveté washed over him. *What could she possibly have done? It was never going to happen.* Zenobia's belief that she could defy the impossible

FREE SOIL

blinded her. He was disappointed with himself for letting her passion influence him. Ryan rushed into the salon. He wrinkled his nose at the smell of chemicals and hot grease.

"Kito, I need to speak with you and Daisy."

"What's the matter?"

"Someplace quiet."

Kito took the money and thanked her customer. "This way," she said, leading Ryan to the back. She caught Daisy's eye and beckoned her to follow.

"Here," he said, giving the letter from Old Ma to Daisy. He sat down and stood up again.

"What does this mean? What cards, what opposition group?" he asked.

Kito said, "Zenobia kept missing Immigration hours, so she was trying to get documents from a soldier in the Mayor's Office, a man named Kimeh."

"Kimeh Browne? She was trying to bribe Kimeh?" asked Daisy.

"Yeah, I mean she was bartering with him."

Daisy took a long, deep breath. "Kimeh Browne is not a mayor. He's a hustler, and he has been one his whole life. Zenobia fell right into one of his schemes."

"He had Zenobia fooled then. Kimeh was trying to hustle money from her to open the clinic. Zenobia hoped he could help."

Kito turned to Ryan, "I swear, I would have said something had I known it was this bad."

"The problem is factions," Daisy said. "Plot and counterplot. Everybody wants power."

"Zenobia has gone back and forth to Yekepa for months. Why is this happening now?"

"Ansa sent a taxi for them with identification cards for Zenobia as a gesture of thanks," Kito told them.

"Ansa?" asked Ryan.

"Who is Ansa?" asked Daisy.

"The Jazz Notes," said Kito. "He plays at the seasons party."

Ryan stared out the window. "Why would he knowingly give Zen something that would get her into trouble?"

Daisy poured a cup of coffee. "The cards are a hustle, only as good as the faction that controls them." Daisy was clear now. "Ryan, invite Ansa to a meeting at my house tomorrow morning. Ten o'clock."

Daisy folded the note from Old Ma and opened it again. "Can I keep this until tomorrow?"

On the ride to Ansa's house, Ryan gaped at American soldiers who were supporting the fragile new government by leading a fledgling unit of mismatched soon-to-be Liberian security forces through military drills. "Left. Right. Left. Right."

"Can't you hear me? I said, Left, Right," shouted the sergeant. These bare-chested undisciplined young men looked comedic. One mistakenly turned and marched in the opposite direction, and Ryan laughed at the sight, until he realized it was a sincere effort. He shook his head.

Ryan heard "Summertime" blasting behind a house when the driver approached Twentieth Street. "Stop where you hear the music."

Ansa was surprised to see Ryan. "Come on in, my man. You want something to eat?"

"No man. I got trouble and I need your help."

"What kind a trouble?"

"Man named Kimeh."

Ansa led Ryan down the street, and when they were near the beach, he asked, "What's going on?"

By the time Ryan finished, Ansa burned inside, his heart

pounded with agony and rage, and the usual hipster musician speech reverted to his original rural dialect.

"This thing is going to blow," Ansa said. "Rebellion is in the air. Things are falling apart. With Doe, people had dared to dream again. The dream is gone again. My wife is a nurse at JFK hospital—doctors and technicians are leaving the country. There is no medicine for treatment. We have plenty of corruption, though."

"Aren't you exaggerating?"

Ansa was almost shouting as he told Ryan about his nephew, the rumors of rapes, and the fear that spooked his family who had lived in the Gbarnga region for generations. "We have to have Liberian solutions."

"So far your solutions aren't working."

"What you see is all reaction to our history." Ansa lit a cigarette and pulled hard as a flurry of thoughts rushed him. He blew out a circle of smoke. He seemed to plead when he spoke again. "We need reforms because we are rich in natural resources and poor in development. Instead of loyalty to tribe, we must become one Liberian people with rules that unify instead of separate. If we can't rely upon ourselves, to build our country, then who do we count on?"

Ryan grew antsy. "Look, Ansa, I can appreciate your situation. Maybe it was a mistake coming to you. Things are becoming dangerous for us. I need to get my wife and go home."

Ansa flicked the cigarette butt across the street. "Like I said, it's up to us to fix our problems, but I am off to Côte d'Ivoire soon as I get my record deal. Don't worry—I know Kimeh is behind the problems in Gbarnga. He stole my money and my family's peace. He has to pay for my nephew. I'll take care of Kimeh as God in Heaven is my witness."

Ryan wasn't sure what he had in mind when he asked Ansa for help, but he knew that he would accept any remedy

Ansa offered. With his hands deep in his pockets, "I need a favor, man. Daisy is planning a meeting tomorrow morning to talk about how to get Zenobia and Tasha back to Monrovia. Can you come?"

"I said I'd handle it myself."

Ryan took his time, measured his feeling, and despite the lump in his throat added, "Then we need to make sure their plan doesn't interfere with yours."

They shook hands.

Ryan was exhausted. As the sun turned orange and the day settled into night, he tried to unwind with a Club Beer. He looked over his and Zenobia's passports and the open return airline tickets.

Ryan looked up when Ezra crossed the street, "What's up, my man?"

"The body's fine."

"Go on in and get a beer." Ryan wanted to be alone with his thoughts and hoped Ezra's visit would be short.

When Ezra didn't move, Ryan went inside and came back with an opened bottle. "Here, man," he said. "After all we've been through, you can go in my house and get yourself a beer."

"Thanks," said Ezra, stalling.

Ryan was giving Ezra only half of his attention, "How's your family? I bet little Ryan is growing."

When Ezra's decayed-tooth smile lit up the porch, Ryan put the documents down. "I'm grateful that you named your son after me," he said as he touched his chest with his hand. "I'm honored." Ryan waited for Ezra to say what was on his mind. "What's going on, Ezra? Is everything all right?"

"Things are not good. Sarah's ma'ket table is low," Ezra said, pointing across the street. "The money she make and the money I make can' reach to pay the rent, to buy gas for the taxi, and then buy our rice to eat. Checkpoints stoppin' people so they can' bring their ma'ket to town. Nobody's money can reach to buy rice and the things they need."

"You need money?"

"Don't shame me."

"I didn't mean any harm, Ezra. How can I help?"

Ezra wrung his hands, twisted the bottom of his shirt one way and then the other. He started back across the street.

"Ezra, you came to say something. I can't help if you don't tell me what's going on…"

"Mr. Ryan," Ezra began slowly. "Sarah and I have somethin' on our mind. About the baby."

"Is he sick?"

"No, the small boy is fine. He's who I came to talk about. Baby Ryan can' always be fine. I don't want him to be a grown'a boy. Sarah and I put it on our mind. We want you and Missy Zenobia to, to—," Ezra could barely let the words fall from his mouth. "We want you to take baby Ryan to America."

"What?" Ryan was standing now. "I couldn't do that! Your child belongs to you; he needs to be with you and Sarah, with Satta. Satta needs to teach him what she's learning."

"Mr. Ryan, I can' give him what you can give him. Satta too big, she know too much 'bout Liberia as her home; plus she coming to go to school. The small boy can grow strong in America, like you." Ezra paused, fidgeted with his shirt again, and stared long and hard at the ground before raising his eyes to meet Ryan's. "Mr. Ryan, I want my small boy to have chance to live before he die."

"I—I have to think about this and talk to Zen when she gets back. Okay?"

"My Sarah like Missy Zenobia; she was kind when she deliver the baby, she pay Satta good dash when she wash the clothes, she teach Satta about numbers and letters, and show her that she is smart and can learn."

Ezra paused, "You and Missy Zenobia have good heart."

"Ezra, this is a big request."

"Then I'm sorry, Mr. Ryan."

"No, no need to apologize. It took a lot for you and Sarah to ask. Let me talk to Zen."

Chapter Fifty-Two

The loud knock snatched Zenobia from her sleep.

"What time is it?" asked Tasha, as she whisked by Zenobia toward the door.

"Midnight."

"Old Ma sent me for Zenobia," said a small boy from behind the door. "She need help with a woman in the village."

"Come on in. You'll have to wait for Zenobia to dress," Tasha said, escorting the boy into the living room.

Zenobia was ready in minutes and followed the boy to a thatch-roofed home where she found Old Ma trying to move a large, older woman onto a pallet. The woman was obese, and it was obvious by the number of children made to stay quiet in the next room that she had had many live births.

"Number six, hypertensive, and I suspect sugar," said Old Ma in the shorthand language the two had developed. "Twelve hours, stopped twice, no water."

"What's her name?" asked Zenobia.

"Fanta."

"Hello-yah, Fanta; my name is Zenobia. I'm going to help Old Ma get you up so you can walk around outside. It's the only thing that'll make the baby come. You want the baby to come, don't you?"

Fanta wanted the baby to come, but she was tired from rearing her family, attending to the greens crop she managed for the local market women This labor was already worse than the others. She was tired.

"One, two, three," Zenobia and Old Ma said, lifting Fanta up at the armpits and standing her on her feet.

Zenobia walked Fanta up and down a beaten path that Zenobia had only seen during the day. It was quiet except for the crickets and bullfrogs, quiet until the next contraction hit Fanta hard. She screamed, "Blessed Jesus!" and Zenobia heard startled babies around the village start to cry.

"That's a good one," said Zenobia. "Let's see how quickly the next one comes." She was walking Fanta outside but heading toward her house.

When the contractions were one minute apart, she walked Fanta into the house where Old Ma had a pallet, boiled water, and lye soap ready.

Zenobia helped Fanta to the pallet and Old Ma checked her blood pressure, which was slightly high. Zenobia helped Fanta sip a cup of tea to bring the pressure down.

Fanta promptly spit the tea out, and Old Ma pushed a second cup to Fanta's lips. "Drink this."

Old Ma checked again—about ten centimeters. Almost fully effaced, the baby was ready to come and still Fanta's water had not broken. "This time, her labor won't stop."

When the next contraction came, Fanta grabbed Zenobia's arm and squeezed so tight, Zenobia was sure her blood would stop circulating. She tried to clamp her teeth into Zenobia's arm until Zenobia pulled back and said, "Breathe, Fanta. If you keep fighting, it will hurt more, and the birth will take longer."

Old Ma switched places with Zenobia. "With the next contraction, I want her to push," Old Ma said to Zenobia.

"When the head crowns, I want you to pinch the sack with your fingernail. You ever do that?"

Zenobia shook her head, "No."

"Today you will. Get a good, strong pinch, though. It's thick, and you don't want to miss. Do it soon as the sack bulges."

When Fanta let out a yell, Old Ma said, "Take one big breath. Now push, Fanta, push long air through your lips. Don't clench your teeth. Open your teeth and put your lips in a circle like this." Old Ma demonstrated. "Push now," she said. "Okay, Zenobia, snip."

The water gushed and the mucous plug landed on the pad of sheets where Old Ma had planned. "Is her water clear, Zenobia?"

"Yeah, I see the head."

"Okay, Fanta," said Old Ma. "The next contraction should bring your baby's head out. You ready, Zenobia?"

"I'm ready."

Fanta yelled again, and when the baby's head popped, Zenobia could see the cord wrapped around its neck. "I got a cord," she said.

"How many times?" Old Ma asked.

"Once; don't worry, I got it," said Zenobia.

"Listen, Fanta. The cord is wrapped around your baby's neck. Zenobia is going to get the baby out, but you have to be still, no matter how much it hurts. It's going to feel like fire soon. Even then, you be still. You hear me?"

Though Fanta liked drama, she knew when to stop. She bore down and pushed with the next contraction.

Zenobia brought the cord over the baby's head as she turned it, and with the last contraction, she pulled a curly-haired baby girl from Fanta.

Old Ma placed the baby on Fanta's chest while Zenobia cut the cord.

Fanta's husband, happy to have a baby girl, stood spellbound, wishing he could get Fanta to mind him the way Old Ma had.

※

Fatigued, Zenobia placed a birthing basin, like a head load, on her head and grabbed a bag of baby clothes. With one hand holding the basin steady and the other gripping the bag, she ran from house to house looking for Old Ma.

At the first house, an expectant mother's water had broken; she was dilated two centimeters and had hours of labor to go. "I'll be back," Zenobia told the woman.

The next woman had dilated three centimeters. "I'll be back," Zenobia told her.

Zenobia couldn't keep up: one—four centimeters, another—six centimeters, eight centimeters, and on and on.

Hundreds of pregnant women, ready to pop, turned, and walked away from Zenobia. "Wait," she called. "You are pregnant with possibility, with hope. You have to have your babies!"

She tried to run after the women and stopped when one called to her, "Come, my baby is coming."

Zenobia ran to her and discovered the woman wasn't ready. "You still have more labor."

One mother yelled, "It hurts!"

Zenobia yelled back "Breathe!"

The sound of women panting echoed into the night against the racket of bullfrogs.

"Breathe, just keep breathing," she told each woman.

"You can do it! Breathe for your life!" Zenobia yelled repeatedly.

Zenobia squatted into position to deliver a woman ten centimeters and fully effaced. The baby's head was crowning so fast that Zenobia barely had time to unwrap her supplies. The baby came forth and laughed, showing a full set of teeth, and then he drew back, deep into the comfort and safety of his mother's womb.

"Zenobia. Zenobia, wake up," called Tasha. "Old Ma is here for you."

Zenobia woke from her sleep feeling as if she had wrestled with an imp all night. She shook off the dream, happy that her day was not going to begin with delivering hundreds of babies.

"This way," said Old Ma, leading Zenobia in a new direction. They walked away from manicured lawns and paved roads—away from the mud-walled village, plastic mats, and sponge mattresses, and soon stood at the foothills of Mount Nimba.

They hiked through a canopy of rain trees that led to a colossal tree that marked the mouth of the forest. Zenobia had to refrain from bowing to its magical spirit.

"It's a baobab tree," said Old Ma, "The tree of life. No matter how often people strip her bark, she heals herself, produces new bark, and continues to grow. We have a saying. 'Truth is like a baobab tree; one person's arms cannot embrace it.' We call her Mother.'"

"Mother looks upside down," said Zenobia, referring to leafless branches that waved and stretched flamboyantly, like roots, toward the sky.

"That's one thing that makes Mother special. She's probably a thousand years old, and during rainy season, she stores enough water in her branches and trunk for a whole village to drink during the dry months. I've even seen people use her trunk for shelter."

Zenobia tilted her head back and let her eyes follow the tree's limbs, which grew in wild, twenty-foot irregular projections. She walked around the tree, tracing its smooth, shiny trunk with her fingers.

"Mother is bare most of the year," said Old Ma. "Soon buds will appear, a sign that rainy season is coming. That's when she brings forth three months of leaves and enough fruit for the entire year."

Old Ma removed a Bowie knife from its leather cover, reached high above her head, and cut a section of Mother's bark.

"This makes excellent medicine for fever and swelling," she said, wrapping the bark in newspaper, and sliding the knife into a thin sleeve she'd sewn into her skirt. "Come on, we have a long day ahead."

To Zenobia, the air was green, wet; it smelled alive despite the putrid odor of decayed trees and the unmistakable scent of dead animals. Brown leaves and twigs crunched under her feet. She jumped. "What's that? Sounds like somebody calling us."

"Howler monkeys—they are announcing our arrival to the forest residents," laughed Old Ma. "Most people think a forest is quiet, but as you can see, it's busy and loud. Shhh," she said. "Listen."

Zenobia looked up at the sound of a crow's caw, but she could not distinguish the singing warblers from parakeets and whippoorwills that called to each other across treetops.

Old Ma led the way through a pine grove that led to dogwood, juniper, and mangrove trees that grew amid thick ferns. She clipped leaves from milk thistle. "This cleans the blood and gets rid of jaundice."

A tailless toad wriggled across Zenobia's foot when she tried to pick some of the thistle. Trying to get out of its way, she tripped over decayed roots and fell face forward toward a stump, where her view of the forest floor—a worm darting beneath a rock, two spiders weaving webs around the base of a milk thistle, beetles nibbling away at a chrysanthemum bush—intensified. Old Ma didn't want to bother the spiders so she decided to get the rest of her thistle on the way home.

Upright again, Zenobia tasted the bottom part of the water root tree that Old Ma held out, coaxing her to suck.

"It's cool water!"

"You'll never die of thirst where there are water root trees." Old Ma put root pieces in her bag and then led Zenobia past a wall of moss; she climbed down an incline where the two had to step over a crevice covered with creeper vines and tightly coiled roots.

Zenobia was afraid to get her foot caught in the webbing. "You gotta look high and low," said Old Ma.

Streams of sunlight appeared and disappeared through trees as they moved in silence, Zenobia out of breath, Old Ma focused on her task.

At an evergreen, Old Ma examined the bark, and seeing it needed to heal from previous cuttings, she moved on. "This bark grinds real fine and makes a tea that's good for the male sex gland and bladder problems."

She cut a limb from a shrub near the evergreen; broke it into six-inch pieces, and gave one to Zenobia. "Grind this, put it under your husband's pillow, and he will never leave you for another woman."

"He already knows what will happen if he tries to leave me for any reason," Zenobia said, laughing, her hands balled into fists.

They went from plant to plant, collecting berries, leaves, and snapping tree bark to make medicines for skin rashes, menstrual cramps, burns, pleurisy, and infections. Old Ma gathered Christmas bush leaves, the plant used to make the paste for little Boima's head.

Standing under a thirty-foot tree, Old Ma caught ripe

kola nuts as they fell. When she handed a nut to Zenobia and told her to chew, Zenobia coughed and gagged. "It's bitter."

Old Ma chuckled knowingly. "It's a stimulant, like coffee, but there is no better treatment for diarrhea or dysentery."

Zenobia slowed down a bit, and Old Ma grunted, "Come on, there's a clearing on the other side of those broad leaf trees. We'll rest when we get there, but first, I want to show you something."

The two stopped at a giant mound. Zenobia hadn't seen anything like it: holes and burrowed columns made the mound that was almost her height look like an apartment building made of dirt.

"It's a termite hill," said Old Ma. "They've left the colony; in fact, we couldn't get this close if they were still in there. The loud drone of workers would keep us away."

Old Ma knelt beside the hill, scooped large handfuls of saliva-drenched termite clay, and put it into a plastic bag. It was her favorite poultice for taking the pain out of any sting, healing a rash, and drawing infection and heat from an abscess. "Ant hills work, too," she said. "Just never approach either until you know all the insects are gone."

"What makes the clay from a colony so special?" asked Zenobia.

Old Ma chuckled. "It's the remains from millions of workers. There's healing in the life they had."

Next, Old Ma plucked several blades of grass and rubbed them between her hands. She showed Zenobia how to clean her hands the same way and pointed to a fallen petrified tree trunk where the two sat down to eat berries and suck water root for lunch. Cicadas and crickets chirped, and the babble of a distant waterfall penetrated the stillness that fell between the women.

"Zenobia, what brought you to Liberia?" Old Ma asked after a long silence.

Zenobia wanted to ask Old Ma what she meant, and thought better of insulting Old Ma by playing dumb. She fixed her eyes on an army of ants, moving together as a single unit to pick up the discarded water root, and hauling it away. "I came to open a clinic," she started, and then twisted her bottom on the tree log.

"What happened?"

"I spent almost two years working on a building instead of doing the work I came to do."

Old Ma waited.

"At home I was torn between pleasing my grandmother and doing what I loved. I was so confused that a baby in my care was born with lead poisoning. I blamed myself and wanted to make up for the mistake. I expected things to be different here, or at least that it would be easier to follow my dreams."

"And are things different?"

The question ripped through Zenobia's veneer. She started to sob into Old Ma's bosom, letting go of all the guilt and self-pity she had harbored.

When Zenobia was composed again, Old Ma sucked on another water root and pushed, "Are things different, Zenobia?"

"It's different trouble, and kind of ironic that I got distracted here too."

"Looks to me like you brought your troubles with you."

"Part of me wants to stay committed to what I started and the other part doesn't want to be proved wrong for coming here in the first place. It's just that Liberia is so full of…" she looked at Old Ma. "She is pregnant with possibility and hope, yet she's not delivering. I'm a midwife, Old Ma; my job is to help people deliver their future."

Zenobia slumped her shoulders. "I'm stuck. And scared."

Old Ma put her arms around Zenobia. "Zenobia, you have to be delivered before you can deliver anyone else."

"What about you, Old Ma? Is this your life? Did you ever want to be married or have a family?"

Old Ma twisted her mouth and began slowly. "I loved a man named Hershel Williams. His home was in Monrovia. During the week, he ran the mines and lived in Yekepa. He was married, though, and had a sickly daughter with polio. The doctors here connected him with the best care in the world. He sent his daughter to Ohio, where she received experimental treatment and rehabilitation. The Iron Ore Company helped with the bills."

Zenobia hoped that Old Ma didn't see her rapid breathing.

"One night Herschel rushed back to Monrovia for his daughter's birthday, because he had always felt bad that Kito had to be away at hospitals for long periods. She was, after all, a daddy's girl. It was an afternoon during rainy season. The roads were terrible; his driver swerved to avoid a watery ditch and ran head-on into a tree. They were killed instantly." Old Ma paused, "I've never loved anyone else."

"Zenobia," Old Ma said, and looked Zenobia head-on. "This is about you. The way you are with women is a gift. What you shared with Esi, Fanta, and the mother whose baby you breathed life into. Even Sarah. All this time I've been shielding you from women who had been cut, but when it was time, your gift led you through the experience—it's all your calling. Your touch gave those women a glimpse at hope, and that hope will manifest in the way they touch their children, their families, their neighbors. Your calling is a gift from God. You take it with you wherever you go, Zenobia. It doesn't matter where you are.

"Hold onto this moment. You will return to it at other

times in your life when you are at a crossroads, or stuck as you call it. Ask yourself if you are using your gift, if you are sowing your gift into others the way you have done here. If the answer is no, choose your gift."

Old Ma gathered their sacks bulging with medicine and wisdom, and on the trek back to the mouth of the rainforest, she collected toothache leaves, turpentine bush twigs for worms, and roots for spiritual clarity.

"Zenobia, your strength is not in holding on—it's in knowing whether what you are holding onto serves your gift. And you are right about Liberia. She is pregnant with possibility, but like any pregnant woman, she has to believe that the fruit is worthy of the hard labor it takes to attain. Liberia is at a crossroads—she can disintegrate or build."

Zenobia asked, "How do I know what decision to make? What if I'm not sure if I am using my gift?"

"You will know, Zenobia. You were born knowing. The things you call trouble are only there to show you what you already know. Pay attention."

At the mouth of the forest, Zenobia closed her eyes. She circled the baobab tree, pulled the citrine from her waist, and left it there as a gift for the lessons she had learned.

Chapter Fifty-Three

Daisy canceled all morning appointments and brewed coffee for the meeting.

"Ma, I'm frightened," said Kito. She had become as much afraid of knowing about her mother's clandestine activity as not. "Our clients whisper about private meetings at the salon. What are you involved in?"

"Listen, Kito. Some things are better not known. Nevertheless, you are right to be concerned. Things are worsening by the day. The government is rewriting the law—with no accountability for human rights. With his petty motives, Doe will have the worst corruption of all time. Electricity and water are decreasing, and I'm telling you, no way am I going back to hauling water from a well and heating styling irons with hot coals." She paused, quivering at the thought. "I was waiting for the right time to reveal my plans to sell the shop. We are moving to Farrow."

"Sell the business? Move—Farrow?"

"Kito, we have to leave. Liberia is spiraling out of control. When she self-destructs, we'll be gone."

"Everything we have is here, Daisy."

Daisy kissed her daughter on the forehead. "CeCe is managing our investments in the States. We have plenty."

The doorbell rang just as Kito asked, "How long have you been planning all this?"

"We'll talk later, sweetheart."

✦

"Good morning, Ryan," said Daisy and directed him toward the refreshments.

"Who Owns the Land? My Papa's Land, Who Owns the Land?" reverberated from a taxi outside. Ansa snap-shook New York's hand. "Thanks, man, for giving me your per-sonal hire," said New York. "I been saving my fare money to go to New York, and when I get there, my heart will be sat-is-fied."

"Sounds like a good plan, my main man, long as you leave after me," said Ansa, shaking New York's hand and slapping his back.

"Morning, Ma'am," Ansa said to Daisy, straightening his posture and speech.

Ryan looked to Daisy. "Ansa is from Gbarnga, and he is well known across Liberia."

Kito interrupted, "I'm the most logical person to go. I can throw my father's name around, and if that fails, I can always tease one of the soldiers; make him think I'll be nice to him, if he's nice to me," she said, making a pleasure-seeking gesture.

"Stop it, Kito," said Daisy.

"So how will you get Zenobia through the checkpoint?" Ansa asked.

"Kito is on to something. I can arrange to have her escort Tasha and Zenobia into Côte d'Ivoire," said Daisy. "I have friends there who will take them in."

"You can meet them there, Ryan. Or you can have them travel south from there and reenter Liberia through Cape Palmas."

"Are there rebel checkpoints to the south?" asked Kito.

"Yes," said Ansa. "Checkpoints are everywhere, and

there are no government controls. Money is the hustle. In Gbarnga, though, I am sure factions are fighting to control the region that leads to the Guinea border."

"Kito can get them into Côite d'Ivoire using Mrs. Williams' friends," Ansa continued. "I'll find the best border checkpoint and let you know by tomorrow night. Kito can leave after that. Okay?"

Daisy said, "Sure. Today is Sunday. Kito can leave for Yekepa Wednesday morning."

"Sounds like a plan," said Ansa.

"Thank you for coming," said Daisy, leading Ansa out.

"Are you all right, Ryan?" Daisy asked when she returned.

"It's just that I let my guard down, and Zen is so stubborn."

"Don't think for a minute that you could have done anything to stop her," said Daisy. "No one could."

"Thanks, Daisy."

"Wait, Ryan. Have you met the woman Old Ma? She mentions me specifically in the note."

"All I know is that Zen came to life when she started with Old Ma."

Kito yelled from the dining room. "Zenobia delivers babies with Old Ma for the Mats to Mattress Program. She probably heard how resourceful you are."

"Zen speaks very highly of her," Ryan continued.

"I see."

Chapter Fifty-Four

By the time she arrived at Tasha's apartment, all energy had drained from Zenobia.

Tasha rushed Zenobia with the news. "School officials came this afternoon with a bulletin of Embassy and State Department announcements in ten different languages. They all asked expatriates to leave Liberia."

"Are you afraid?" asked Zenobia as she put her bag of herbs and medicine away.

"No! Messes up my plans is all."

"I thought you didn't have any plans."

"That's what I mean. I gotta make some."

"What about you?"

"Ryan has to get me out of Yekepa first."

"Do you ever think about Sarah?" asked Tasha. "We never talked about it. I felt so sorry for her that night. Still do."

"There is so much to understand about people."

Tasha threw her hands into the air. "What is there to understand about something like that? I will never understand it."

"My grandmother warned me that being a midwife would show me ugly things. Even so, I know she never saw a circumcised woman. I do not understand, though, how mothers keep that slaughter going. If just one mother said, 'no,' it would change the practice. I hope Sarah stands up for Satta. I just don't know if she has the strength."

Chapter Fifty-Five

Ansa went strait to Kimeh's house when he hadn't shown up at the office for the second time, and he wouldn't let Kimeh rush off without agreeing to meet Tuesday morning.

When Kimeh arrived an hour late, Ansa explained his own distance with, "I have a touch of malaria."

"Sorry 'bout the money biz'ness," Kimeh started. "We were so tired after the reception, all the drinking and dancing. My wife rushed me before I paid you." He pulled bills from his pocket and peeled off one hundred dollars.

"No sweat," said Ansa, steadying his hand. "What's important, my man is that we have an understanding."

He rubbed his hands together. "Yeah, an under-standing."

"Listen, man, I need a favor," said Ansa, hitching his pants and looking around for Kimeh's men.

"Anything for you," said Kimeh, relieved there wasn't pressure for more money.

"In fact, I have a biz'ness idea," began Ansa. "You see, some band members were stopped on the road to Yekepa, at the Gbarnga Checkpoint. They were going to see a couple of honeys, if you know what I mean."

"Yeah, honeys."

"Well," continued Ansa, "There're some pretty heavy-duty brothas up there, talking about Kimeh's pass card ain't worth nothing, wouldn't let my guys through to see their honeys. Can you believe that?"

"Never," Kimeh said, trying to hide his embarrassment.

"I sent some friends over to talk sense to the men, but they wouldn't listen, said they wouldn't talk to anyone but you, Kimeh."

Kimeh tightened his belt around his weasel waist. "I been busy, maybe I can send...."

"You, man—nobody but you," said Ansa, and slapped Kimeh's knee.

"That's right, me. I can tell them my idea to merge," Kimeh said, raising his hand in celebration. "I've been looking for this chance. When can we go?"

"I'm ready. My truck is downstairs."

On the ride to Gbarnga, Kimeh chattered—his daughter had married a rich Nigerian; the roads worsened with every rainy season—mostly he talked about swindling foreign investors who dreamed of getting rich off Liberian diamonds.

Ansa slowed down a mile and a half before the Gbarnga Checkpoint. Branches scraped the roof of his truck as he drove into a grove of trees and high grass.

"We'll have to walk from here," said Ansa. He put the truck in park and left the motor running.

"Where are my men?" asked Kimeh, nervously. "I haven't seen anyone since we started."

"They're at the meeting," said Ansa. "New checkpoint guards have been trying to talk your men into joining them. You know it's all about money, Kimeh. That's why you have to talk them into joining you, my main man."

Kimeh swelled his chest and stepped out of the truck behind Ansa.

"I'll go in there and convince them that there is no power in two, power is in one. I'll tell them how I get money, and watch them rush to fall behind me."

"You should be in charge of the entire region. Spread your men from Monrovia to Yekepa."

Kimeh followed Ansa through a thicket of tall grasses and shrubs. Leaves and branches moved to the mild, dry-season breeze, and to the quickness of the men. "You got a cigarette, man?" asked Ansa, as they approached a small shanty nestled behind the brush.

"I was going to ask you," said Kimeh. "Meetings make me nervous—never know how they are going to turn out."

"I'm going back to the truck to get my cigarettes and lighter," said Ansa, digging deep into his pockets as if either might appear. "Go on ahead, man. I'll catch up to you. Everyone is in that house."

The air was still except for the slight rustle of dried grass that crunched beneath Kimeh's feet. Ansa backed into a banana grove and held his breath as he crouched and watched through giant leaves.

Half a dozen men shattered the quiet air when they took aim at the target. Ansa closed his eyes and imagined each man squeezing his trigger. He heard the sound of steel sliding against steel, a hammer drop, and indiscriminate popping sounds, the crackle of sniper gunfire, a hail of bullets whistling through the trees, and even a rocket launcher. Then he backed himself further into the leaves, almost tripping over fallen bananas, until the smell of gunfire and singed vegetation overwhelmed him. The sound of men scattering through the grass and into the forest signaled his exit. He lunged toward the truck.

That's one piece of corruption I don't have to worry about.

Ansa could not mount the road; his tire was lodged deep inside the very gully that had helped him hide. He gunned the engine. Nothing. He climbed out, lifted the chassis, and perspiring profusely, he pushed it free.

By the time Ansa reached the Gbarnga Checkpoint, jeeps were heading in the direction of the gunfire. *That'll keep them busy for a while.*

The few remaining guards waved to Ansa. "Where you playing next, my main man?"

Ansa raced into Yekepa and straight to Gertrude. "Hey, babe, I'm looking for Tasha—she teaches at the International School."

"Unit number seven.

"Is her friend there too?"

"If she's not in the village."

Ansa rolled his truck up to Tasha's front steps and stopped without parking.

"Tasha, Zenobia, open the door," he yelled.

"It's Ansa," Tasha said to Zenobia.

Tasha asked, "What's going on?"

"I came to get you. How long will it take you to pack and leave?"

"Slow down, Ansa. Tell us what's going on."

Zenobia listened tippy-toe over Tasha's shoulder while Ansa told them about the note from Old Ma, the plan made at Daisy's home, and Kimeh's accident.

"We have to pass the checkpoint while I can get through on my popularity," said Ansa. "Plus, we need to get to Monrovia before Kito makes a useless trip. Just tell me what you want to put into the truck."

Tasha was pacing. "I haven't made up my mind. I could visit my parents. I'm not sure," she rambled.

"The Embassy said leave. What more do you need?" asked Zenobia.

Ansa shrugged his shoulders. "You have an hour, because we have to be in Monrovia by morning."

Zenobia had packed and was rolling brochures and securing them with a rubber band when Tasha shrugged and said, "Why not?"

When the truck was loaded, Zenobia asked Ansa to drive to Gertrude's. "I need to leave a message for a friend."

Zenobia took out a "Breast Is Best" flyer and wrote Grandma Jones's address and telephone number on the back. On the bottom of the paper, she wrote, "I know what decision to make about my gift. Thank you."

"Please give this note to Old Ma," she told Gertrude.

Chapter Fifty-Six

Kito and Daisy arrived early Wednesday morning. Ryan had hired a driver and paid Kito's expenses. Daisy rehearsed the plan with Kito and gave her the names and addresses of every known relative and friend on the West Coast of Africa.

"If you get into a situation, use any name, living or dead. And don't take unnecessary chances," Daisy told Kito for the umpteenth time.

As Ansa turned onto Airfield Road, Zenobia leapt out and bolted up the steps before Ansa could stop.

She rushed into Ryan's arms. "I love you. I missed you so much. I am ready to go."

"Me too, me too!"

Ryan held onto Zenobia as if he was afraid she might slip away from him.

Kito jumped around in circles, "I was on my way to get you. How did you get here?"

"I had to hide in the truck. Ansa said Kimeh is dead."

Daisy took in every word. "And Old Ma?" she asked Zenobia.

"Daisy, Old Ma is fine." Zenobia grabbed Daisy and

held her for a long time. "Old Ma is doing great work, she saved my life in more ways than I could have imagined. And, Daisy, she sends her esteemed regard to you."

Ansa unloaded his truck. "I'll say my good-byes right here."

Ryan and Ansa said everything they needed to say when their eyes locked. Ansa drove away.

As Kito and Daisy left, Daisy warned, "This doesn't change anything, Ryan. You must leave soon."

"Come, Tasha—you are staying with us," Daisy said. "Ryan and Zenobia need their privacy."

علم

"Zen," Ryan said, pulling her into the bedroom, "There is so much to talk about."

"I can't hold it. Ryan, I gotta tell you about Kimeh and the checkpoint," she began and told him all she had learned in the rain forest.

"I am so sorry I kept so much from you. It's just that..."

Ryan had to push through Zenobia's excitement. He told her about Ezra's request. "I don't know, Zen. I always imagined starting a family with my own seed. How do we tell little Ryan that we left his parents in Africa? What if after we've loved him he wants to leave us, and come back to Ezra and Sarah?" He rubbed his head, "I'm stumped on this one."

From the time Zenobia had pulled baby Ryan from Sarah's scarred loins, she had felt a part of him, but taking him to Farrow was another matter.

"I haven't even imagined myself pregnant, let alone raising somebody else's child. I do know this," she said, inhaling the hint of sandalwood at Ryan's neck. "I love you, and I'm thankful that you are in my life." With Zenobia tucked neatly under Ryan, they slept.

The morning after Zenobia returned Sarah sent Satta to the market in her place. Sarah held her son close. She looked deep into his eyes and examined every inch of his body. He was perfect. She pressed his heart to hers and recounted the day her mother was dying from malaria fever. "I will never let a child of mine know the pain I suffered," she told her weak mother.

From the day her mother refused to hear Sarah say *"no,"* Sarah did not express love toward her in the way of a daughter.

"My love for you was showed in your cuttin,'" her mother had said. "You can' marry if you are not clean and pure. Without husband, you can' manage life."

"It hurt deep. It still hurt. You took somethin' without askin' and it make me think I can' have what I want in life."

"Sorry ya. Sorry," her mother had said before she slipped away.

Sarah looked into her baby son's eyes again and traced his face with her fingertips. *My children will live and not die. They will have a good life.* She handed the baby to Ezra, straightened her back and marched beyond the aloe plant and across the street. With determination, she knocked.

"Come in, Sarah," said Zenobia, and returned with a Coca Cola.

"I know Ezra talk to Mr. Ryan about the baby, now I talk to you," she said. "My brother was shot at the rice riots, now he carry gun. The gun is too big for him, but it make him feel big; the gun give him power. With the gun, he mark territory on land he can never own. One day, a taxi will come tell me my brother dead or he kill somebody—either way, he dead. I don't want my baby with gun. To the ma'ket, all the people talk of fighting. I can' see the fighting stop. When I hold my baby and look into his eyes, I can' see him live I want my baby to live without gun," said Sarah, tears pooling under her chin. "You help me one time. You take my baby to America, I can breathe again. I want him to have good life with you. I owe you my life."

Zenobia wasn't sure what to say. "What about Satta?" she asked, stalling.

Sarah dropped her head.

"I'm sorry," said Zenobia, "I only asked because—."

"No mind—it's okay," said Sarah, summoning courage. "My mother said it is our way, but I will save Satta. It will never happen to her."

Zenobia couldn't feel her own heartbeat. She was sure she wasn't breathing, and for several minutes she just sat while the room seemed to swirl around her. Somewhere inside came a cough, bringing her back to herself. Still, she didn't know what to say. The responsibility of loving and raising baby Ryan suddenly seemed minuscule compared with all that Sarah had said.

Ryan, who had been standing within earshot, joined Zenobia, holding her on the couch so she wouldn't topple over.

"Satta can make it 'cause she a girl, but the boy, I can' see him make it. My baby can' live here. Out of love for my family I ask you to give him what I can'."

Zenobia walked onto the porch. She looked up and down Airfield Road and saw for the first time something other than her dream. She saw what Ryan had seen through his camera lens all along. No matter what challenges they faced in America, Zenobia knew that she and Ryan could offer baby Ryan more.

Zenobia thought about "Mother," the tree of life, her wisdom, strength, and Zenobia's own sense of awakening.

Back inside, she grabbed Ryan's hand. Together they agreed.

Ryan said to Sarah, "Zenobia and I have love in our hearts for your whole family. Of course, we will take the baby."

That night, the prophetess ran naked through the streets. "Wake up. Wake up. It is coming—looting in the streets, warlords, government graft and corruption," she cried. "Doe assassinated, war, rogue army, blood diamonds, child soldiers, killing, dying, hundreds of thousands of Liberians will die. Wake up or we will cry blood tears. I'm telling you, pray for Liberia, beautiful Liberia—her land, her people, pray for Liberia."

Chapter Fifty-Seven

Zenobia stayed secluded and used the weeks to bond with baby Ryan. With Daisy's help and a proper dash, Ryan obtained custody and travel visas for the baby. Ezra drove Zenobia and Ryan to the airport, with Sarah kissing and hugging her baby good-bye for the last time. At the airport, Ezra held Sarah and softly wiped away her tears with his fingers. Satta stood on the tarmac and waved.

Zenobia promised Ezra and Sarah a letter with pictures every month; Satta would read them, and pen letters to baby Ryan from his parents. Ezra and Sarah said, "Good bye, Zenobia and Ryan," in unison as they waved.

When Zenobia and Ryan climbed aboard Pan Atlantic Airlines, Kito, who was returning to Farrow, accompanied them. Always Beautiful and Daisy's house were posted for sale. Tasha had already left for Chicago. Ansa and his family were in Côte d'Ivoire.

Ryan soaked in the news from America as he flipped through magazines. A January 5, 1981, *Time Magazine* article named Ronald Reagan "Man of the Year" for his smooth and graceful rise to the most powerful position in the world. The article described Jimmy Carter's loss to Reagan and return to Georgia.

Ryan filled Zenobia in on the news about America's economy. "There is inflation at home. People are afraid of losing jobs; they're using their savings to live on."

"That'll feel different. We bought a lot with a little in Liberia. It's going to be tight, Ryan, especially with a baby. Are you nervous?"

Even though the weight of responsibility had settled on Ryan's shoulders, he said "No. I can't imagine a bigger challenge than what we have already faced. You said delivering babies is a miracle. You and I, on this airplane, is a miracle." He leaned over, and Zenobia, fussing with the hair of his beard, lifted her head to plant a kiss. "I'm ready to care for my family," he added.

As the plane burst through the clouds, Ryan watched Zenobia kissing and loving their bundled son while baby Ryan smiled and blew bubbles back at her, something she had recently taught him.

Zenobia held Grandma Jones's final letter between her fingers. She read where Grandma Jones couldn't contain her excitement over Zenobia's return. "We're waiting on you, precious, and we're planning a big dinner," Grandma Jones had written. She could barely wait to welcome her great-grandchild into the Jones family.

For Further Reading

Free Soil is a work of fiction borne out of my imagination after living in Liberia from 1979 through 1984. My intentions here are to examine part of the human experience—the land, people, and situations—I knew there, to bring to light the underside of layered and historical class division and oppression, and to dramatize the story with integrity.

The genesis of this writing occurred one day in Monrovia as I ate falafel and hummus in a dimly lit Lebanese restaurant. I was reading the *Daily Observer Newspaper* about bans on imported rice, poverty, political party mergers, and failed insurgents, and somewhere deep in my spirit I wondered, *Why am I here at this time?* Suddenly I realized that God had a greater purpose for me to fulfill because of this experience. I then gathered newspapers, photographs, letters and cards, a Peace Corps Manual, and random receipts and then stuffed them into a box, which I held onto for almost twenty years. These items became the texture for the situations within these pages.

People and events from Denmark Vesey to Blacks in the American Antebellum South to Liberia's rice riots, the coup d'état, and the beachfront execution are all documented in history. The characters are fictional, and it is important to note that my lens is that of an African American.

If you are interested in knowing more about the history behind *Free Soil*, here are some of the books, documentaries, and websites I used, and places I visited.

Bibliography

Allen, Philip M. and Segal, Aaron (1973). *The Traveler's Africa*. New York: Hopkinson and Blake Publishers.

Blight, David W. (2007). *A Slave No More: Two Men Who Escaped to Freedom, Including Their Own Narratives of Emancipation*. Florida: Harcourt Books.

Doyle, Barbara, Sullivan, Mary Edna, and Todd, Tracey (2008). *Beyond the Fields: Slavery at Middleton Place*. Based on the Exhibit: Beyond the Fields: Slavery at Middleton Place. Middleton Place Foundation.

Edwards, J. W. Inc. (2006). *Douglass: The Narrative of the Life, Frederick Douglass*. Michigan: Borders Classics.

Egerton, Douglas R. (2004). *He Shall Go Out Free: The Lives of Denmark Vesey, Revised and Updated Edition*. New York: Rowman & Littlefield Publishers, Inc.

Freehling, William W. (1966). *Prelude to Civil War: The Nullification Controversy in South Carolina 1816–1836*. New York: Oxford University Press.

Hurmence, Belinda (Eds.) (1984) *My Folks Don't Want Me To Talk About Slavery, Twenty-one Oral Histories of Former North Carolina Slaves.* North Carolina: John F. Blair, Publisher.

Hurmence, Belinda (Eds.) (1994) *We Lived in a Little Cabin in the Yard.* North Carolina: John F. Blair, Publisher.

Robertson, David (1999). *Denmark Vesey: The Buried History of America's Largest Slave Rebellion and the Man Who Led It.* New York: Alfred A. Knopf, Inc.

Rhyne, Nancy (2005). *Before and After Freedom: Lowcountry Folklore and Narratives.* South Carolina: History Press.

Smith, Margaret Charles and Holmes, Linda Janet (1996). *Listen To Me Good: The Life Story of an Alabama Midwife.* Ohio: Ohio State University Press.

Still, William (2007). *The Underground Railroad: Authentic Narratives and First-Hand Accounts, Edited and with an Introduction by Ian Frederick Finseth.* New York: Dover Publications, Inc.

Tindall, George Brown (2003). *South Carolina Negroes: 1877–1900, With a New Introduction by the Author.* South Carolina: University of South Carolina Press.

Waters, Andrew (Eds.) (2002) *Prayin' to Be Set Free: Personal Accounts of Slavery in Mississippi.* North Carolina: John F. Blair, Publisher.

Wilson, Charles Morrow (1947). *Liberia 1847–1947: Africa's Only Republic...An Experiment in Democracy.* New York: William Sloane Associates, Inc.

Wood, Peter H. (1974). *Black Majority: Negroes in Colonial South Carolina From* 1670 *Through The Stono Rebellion.* New York: W.W. Norton & Company.

Television Broadcasts

Stack, Jonathan and Brabazon, James (2004). *Liberia: An Uncivil War.* USA.

Zvi Dor-Ner (Producer)WGBH Boston, PBS Special(2002*) Liberia: America's Stepchild: The Untold Story Of America's African Progeny.* USA

Newspaper Sources

New Democratic Weekly. July 18–20, 1983

Daily Observer. Various newspaper editions from 1980–1984.

Electronic Sources

The African American Mozaic. (n.d.) Retrieved from: http://www.loc.gov/exhibits/african/afam002.html

American Colonization Society. (n.d.) Retrieved from: http://personal.denison.edu/~waite/liberia/history/acs.htm

Black Masters: The Misunderstood Slave owners. Retrieved from: http://findarticles.com/p/articles/

Black over White: Negro Political Leadership in South Carolina during Reconstruction by Thomas Holt. Excerpt retrieved from: http://books.google.com/books?

Charleston History (n.d.) Retrieved from: http://www.google.com/search

History of Liberia: A Timeline (n.d.) Retrieved from: http://memory.loc.gov/ammem/gmdhtml/libhtml/liberia.html

Liberian Colony from the Liberian Collections Project. Indiana University Bloomington. Retrieved from: http://onliberia.org/lib_colony.htm

The Liberian Constitutions: 1820, 1839, 1847, 1984 from http://onliberia.org/con_index.htm

Report of the Presidential Commission on National Reconstruction, June 12, 1979. http://wsm.ezsitedesigner.com/share/scrapbook/52/522852/Report_on_National_Reconstruction__Brownell_Commission_.pdf

Republic of Liberia. Truth and Reconciliation Commission Final Report from https://www.trcofliberia.org/reports/final/trc-of-liberia-final-report-volume-ii.pdf

Rice and Indigo in South Carolina (n.d.) Retrieved from: http://sciway3.net/proctor/state/sc-rice.html

The Role of the Bassa in Reshaping Liberia from http://www.uniboa.org/reshaping.html

Role of Emigrants that have been sent to the colony of Liberia, Western Africa, by the American Colonization Society and its auxiliaries, September, 1843. Transcribed from "Information relative to the operations of the United States squadron on the west coast of Africa, the condition of the American colonies there, and the commerce of the United States therewith," 28th Congress, 2d. Session, S. Doc. 150, serial 458. Retrieved from: http://ccharity.com/liberia/index.htm

South Carolina Antebellum Period 1784–1860 (n.d.) Retrieved from: http://www.sciway.net/hist/periods/antebellum.html

WHO/World Health Organization. Female Mutilation from http://www.google.com/search?hl=en&client=firefox-a&rls=org.mozilla%3Aen-US%3Aofficial&hs=ZpJ&q=world+health+organization+against+female+mutilation&aq=f&oq=&aqi=

Places to Visit

The Aiken-Rhett House is an intact double home and slave quarters displaying life in Antebellum Charleston. The virtual tour exhibits history and floor plans. Built in 1817, the house is located at 48 Elizabeth Street in Charleston, SC.

The Charleston Museum. 360 Meeting Street, Charleston, SC. Exhibits: When Rice was King and from Slavery to Sharecropper.

Geechee Tours to Sapelo Island, Georgia, the fourth largest Georgia barrier island. Its history dates back 4,000 years. http://www.gacoast.com/geecheetours.html

Gullah Tours explores the places, history and stories that are relevant to the varied contributions made by black Charlestonians. Charleston, SC. Alphonso Brown, Guide and Lecturer.

Middleton Place demonstrates rice field, rice mill, slave chapel and cemetery, and permanent exhibit, Eliza's House, an historic dwelling once occupied by former Middleton slaves.

Old City Market, build in 1841. Market Street between Meeting and East Bay Streets. Charleston, Sc.

Old Slave Mart Museum: Recounting the story of Charleston's role in the inter-state slave trade. Six Chalmers St., Charleston, SC.

Sights & Insights Tours, Inc. explores Charleston's Black history and Gullah/Geechee culture. Charleston, SC. Al Miller, Guide and Lecturer.